Praise for *Season of the Gods*

"*Casablanca* is, among other things, an accidental masterpiece that remains a primary testimonial to the studio system. Robert Matzen's novel about the film's chaotic production is like the movie in that it's both entertaining and a moving love story about a lost paradise: Hollywood."

Scott Eyman, author of *Charlie Chaplin vs. America* and
Cary Grant: A Brilliant Disguise

"Absolutely fascinating! Robert Matzen is known for his meticulously researched nonfiction, but his first foray into fiction is not to be missed. You may think you know the beloved film *Casablanca*, but you'll be riveted by this story behind the story. *Season of the Gods* is must-read fiction for lovers of old Hollywood."

Brenda Janowitz, author of *The Audrey Hepburn Estate* and
The Grace Kelly Dress

"Robert Matzen's intimate knowledge of the studio system era at Warner Bros. combined with his storytelling acumen brings the backstory of the making of *Casablanca*—the greatest Hollywood movie of all time—to life."

Alan K. Rode, author of *Michael Curtiz: A Life in Film*

Praise for *Dutch Girl: Audrey Hepburn and World War II*

"A vivid, moving, and persuasive account of a harrowing time that the actress seldom discussed . . ."

The Wall Street Journal

"A master storyteller, Matzen has given us a great story—intimate, intense, and unforgettable."

Foreword Reviews

T0038837

SEASON OF THE GODS

Also by Robert Matzen

Warrior: Audrey Hepburn

Dutch Girl: Audrey Hepburn and World War II

Mission: Jimmy Stewart and the Fight for Europe

Fireball: Carole Lombard and the Mystery of Flight 3

Errol & Olivia

Errol Flynn Slept Here (with Michael Mazzone)

SEASON OF THE GODS

A Novel

Robert Matzen

GoodKnight Books
Pittsburgh, Pennsylvania

GoodKnight Books

Published by GoodKnight Books, an imprint of Paladin Communications, Pittsburgh, Pennsylvania.

ISBN 978-1-7352738-7-7

Library of Congress Control Number: 2023934162

This book is based on actual events and people as reflected through documentation. The scenarios are fictionalized.

Book and cover design by Sharon Berk

Cover illustration by Andrea Carvajal

Photo of Robert Matzen by Annie Whitehead/Harvesting Light Photography

Printed in the United States of America

To Irene and Aaron, for lives well lived

Now Dawn, the Yellow-Robed, scattered over all the earth. Zeus,
who joys in the thunder, made an assembly of all the immortals
upon the highest peak of rugged Olympos. There he
spoke to them himself, and the other divinities listened:
"Hear me, all you gods and all you goddesses: hear me
while I speak forth what the heart within my breast urges.
Now, let no female divinity, nor male god either,
presume to cut across the way of my word, but consent to it
all of you, so that I can make an end in speed of these matters.
And anyone I perceive against the gods' will attempting
to go among the Trojans and help them, or among the Danaäns,
he shall go whipped against his dignity back to Olympos;
or I shall take him and dash him down to the murk of Tartaros,
far below, where the uttermost depth of the pit lies under
earth, where there are gates of iron and a brazen doorstone,
as far beneath the house of Hades as from earth the sky lies.
Then he will see how far I am strongest of all the immortals.
Come, you gods, make this endeavor, that you all may learn this.
Let down out of the sky a cord of gold; lay hold of it
all you who are gods and all who are goddesses, yet not
even so can you drag down Zeus from the sky to the ground, not
Zeus the high lord of counsel, though you try until you grow weary."

—Homer, *The Iliad*

CHAPTER 1

It was homework for Irene Lee to go and see *Watch on the Rhine* at the Martin Beck Theatre. Lt. Jack Janowitz hadn't seen it and was about to ship out, so what the hell, kill two birds with one stone. Irene pulled some strings and got two tickets for the matinee. Afterward, on a beautiful autumn Sunday afternoon, she and Jack walked along Seventh Avenue to Sardi's on 44th for an early supper.

Lately, Irene had been spending a lot of time thinking about war. She wondered what New York City would be like if German bombers appeared in the sky as they had over Rotterdam. She imagined German troops in the streets, fighting building to building. Of course, there wasn't a war and maybe there wouldn't be a war, but Europe was conquered and much of the Far East, and there were Germans in U-boats right out there in the Atlantic, so nobody knew what was next, and all this flashed through her mind as she walked along Seventh Avenue beside the Navy man before they reached the restaurant.

Irene didn't want to hit Jack's wallet too hard, so she ordered filet of sole Florentine at $1.25 and onion soup at 40 cents, and he had the chicken chow mein. As they waited for their food, neither found much to talk about on a first—and inevitably last—date.

"Gladys says you're leaving soon?" said Irene.

"Shipping out tomorrow," said Jack. He wasn't what you'd call handsome, and the crew cut gave him a teddy bear sort of a look, but the uniform certainly didn't hurt.

"Shipping out for where?"

He pulled a paper from his jacket pocket, unfolded it, and read, "Casco Bay, Maine. The U.S.S. *Truxtun*."

"Pardon me," she said, "but the only thing I know about the Navy is what I learned from movie scripts. Is this *Truxtun* an aircraft carrier? That's a reference to *Dive Bomber* with Errol Flynn, by the way."

"I saw *Dive Bomber*," said Jack. "And I wish the *Truxtun* was a carrier. She's an old tin can from the last war. That's a reference to a destroyer, so we'll be out there escorting convoys. I can't say I have a good feeling about it."

"You mean because of the ship that got sunk by the U-boat—was it yesterday?" asked Irene. She had seen the headline in the *New York Times*.

He nodded. "The *Reuben James*. I can't stop thinking about her. I went through the Academy with one of the guys on the *James*, Pete Protin, and from what I hear, the torpedo hit the forward magazine. She had depth charges strapped on the deck, and they snapped loose as the ship went down and exploded in the water. I mean, what chance does a guy have in that?"

Irene couldn't begin to imagine. In fact, it took a moment of silence to comprehend what he had just said. "So, no word about your friend?"

"No word about anybody," said Jack. "There were some survivors is all I know. Forty maybe, but a destroyer carries 150."

Irene had agreed to this date because her pal Gladys, who worked in Irene's office, was worried about her kid brother in the big city. So Irene had offered the favor of a blind date for an afternoon, and then she would send the guy on his way.

"It sure sounds like we're at war or are gonna be," said Irene as the food arrived. "Very scary."

"I was finishing up at the Academy when the Germans invaded Russia," said Jack as he crumbled crackers on top of the chow mein. "One of my instructors explained Hitler's strategy almost like a chess match, with a map of the world as the board. He said the Germans would conquer Russia and then send those troops to North Africa. When they beat the British there, the Nazis will have oil supplies from the Caucasus and from Libya. And that will be checkmate for us."

Suddenly, Irene didn't feel much like eating, which Jack noticed. "I'm sorry to be all gloom and doom, Irene. Here." He reached inside his jacket and pulled out another piece of paper and unfolded it. "I thought about questions to ask you about show business. I mean, you work in the movies. Like, in the movies!"

All at once she found Jack Janowitz adorable for thinking she was important enough for him to sit around dreaming up questions to ask. His voice had raised an octave when he started talking about the movies, and he no longer seemed a guy of twenty-four about to go off on the high seas but more like a kid of fourteen.

"Question number one," he said, looking at his list, "what's Ann Sheridan really like, and can I have her phone number? Oh, that's question two."

Irene laughed so hard she had to cover her mouth with her linen napkin. "If this was our second date, I'd be insulted, sailor," she told him. "Sure, I know Annie. They call her Clara Lou and she's a stitch. And no, you can't unless your sister can scrounge it."

He reacted as if he didn't really expect to land Ann Sheridan's phone number. "Question number three, do you get to sit and watch all the pictures be made?"

"Oooh, that's a good one," said Irene. "I would like to, but I don't. My job happens before the pictures are made. I find the stories and work with the writers to get the scripts written. All that's done before the cameras roll because the actors need to know all their lines and all about their characters beforehand."

"Oh," he said as he sat slowly deflating. "But Gladys says you go out west to the studio a lot, and so I thought you'd, you know, do exciting things out there."

"Words are exciting, fella! Where would the actors be without words? Where would the studio be without stories? Look around this place. Without stories, there would be no Broadway, no Sardi's. I'm right there in the middle of the fight."

He nodded thoughtfully. "So, you're sort of the brains of the operation."

There it was again, that adorable Jack Janowitz something. She couldn't tell if he was being serious or pulling her leg, so she pressed on. "I might go through a stack of plays and find one out of thirty or forty that's worth sending to my boss at the studio. *Watch on the Rhine*, for instance. That's a cinch to be made into a picture, and so I'm sending the script on to Burbank. *The Man Who Came to Dinner*—same thing. That's being shot now, with your girl Ann Sheridan. A lot of my job involves looking for plays that the studio will make into pictures. Get it?"

"Got it." He looked down at his paper, and said, "Question four. What's Lana Turner really like, and can you get me her phone number?"

She allowed Jack to see her roll her eyes. "Lana Turner works at MGM, which is nowhere near Warner Bros. No, I haven't met her, but I'm beginning to understand your tastes."

An hour later, they shared a cab up to her apartment building on Central Park West, then stepped out into the chilly air for the moment of truth. She had already decided that if he wanted to kiss her goodbye, that would be fine, despite their seven-year age difference. The kid was defending the nation on the high seas, and he was a sweetheart—Jack and his list of questions. He was a good ten inches taller than she was, with her three-inch heels offsetting the difference a little. Still, standing-up kisses were always an adventure for tiny Irene Lee.

"Well, thank you for babysitting me, Irene," he said, removing his white officer's hat.

She laughed. "Is that what you think I was doing? Babysitting you?"

"That's what Gladys said you were doing."

"I think you're a fine young man and a handsome officer, and I had a very nice time," she said. His eyes showed fear, but here it came. He leaned down and brought his mouth to hers. She knew she was a good kisser and thought she'd give him something to remember, but he seemed to have beaten her to the impulse. His tongue shot into her mouth and started exploring. But what the heck. She reached up and placed a hand on each of his biceps to gain a little control of the situation and French-kissed him back. In the next ten seconds, she figured she had taught him a thing or two about the art of the kiss.

When it ended, he seemed not to know where he was for a moment. She said, "If any of your babysitters ever kissed you like that, maybe I'll buy your story and have it made into a movie."

"No, ma'am, not ever," he said, catching his breath.

She smiled her most winning smile. "All right then, anchors

aweigh, sailor, and thank you again."

He replaced the hat on his head, gave her a smart Annapolis salute, and said, "Yes, ma'am!"

She returned the salute and said, "Good luck, Jack."

"Thanks," he said, got in the cab, and was driven off.

By 6:30 she was out of her clothes and into a robe to read the last of the scripts she had promised herself she would finish over the weekend. She stretched longways on the sofa, put a cushion behind her head, lit a Chesterfield, and slipped on her glasses to read the cover. EVERYBODY COMES TO RICK'S, by Murray Burnett and Joan Allison. Unproduced, from the slush pile. Expectations: zero.

She opened the cover to see the play was set in Casablanca, French Morocco, then stretched her mind back to ninth-grade geography class to remember exactly where that might be. Northwestern coast of Africa, maybe? Then she heard Jack's voice in her head: "One of my instructors said the Germans would conquer Russia and then send those troops to North Africa. When they beat the British there, the Nazis will have oil supplies from the Caucasus and from Libya. And that will be checkmate for us." She felt a push of energy to get going on this one.

Exactly 110 minutes later, as she read the stage direction CURTAIN FALLS at the end of Act 3, Irene felt a burst of chills at the base of her spine and a ringing in her ears. She had always known she was intuitive. She could feel ghosts. She could sense when someone was lying or telling the truth. Now that sixth sense was sending up skyrockets, which made her stare down at the bradded document in her lap. She couldn't say it was all that good, confirmed by the fact nobody had taken a chance with it. But this play had power. It kept her attention from beginning to end, and she found something compelling in the character of a cynical American hiding out in a Casablanca nightclub—tingles-along-the-spine, ringing-in-her-ears compelling. And the location—no one could argue with the location in North Africa, the place on Jack's world map where Hitler would call checkmate.

She held the script in both her hands and said, "Mr. 'Everybody Comes to Rick's,' I am going to introduce you to Mr. Hal B. Wallis. He's not the friendliest man, but I think you two might have something to talk about."

CHAPTER 2

Hal B. Wallis would be the first to admit he wasn't the friendliest man, but then nobody paid him for niceties. They paid him to sit as the top warlord at one of the top studios in Hollywood. He was about to start shooting a new Warner Bros. picture called *Yankee Doodle Dandy*, a look at the life and career of Broadway entertainer George M. Cohan. First thing on a Monday morning, Hal's receptionist, Sally, buzzed in to see if Hal would take a call from Bill Cagney, brother of the man set to portray Cohan.

Hal asked Sally to put the call through, assuming Bill wanted to know the logistics—shooting schedule, wardrobe tests, etc.

"Hi, Bill, what's up?" said Wallis.

"Listen, Hal," said Bill Cagney on the other end of the line. "Jim's digging into the Cohan script and he's going to need some changes. We thought—"

"No! Certainly not, Bill," Wallis cut in. "I've already handed this script out to the departments for preproduction. It's just not possible to make changes, so don't ask me."

Wallis heard scuffling on the phone, then a new, higher-pitched voice. "Hal? It's Jim Cagney. I've got to have this script reopened. You've got to let the Epstein brothers get in there and fix it. I trust those boys. I want them to do whatever it takes."

Hello, Monday, thought Wallis. For all James Cagney's talent, what a monstrous pain in the ass he was. "I'm not going to argue with you, Jim," said Hal in his most measured tone. "As I told Bill, this script is final."

Jim Cagney shot back, "Cohan is supposed to be this showman, this light entertainer. A brilliant satirist. And what you've got right now is a two-hour obituary. There's nothing for an actor to interpret. It's got zero charm, and if anybody knows how to add charm, it's the Epsteins." After years with the incendiary Cagney, Wallis didn't want to fan the flames, so he forced himself to hold silent. "Think it over, Hal. You know where to find us." And then Wallis heard *click!*

He felt himself sweating, and he didn't like to sweat. Hal prided himself on a mastery of emotions, a secret power that gave him leverage over everyone and everything at the studio, up to and including the actors and even the chief, Jack L. Warner.

Sally buzzed him again; was it Cagney calling back to apologize? "Yeah?" he said.

"I've got Miss Lee on the phone from New York," said Sally. Hal's first impulse was that Irene could wait; his second impulse won out—maybe Irene could guide him through this mess with the Cagneys. He told Sally to put the call through.

"Hello, Renie," he said, trying to be pleasant.

He heard only static on the line, and then she said, "Oooh, somebody got up on the wrong side of the bed."

He didn't feel the luxury of pleasantries. "Cagney wants the boys to punch up *Yankee Doodle*. Punch it up or he walks."

"Punch it up how?" she asked.

"Humor," he replied.

More static on the line. "I think he's right," she said.

"You approved that script!" Wallis shot back.

"We all did, because we couldn't deal with Cohan anymore," said Renie. "But in the back of my mind I was thinking, this thing's awfully grim. I figured maybe Cagney would improvise some bits of business like he usually does. You know, to lighten things up."

"Maybe in the old days," said Wallis, "but not anymore. The little bastard just hung up on me when I told him no to script changes."

"Ouch," said Lee. Hal could hear her light a cigarette and blow out the smoke. As usual she was a tornado flattening Kansas. "You want my advice? Of course you do or you wouldn't have taken my call. Get the boys on the phone and tell them to add some laughs. And they'll tell you they don't want to be involved because they've heard that Cohan is a pain in the ass. Then you tell them I said they have to drop everything else and do it."

As usual, she had gotten under his skin in 100 words or less. And yet, he had been inclined to take her call and canvass an opinion. At length he said, "It's bad business to reopen scripts that have been sent out to the departments." He thought another moment and sighed. "But if you say Cagney's right and the picture will suffer, then I'll think about bringing in the Epsteins."

"Do you want me to call them?" she asked.

"Listen, I'm the head of production at Warner Bros., and I don't need to throw my story editor's name around to get things done. I'm in charge. If I think it's the right move, I'll call the Epsteins." He realized his harshness; he pulled back. "What were you calling about, anyway?"

"A play I read last night. I want you to buy it."

Wallis grabbed a pencil and prepared to write. "What theater?" he asked. "Who's producing it? Who's starring?"

She hesitated. "Nobody's bought it. It's unproduced. It's about an American who owns a nightclub in Casablanca and runs into his old flame."

"Come on, Renie," he groused. "No press? No track record? No stars? Pass."

He heard her laugh and sing into the phone, "You'll be sorreee," which he knew to be code for, *You haven't heard the last of this*.

"Say goodbye, Renie," he sighed.

"*Au revoir*, Renie," she said on cue, almost like a song, and he set down the receiver.

Alone again with his thoughts, Wallis considered other ways out rather than giving Cagney what he wanted. But he knew no other actor on the lot could step into the Cohan role. And production was set. And buzz for the picture was strong. And yes, the script had taken months to develop by one of his top writers working directly with Cohan. Wallis wondered if maybe he had lost his perspective on it.

He leaned back in his chair and, as always, his eyes drifted to the plaque hanging on the wall to his left. The plaque bore a quote by Ralph Waldo Emerson that read: "Do not be too timid and squeamish about your actions." Hal leaned forward with a leaden arm to pick up the phone and buzz the desk outside his office.

"Sally, will you find Philip Epstein for me, please?" he said wearily. A little part of Hal allowed himself to be bothered by what he was doing, but this was business—serious studio business.

Hal chose Phil Epstein to talk to because at least a person could reason with Phil. Sure, Julius was the senior brother in terms of studio experience, but Julie lacked Phil's grace. Yes, that was it. Julie was brash, unpredictable, which made Phil the safer play.

It took several minutes before Sally located Philip Epstein and got him on the phone, meaning Phil wasn't where he was supposed to be, which was in his office one building over, working regular hours. Which likely meant Julie wasn't there, either. Wallis picked up the receiver on Sally's prompt and waited.

Ten miles away, Philip Epstein sat on the living room rug at his house on Holmby Avenue in Los Angeles. Beside him sprawled his little boys, Leslie, age three, and Ricky, age two.

Dad had bought his sons a tin gas station almost a foot and a half long and had just completed its construction. Phil had inserted tab A into slot B and so on until his fingers bled. "We're open for business, boys," said Phil as he blotted blood with his handkerchief. Leslie sat up and pushed a lead Packard along the floor toward the station. Ricky lay on his stomach and stared at a toy Cadillac.

"Yes, that's right, pull up to the pump like we always do," Dad said to Leslie, and the child drove his car onto the gas station lot. The boys' mom, Lillian, drifted in from the kitchen and watched the action for a moment with a smile on her face.

"Ding-ding!" said Phil as his son drove his Packard over an imaginary hose that activated an imaginary bell and then parked in proper position beside the pump.

"Fill 'er up!" said the boy. Or what translated to "Fill 'er up!" which Phil invariably would say to any attendant in real life at any gas station. Phil looked up at Lillian; wow, she was beautiful, he thought every time he looked at her. Every single time. Her painted lips showed faint amusement at the goings-on.

"Fill 'er up! Yes, sir!" said Phil, maneuvering a three-inch lead gas station attendant into position. "Ding, ding, ding," he said slowly as the Packard gassed up. "Let me get the windshield for you, sir. Can I check the oil?"

Leslie shook his head no, the oil's fine. Or maybe no, my mind is wandering; Phil couldn't be sure. Meanwhile, Ricky had rolled onto his back and held the Cadillac up high and stared at it. Next it would go into his mouth.

In the kitchen the phone rang, and Lillian moved off to answer it.

"Don't you need any gas today, Ricky?" asked Phil. Ricky ignored him and stared at the car and the ceiling beyond.

"Yes, he's right here," Phil heard Lillian say from the kitchen. She hurried into sight. "It's Hal Wallis," she whispered with urgency.

Phil's heart skipped a couple of beats because it wasn't exactly usual to get a call at home from the most powerful guy at the studio. He climbed to his feet, touched Leslie's cheek, told the boys to play nice, walked to the kitchen, and picked up the receiver. Phil knew Julie would be arriving soon for the drive to the studio since they liked to get there in time for lunch at the writers table in the commissary. Because this was Hal Wallis—hirer and firer of writers—Phil paused, drew in a breath, and wiped his mind clean. He would be upbeat and wish Hal a good morning. But what came out of his mouth was, "Hal, are we in trouble?"

"Usually, yes, you are," said Wallis without humor on the other end of the line. "Interesting I should find you at home and not at your desk, Phil."

Phil's mind shot through any number of excuses, but before he could utter one, Hal continued, "Listen, I need you and Julius to do some fix-up work on a script."

Alarm bells went off inside Phil's brain. There was one script he and his brother definitely did not want to be involved with— Phil and Julie had talked about it just yesterday—and so Phil couldn't take any chances. "Well, as you know, Hal, we are working on the de Havilland picture right now—"

Wallis cut in, "The Cagneys want you guys on *Yankee Doodle Dandy* with an eye toward adding some humor."

Bingo. The script they wanted nothing to do with. Dread poured over Phil because he and Julie had been listening to their colleague Bob Buckner moan and groan for months about working with George M. Cohan, the self-professed great entertainer. The brothers believed if they got involved, everything they came up with would be reviewed and rejected by Cohan, so really, why bother?

"I heard the script was final," Phil parried. "I heard you already sent it to the departments."

Another hesitation from Wallis. "It was. I did." Every word seemed to pain him.

"Soooo . . . ?" Phil inquired.

"So, Jimmy just now read it and said it needs the Epsteins," said Wallis with impatience.

"What does Renie say?" Phil asked a little too quickly, and he realized it at once.

"It doesn't matter what she said!" Wallis snapped. "Get in here and get to work. And don't let me catch you at home again, Phil. I want you in your office during business hours. Both of you."

"On our way," Phil said optimistically.

"Goodbye, Phil," said Hal Wallis, and Phil heard an angry click as the line disconnected.

Before he could hang up the receiver, he heard his brother honk his horn in the driveway, signaling it was time to leave. Phil grabbed his briefcase, looked into the living room, said, "Bye, boys!" and kissed Lillian goodbye. Halfway out the door he paused, came back in, wrapped Lillian in a proper clinch, and planted one on her like he meant it. She responded as if she meant it too.

Julius Epstein's black Buick Roadmaster sedan sat in Phil's driveway, purring, as Julie awaited his brother and reflected on the morning, which included a nice long run from his house on Homedale Street all the way to the Bel Air gate and back. Running kept the ticker in shape and allowed him time to commune with nature while thinking about whatever script they were working on. He had gone home and showered in no great rush, and now they just had time to get to the studio for lunch. If, that was, Phil came out on time. And in a moment, there was the other Epstein, wearing a navy-blue blazer over a tan dress shirt with a navy tie. Phil favored solid colors; Julie, stripes or checks. It was odd how different the twins could be in some ways, as with how they dressed, yet few seemed able to tell them apart.

Phil slid into the passenger side of the bench seat, set his briefcase between his knees, and as Julie put the car into reverse and backed into the street, Phil said, "I just got off the phone with Mr. Wallis."

Julie's foot hit the brake and the car held there, blocking both sides of Holmby Avenue. He looked into his brother's face for signs he was kidding, especially with the way he had said *Mr. Wallis*. All Phil said was, "You're blocking traffic."

Julie said, "There isn't any traffic." He studied Phil another little while, got a let's-get-going expression and jerk of the head from him, and put the car in gear. He drove up to Beverly Glen, where he could get some speed going.

With the side streets out of the way, Julie said, "All right, what did Mr. Wallis want?"

"Guess," said Phil.

The answer came to Julie in less than three seconds: the Cohan thing. "Shit," he muttered.

"Exactly," said Phil.

"Did you tell him no?" Julie demanded as he hung a right onto Sunset Boulevard.

"Of course I didn't tell him no!" said Phil. "You didn't hear him—he's pissed at Cagney and we don't need him pissed at us."

"Shit," muttered Julie again, and he stepped on the gas, heading for the Warner Bros. studio in Burbank.

After lunch at the writers table in the Warner Bros. commissary, the Epsteins walked to the Writers Building and climbed the steps to their adjoining second-floor offices. Inside the door sat the desk of their secretary, Alice Danziger, and on sight of them, she made eye contact with Julie and held out the screenplay for *Yankee Doodle Dandy*. "Here, for you," she said. "And Miss Lee called from New York and ordered me to call her back and put you on the line the moment I saw you. You specifically, Julie."

"Oh yeah?" said Julius. "Well, who's your boss, us or her?"

Alice laughed and went on laughing as she dialed the operator and asked to make a person-to-person call to New York City.

As she held the phone to her ear, she looked from one glum brother to the other and said, "What do they want you to do, bump somebody off?"

"Save *Yankee Doodle Dandy*," groaned Phil.

Julius said, "The love story stinks. And the plot stinks. And it's got no laughs."

Alice said, "What's the problem? You guys are always fixing scripts. Always adding laughs."

"We never had to deal with George M. Cohan before. He demands total control, and we'll add some laughs and he'll take them right back out again."

Alice gave a shrug as she still held the phone to her ear. "So don't show him," she said. "It's your bargaining chip. 'Sure, we'll do it,' you tell Mr. Wallis, 'but you can't show Cohan.'" Alice shifted in her seat.

"Stand by for Julie Epstein, Miss Lee," said Alice, who then held the receiver out for Julie.

Julius reached for the phone and sighed, "This is Julie."

"Oy," said Lee on the other end of the line. "All you guys sound like you're helpless out there without me. Listen, I know Hal talked to Phil, and I know the script was dropped off. Just shut up and get to work. No bullshit. No dragging your feet. You know exactly what needs to be done, so do it."

Julie felt himself rock back a step. "You usually aren't this mean," he said.

"Trust me when I tell you, there are times to mind your P's and Q's, and this is one of them. Hal's mad enough that you guys weren't in your office when he needed you."

"What's the time frame?" Julie asked.

"It's already been sent out to the departments," said Renie. "What's that tell you?"

"That they're ready to start shooting in a couple weeks," Julie allowed. "But Renie, do you realize the work? We've read the thing—it's got no laughs."

Irene said, "You know what Hal would say. Hal would say, 'That's what we pay you for.'"

Julie gave Alice a glance; she sat slicing letters open with a pearl-handled opener. "Well, how about this, Renie. Since we're pressed for time, how about if our rewrites don't get shown to Cohan? We write it; you and Hal approve it. Deal?"

"Do you want to get me fired?" said Lee.

"Do you want to get us fired?" returned Julie.

Renie fell silent a moment. "I guess maybe we could collect the rewrites and sit on them. Wait until there's no time left to send blue pages back and forth by air mail." Another pause. "Yeah, okay, Julie. Get started. I'll try to handle Wallis. But you didn't hear me say that."

"Thanks, boss," said Julie. The call ended and he handed the receiver back to Alice, who gave him a jaundiced eye. "Thanks for the idea, Alice," he said.

With the deal in place, Alice watched as Phil pried the brads out of the *Yankee Doodle* script and divided the loose pages into Acts 1, 2, and 3. As usual, he got down on hands and knees to place three piles of pages on the floor, and then sat Indian style. Julie joined him and they started reading.

After a while, Julie said, "Do you realize there's no girl in this picture?"

Phil snapped his fingers. "That's right. He had a messy divorce and his second wife was a floozy, so he said no women in the script."

"Bullshit," said Julie. "We're writing in a girl."

"Let's make her a hot one," said Phil, who looked over at Alice. "Pencil."

She tossed him one, and that's how it began, the great last-minute rewrite of *Yankee Doodle Dandy*. They showed up at work in the morning and revised scenes in pencil for Alice to type up on blue paper, signifying rewrites. The blue pages then went straight to Jimmy Cagney, who loved them!

"See?" Cagney enthused. "This is why I demanded you guys!"

Alice was a witness to the birth of Mary, the fictional girl-friend and then wife of George M. Cohan. The boys added humor to Cohan's meeting with the man who would become his writing partner, Sam Harris, and inserted gags when Cohan and Harris meet up with hapless Broadway backers Dietz and Goff.

On a morning ten days into the rewrite, Alice sat typing up the pile of new script pages they had concocted. She hadn't quite gotten the hang of functioning with her bosses in the office every day, so she paused from typing to drink her third cup of coffee of the morning and reflect on life at Warner Bros. after two years behind the lingerie counter at Bullock's. Many of the secretaries, stenographers, and typists on the administrative side of the studio envied Alice her ringside seat between two such cute and passion-ate fellows as the Epstein brothers, with their dark eyes, match-ing muscular builds, and athletic swagger that made each brother worthy of a second look. But both Epsteins were married, with children, although Julie's union was rocky at best.

Today the boys were especially geared up, and as Alice sipped her coffee, watching them, she didn't notice the figure moving in beside her.

The lanky Hungarian Michael Curtiz, an odd man in his for-ties, had wandered into the office. He wore a safari shirt, riding breeches, and knee-high boots, which likely meant he was in the middle of directing a picture, and Curtiz would soon be directing *Yankee Doodle Dandy*, so Alice knew his visit was no accident. He stood too close for her comfort, preoccupied by the arrangement of flowers sitting on the corner of her desk. She always kept a fresh bouquet there, and Curtiz carefully adjusted the blooms until they achieved perfect balance in the vase.

Owing to all the hit pictures he directed, Curtiz had gained a lot of power on the lot, which meant the girls in Administration respected him, but a number didn't like him, Alice included. Rumor had it he made sure a number of girls were kept on the payroll so they would be available for lunchtime funny business—and he was married!

Now Curtiz surveyed Alice, and she felt flattered and repulsed all at once. He smiled and touched her chin in a way meant to charm her; she wasn't charmed. She set down her coffee cup and resumed typing, and Curtiz turned his attention to the twins on the floor surrounded by the most important document within a twenty-mile radius—the screenplay of *Yankee Doodle Dandy*.

"How's it going, boys?" he asked in an accent that could at times prove impenetrable. Alice stopped typing and pretended to struggle with Julie's handwriting, but she just wanted to witness her bosses dealing with Curtiz. Or, rather, the top director at Warners dealing with her bosses.

"We're up to the part we hate," said Phil.

"What part you hate?" asked Curtiz, kneeling beside the boys.

Julius took in hand two sheets of paper. "The dead zone after the parents get old and Cohan and Harris split up. I don't know what the hell Buckner was thinking, but his story dies the minute Old Man Cohan dies."

Curtiz grew sour and shook his head from side to side. "Father dies and there is no tear in the eye. There should be death scene to make tear in the eye. Walter deserve death scene." Alice knew that character actor Walter Huston was to portray George M. Cohan's father, Jerry.

Just then Alice enjoyed a silent eureka moment: the Hungarian Michael Curtiz sounded like Bela Lugosi in *Dracula*. And sort of looked like him as well!

After a quiet time staring at the two pages in question, Julie exclaimed, "Shit!" He got up on his knees and rifled through a pile of script pages over near the wall. He looked at Phil and said, "We need to repeat a line from earlier."

"Which line from earlier?" asked Phil.

Julie said, "We put Dad on his deathbed and George comes in. Dad's delirious and wants to know how the family performance had gone this evening. George says, 'It was great, Dad. The audience loved us.' And Dad says, 'Did you thank them?' And George says, 'I sure did. I said—'"

Phil cut in to state the obvious: "My mother thanks you, my father thanks you, my sister thanks you, and I thank you!"

"Then, boom, Dad dies!" said Julie. "Imagine Cagney playing that scene!"

"Oh my God," murmured Curtiz. "Imagine Walter playing that scene."

Julie looked at Phil for a reaction; Phil was staring off at the far wall. Truth be told, Alice liked Phil better than Julie, because Phil had such a good heart. And Phil was honest to a fault. Phil said, "It's pure corn."

Julius glared at his brother. "Yeah, but it'll play."

"It's pure brilliant!" said Curtiz. "I'll make it play. There will be the tear in every eye the way I shoot it."

Curtiz stood and clucked his tongue slowly, smiling in admiration at what he had just witnessed from the two brothers, and headed for the door. Before Alice, he stopped and bowed. "Good morning, lovely secretary." There it was again, confirmed for Alice—the delivery of Bela Lugosi.

At the door as he walked out, the Hungarian said over his shoulder, "I love you guys!"

In six weeks of work on *Yankee Doodle Dandy*, Alice watched many such acts of genius as the boys nuanced the screenplay into a thing of warmth and sincerity. She would remember their work some months later when *Yankee Doodle Dandy* premiered and the Epsteins didn't get a screenplay credit along with Robert Buckner. Alice asked them if they weren't bothered.

With a benign shrug, Phil said, "Sooner or later, Wallis or Renie will send something our way."

Later on, Alice would remark to herself, *Did they ever.*

CHAPTER 3

Irene's first stab at transcontinental airplane travel was a marvel and allowed her to sit in comfort and watch America pass beneath the wings of a DC-3 airliner. At LaGuardia she had bought the *New York Times* and over Pennsylvania read a story about Yugoslavia, where the Nazis had rounded up 8,100 hostages, including intellectuals, clergy, and students, and executed them. The article labeled it "ruthless Nazi extermination of Serbs." *So this is what the refugees inside Rick's have fled,* she thought to herself. It stunned her, here amidst the luxury of U.S. extravagance to imagine the brutality in Europe.

The miles added up and by the time she reached Burbank, she agonized as she rubbed her backside and clomped down metal stairs yet again. *Seventeen hours from coast to coast, my ass.* Nine legs of hedgehopping cross-country from New York. TWA Flight 3, a Sky Club, promised seventeen hours from coast to coast, which didn't dwell on the details of very loud engines and a very cold cabin at 10,000 feet. Now, finally, she had made it back in time for executive portraits in the Warner Bros. still studio, the annual ritual, and one that made her feel part of the hierarchy.

There wasn't time to stop off at her apartment on Franklin; she must head straight for the studio to make it by 10:15, her appointment time. She found a cab and settled into the back seat, luxuriating in the warmth of that California sun. Nothing like it. She loved the palm trees and had always loved them, and she allowed her mind to drift during the straight shot south on North Hollywood Way. With a left on Alameda, the cab pulled up at the front of the studio Administration Building, and it was that simple: LaGuardia to the portrait studio in less than a day. She glanced at her watch. It was 9:55, so twenty minutes to spare. But she thought to herself that next time she would take the train. Flying, thought Renie, was for the birds.

She lugged her suitcase through the guts of Administration and out the other side, past J.L.'s tennis court and the edit bays onto First Avenue for the short walk to the little building where they took portraits of movie stars. She would spend fifteen minutes getting her face back together and fixing her hair; then she would smile prettily yet again and hang on the wall as the only female executive at the studio, not officially in the chain of command, mind, but an executive either way. Irene reported directly to Wallis. Technically, Wallis reported directly to Jack L. Warner, and Jack, the chief, reported directly to his big brother Harry, who reigned in the New York office.

Inside the calm of the portrait suite, Scotty Welbourne, one of the studio photographers, led her to the makeup room, traditional in setup, with a makeup mirror ringed in the orange glow of light bulbs. She hefted her suitcase onto the table and snapped it open, pulled out a hairbrush and makeup bag and set to work. So nice, so quiet. Despite the fitful sleep on an airplane less than five feet from two growling engines, she now felt rejuvenated, and the portrait would show it.

The mere act of brushing her chestnut hair relaxed her. Only one ingredient was missing. She reached into her purse and pulled out a cigarette and lit it. There, perfection. She went on brushing out her hair.

A tenor male voice sounded over her shoulder: "Oh it's you." She glanced in the mirror and her stomach dropped. It was the chief, Jack L. Warner, standing in the doorway.

"Oh good morning, Chief," she said as cheerfully as she could muster.

He pushed into the small makeup room and said, "I've got a bone to pick with you, young lady."

One never expected pleasantries from the chief because he always had a bone to pick. She knew from experience not to react on instinct. She drew in a breath, let it out, and set her brush down beside her makeup. Then she waited a second and turned to face him, making sure to look him in the eye. "Yes, Chief?"

Jack Warner was a round-faced man, beautifully coiffed, with an Errol Flynn moustache. He could easily have been someone's banker or tailor. He appeared respectable, ordinary. He was neither.

"All of a sudden last Friday, I see a script full of blue pages on my desk. It was the Cohan picture, with changes from the Epsteins."

Oh shit, thought Irene. Today was the day cameras would roll.

"You knew I had an agreement with Mr. Cohan that he would see any script changes before we started production," said Warner.

Irene returned to brushing her hair in the mirror. She knew better than to make direct eye contact at such a moment. "Mr. Cagney needed some rewrites," said Irene into the mirror, "and he knew the Epsteins could give the script some help."

Warner moved close to Irene, just three feet away. "I asked Wallis about it, and he claimed he knew nothing. I've dealt with

Hal for years and I believe he was genuinely unaware about the scope of these rewrites. That means it was your doing." He clasped his hands behind his back. "I don't think you have any idea how embarrassing this is, having to go to Mr. Cohan and explain these changes. Or the legal bind for the studio."

Irene had earned her reputation at the Fox studio ten years earlier, at twenty-one, when she faced off against Erich von Stroheim in a story meeting. She had known she was right then; she believed she had done the correct thing here. She drew in a sharp breath and said, "I think we both know Mr. Cohan was killing this project. He had some skeletons he wanted kept in the closet—who doesn't? But the bottom line is, it was going to be a bad picture."

She could see Warner's surprise at her counterattack, so she kept going. "Mr. Cagney pointed out the obvious: the script was weak, and all I wanted was to turn out the best picture possible."

When she stopped speaking, he went on staring at her in the mirror—assessing, she thought. "I understand that part," said Warner. "Wallis agreed to let the schmuck writers open up the script. But it was you who took it upon yourself to sit on their changes until it was too late to send anything to New York. Is that it?"

What could she say? He had her dead to rights. She shrugged. "That is the gist of it. Yes."

She became aware that Scotty Welbourne was hovering about. It was time for Irene's portrait sitting, but Scotty was a company man who knew to keep a distance.

Warner reeked of cologne. It was good cologne but there was too much of it for a small room. It was Pour Un Homme de Caron, she was certain—Rouben Mamoulian had worn it when they were together. She felt her stomach grow sour.

"I had Legal pull your contract," said Warner on a new tack.

"Did you know it's up next August first?"

Of course she knew that. But why did Warner care? "Yes," was all she said.

He turned away and stared off at the entrance to the make-up room, where Welbourne was standing. In an instant Scotty vanished. Warner always wore nice suits, very well tailored, and this one, a brown tweed, was no exception. He still had his hands clasped behind his back. He turned to face her once again.

"I believe there are a dozen men who could step in and do your job," he said coldly. "Do it better than you."

"We disagree there, Mr. Warner," said Irene. "I know I'm good at my job."

"And you've no right to play god. There's only one god here." Actually, Renie thought, there are two, counting Wallis.

Warner walked toward the door and said over his shoulder, "If Cohan asks about the script, I will send him the changes—"

"Why would you do that," she called, "if you know it's going to make the picture inferior?"

He stopped at the door and turned. "Because he could sue us! And a lawsuit is bad business," said the chief. "If we happen to get lucky and Cohan doesn't sue us, then I won't fire you at once. I'll wait until the end of your contract and make sure it's not renewed. How does that sound?"

"Awful!" she responded automatically, as if his question weren't rhetorical.

"Good, we understand one another," he said, flashing a toothy smile as cold as Idaho. He silently walked away, and with a trembling hand, she powdered her face, applied fresh lipstick, and sat for the worst portrait of her life as Jack Warner observed, awaiting his turn.

CHAPTER 4

Transplanted New Yorker Stephen Karnot stepped out his front door in Los Angeles at 8:10 into a beautiful morning on North Laurel Avenue and began his commute to Burbank on Monday, December 8, 1941. Luckily, his car knew the way up Crescent Heights to Laurel Canyon Boulevard, then up and over the mountain and into the San Fernando Valley, where a right turn put him onto Moorpark, which took him due east to Warner Bros. The morning promised a fair and cloudless day with temperatures easily topping eighty degrees.

He parked his car like every other day, slipped on his jacket and adjusted his bow tie, crossed the street, and walked in the main gate, one individual among the anonymous masses filing in. The technical people—lighting men, electricians, carpenters, camera crews—had already reported, and now the administrative people had begun arriving—men who ran the business side, women from the massive secretarial pool, and, of course, the writers.

A left turn sent Stephen strolling on toward the Writers Building on the corner of the lot, near the front office. He passed deep green hedges and sapling shade trees, also of deep green, and manicured lawns and shrubbery that gave this place a homey quality despite the cutthroat nature of the business run in the Administration Building off to his right.

Even for a Monday morning, the grounds seemed downright somber, and Karnot's mind drifted back to the previous day spent with wife Billi, both of them tethered to the radio for reports of the air attack against Pearl Harbor in Hawaii. Here on the morning after, it was the unknowns that rattled people. He caught snippets of conversation all along the way.

"Dirty Japs."

"Where do ya think they'll hit next?"

"They're going to invade!"

". . . bomb Los Angeles."

". . . aircraft plants in Santa Monica."

". . . imprison us all."

The world looked so different this morning. War had already been raging in Europe for more than two years, and even after Hitler had begun his invasion of the Soviet Union and Nazi armies blazed east through the Ukraine, the United States had kept blinders on and conducted business as usual. Yesterday it all had changed, with the American Pacific fleet destroyed at its moorings, or so the reports said.

In the quiet of morning, it didn't seem possible so soon after the attack that the lights would be clicking on and the cameras rolling. James Cagney would be shooting *Yankee Doodle Dandy* today, and Bette Davis and Olivia de Havilland would make *In This Our Life*; Cary Grant and Priscilla Lane should be entering the home stretch of *Arsenic and Old Lace*. At the corner of the lot where the writers held court out of harm's way, the crowd had thinned, and Karnot didn't see much more than groundskeepers and messengers this morning, everyone looking glum and moving with due sluggishness.

He entered the Writers Building at 8:40 and walked down

the quiet hallway toward the boss's office. It wasn't an easy walk because his boss, a little woman of five-foot-nothing, scared the hell out of him. He felt vulnerable in that office, mauled and over-matched and instantly exhausted. He always tried to get in and out with a minimum of eye contact and conversation, and sometimes succeeded. In mere seconds he could feel his underarms getting wet as he neared the door of the Warner Bros. story editor.

He drew in a deep breath, rounded the corner, and there ahead he saw the boss sitting at the story editor's desk.

"Good morning, Renie," said Karnot.

Irene Lee hunched over her typewriter, erasing an error in a memo. She looked up, annoyed, saw him, said nothing, and went on erasing, then in a quick spasm whipped the memo out of the typewriter, crumpled it furiously, and flung it into her wastebasket. She sat back as if to calm herself, enforcing a deep silence.

There it all was, in a nutshell, the little bundle of furious energy known as Irene Lee or, more commonly, Renie.

Karnot felt like he had strayed into the lion cage at the zoo. He moved slowly, quietly, to the slush pile to pick up three or four scripts and treatments to look at, and then he would tiptoe out without a word. It's what script readers did—they analyzed scripts that had made it inside the studio walls. It was kind of ironic that the lowest-paid employees in the building performed jobs on which the entire studio relied.

"No you don't," said Irene, brightening all at once. She slid the heavy-rimmed glasses that had been resting on her nose up on top of her head. It was like lifting a curtain and revealing a work of art. "Talk to me, Stephen."

He stopped and turned. "Talk to you about what, Renie?"

"You're not going to drop everything and enlist, are you?" She had enormous brown eyes that she used to bore right through a man; they went with a wide, well-proportioned face.

"The thought did cross my mind," he said.

"Well, try to resist the urge, please." She began shuffling through the wire inbox on the corner of her desk. "I've got something special I need you for," she said, grasping a large manila envelope from the stack and giving it a yank. "This just came in from New York." She ripped open the envelope to reveal a script of about 100 pages. She held it tightly in her small hands, and those big, dark eyes sliced through his consciousness. "Now, listen. This one was already important, and then yesterday happened," she said, and her eyes grew sad, as if she might cry. "Now it's the most important script in the world, and I really need you to like it. Do you understand me?"

Oh, did he ever. "Who wrote it, your brother?" he kidded.

"Nooooo," she said, deadpan, "it's a play, unproduced. And I do not know the authors, for your information, Mr. Smarty-pants. But I've got a feeling about it—I read it in New York and the more I thought about it, the more right it felt, so I had 'em send it over."

Irene usually worked in New York, but she kept an office in Burbank and would stop in for weeks at a time. Those weeks, everyone was on their toes.

She handed him the script and he felt its heft. He gave the cover a glance. "'Everybody Comes to Rick's.' Just tell me what you want me to do," he said.

She lit a Chesterfield, took a drag, held it in her lungs, and then shot a stream of smoke out the side of her mouth. "I want you to give it your usual eagle eye and write a dynamite summary." She paused to pick a bit of tobacco from the end of her tongue. "I'd like Hal to see this right away. He's going to want war stories, and this will fit the bill."

"Oh, a flag-waving spectacle, eh?"

She shook her head. "Quite the opposite. You'll see."

"I'll aim for this week," he said, nodding.

She said with gravity and in a burst, "Oh, it better be this week. And, if it's not too much trouble, knock his socks off for me."

"Knock his socks off," repeated Karnot. "Got it."

As he turned to leave, she said, "Thursday's better than Friday." He turned back, and she added, "I know you, and this week means Friday, but Friday isn't good enough. Thursday's better."

"Understood, boss," he said.

She hesitated. "There aren't a lot of people around here I can trust," she said quietly, glancing past him out the door. "Just help me out, okay?"

It was a very un-Renie-like moment, and it touched him. "Okay."

She allowed a genuine smile, then pivoted in her chair back to the typewriter and grabbed a clean interoffice form from the stack. She slid her glasses down to working position. On the communication form she set before her were lines at the top that read "To Mr." blank and, below that, "From Mr." blank. As was her practice, she hand-corrected the form to read "From **Miss**" before ratcheting the form into the typewriter and typing Lee.

She similarly expected that everyone in the building up to and including Hal Wallis would correct the "To" line to read ~~Mr.~~ **Miss** Irene Lee.

"And don't enlist until after you finish the synopsis!" was the last thing she called before banging away on the keys.

Drifting along the hallway toward his first-floor office, Karnot studied the stage play "Everybody Comes to Rick's." He knew

Renie back in the days when he had been a writer and director off-Broadway. Until, that was, the government had identified Stephen and first wife, Greta, as Communists, which ended the marriage and drove him west from New York. But Stephen had remade himself, married another, safer girl, and sought a fresh start in Los Angeles at Warner Bros.

Karnot stepped into his seven by nine office, hung up his jacket, opened his office window, and stood for a moment feeling the cool morning breeze. He sat down at his desk at 8:51, lit a cigarette, and turned to the cast of characters of "Everybody Comes to Rick's," as in Rick's Café, Casablanca, French Morocco, summer 1941, "an expensive and chic nightclub which definitely possesses an air of sophistication and intrigue." He read the cast: Richard Blaine. Sam the Rabbit. Luis Rinaldo. Lois Meredith. Captain Heinrich Strasser. There were sixteen speaking parts in all.

By now the building had come to life. A radio snapped on and the voice of FDR filled the space. The sound distracted Karnot, and he watched four of his colleagues huddle around the radio in the adjoining office; others in the vicinity had remained in their offices but no typing could be heard, which reflected keen interest in what Roosevelt had to say. All heard the president address a joint session of Congress to recap the bombing of Pearl Harbor and other attacks that had taken place the day before across the South Pacific. Roosevelt asserted that a state of war existed between the United States and the Japanese Empire, and he asked Congress for a formal declaration. Just like that.

The script reader assessed the ashen faces around him as it sunk in for all. The world was at war.

FDR's speech ended to wild cheers from a united Congress; scattered applause within the Writers Building could be heard as well. Then the radio clicked off. Karnot's eyes drifted from his gloomy colleagues down to the script that sat before him. With the world instantly a changed place, Karnot knew that Renie was right: the big boss, Wallis, would be wanting properties featuring wartime plots. As usual, Renie had been two steps ahead and Stephen returned to sweaty French Morocco for the long haul.

Karnot began to read Act 1, about Rick's, the most popular nightclub in Casablanca. The piano player at Rick's, a Negro named Sam the Rabbit, was the typical comic relief and effete to boot. The clientele at Rick's included a tide of European refugees on the run from Hitler who had ended up in Casablanca as the last stop before Lisbon and freedom.

Karnot read about an elegant Spaniard named Ugarte who held two letters of transit: *carte blanche* papers that could guarantee any refugee safe passage out of Casablanca with no questions asked.

Ugarte asked if Rick would keep the documents safe for an hour or so because even though Rick despised Ugarte, the Spaniard saw Rick as the only man in the city that could be trusted. Rick said yes, took the papers, and slipped them in his pocket.

Luis Rinaldo, prefect of police, was introduced. Rinaldo and Rick revealed the American's backstory—leaving Paris and his wife and two children for Casablanca in 1937 under mysterious circumstances. But the subject of the evening was Rinaldo's latest one-sided romance—he traded sex with young, "unawakened girls" for exit visas. Rinaldo had his sights set on Annina, Bulgarian refugee bride of naive Jan. A German officer was introduced, Captain Strasser, who arrived to witness the arrest of Ugarte for selling exit visas. Ugarte was captured and led out just as Czech newspaper publisher Victor Laszlo walked into Rick's with a beautiful American woman named Lois Meredith on his arm. Rick's stunned reaction at seeing Lois made it clear that she was the reason he had fled Paris and his old life in 1937. Act 1 ended later that night with Rick alone in the closed café, drunk. He ordered Sam the Rabbit to play the favorite song of Rick and Lois in the old days, "As Time Goes By."

As he read, Karnot pulled a fresh yellow legal pad from one of the stacks found in every office in the Writers Building and started to make notes about the cast of characters.

The pages of Act 1—thirty-seven of them—had one after another placed Stephen Karnot into an ever-deeper trance. He reached for a cigarette to find the empty pack already crumpled next to a full ashtray. He couldn't remember smoking all the cigarettes or crushing the pack. Around him the offices sat in empty silence and out the windows the sun slanted low in the western sky. It was 5:25 and he had told Billi he would be home by 6:00.

Karnot could begin to understand Renie's interest in the international characters and their conflicts inside the smoky adult playground. He looked up and there she stood, the boss, leaning against the frame of his open door and playing with the pearls around her neck. For someone so imposing, intimidating even, she remained a toy-sized woman.

"Well?" she asked.

"I assume this is the straw that stirs the drink—the letters of transit?" he asked, and she nodded. "I haven't seen the *carte blanche* used since Dumas did it in *The Three Musketeers*." He thought some more. "The setting in North Africa's interesting, given the fighting in Libya."

"Isn't it?" she said encouragingly.

He referred to the notes on the pad before him. "I like the

characters so far. I like the setting, the mystery, and the desperation. There are a lot of good things here."

Her guard was down; her face could be softly beautiful at times like this, and he watched her let out a long breath. She smiled in peaceful satisfaction as if to tell him, *See? If you play ball, I'll play ball.*

"In my head, Raft is already Richard Blaine," said Stephen. "Mary Astor could be right for Lois, the American woman."

"Write it all down," said Renie, "and let's keep talking."

"Yes, let's," said Karnot, and with that Irene walked away from his door. It occurred to him that if his boss planned to breathe down his neck until he finished, it would be a long week, so he stood on stiff legs, slipped on his jacket, closed the windows, and went home.

CHAPTER 5

At 8:50 Tuesday morning, Karnot was back to the task and into Act 2, Scene 1: the next morning at Rick's, after Rick had been reunited with Lois, the woman who had wrecked his life in Paris. In a shocking twist, Rick and Lois had spent their first night together making love in his apartment over the club.

Karnot turned page after page. Over breakfast, Rick and Lois revealed their history together, and Rick decided that she must leave Laszlo and she agreed. Rinaldo entered and revealed that Lois had spent the night with Rick only to obtain a letter of transit to get Lois and Victor out of Casablanca. "You bitch!" Rick growled at her. It was the end of Act 2, Scene 1.

Karnot closed the script, set it down, and rose from his chair. His knees creaked from sitting so long. He lit a cigarette and smoked it as he looked out at the hints of suburban Burbank he could see past the thicket of palm trees and shrubberies of the Warner Administration landscape. No way around it; Karnot was rattled because venturing into Act 2 had changed everything about the job of recommending this play. This dirty story about sexual relations—the horny French police captain who chases jail-bait and the American adulterers—simply couldn't be filmed.

He needed time to figure out these complexities: what he would say to Renie and how he would say it. Stephen decided he would take a walk down to the back lot, maybe New York Street or European Street—wherever nobody was shooting today—and do his thinking there. Yes, good plan. He shoved the remaining half-pack of cigarettes in his pocket, grabbed his jacket off the hook, and—

—smashed headlong into Renie as she rounded the corner coming into his office while he rounded the corner going out.

The collision rocked Irene back on her heels. It took a couple of seconds before she realized he had landed on her instep, and she leaned into the wall and moved her ankle around, testing for a break. Irene didn't usually stop to consider how much smaller she stood than the men in the building; moments like this reminded her. Luckily, she was solidly built—good Pittsburgh stock and a lot stronger than she looked. She took a step back and checked her clothing for damage. This was her favorite new outfit, tailored like one she had seen Joan Crawford wear in *When Ladies Meet*—a striped jacket over a simple shell, with wide-legged pants. She and Joan were exactly the same size; they had once talked about it in the ladies room at the Trocadero and marveled at their similar frames, each just five feet even, and both had made it in a man's town.

Irene worshiped Joan, who was among the gods, earning $3,000 a week at MGM. And as the boss of the Warner writers and the one who approved all stories bought by the studio, Irene made a lousy $500—less than many of the writers working under her!

"Where's the fire, buster?" Irene asked Karnot as she composed herself and flexed her ankle. He hovered there like a big goof, a foot taller than she, with his bow tie knocked crooked and a look of embarrassment on his face. Irene could sense he was taking it on the lam because of something related to his current assignment; she just didn't know exactly what.

He sighed. "I wanted to take a walk and think, that's all. I thought maybe the back lot."

She glanced into his office and saw the script opened on his desk. She looked up at him and smiled indulgently. "Let's both walk. Let's both think," she said brightly. She began moving toward the staircase, her foot still smarting. Three-inch slingbacks didn't help, but it was all in a day's work. She looked over her shoulder and he stood unmoving, so she gave a head nod that invited him to tag along. He followed obediently, and they walked out the center terrace doorway and clomped down the outside stairs into a warming December midday.

Irene had spent a semester at the lovely campus of Carnegie Tech in Pittsburgh, and the grounds at Warner Bros. Administration reminded her of those days. On that corner of the lot, all was green, quiet, and dignified. But a left turn onto First Street changed the view into one of factory sprawl. Irene walked along, a carefully practiced stride—confident, level, with just the right arm swing. Karnot strolled slowly beside her like a schoolboy on his way to the principal's office, hands in pockets and head down. They passed the star bungalows on their left—even the most seasoned employees craned necks for a glimpse of Errol or Bette, but nobody was sighted, worse luck.

Irene and Stephen passed the Makeup Department on the right, then the commissary, and she kept leading him deeper, toward the back lot. To their right as they walked loomed the soundstages, symbols of Jack Warner's industrial might. The Warner brothers had constructed their soundstages one next to the other until there were now a dozen and a half, and they were designed to be busy and stay busy. At Warner Bros. everybody worked with a single-mindedness born of the need to keep these stages humming. Justify the cost of construction and turn out product. Irene was cognizant of this fact every day, and if the knowledge faded, Hal Wallis would remind her.

Irene led Stephen onto New York Street, with neither saying a word. There were sawhorses up at the head of the block and a young production assistant hurried out to stop the interlopers.

"Sorry, we're about to roll," he told them, but then he didn't need to.

Clues of a working production were abundant, from the lights and reflectors halfway up the block to the camera on a dolly with its scurrying crew and the players in the process of being blotted and coiffed by makeup staff that hovered like bees. Irene recognized Ann Sheridan as the female on the production, which meant they were working on *Juke Girl*.

The pair kept walking until they reached the quietest part of the lot. They stood in the shadows created by the Nottingham Castle facade that had been used in *The Adventures of Robin Hood*, the gate and turrets that Errol Flynn, or rather his double, had so easily scaled on a rope four years earlier. Now, all was quiet. No Robin Hood or merry men or Prince John's soldiers or Erich Korngold music blaring out the action. There was just a hint of a breeze, the cool of the shadows, and the music of some songbirds.

Irene leaned against what looked like a stone wall, but then she withdrew, realizing it wasn't nearly as sturdy as it looked. She brushed grit off her jacket. Karnot rested his hand on the metal of the heavy gate only to pull that hand back.

"Huh," he said. "It's not metal; it's wood."

"The magic of Hollywood," she said, and then, to give him a little jolt: "How was Act 2?"

He shoved his hands back in his pockets, and she watched him arrange his thoughts. "It's exotic and mysterious. The conflicts are obvious; boy meets girl. Boy loses girl. Boy ends up a bitter derelict in Casablanca. Then there's the visa thing. Letters of transit," he corrected.

"I agree with you," said Irene. "A very strong setup."

"But . . ." he said, and the word hung in the air. An impulse made her dig into her jacket pocket and pull out cigarettes, tap one against the pack, and stick it between her lips. She snapped off a match and struck it, and the flame hissed. She dragged deeply.

"I know you believe in this story, but how do we account for all the problems?" He paused, and then words escaped him in a rush. "Your police captain preys on virgins and gives them safe passage out of town if they will have sex with him."

She allowed the smallest shrug that acknowledged, *Yeah, you've got me there.*

Karnot seemed emboldened. "Self-pitying Rick, who's full of bitterness at Lois for her past actions, still wants to make love with her. Why? She's cruel and unrepentant; it's as if he wants to suffer some more." Karnot shook his head in disapproval and said, "I think they call that sadomasochism."

Irene had smoked down the cigarette in long inhales until it was a stub, lit a new one with the old, and regrouped herself. He looked at her as if to ask, *Have you heard enough? Are we done?*

"No, no, keep going," she said.

"Okay," he said, "so then it's revealed that Lois, for all her talk of love and 'darling this' and 'darling that,' only slept with Rick to obtain letters of transit to get out of Casablanca with her husband!

So in sixty pages we have, one, a police official molesting virgins or inveigling them for sex."

"Oooh! Great word," she exclaimed.

"Two, sexual intercourse between unmarried people bordering on sadomasochism. Three, married woman exchanging sex for visas." He now held up three fingers, looked down at them, then over at her, and exclaimed, "And I'm only halfway through the play!" He was quiet a short moment, then added, "Oh! And Rick is insufferable and very feminine in his emotions. How would the audience feel about Raft or Cagney playing such a character?" Now he held up four digits. He said again, "Halfway through."

There in the December shade Irene felt a chill, not an intuitive chill but rather a garden-variety chill, and she folded her arms over her chest. "You're not telling me anything I haven't already considered," she responded. "But it's such an intriguing premise, and it's Vichy France, friendly to Germans, and the American is there in the middle of it. All of it happening in what may be the most important spot in the world. If it's done right, this one's got a world of potential. I can feel it."

"There's one Nazi, and he's got only a few lines."

"But the people," she pleaded. "The humanity gathered in Rick's, as if they're drowning and this is the lifeboat. Do you see? If you focus on boy meets girl, you miss so much about the larger story."

Stephen stared off at the mountain next to the back lot. "Yeah. What's going on in Europe. Extermination. Yeah. I understand."

"Thank you," she said, suddenly feeling better. "I need you to finish reading and see if you can find enough positives so Hal wants to buy it. Once it's bought, then the guys who work upstairs can fix all those problems you listed." She glanced at her wristwatch and started retracing their steps. "Come on, you've got work to do."

Ten minutes later, after she had returned to her desk, the phone rang.

"Irene Lee," she answered.

"Renie, it's Marjorie," whispered a voice. Marj Kershaw had dated Irene's brother Robert for a while but ended up hating him—but Marj hadn't held Robert's shortcomings against Irene and they became friends.

"Marj, why are you whispering?" said Irene.

"Because I've got a scoop for you, that's why, and I can't tell you, but I have to tell you." It was all a low, desperate whisper. Marj worked for a junior partner in the office of attorney Loyd Wright some blocks over from the studio.

"I love it!" Irene said softly. "What have you got?"

"Wallis wants to renegotiate his contract with Warner Bros. He wants to be bumped up to executive producer and hand off some of his duties to other producers at the studio. If he doesn't get what he wants, he's going to leave!"

"Holy shit!" said Irene. "Are you sure about that?"

"One hundred percent," said Marj.

"Oh my God, I owe you! Thanks, Marj."

"Okay, bye," whispered Marj, and Irene's mind careened through a racetrack of thoughts. She had been entertaining this crazy idea that she could become a producer at the studio, the one who lined up the talent and the director and executed the plan for a picture. There weren't any women producers anywhere in town that she knew of, which made the idea perfectly perfect. So, if Wallis really did get bumped upstairs, he would be needing a producer for this Morocco story if, that is, Wallis were to buy it. Sure, it was pie in the sky to think about these things, but she wasn't just some dreamer in Iowa City; she was the story editor at Warner Bros., already on the inside, so who knew?

At roughly the time Irene hung up the phone, Karnot sat down with Act 2, Scene 2, fresh cup of coffee in hand.

That evening in the club, Rick had regrouped from sex and spatting with Lois. Rinaldo informed Rick that Ugarte had committed suicide in jail, but the letters of transit he had been carrying were not found, and Rinaldo suspected that Ugarte had given them to Rick. Just then, Victor and Lois entered the club. Rick accused Victor of sending Lois to seduce him to obtain a letter of transit, but this news stunned Laszlo, indicating he had done no such thing. Meanwhile, Rinaldo tried to get young Annina Viereck drunk on champagne, causing her enraged husband to punch Rinaldo. Rick hurried to the wall switch and shut off the lights to the club. When the lights came back up, the Vierecks had vanished. An enraged Rinaldo ordered the club shut down and searched for the Vierecks, but the police couldn't find them. Rinaldo stormed off and only then did Sam open a secret compartment in the wall. Out stepped Jan and Annina Viereck.

Karnot read the words CURTAIN FALLS and stared at the page. Then, with combustion building, he jumped up from his chair and zoomed down the hall to Renie's office where she sat phone in hand, talking. He stopped short and waited, a tea kettle ready to whistle. In another minute she said "Bye-bye," and hung up the phone.

Karnot said, "The mood was tense and the pages were flying by. And then, all of a sudden, our authors gave us a cheap plot device from the last century. The lights go out and two characters vanish from the stage."

"Granted," said Renie. "A cliché."

"And Rinaldo is turning out to be a creepy man," said Stephen. "I liked him until the part with Annina and the champagne and trying to get her drunk as a prelude to sex."

"It's honest," she said with a shrug. "Men use alcohol to loosen up women. Whether you like Rinaldo or not, there's depth to these characters."

That evening, Stephen and Billi hung blackout curtains, then hovered over the radio to hear FDR's fireside chat about Pearl Harbor. It was quiet and utterly still in their neighborhood, and with windows opened, they could hear the echo of a dozen radios within earshot, all tuned to the president.

On Wednesday morning, December 10, with the voice of FDR still in his ears, Stephen placed two packs of Lucky Strikes beside the ashtray on his desk, sat down and adjusted his seat, then opened the script to Act 3, set in Rick's the evening after Jan and Annina had vanished.

The club was still closed by order of a vengeance-seeking Rinaldo. Rick, who continued to provide shelter to the Vierecks, sent Sam out to buy four plane tickets. Lois entered the club to tell Rick she was staying with him, and Victor could go on without her. Rick worked with Rinaldo on a trap for Laszlo: Rick would offer Victor the letter of transit and when he took it, Rinaldo would arrest him, leaving Lois in the clear to stay and live with Rick. But at the critical moment, with Victor's hand grasping the letter, Rick pulled a gun on Rinaldo and held him there to allow Victor and Lois to escape from Casablanca along with Jan and Annina. Lois wanted to remain with Rick, but he said no, and

Victor took her away. With the four safely flying overhead on the plane to Lisbon, Rick tossed his gun on the table and faced arrest by Rinaldo and the German, Strasser. FINAL CURTAIN.

Karnot sat unmoving as he digested all he had experienced from this play. He scribbled some final notes, then picked up the phone and dialed three numbers.

"Miss Lee," said Renie crisply on the other end of the line.

"Karnot here. I've finished."

There was a pause, and he heard the phone bang against what he presumed to be her shoulder. Renie said, "I would love to go strolling to Nottingham again, but I'm swamped. Do you feel you can you sell me in a hundred words or less?"

"Well," he said, referring to notes just written, "it's suspenseful and psychological. For a hundred pages where people are sitting around talking, the plot is wound tight. It's a natural for Raft or Garfield or Bogart. And Lois is Mary Astor all over. For all the censor problems, it's got a shitload to offer. It's colorful and timely. I'd put all that under the headline, 'Sophisticated Hokum.'"

"Dynamite, my friend!" she exclaimed. "Write it up by lunch tomorrow, will you please?" Then she added, "I love you, Stevie!" and hung up.

As he ratcheted a sheet of paper in his Royal and hit the carriage return a few times, he sighed in relief that he had passed the first test—the Lee test. Now he would rely on inspiration from the good things in the story to knock the socks off Hal Wallis because that was the true bottom line of this exercise: Stephen Karnot felt allegiance to Renie that he couldn't explain. She had trusted him, and now he was happy he could deliver.

CHAPTER 6

This December Friday, with America at war for five days now, Hal Wallis walked out of his estate on an expansive corner lot in Van Nuys where he lived with Louise Fazenda, his actress-wife, and their son, Brent. As always, there was plenty to occupy his mind as he set film canisters in the back seat of his Packard and prepared for the commute to the office. He slid into the driver's seat and set off eastward through the lush terrain of the San Fernando Valley, passing orange groves and farm fields heading for the studio where he would spend the next ten or twelve hours, at which point he would load new cans of film, the dailies, into his car to screen at home for another couple of hours and make notes for the directors, and then start over again the next morning.

Wallis pulled into his favorite parking spot just before nine and made his way into the Administration Building and up the stairs to his office down the hall from Jack L. Warner—as far away from the chief as possible. First thing, he called in his assistant, Paul Nathan, with a stenographer. Nathan brought a script and some other papers in and set them on the boss's desk.

"What do I need to know about, Paul?" said Wallis to Nathan.

Paul was a handsome young guy, well-groomed and sharp as a tack. "As you know," began Nathan, "one of our female stars is nailing one of our directors."

Wallis knew too well. Olivia de Havilland was having an affair with John Huston, Walter's kid, who was directing the Bette Davis picture. This was a new kind of problem, especially from de Havilland. "Yeah," said Wallis, "what about it?"

"Bette is noticing," said Nathan simply. It was a loaded three words.

"Wonderful," said Hal. He barked at the stenographer—all these gals were anonymous, interchangeable, and he didn't bother to learn their names: "Memo to John Huston. Subject: In This Our Life. Watched the rushes and you're still favoring de Havilland and giving her the best coverage, at the expense of Bette. Stop it, John. Miss Davis is going to catch on very soon and walk off the picture." Wallis thought another moment and added, "And stay out of Livvie's dressing room. And everything else of Livvie's. She's a contract player, not a courtesan." Hal thought a moment. "No," he amended for the stenographer, "scratch the last part. Just end with the part about Bette walking off." He turned back to Nathan. "Next?"

"Sherman is six days behind schedule on *Juke Girl*." It was all Paul needed to say.

"Memo to Vincent Sherman," snapped Wallis. "Subject: Juke Girl. Vince, you're doing it again. I have warned you on every picture you have directed to pick up the pace. Now I am warning you again. Six days behind schedule is unacceptable, and you must recover some of those days. Send me a list of efficiencies you will employ to make this happen."

Hal dismissed Paul Nathan and the stenographer and opened his mail, small envelopes first. In a while, a knock at his opened door signaled the arrival of Irene Lee. He watched her sashay the eighteen feet from the door to his desk. Wallis admired every stride. Anytime she was in sight he cleared his mind and just took her in, and there was no question, she knew it. Today, to his delight, she wore a suit with a skirt that showed some leg. She reached his desk and stopped, scanning the piles of scripts, memos, and envelopes on its surface.

"Aha!" she said. "So you haven't looked at this yet." She tapped a bundle resting before him that included a script and synopsis that sat under the remainder of unopened envelopes.

He sized up the situation in a glance. "No, but it sounds as if I had better," he said.

"I'd appreciate it. When you've got the gist, call me and we can talk at lunch." She spun slowly, managing to give her head a small toss that caused an enticing bounce to her shoulder-length chestnut hair. Then she walked back to the door at such a pace that he could take in the shape of her calves, which were enhanced by back seams in her stockings, and work his way up. As usual, he thought, *Quite a swing on that back porch.*

"Thanks, Hal," she called without looking back and she was gone, the scent of Chanel No. 5 lingering in the spot she had just occupied.

He had always been attracted to her, from the first instant, years back. He didn't know if she shared the attraction; sometimes she seemed to, but nothing had developed and he didn't push it. That created the problem: he knew she was a flirt whenever flirting would help her cause. The face and body and wit, and the hair, the way she walked, the perfume—all were weapons in her arsenal. It seemed that she calculated her sex appeal down to whether the day called for something to show off her legs or for trousers to lounge in. As a result of all he knew about his lady story editor and all he didn't know, Wallis had never made a move. Nor had she ever made one. She merely offered herself up for his viewing pleasure, all the while hinting that going for a test drive would result in the ride of his life.

Had anyone walked in, they would have wondered at the smile on his face, for in the Administration Building, Hal B. Wallis rarely smiled or had anything to smile about. Then he snapped himself out of the Renie reverie to take script in hand. He looked down at its title, "Everybody Comes to Rick's." He pulled away the script analyst's memo and one-page story brief that were paper-clipped to the cover. Behind the bundle of script pages was a hefty synopsis. Hal saw the name Karnot—oh, the Commie. He read the memo: "Excellent melodrama. Colorful, timely background, tense mood, suspense, psychological and physical conflict, tight plotting, sophisticated hokum. A box-office natural for Bogart or Raft in out-of-the-usual roles and perhaps Mary Astor."

Wallis sat back in his chair, lit a cigarette, and read the synopsis. Rick seemed a strong lead character. The café as a "powder keg of political tension" grabbed him; Karnot the Commie knew how to write a synopsis. Letters of transit, okay. But when the beautiful Lois Meredith enters, it all goes sideways. The married American woman ends up sleeping with Rick? The Breen Office would kill the script dead in its tracks. But Irene had obviously seen something of promise here, so Hal kept reading.

The love triangle between the jaded American, his lost love, and her Czech husband seemed fertile ground. The American felt like a Bogart part—the cynical, strictly neutral, and self-serving hero. These were aspects of the new Sam Spade persona the studio wanted to cultivate for Bogart. But could Bogie carry a full-fledged romantic role?

Wallis glanced at his watch to see it was already 12:30 and

time for lunch. He thought of Renie and rushed through the remaining lines of the story summary. He called Lee at 1:05, and they walked to the Green Room on what had become an ice cream sundae of a day, wall-to-wall blue sky and a temperature somewhere around seventy-five. As they sat at their usual table, Ruthie, their waitress, set down Hal's usual iced tea and Irene's usual coffee. Renie added two splashes of cream and two heaping spoons of sugar. Hal ordered a salad and a hot roast beef sandwich; the lady ordered a bowl of seafood bisque and half a Reuben.

After Ruthie had turned away, Irene said expectantly, "Well?"

Wallis sipped his iced tea. "Why don't we cut to the chase, Renie: Just tell me what you wish I would be thinking."

Renie gave a sigh. "When I first laid hands on the play in New York, it got under my skin," she said. "I thought about it on the plane, and thought some more, and then last Friday I asked them to send it over."

"But you said it's unproduced. As in, nobody wants it—"

"—yet," she finished. She drank a quarter of the cup of coffee in a gulp; it was difficult to imagine an Irene Lee even more awake than usual. "I challenge you to tell me what this play hasn't got. Exotic locale, skulduggery, sex, intrigue, Nazis, and people fleeing them."

"And a love angle we can't film because the censors won't let us," said Wallis. "From what I can tell, it's a hundred pages of people sitting around being miserable in Morocco. Helluva title, 'Misery in Morocco.'"

She gave him the look.

"Beyond that," he added, convincing himself and, he was certain, her, "we've got our roster set for the year, so 'Misery' would have to be shelved until next year."

"Nope," she said with emphasis, and added another scoop of sugar to her coffee.

"What do you mean, 'nope'?"

She stopped all movement to focus on him. "Now is the time for this story. I feel it. Don't you feel it? North Africa's important—they're fighting over the oil in Libya right now, the British and the Germans."

"So, I'm supposed to wreck my entire schedule to make a picture out of your unproduced play because of North Africa?" It was more challenge than question.

She thought a moment. "Yes." She glanced over one shoulder and then the other to insure no one was on the verge of floating within earshot. "And the other reason is that your contract with the studio is up in, what, March?"

He stirred his tea. "April."

She said just a touch more than under her breath, "If you leave, you'll need something to produce. And this would be it. You could buy it back from the studio."

"Who said anything about leaving?" he whispered. "Who have you been talking to?"

She shrugged. "You have sources; I have sources. Mine say you want a promotion, or you head for the door."

Wallis felt himself color about the face because Renie had just hinted at—in the Warner Bros. executive dining room no less—his master plan. She didn't seem to know the details, which were that he was negotiating to become a partner at United Artists. In his many years in Burbank, Hal Wallis had made Jack Warner and the other brothers uncounted millions by producing hit after hit, working long days, serving as loyal company man to a son of a bitch. And to Hal Wallis, that was Jack Warner: a well-dressed, uncouth, narcissistic son of a bitch. And if Hal were to stay, it must be on very favorable terms.

"I grant you, 'Misery in Morocco' is a lot of yakety-yak at present," said Irene as Ruthie set down the soup and sandwich, and salad and hot roast beef. Everything moved fast at Warner Bros., including food service. Bosses like Wallis and Lee demanded to be served at a lightning pace so they could eat fast and get back to their offices for the afternoon. Fast.

"I say again, this one has potential," Renie went on uninterrupted. "It's got what it takes as an A picture."

He decided to stop arguing because what else did he have Lee around for if not to offer such counsel? And his gravy was getting cold.

He took a deep breath and looked into her brown eyes. "Okay, give me a week to figure out my . . . situation. I'll study Karnot's analysis and think about it."

"Okay!" she sang. "But if we found 'Misery in Morocco,' anybody else in town could find it too. And if somebody else skunks us, Hal Wallis, you will never, ever hear the end of it. I promise."

CHAPTER 7

The week of December 16, 1941, Secretary of the Navy Frank Knox disclosed that almost 3,000 Americans had been killed in the Japanese attack on Pearl Harbor. News photos of the destruction ran in the *Los Angeles Times* throughout the week, as did stories about Wake and Midway Islands where U.S. forces were getting clobbered but continued to hold out against enemy attack. That Friday, Congress passed the Conscription Act, and all men from eighteen to sixty-four were required to register for the draft. That would begin to have a direct impact on the picture business as Warner Bros. performers and technicians went off to war.

The war had taken Hollywood in a firm grip. Like every executive at every studio, Hal Wallis needed war-related properties that could be developed into quality pictures; he needed them whether or not he stayed at Warner Bros. But did Renie's Morocco story fit the bill as a wartime picture, and was she correct that he must move forward and make it as soon as possible?

Wallis heard a rapping on the frame of his open office door. He looked up; it was one of his producers, rotund, energetic Jerry Wald. "Did you hear about the Jap subs off the California coast, Hal?" Jerry asked as he charged into the room, all bluster and enthusiasm. "They're right off the coast!" Wald had a voice that was almost soprano, especially when he got going.

"I hadn't heard about Japanese subs, Jerry, but have a seat. Let's talk."

"Sure," said Wald as he ambled over to one of the two chairs before Hal's desk and plunked his wide frame down, causing his jacket to gap and expose a wrinkled white shirt.

Hal's mind swirled this morning. He had one foot in at Warners and one foot out, way over at United Artists. As much as he despised Jack Warner, if he moved to UA, he would feel the loss of the Burbank support team, from the Warner stars to the writers and the producers working under him—like Jerry Wald. Hal would be starting from scratch if he flew the coop, and that might have him working fourteen-hour days far into the future.

The precarious position affected every decision, and he couldn't reveal any of this inner conflict to his producers, particularly an operator like Jerry. Wallis said, "I'm considering buying a stage play, but I want to be careful."

"What kind of stage play?" said Wald, lighting a cigarette. Jerry was always in intelligence-gathering mode, which was fine. It meant he cared.

Wallis picked up the script. "A story about an American expatriate who runs a club in Morocco. It's a thing out of New York."

"Nah. You should be buying war stories," said Wald.

"This Morocco thing is a war story. It's Vichy Morocco with a heavy Nazi influence."

"Hmmm," said Wald. "You want me to take a look? Opinions are free."

"That's exactly what I want," said Hal, rubbing his stubbly chin. He picked up his phone and pushed a button. When he heard Paul Nathan's voice, Hal said, "Paul, do me a favor and send a memo to Miss Lee. Ask her to have some copies of that script

'Everybody Comes to Rick's' and Karnot's analysis sent around to some people. Jerry Wald and also some of the writers. She knows who to involve. Thanks." Wallis hung up the phone, aware of a knot in his stomach.

Jerry stood and stamped out his cigarette in Wallis's ashtray. "I'll give your play a read right away," he said as he headed for the door, where he turned back and shot a finger at Wallis. "You're the best."

The next morning, Phil Epstein slouched at his desk with his feet up when a knock sounded at his office door.

"Yeah," Phil called to the visitor without bothering to see who it was. He was reading the *L.A. Times* and had spotted a headline that Santa Anita wasn't going to open on New Year's Eve. He and his brother had just been talking about going there for opening day.

"Hey, Julie!" he said loudly.

"Yeah?" said his brother in the next room twelve feet away.

"They canceled the Rose Bowl 'cause of the war! And the whole Santa Anita season!"

"Motherfuckers!" Julie exclaimed from the adjoining office.

The Epsteins loved driving out Colorado Boulevard to Arcadia and making a day of it, with or without their wives. Usually without.

Phil had already forgotten about the knock on his door; his opened newspaper obscured the identity of the person who had entered.

"Jesus, you guys!" said a familiar, high-pitched voice. Phil lowered the paper to see Jerry Wald standing before him wearing a pained look on his mug. Wald was a round man with a round face, dark skin, and wore his black hair slicked back. Every suit he owned looked like he had just slept in it.

"What's the matter, Jerry?" Phil wanted to know.

"What if I was the chief," hissed Wald, his voice especially high, "walking in to see a writer sitting here reading the paper with his feet up?"

Wald was easy to fluster and owned a paralyzing fear of Jack Warner. Jerry thought that since he had been involved in bringing first one and then the other Epstein onto the lot, their antics would come back to bite him. Which both brothers found hilarious.

"All it would take," said Wald, that voice pitched like Walter Winchell in a desperate whisper, "is one instant where he saw you with your feet up on the desk, reading the paper, and your goose would be cooked. And so would mine."

Julie's voice in the other room called, "Did somebody on the Warner payroll just say somebody's goose would be cooked?"

"Yep, clichés are flying," said Phil, who could feel his brother's blood heat up. Phil carefully folded up the paper and laid it on his desk. "What can I do for you, Jerry?"

"Little favor. Just a little one," said Wald, who was as transparent as the windows, and Phil could see that this favor wouldn't be a little one; what was coming was going to be a big favor. Wald held in his hand a script. "Give this thing a good read and tell me what you think, will you?" He paused. "What you both think."

"What is it, Phil?" Julie called expectantly from the other room. He had been listening; Julie's hearing was excellent.

Phil stuck out his hand, and when Wald hesitated, Phil wiggled his fingers in universal sign language for fork it over. Wald handed him a mimeographed script and a mimeographed story synopsis.

Phil gave both a quick inspection. "It's a stage play, Julie," he reported. "A stage play and one of Karnot's story summaries."

"Oh, the Commie," called Julie.

"'Everybody Comes to Rick's,'" Phil read from the cover. "Jer wants us to tell him what we think."

"Ha!" called Julius. "Jerry wants you and me to tell him what he thinks!"

"I came to the same conclusion, Julie," called Phil. Wald had been riding the coattails of the Epstein brothers for years. Back when Julius was an unknown writer in New York, he and Wald had collaborated on a story synopsis that made its way to Warner Bros., and the studio had bought it—after Wald had removed Julie's name from the cover page. So then when Wald had gotten himself a job as a screenwriter at Warners without an iota of talent for writing, he was forced to import Julie from New York City to serve as his ghostwriter. The arrangement had worked for a while, but then Julie forced Wald's hand and began to get cowriter credit on the stories, and Warner Bros. had hired him. Suddenly, Wald didn't have anyone to ghostwrite for him, and so he snuck Phil into town from Pennsylvania until Phil also forced Wald's hand, and now both Epsteins worked at the studio. And even though it had become unofficially official that Jerry Wald couldn't write, his chutzpah, sense of story, go-getter work ethic, and charming personality had allowed him to thrive as one of the lot's most promising young producers. It took brass balls for Jerry to continue to rely on the smarts of the Epsteins, but that's one thing Jerry had as a pair: brass balls.

Phil could sense they were overdoing it, giving the business to Wald. Julie could be especially brutal. "Okay, so we'll look at this play for you, Jerry," said Phil quietly. "As a favor."

"I appreciate it, you guys," said Wald, who pulled a handker-chief from his pants pocket and blotted his forehead. In the mean-time, Julie had drifted up to Phil's door and stood behind Wald. "I want my own copy," he said over the producer's shoulder.

Jerry turned, pushed his way past Julie, and said, "There's a war on and paper is precious, Julie. Share." As he passed Alice sitting at her desk, Jerry added, "Morning, doll," and was gone.

Phil held up the script in one hand and the twenty-page syn-opsis in the other. He looked at his brother and said, "Pick one."

Julie grabbed the summary. "The short one."

"Goldbricker," said Phil.

Philip Epstein spent the next hour reading in silence. He knew his brother must be interested in the summary because Julie hadn't uttered a sound, which must have delighted Alice.

Suddenly Julie called, "I'm done. Trade me!"

Phil looked at how many pages he had gone through, and how many remained. He snapped, "I'm not even halfway through! Rick is just meeting this Laszlo guy!"

"You want me to tell you how it ends?" said Julie.

"No! Shut up and let me read!" said Phil.

As he moved to Act 3, Phil could feel his brother's impatience in the next room. They had just gone to see the United Artists picture *The Corsican Brothers*, an Alexandre Dumas story starring Doug Fairbanks Jr., in dual roles with trick photography. The sto-ry concerned Siamese twins separated at birth who when one is injured the other feels pain. To the world, this was a supernatural story; to the Epsteins, it was life.

Julie wandered into Phil's office to "borrow the *Times*," he said, but he was stealing glances to see how much progress his brother had made on the script. He shuffled back out noisily, newspaper in hand. Phil could hear him turning the pages of the paper next door. Turning each with a flourish.

Phil read how Rick was making a deal with Rinaldo to arrest Laszlo as he took possession of one of the letters of transit. The idea was that the Vierecks would fly to Lisbon with the other letter. But as Rinaldo attempts to arrest Laszlo, Rick pulls a gun on him, and Laszlo and Lois escape and fly out of Casablanca with the Vierecks. And Rick—

"He what?" exclaimed Phil. "He throws his gun on the table and allows himself to be arrested by Strasser!" Phil riffled back three pages and read it over to confirm what he was seeing. "What the hell did he do that for?"

In a moment, Julie was standing in the doorway to his brother's office. "I could have told you that's how it ended."

Phil looked down at the last page of the script, feeling that the play's writers had betrayed him. "It's slow as shit," he said to Julie. "And then the hero just quits." Phil thought another moment. "But it's kinda racy. And that makes it," he said, holding a finger up like Clarence Darrow, "unfilmable."

"Right!" said Julie. "Un. Fucking. Filmable. I love that!"

The suite of offices was remarkably quiet as the brothers digested the story they had just consumed, the short version and the long. Neither had to say aloud that he thought the play was crap; like most things, the information passed between them at a frequency somewhere near the whistles only dogs could hear.

"But if it's crap," said Phil, "why are we, you know, thinking about it?"

"Yeah, that's bothering me, too," said Julie. "You know what got to me?"

"What?" said Phil.

"The desperation of the people to get out of Casablanca. We've got it easy here; for people in Europe, every day is life or death."

"Jews, you mean," said Phil.

Julie nodded silently.

He handed his brother the story synopsis and Phil handed Julie the script. Then the offices grew so quiet again that Phil noticed Alice tiptoeing over and looking in first at Julius in his office and then at him in his, like a sitter checking that the baby is still breathing. Alice stood between them so each could see her and said, "How long have I worked for you? I have never seen you so interested in something, in anything, that you missed lunch at the writers table."

"Shit, what time is it?" Julie asked urgently.

"It's a quarter of two," said Alice.

Phil stared at Julie, his face ashen. "Are you thinking what I'm thinking?"

"That lunch is the most important hour of the workday?" said Julie. He still held the script in hand, and now his face turned sour as he stared down at it. "This thing stole our lunch!"

Phil felt the same way: their lunchtime sessions at the writers table were sacrosanct. It was the only fun anybody could have at this prison of a studio, and the fact they had missed it led Phil to marvel, "Jerry actually brought us something good."

"Is it good, Phil? Is it?" Julie asked. "This Rick character is a big baby. A goddamn loser! He pisses and moans over some woman who's a tramp, this Lois, and then throws in the towel and gives up! And it's a play, so all they do is sit around and talk."

Phil watched Alice return to her desk and begin to file her nails, but she was watching him over her glasses. "It made you miss lunch," she tossed off, casually, "and you admitted yourself, the thing about the refugees could be important to show."

"Maybe it is good," said Julie to Alice.

Phil stood up and began to pace out from his office, through the common area where Alice sat, into Julie's office, and back out again. "If you toughened Rick up, you'd have Bogart," said Phil as he paced. "But it's only got one Nazi."

"We could add some," said Julius. "The more the better. It could use some spies in the shadows. Dark and moody, like *Algiers*, with guys in fezzes. And belly dancers."

Phil snapped his fingers. "*Algiers*—exactly!" He continued to pace. "And I gotta say, I like the chemistry between Rick and Rinaldo. They're like friendly enemies."

He could see that Julius was warming to the task; Phil loved when his brother got going. "If we're talking *Algiers*," said Julie, "then we need somebody like Hedy Lamarr or Sigrid Gurie, in a gold thing with her tits hanging out."

"Definitely some tits," said Phil. "Women in gold, yeah." He stepped out of his brother's office and eased over to Alice's desk. "Can you bring us a couple of pastrami sandwiches, Alice?"

"And Cokes," called Julius.

Phil pulled out a five and said, "And get yourself a little somethin'."

Phil laughed when Alice glared at him, took the five, and stormed off. He knew that she knew she was better than this, but she did it anyway. Alice was a trouper.

Julie came in to sit opposite Phil at his desk and they began to formulate exactly what they wanted Jerry Wald to think about this property, because one thing was sure: without either uttering the words *we want this job*, both knew they had to be the writers adapting "Everybody Comes to Rick's" for the screen.

CHAPTER 8

At a quarter past four on Christmas Eve 1941, Wallis sat in his office facing a seated Jerry Wald. As the afternoon waned, a Wednesday afternoon, Wallis held a paper in hand and said, "I was very interested in what you said here about giving it the look and feel of *Algiers*." Hal loved the way Jerry could capture the idea of a picture in a sentence or sometimes in just a word. "*Algiers*," Hal murmured again, looking off. "That's inspired, Jerry. That really got me to thinking."

"That's what you pay me for, boss: ideas," said Jerry, shooting Hal with a thumb and forefinger. "I'm seeing it as dark and moody, full of shadows, maybe some spies, definitely more Nazis. And women, exotic women like the way they used Hedy Lamarr and Sigrid Gurie in *Algiers*. Gorgeous women. Imagine Ann Sheridan in some of those getups. You know, costumes, in gold."

Hal rubbed his chin, annoyed that he had just shaved and yet needed a shave. "*Algiers* was too highbrow for the second-run theaters," Wallis thought aloud, "but it had style. And it got some award notice from the Academy. If we went for the *Algiers* look and feel, maybe we could turn this play into something."

"I'm enthusiastic about it," said Wald. "Have you gotten a price?"

"Yeah, $20,000," said Hal.

"Did you ask the chief?"

"I sent Mr. Warner a memo," said Wallis. "Jack said, 'Get some opinions,' which I'm already doing, 'and then make a decision.' He said if it's thumbs-up from you guys, go ahead and buy it."

Wallis looked up at the Emerson plaque, then reached over and picked up the phone and dialed three numbers. He heard Irene Lee pick up. "Hello, Renie?" he said into the receiver. "Go ahead and buy the Morocco story, will you?"

He heard her give a little whoop into the phone. "You won't be sorry," she told him.

He smiled. "I had better not be, or you will never hear the end of it." And he hung up the phone.

Irene Lee sat back at her messy desk and put up her feet. For once in her life, she allowed a moment, just a moment, to admire the new navy blue slingbacks she had bought on her way home the previous evening—the kind Joan would wear. Irene sat back, breathed, and relished a watershed moment. She lit a Chesterfield and savored it. In this little sliver of time, the dark figures she always contended with, the demons she had been beating back all her life, crept back into view. She grappled endlessly with one of them, the perfection demon, and couldn't accept her own imperfection. And yet she had to be perfect. She must be perfect to keep up with her perfect brother Robert, three years older, Mother's favorite. By the time Irene came along, she could only stand in the shadow of the flawless Robert, good-looking, charming, talented Robert who became a musical prodigy on the violin, then excelled at Dormont High in Pittsburgh. He became a legend there—of course—and easily won a scholarship to the Curtis Institute of Music in Philadelphia.

At every step in life, Irene had bobbed in his wake. "Oh, you're Robert's little sister," she had heard a thousand times, and she would smile prettily and acknowledge the hated fact. Irene became a good pianist but didn't win any scholarships. She tried theater in high school and joined the Pitt Players as she attended Carnegie Tech, but she was only good and failed to earn lead roles. She just wasn't Robert.

But Warner Bros., well, that was a different story. She remembered reading *The Iliad* in high school, and she had come over the years to see this, the studio, as Mount Olympos. Even though in theory Jack Warner reigned supreme, it was really Wallis who played Zeus and kept the other quarrelsome gods in line. The entire world looked at this studio and its stars as the gods, and Wallis kept them all in line. And just one moment ago, Zeus had smiled on Irene.

She sat back and dragged on her cigarette in a reverie that she decided to extend another five minutes. She thought about Joan, who had saved Irene from a life of anonymity. Irene first saw Crawford in *Our Dancing Daughters* in high school and fell in love with everything about her. Joan was perfect like Robert but not threatening like Robert. From Joan, Irene learned about makeup, hairstyles, and dressing for success. She learned that Joan was short too, just five feet tall, but commanded the screen anyway, and so Irene learned to walk like Joan, in a way that gave her the appearance of being self-assured and sexy and tall. She trained herself to talk like Joan, losing that clunky Pittsburgh accent. All of it worked. Irene thought about the move to New York City and the drive of a twenty-one-year-old to get a job in the picture business, which eventually led her to Wallis, who offered her a job at Warner Bros. in the story department.

It was right around then that she invented the concept of the perfect picture. She could never be perfect, could never be Robert. But what if she, Irene Lee, could be part of creating a perfect motion picture? What if she were to find the magic property and serve as producer and watch it go on to win awards? That would be something no story editor, let alone no woman, had ever done in Hollywood. It could be *The Adventures of Robin Hood*, but better. *The Wizard of Oz*, but better. *The Grapes of Wrath*, but better. Not just better. The best. Perfect. Her perfect picture.

She thought about closing her door in case any of the writers saw her lounging, but the hell with 'em. At times like this, she always thought about her lifetime of rage that exhausted her. She raged for having Russian immigrant parents named Levine. She raged at her mother for loving Robert more. At being born a Jew. At being born a girl, being short and slender, having ambition but no singular talent. She raged because God made her a second-class citizen in a world of men. She raged every time a man condescended to her, or put the make on her, as if any old line would work on Irene Lee, the little Pittsburgh Jew girl who hero-worshiped Joan Crawford.

Irene had her secrets, like planting stories about herself in the Pittsburgh newspapers. One of her high school pals from Dormont worked at the *Pittsburgh Press*, and they conspired to run little stories about Irene that her mother would be sure to see. Irene Lee talks back to Erich von Stroheim during a Fox story conference. Irene Lee becomes a story supervisor at Fox. Irene Lee named assistant story editor at Warner Bros. Then the big one, in 1933: a two-column feature detailing Irene Lee's denial that she was engaged to wed famed director Ernst Lubitsch, complete with an Irene glamour shot. Take that, Robert! Of course, Lubitsch would be surprised to learn how close to wedlock he was with a girl he considered nothing more than his current playmate. And wasn't Mother scandalized enough to forget about Robert for fifteen full minutes?

Soon Irene would have to call Roy Obringer in Legal and have him contact Wharton & Gabel, who represented the authors and their play, "Everybody Comes to Rick's." But not just now. Now she needed to savor a little longer. Hal's call from upstairs to approve the purchase of the play she had found validated her. Yes, that was what she felt, twenty grand worth of validation that on something big, something where she had stuck her neck out, Irene Lee's opinion meant something. It didn't matter that the play had gone unproduced, and sure, she'd had to twist Stephen Karnot's arm behind his back for that positive story review. She dabbed a finger with her tongue and wiped a smudge off the leather of her left shoe, by her little toe. If there were a bottle around, she'd have poured a slug of whiskey to celebrate. She felt suddenly like a parent, a guardian maybe, to this oddball of a play, but she continued to have a feeling about this one. Such a strong, ringing-in-the-ears feeling. This one was something. Hell, this one might be bigger than the engagement to Ernst Lubitsch.

CHAPTER 9

Arthur Wilson lay in his bed, awake in the night, as wife Estelle snored gently beside him. He grabbed the alarm clock beside his bed and tilted it toward a sliver of light beaming through the drapes: 4:20 in the morning, meaning the alarm would ring in forty minutes. In the muffled distance with the bedroom windows open, he could hear an occasional delivery truck changing gears on Beverly Boulevard a block to the south. Other trucks roared by on Temple a block to the north. In a perfect world he would doze again, but this world wasn't perfect. He had been wrestling with Morpheus for decades now and losing most bouts, but then Arthur was a worrier. He did not like living in this rented bungalow. Estelle deserved better than Filipinotown. And so he fretted. Lying in the dark, he kept two-four time to the tick-tick of the clock and wished Estelle would follow that same tempo. She did not. Estelle sawed logs to her own beat with every delicate inhale.

Arthur had been fretting a lot about the war, but not this night. This time his troubles centered around the decision to follow advice from Orson Welles and come to Hollywood, the land of opportunity. Arthur kept experiencing flashbacks to two years earlier—two years exactly—at the Martin Beck Theater on Broadway. He had played Little Joe Jackson in *Cabin in the Sky*, and his performance had fit right in with greats that included Ethel Waters,

Rex Ingram, and Katherine Dunham. In his mind's eye, Arthur could still see past the footlights, the audience out there, packed houses of 1,300 a night for twenty weeks. He loved it, simply loved it. Good, steady work and the opportunity to perform—that's all he asked. That's all he ever asked or wanted. And he could think back beyond *Cabin in the Sky* to years on the stage in Harlem, the Lafayette Theater mostly, and before that to cabaret work in Paris and Marseilles. The memories flooded his mind in the night, and he couldn't shut them off. Sometimes he didn't want to. He just lay there and listened to the applause and felt the love.

Now, here he was in Hollywood the week between Christmas and New Year's, the only Negro contract player in the employ of Paramount Pictures. He was starting at the bottom again despite a resume as long as his arm, starting at the bottom at age fifty-seven in a town that hadn't exactly thrown open its arms to welcome him. He had signed with Paramount for $350 per week, which had allowed Arthur and Estelle to move to an area of Los Angeles not too far from the studio. Arthur liked to work, and he had sat idle until finally getting a part in a picture; he had started yesterday and would finish today or tomorrow. His overactive mind replayed the previous day on Stage 14 working for a pleasant director named Mr. Lanfield and the lively and wise-cracking Bob Hope. Arthur's entire day had been spent dressed as the porter of a passenger train watching Hope deliver dialogue with British actress Madeleine Carroll; hours of standing there reacting. By the end of the day, he'd been exhausted, his back aching, and now here he was, unable to sleep.

At one minute to five he debated whether to push the button of the alarm so it wouldn't wake Estelle, but he would be needing breakfast and they had agreed she would cook it, so one minute later when the bell sounded in high A, he remained abed while Estelle shuffled first into the bathroom and then a few more steps to the kitchen.

"You have another full day today, Dooley?" she asked him forty minutes later after he had bathed, shaved, and dressed. She scraped scrambled eggs onto his plate from a blackened old skillet that had survived every move they had made and probably the Civil War before that.

"Yeah, full day," he answered. "Until five, remember," he added to remind her of wartime hours at the studio—production must end at five o'clock by law so people would be off the streets by nightfall, when blackout conditions began.

There was no further conversation until after she had set two pieces of white toast on the other side of the plate in front of him, which he barely buttered because of the way the stick of butter was dwindling, and talk was there wouldn't be any more butter because of rationing.

"How they treatin' you?" she asked as she poured coffee into both their cups from the percolator with a big old dent in its chrome.

"The director's very nice," said Wilson. "Man named Lanfield. Sid, I think. They call him Sid. He's a very respectful fellow, very cheerful and funny."

"Hopefully they won't have you on your feet all day again," she grumbled as she seated herself beside him.

He wished for bacon but there wasn't any to be had; at least Estelle couldn't find any this week in Filipinotown. Shortages brought on by the war were already hitting the food supply, and the holidays hadn't helped. He ate all the eggs and both slices of toast and made himself some more toast because he knew he would need fuel for the six or seven hours until lunch, and white bread still abounded in stores.

After breakfast he brushed his teeth, tied his tie, and picked up a dress shoe to slip it on and cringed at the scuffs. He rooted out a tin of Cavalier shoe polish and a rag and did his best to shine away the scuffs. It wouldn't do to be seen at work looking run-down when he hoped for better parts in more pictures, especially when he wore his own shoes as wardrobe. Still, Paramount was a fine studio, and he was proud to work there.

At 6:25 he reached the front door to receive a warm smack on the lips from Estelle. "Break a leg, Dooley," she said for the second day in a row, and with his heart bursting with love, he headed out onto Council Street and down to Beverly, where he hopped on the streetcar heading west and hopped off twelve minutes later at North Van Ness. From there he strolled up to Melrose and then turned toward the main Paramount Gate.

It was a white studio. Bright white. The gate, the administrative buildings, the soundstages, and the people. Very white. He took great care to avoid eye contact as he walked toward the Makeup Department to be prepped, then Wardrobe for his porter costume, then one more walk in the cool of the morning to Stage 14, where the train station set was being lit for another round of takes. He had experienced all manner of work on stages spanning half the globe, but the buzz of a Hollywood set before the camera rolled could only be compared to a hornet's nest. Inside the sound-stage, people swarmed around a number of full-size Pullman cars. Up ahead past three of the cars, at the spot where he had worked the previous day, men with tape measures and light meters called back and forth with the camera operator. The set designer looked through the camera's eyepiece and called out to set dressers making final background adjustments. Gaffers ran cable to the lights that had been carefully locked off from the day before for continuity. The men adjusting the lights conversed with men judging the quality of the light. Over a ways, Bob Hope paced back and forth and ran lines with himself, then glanced down at script pages and mumbled dialogue. A makeup girl stopped him and applied powder, then Hope paced anew and mumbled some more.

Off at the edge of the stage, dozens of extras smoked cigarettes and waited. They were train passengers, men and women, conductors, and porters. All knew to stay out of the way and by their nonchalance and the way they chatted with one another, it was clear they had been doing this for years.

Near the focal point of the action, the other star in the scene sat in a camp chair with her name on it: Madeleine Carroll. She wore a navy dress with a plaid, full-length coat over it. On her bright blonde hair rested a beret. Carroll wore reading glasses and quietly studied her script, legs crossed, showing an exquisite ankle above slingback pumps. Dooley was careful not to make eye contact, but he decided ankle contact was okay, so he lingered for a moment on a very fine sample of an ankle.

"Dooley! Good, over here," called a voice that shook him from his reverie. Director Lanfield, a trim man of about forty, had dressed well in a pressed shirt, tie, and sport jacket. He held the script in his hand, the proper pages folded back.

"Yes, Mr. Lanfield," said Wilson and hurried over the thirty feet to yesterday's mark in the concrete floor of the stage, an X in black tape. Next to him loomed a full-size passenger railcar.

"Now, yesterday," said Sid Lanfield. "Yesterday you were great. You're just confused. Bob Hope's character confuses you. He's got this frantic energy because Madeleine has been driving him crazy, and your bit of business, the way you reacted to Hope, was perfect. Just perfect. We're going to pick it up from one of their exchanges and finish the scene. There's just a bit more back and forth, and you remember that deadpan you were giving Bob? But as the dialogue progresses, you grow a little curious as to what these folks are going on about. So, we'll try it and get your natural reactions, and then we'll adjust. You okay with that?"

"Yes, sir," said Wilson quietly. "Increasingly curious. I can do that."

Director Lanfield provided a look at the script. "There's some back and forth—she'll feed Bob his lines—the camera will be on you and Bob the whole time. She says, 'Don't forget to take your pills. And that green stuff, take lots of that.' Then Bob says, 'Okay, but don't you drink anymore—you've got quite a snootful.' At that point, hearing him say that, I want you to give the camera a bit more of a reaction." Lanfield put a hand on Dooley's shoulder. "Just follow along; give me natural takes. A little alarmed at the strange conversation. Then Bob will notice you and do some business, trying to explain what's going on. You just stare at him. We'll be rolling through it. Then your cue is when he turns on his heel to board the car and says, 'Come on, let's go!' You give a couple of long beats and look up toward Madeleine's mark, and then follow Bob inside." Lanfield squeezed Dooley's shoulder. "Got it?"

"Yessir, I got it," said Dooley. He felt his heart should be racing, but it wasn't. It was a job he could do. He could do a lot more, but this was what Paramount needed today.

Lanfield spun around and when he did, he gave a head nod to the assistant director.

"Okay, camera rehearsal!" screamed the assistant director. "Positions, everyone!"

Lanfield looked back at Dooley. "And don't be afraid to have some fun with it," he said. Dooley acknowledged his understanding with a firm nod.

"Quiet on the set!" screamed the AD. "Extras walking through, position one!" Then the assistant assessed the stage as everyone grew still.

Bob Hope had moved in next to Wilson but deep in the character and moment, gave him no notice. Twenty feet away, Carroll stood facing Hope, script in hand, still wearing black-rimmed glasses.

"And—action!" said Lanfield.

Hope called out his dialogue to the distant Carroll. She fed lines back. Wilson performed by doing little more than nothing. He relied on his face to paint a picture while discreetly looking at Hope. The scene progressed. A few extras walked past on cue. Hope suddenly looked at Dooley, and the eye contact nearly electrocuted Wilson. It was the first time in all these hours over two days that Hope had acknowledged him. Hope did his business, then said stridently, "Come on! Let's go!" and spun on his heel. He walked into the Pullman car, and Wilson did as instructed—looked off at Carroll and then after Hope and followed him inside.

"Cut it," said Lanfield calmly.

"Cutting!" screamed the AD. "Okay, extras walking through, back to one! We will be rolling camera in a moment!"

Hope returned to his mark. His face showed no emotion. Lanfield walked up to Dooley and as he did, Hope angled the script in the director's hand so he could do some final cribbing.

"Dooley, perfect all the way through. After Bob says, 'Come on, let's go,' give it one less beat. Look at Madeleine, little shake of the head maybe, and follow Bob in. Okay?"

"Sounds good, yessir, Mr. Lanfield," said Dooley.

They nailed the scene in one take, and Lanfield said calmly, "That's a buy, print it," and asked for a backup.

As they shot the reverse with the camera on Carroll, with the mob of extras walking through the busy train station, Dooley was no longer on camera and proceeded to Stage 9, interior a sleeping car, for his next scene. Still dressed as a porter, his character would be in the sleeper car walking a tray with a dead fish up to Hope, who was playing a scene with a train conductor. Now Wilson had a line: "Here's your fish, sir."

Four-and-a-half hours later, with Hope shooting on Stage 9, a fresh-faced production assistant found Dooley waiting and said, "We're a little behind. You can go, Wilson. We'll need you again at seven in the morning."

"Yes, sir," said Wilson, who then walked out of Stage 9 into the late afternoon sun and headed back to Wardrobe to change into his street clothes.

Another difficult night followed, during which he lay there retracing his steps through the Harlem of 1930 and '31 and '32, savoring those exciting times. It was the worst of the Depression, but then he was colored, and colored people had had so little, there was little to lose. He recalled touching the Tree of Hope beside the Lafayette Theater. All the Negro performers who worked there would touch the tree, and Wilson mused to himself as he lay in the dark that maybe, just maybe, it had worked. In three hours he was back in his porter costume for one more day on Stage 9.

In a corner of the mammoth soundstage, he found a white actor in a train conductor costume speaking with an older Negro dressed as another porter. Wilson walked up to them.

"How ya doin'?" bellowed the conductor, a man with a wide,

weathered face that Wilson had seen in any number of pictures, always playing a cop.

"Wade Boteler," said the man, shifting his cigarette from his right hand to his left to shake Wilson's hand. The white man's grip was firm.

"Charles Moore," said the Negro quietly with a smile, and he shook hands with Wilson.

"Dooley Wilson."

"You're the new guy," boomed Boteler. He was a very jovial fellow. "*Cabin in the Sky*, right? Glad to know ya."

Wilson gasped inside at such an acknowledgment but didn't want to let it show. To be spoken to by a white actor and to be recognized for *Cabin in the Sky*—Wilson shuffled awkwardly from one foot to the other.

"*Cabin in the Sky*," murmured Charles Moore with quiet reverence. "My oh my, that's wonderful."

"Don't you be modest," Boteler scolded Moore and said to Wilson, "Charlie here was in twelve pictures last year. He's practically a real porter by now. If he washes out of the business, he can always get a job on the *Super Chief*!"

Moore laughed sheepishly and elbowed Boteler in the ribs. "Wade only mentions my twelve pictures because he made thirty last year! This guy was in thirty pictures in a single year! And big pictures too. He works with Jimmy Cagney and Errol Flynn."

Boteler snorted happily. "I walk on and walk off, with a line here and a line there. I do the tough guy and the slow burn. But I'll tell ya—it bought me and my wife a house! We set up shop in Glendale, thanks to thirty walk-ons as a cop." He finished his cigarette with a deep drag and dropped it to the stage floor to step on it. "We day players gotta stick together, right?" He gave first

Moore and then Wilson a light jab in the ribs.

For the first time since he had hit town, Dooley felt like a part of something. He thought of Estelle and their own dreams of owning a home. In a moment the AD called, "Places!"

"Oops, gotta go," said Boteler, and he hurried over to the camera and the set, the sleeper car where he performed a bit with Hope, who was ensconced in an upper berth. Back and forth they went and Wilson watched, mesmerized at the talent of the two men. Boteler hadn't even been studying his script but rattled off his lines with perfection, even cuing Hope a couple of times.

After the printed takes were confirmed, an assistant cameraman called, "The gate's clean!"

Lanfield searched about the soundstage. "Dooley! Where's Dooley?"

Wilson hurried past the camera into the middle of the sleeper car set and stood at the director's side.

"Yes, Mr. Lanfield," he said.

Lanfield pointed to Dooley's mark at camera left, up the sleeper car corridor. "There's position one. The gag is, Bob's got a pet penguin he needs to feed. You walk the serving tray with the fish up the aisle to Bob and Lyle. I need your delivery to be nice and bright. 'Here's yo fish, suh!' Then the boys go back and forth and when you hear voices call from off-set, you look surprised and walk off."

"Yes, sir," said Wilson.

They did a rehearsal and then Lanfield ordered the camera to roll. Dooley stood in position one, ready for his first line as a Paramount player. He could feel his heart beating, nice and steady and slow.

"All right, let's shoot this!" called the director. "Camera."

"Rolling!" called the cameraman.

The sound assistant stepped in front of the camera and placed a clapboard before the lens. "Scene 30, take 1!" he called, and snapped the clapboard.

Lanfield let the assistant step clear. Then, "Action!"

Dooley held the tray at shoulder level and smelled a dead bass right next to his nose. He walked about twelve feet up the aisle of the sleeper car, concentrating to balance the tray up above his shoulder. He reached his mark before Hope, who sat in the upper berth, while Wade Boteler held his mark three feet away.

Wilson gave Hope a glance and said happily, "Here's yo fish, suh!" and removed the lid from the plate with the dead fish.

Boteler took one look at the fish and bellowed, "Raw!" at Hope. "What are you doing with a raw fish?"

"You put it under your pillow," stammered Hope. "It makes your dreams come true!"

Then a visual cue from the AD brought complaints from other passengers in the car, which were voices of extras off-camera.

"We're trying to sleep!"

"Quiet!"

And Dooley gave Hope and Boteler a confused look and drifted off camera.

"Cut!" called Lanfield. "Perfect! Beautiful! Print that one and let's shoot a backup."

They did it again, just as perfectly. The AD barked, "Redress for Scene 31!" and the crew set into instant motion, moving lights and cables, dollying the camera into a new position. It was all done quickly without a wasted motion, in minutes.

Dooley stood watching it all with Charles Moore and thought, *I can only hope our army runs this efficiently.* And then the camera assistant was checking his light meter with the director of photography, a man called Bill.

Lanfield hurried over to the two porters as they waited and watched. "Okay, now listen," he told them. "You two get the payoff for the entire sequence. Up until now we haven't seen the penguin in his pajamas, which has been the talk of the train, this penguin, in pajamas. But now you two are going to see him walking up the aisle. He's not a figment of somebody's imagination; you see him. You both see him, but Dooley, you get the line. 'Lookee here!' Nice and bright. You are, sort of, enchanted to see this penguin. Okay? So try it for me, will you? 'Lookee here!'"

Dooley closed his eyes and tried to picture what he would see—a penguin in pajamas. "Lookee here!" he attempted.

Lanfield's brain processed the line. He shook his head. "No, lighter. Like you're seeing maybe a . . . a . . . leprechaun. You know? It's adorable, this penguin in pajamas, and unexpected. And of course, you've never seen a penguin before—they don't have penguins where you come from, right? Try it again."

The director's words found their mark. Dooley understood. "Lookee here!" he said almost breathlessly.

Lanfield threw up his hands as if signaling a touchdown. "Perfect!" He turned to Bill and the AD and said, "Don't waste time on a rehearsal. Let's shoot it right now. Dooley, Charles, you're over here," and he pointed to a curtained-off area that was to serve as a galley for the train's porters. They stepped into the curtained-off area. "Okay, you are working at the galley, doing something at the counter. Charles, a little bit of business at the counter, no looking up yet. Ready?"

"Speed."

"Scene 31, take 1."

"And—action!"

Dooley pretended he was cutting a sandwich at counter level. Lanfield whispered just off camera, "Now, to your right, you see the penguin! And you see him too, Charles! Give me a take, and then, Dooley, your line."

Dooley did as instructed, looked to his right. There was no penguin, but the AD held his fist at knee level along the aisle. Dooley gave it a beat and said, "Lookee here!" He delivered it quietly, with astonishment, almost under his breath. He kept his gaze fixed on the assistant director's fist. Out the corner of his eye, Dooley could see Charles reacting, his eyes wide in wonder.

"And—cut! Beautiful! Print it!" said Lanfield. "One more and then we'll shoot the reverse! Camera, roll again."

An hour later they wrapped for the day, and the production assistant closed Dooley Wilson out of his first picture under contract, *My Favorite Blonde*. He had done his job brightly, on cue, no flubs, right to expectations. He was the perfect comic relief, with not one foot of film wasted on his account. He could only hope somebody at Paramount had noticed because he dearly wanted that house. Yes, sir, that would be a wonderful thing, to take Estelle away from the trucks and noise of Filipinotown. Maybe they could find a quiet corner of the world somewhere, maybe in Glendale, near his new friend Wade Boteler. Dooley walked through the Paramount gate that day, stopped, and looked back toward the white soundstages at the realization he never had actually seen the penguin wearing pajamas.

CHAPTER 10

Nineteen miles east of Paramount, Julius Epstein reported for work on the Warner Bros. lot at 11:30 Tuesday morning. Just after he had passed through the Barham gate, a familiar voice, an angry tenor voice, called from behind him, "Hey! You! Schmuck! Hold on a minute!"

Julie stopped and turned in time to experience an oh-shit moment. Bearing down on him like a P-40 came Jack Warner, walking with purpose to reach the spot where Julie stood.

"Hey, Mr. Warner, how's tricks?" Julie offered with great cheer. Julie had awakened in a good mood. He had run six miles through the quiet streets and then showered and dressed in time to reach the studio for lunch. Now he realized he should have expected the Warner ambush—the chief lived for such moments, looking for someone to bully.

When he reached Julie, Jack glanced down at his wristwatch, stood silent for a long beat, and then said in his familiar, staccato tone, "What are you doing reporting for work at lunchtime? Working hours for the writers are nine to five, with no exceptions!" Warner had the rat-a-tat-tat delivery of a typewriter, just as loud and just as fast.

Phil and Julius had often discussed the fact that the chief didn't scare Julie. Phil had respect for the chief, but the chief just aggravated Julie, who resented authority all the way back to first grade when Miss Glod sent him for a paddling by the principal because he refused to put up his hand before speaking in class. So Julie's inclination was always to give it back to the head of the studio as good as he got. Phil would cringe at his brother, but as God was his witness, Julie couldn't help himself. In response to Warner's verbal assault, Julius looked at his own watch and said, "Yes, Chief, it's 11:30 and I'm coming to work. And it's 11:30 and you're coming to work. So, and I say this in all seriousness, let's call it a wash and I won't mention it again if you won't."

The chief said, "I happen to own this place and I can come and go when it suits me!" He pointed at the water tower looming above the lot with the Warner Bros. shield emblazoned across it; he was always showing somebody the goddamn water tower. "You see that? There's a W and a B." He said it slowly, theatrically. "That stands for Warner. Brothers. That's my name up there, kid, not yours."

Julius did as directed and admired the water tower. "Are you offering to add our name up there? E.B.? Epstein. Brothers. Because I'm telling you, Philip will be thrilled. Honored and thrilled."

"And that's another thing," raved Warner. "I never know which goddamned brother I'm dealing with. So, you're Julius. Fine. You are on report, Mr. Epstein. Mr. Julius Epstein."

Julius lost his breath. "What does that mean," he asked, "I'm 'on report'?"

"Just what it sounds like," said the chief. His arms were involved now; he waved them in anger. "I'm putting the gates on notice that the Epsteins are to be here at nine. Not ten, or eleven, or twelve. Nine! The carpenters and painters come onto the lot long before nine, and the least you and your brother can do is respect the real workers who make your salary possible!"

Julius said before he could think about it, "I doubt a carpenter can come in and knock together a script."

"Listen, smart guy," Warner said; he was now chin to chin with Julius. "I can throw a pencil out my window and hit a writer. You are that replaceable! Think about it!"

Warner had turned a bright shade of red by the time he stormed off. Julius imagined that Phil wouldn't like to hear about this incident, but that wouldn't stop Julie from telling him. Julie always figured the Epsteins had grown up on meaner streets than any of the Warner brothers of Youngstown, Ohio. Julie also believed that even if the chief fired them, Wallis would hire them back or they'd catch on with another studio.

Julie resumed his stroll toward the commissary and thought about this nine-to-five business. Maybe they weren't the hardest-working men in show business, but to Julie, the results spoke for themselves: the Epsteins wrote hit pictures that made money.

Phil had come in at nine this morning, and he met his brother outside the commissary door. Phil was watching Julie approach and held the door open for him. "What's wrong with you?" Phil asked as Julius passed through. "Hit a puppy on the drive over?"

"No, worse. I ran into the chief. Now I'm on report."

"What the hell does that mean?" Phil demanded. "'On report.'"

"I'll tell you later," said Julius, wincing at the thought of the guards at the gates watching Epstein movements. They were both inside the door now, in the cavernous commissary, assaulted by the din of fifty conversations as they snaked their way over to the writers corner.

They passed Bill Cagney sitting with Jimmy, who wore a tan suit with a newsboy cap. Jim shot Julie a smile and a nod as they passed. "Hey, Epsteins!" called Jimmy Cagney. "Loved the blue pages you sent over yesterday—that business with Harris and Schwab! Keep 'em comin'!"

"For you, Jimmy, anything," hollered Phil. Julie looked back to see his brother grinning like a fool at a Cagney compliment.

The usual Epstein seats awaited at the writers table, which had a bird's-eye view of the comings and goings. The boys had great seats, one on the end, one adjacent, at the long table that held twelve comfortably and up to sixteen on busy days when extra chairs would be crammed in. Today the table was a little more than half full; a lot of the guys were vacationing for the holidays.

"What did we miss?" Julius asked as they sat, Phil on the end.

Next to Julie sat the Scotsman Aeneas MacKenzie, who said in a brogue, "Joe Louis is fighting Buddy Baer on the ninth."

"Don't take Baer," said Phil, studying the menu. A waitress approached, a pretty redhead with green eyes and nice calves, and Julius gave her the once-over to confirm, yes, very nice.

"I dunno," said Bob Buckner farther down the table. "Remember when Baer knocked Louis out of the ring?"

"Yeah, and Louis climbed back in the ring and whaled the tar out of Baer," said Julie. "Tuna salad and a Coke," he said to the redhead.

"Club House and a Coke," said Phil, and the waitress hurried off. Julie loved boxing, but boxing ranked last in Phil's mind now; he sized up a group that seemed too intent on eating. "So, what did we think of the script that Irene sent around last week?"

"That Morocco thing? I hated it," said Buckner, who had a Monte Cristo and french fries. "What the hell kind of story is that? Where the hell is Casablanca, and who the hell cares about some loser pining away for the girl who eighty-sixed him after he ruined his marriage for her?" He paused. "Of all the shit I read in 1941, this one stank out loud."

"Don't sugarcoat it, Bob," said Phil. "Tell us what you really think."

Buckner jabbed a greasy finger at Phil. "There's a good reason this play kicked around so long with nobody buying. It's old and stale and I hate the characters." Buckner specialized in writing for Errol Flynn, so his stock was already high. Then he had written *Knute Rockne—All-American* and become the latest darling of the Writers Building.

Hal Wallis's brother-in-law Wally Kline said, "No matter how the writers would approach those people in that play, the censors would cut off its balls. And that character Rick has already lost his balls. All you're left with is an American who's in Casablanca for no good reason other than he cheated on his wife, which means he has to die at the end. No thanks."

Julie said, "But Wallis bought it, so he must have seen something."

"Yeah," said Buckner, "because you-know-who read it and she forced the Commie to give it a big buildup. Then that idiot Wald put the bug in Hal's ear that this thing was six sticks of dynamite. Now we're stuck. Twenty grand for a big old piece of ham! All I know is, I don't want to make eye contact with Renie when she assigns it."

Julie looked at Phil; Phil looked back in puzzlement. "Did, uh, did anybody else like the dynamic of Rick and Rinaldo?" Phil ventured.

MacKenzie nodded. "It wasn't bad."

Buckner said, "But you can't get that far because the backbone of the story is a sexual affair that broke up a marriage, and now it's a rekindled sexual affair between two people who aren't married. Case closed!"

"The Spaniard and this letter of transit is a pretty good device," Julie offered. He felt like he and his brother were those guys who levered clay pigeons in the air at the shooting range.

Howard Koch, the tallest of the writers and beanpole thin, sliced delicately at a filet mignon and said, "Why not take out all the sex and make it about conscience? A man loses his ideals and then regains them. Make the letters of transit metaphoric."

"Letters of transit don't even exist!" Buckner bellowed. "I called Lissauer and asked! He looked it up and said there's no such thing." And if anyone would know, it was Lissauer. "Wait a minute," said Buckner. His hand hung in the air, demanding quiet; Buckner could be quite dramatic, and now he was doing calculations in his head. "Wait just one minute." He sat there thinking and then said to the Epsteins, "Did you guys set Wald up to pitch this thing to Wallis because you want the job?"

The boys sat there mute.

After a moment of silence, MacKenzie said, "If you want to know the gospel truth, I didn't hate it. Maybe Howard's right. You could build this story into something about, I don't know, democratic ideals. You could turn Rick into some kind of patriot. Or American spy battling the Germans. Make it a Scarlet Pimpernel sort of thing."

Howard Koch jabbed his fork in MacKenzie's direction and gave him a smile. *Touché.*

The group fell silent again. A gloomy Kline said, "I think you could squeeze a story out of that thing sooner or later, but it would be a tough job." Wally and MacKenzie had written the screenplay for the Flynn picture about Custer that had been racking up big numbers in its New York premiere, giving these two extra chips at the table. It hadn't been easy turning Custer into somebody worth rooting for.

"But Wallis owns this story now," said Julius, "and somebody's got to write it."

Buckner flashed his wryest smile, which was plenty wry. "Boys," he said with a flourish as he arose, "I wish you luck." And with that he wiped his mouth with a linen napkin, set it delicately on his empty plate, pushed his chair in for emphasis, and departed.

"Christ, all the time with Cohan has wrecked that man," said Phil. "Don't you guys want to cast this Morocco story? How many pictures have we sat around this table and cast?"

"Plenty," said MacKenzie, "and we never get it right. How about we leave the casting to Steve Trilling?"

"But if we figure out who we're writing it for," said Julius, "that's half the battle. I think it's got Bogart written all over it." The redhead brought Phil's Club House and Julie's tuna salad, and their Cokes. Julie watched her walk away.

MacKenzie said, "Don't laugh, but I think Garfield could do interesting things with Rick. They won't give it to him, but they should."

"Yeah, poor John," said Phil, trying to grasp the many layers in his sandwich. In the process, he stabbed himself with a toothpick and yelped.

Buzz Bezzerides sidled up and took one of the empty chairs. "What's the hottest spot on the Strip for ringing in the New Year?" he asked in a voice that had a gangster's edge to it.

"Ciro's," said Phil.

"Never mind that," Julius said. "We're talking about the play Hal just bought. The Morocco thing."

"Oh, that piece of shit," said Buzz. "What I can't figure out is, why would Hal Wallis spend Warner's money on that, that—" he groped for a descriptor, "—melodrama when he's got one foot out the door?"

Julius wrenched his attention back from the redhead. "Who's got one foot out the door?" he asked.

Buzz said in a low voice, "Word on the street is, Wallis has a deal with UA. It'll be in *Variety* tomorrow."

"Son of a bitch," said Kline. Julius wondered how Wallis's own brother-in-law didn't know what was going on.

"Way to go, Wally," griped Julius. "Your own family doesn't talk to you." All the writers razzed Wally Kline mercilessly for being married to Hal Wallis's older sister Juel.

Howard Koch puffed his pipe and said, "Let's just hope it isn't true." Nobody loved Hal Wallis, the top man who could walk right past a guy on the lot without acknowledging, *Hey, you're one of the writers making me money!* At the same time, everyone respected Wallis for the smarts he brought to every production.

No doubt about it, Buzz had rolled a hand grenade across the writers table. With Hal gone, what would become of, well, everything? Hal had grown accustomed to counting on the Epsteins; they had rewarded him with hits, and so in theory, Wallis would offer the boys jobs at United Artists. Julius let his eyes scan the terrain of a commissary pulsing with life, even during the holidays. Over in the corner, John Huston and Olivia de Havilland sat plastered together like horny teenagers whispering God only knew what to each other. And at another table, Ann Sheridan sat with Reagan and Bob Cummings, all in period costume. This was a great place to be, thought Julius, and suddenly he couldn't imagine leaving it. First the Japs, and now this. What a helluva December.

CHAPTER 11

Hal Wallis sat in his office ruminating about a world gone up in flames. British forces battled Rommel's Afrika Corps in Tunisia. Japanese armies mauled the American defenders of Manila. Japanese subs attacking ships off the coast of California had inspired more blackouts in all the coastal cities from San Francisco on south. And then, even closer to home, there was this: he held before him the new issue of *Variety* and stared at a page-five story headlined, "Hal Wallis-Murray Silverstone Talk Indie Unit Setup for UA Distribution; Also Partnership."

He set down the paper and forced his concentration on a memo just received from Paul Nathan headlined, "Suggestions for a Writer for 'Everybody Comes to Rick's.'" Wallis read down the list—the only names that jumped out were Kline and MacKenzie, who had just done Custer for Errol Flynn. And the Custer picture would be a guaranteed smash hit.

He stared at the title in Nathan's memo—"Everybody Comes to Rick's." Strangely, what popped into his head was Jerry Wald's high-pitched voice comparing this script to *Algiers*. Could a one-word title work for this picture as well? Rick's? No. Casablanca, he thought. Why not call it Casablanca?

When Hal's phone rang in the silence, he felt his heart skip a beat. He picked up the receiver. "Wallis."

"It's Loyd," said a deep voice. "Can you meet me in the cemetery in half an hour?"

"Right," said Hal. He hung up the phone. He read memos for a quarter hour, then grabbed his hat, jacket, and sunglasses, and hurried out, the copy of *Variety* under his arm. He strolled to his Packard—no need to attract attention by rushing—and drove down Barham. He turned left onto Forest Lawn Drive and in a little while, just out of sight of the studio, hung a right into the new branch location of Forest Lawn called Hollywood Hills. The gravel parking area inside the growing graveyard had become a secure meeting spot for Hal and Loyd during these last tense months. It sat behind a row of hedges and shade trees. Playing high-stakes poker with the studio as they were, conversations must not be overheard.

Hal lit a cigarette, sat, and waited. Lazy white clouds floated overhead, and the breeze had a chill to it. He snapped on the car radio and found Benny Goodman playing "Birth of the Blues." He couldn't help feeling optimistic, despite the uncertain global times and the headline in *Variety*.

The song ended, and a news report began. The announcer said, "In France, 6,000 French Jews, including some of the wealthiest and most influential in Paris, were rounded up by the German occupation forces in that city this week, destined for deportation to concentration camps in Eastern Europe."

Hal's light mood darkened, as if a curtain had descended in front of the windshield. "Those arrested were picked up at dawn and taken in motor trucks to police stations where they would remain until the trip to camps in Poland and Russia. It is learned that the figure may reach 8,000 to 10,000 before—"

Hal reached forward and snapped off the radio. Why hadn't it hit him before now? Well, of course, the work. The pictures dominated his every waking moment. But those Jews, the wealthiest and most influential in Paris—Paris!—were picked up at dawn. My God, he thought. He let his eyes rake across the serene landscape, the genteel greenery.

The sight of Loyd Wright's black Cadillac Sixty Special turning into the cemetery interrupted Hal's train of thought, but he found that he couldn't breathe. He simply could not draw a breath.

Wright pulled in opposite Hal, so their driver's-side windows were a foot and a half apart.

Loyd studied the face of his friend as he cut his motor. "What's happened?" he asked in the deep and gentle baritone of a counselor.

Wallis couldn't find the words to respond. Finally, he forced speech and said, "The news. French Jews rounded up, sent to camps. It just—I don't know."

Hal looked into his friend's eyes, looking for guidance, for something, but what could Loyd say? What could anyone say? Loyd shrugged his shoulders and shook his head. There wasn't wisdom for a world this mad.

Wright had the presence of a character actor, somebody's calm and scholarly uncle with a still-handsome face and wavy gray hair. "We could talk business later," said Wright. "You could give me a call when you're ready."

Hal heard himself say, "You're in bed, safe at home and in bed. And they knock down your door and drag you away."

Why had this particular news report gotten to him? Why French Jews? Why now? But it had gotten to him and swept over in a morbid wave. But Hal knew he dared not waste the time of his busy and in-demand legal representative. "The report in *Variety*," said Wallis. "I thought we had better talk. Is there anything new in the negotiations?"

"Roy Obringer and I have been chatting quite a bit," said Wright. Obringer ran the Legal Department and served as Jack Warner's right-hand man.

"And?" said Hal.

Loyd allowed a stockbroker smile. "You have Jack over a barrel. The simple fact is, he can't let you get away. Not the guy behind every hit from *Captain Blood* to *The Maltese Falcon*. His brothers would skin him alive, and he's furious about it, but he'll give us what we want. And that means, when all is said and done, you will stay at Warner Bros."

"On my terms," Hal said, in the form of a question. "Producing the pictures I want and turning everything else over to Wald or whomever?"

Loyd always took in everything, listened to every word, and paused and considered before speaking. He thought and then he nodded. "I have been drafting the key points to present to the studio, and you will, of course, approve every word before they see the document."

"Jack hates me," said Hal.

"From what I gather, Jack despises just about everyone," said Loyd. Wright's caramel voice and elucidation gave every utterance almost biblical importance. Hal loved to hear him speak, especially when the subject was Hal himself.

"I would just like to try making one picture at a time, and then go home and have dinner with Louise and my son," said Wallis. "I want to pick just a few pictures a year to develop and make them all great."

Wright put up a hand to request a pause. "The studio will demand you make six great pictures a year, and we might get them down to four or five."

"Which is still better than the way it works now, where I'm overseeing everything."

A wry smile played at Wright's lips. "I have yet to be convinced you can let others run the productions. You are obsessive, my friend. But we are going to get a great deal—any story you want, your choice of director and talent, studio financing for all productions, and profit participation." He reached in his jacket pocket and pulled out a pack of Beemans, unwrapped a stick, and popped it in his mouth. "Warner Bros. is a luxury car that you have driven with great care," said Loyd, pausing to chew the stick of gum medicinally to soothe his stomach. "I want to see you keep that ride, because if you started over at United Artists, it would mean trading in your luxury car for a—" he glanced down at Wallis's vehicle, "—for a Packard."

"Nice," grumbled Wallis.

Wright pressed on. "United Artists is a charming idea, but you need to stay at Warner Bros."

It all sounded good to Wallis, except for one thing. "I'll still have to deal with Jack."

Wright nodded. "Which you have done for a decade, and you've survived the experience. I would call your relationship with Warner a mutually beneficial one. A very practical one." Wright watched Hal for a reaction and when he didn't see one he said, "Maybe you shouldn't listen to news reports about Europe."

Wallis turned the key to the Packard and pushed the starter. The engine turned over and when he stepped on the gas, the car roared to life. "On the contrary," said Hal. "Maybe I need to pay a lot more attention to Europe. I'm too old to carry a rifle in this war. I guess maybe that makes the pictures my weapon. Maybe I need to craft my pictures as weapons of war." He slipped on his sunglasses, pulled out a cigarette, and lit it. "Yes, counselor. Let's get this done so I can make war pictures. I place myself in your hands. Do what you think best."

Wright smiled an easy smile. "I always do. I will send over a detailed proposal by messenger, say, in two days. You make your changes, and then I'll present it to Obringer."

Wallis slipped the car into gear. "Fine, thank you, Loyd," he said as the car began to move.

"And Hal," called Wright. Wallis braked to a stop. "Happy New Year."

Wallis forced a smile. "Thanks. Happy New Year, Loyd."

Wallis drove back to the studio, parked in his spot, and walked inside the Administration Building. Six thousand Jews, wealthy and influential, or was it eight thousand or ten thousand? Thousands of souls rounded up and sent away, and would they ever see their beloved Paris again?

Wallis headed straight to the first-floor office of the story editor.

The door stood open and there sat Renie in her reading glasses, marking up a script with red grease pencil in heavy strokes. For this task she had removed her jacket and rolled up the sleeves of an off-white blouse. A cigarette dangled from her lips and she squinted against its smoke. He rapped gently on the doorframe with his knuckles. She glanced up over the glasses, saw it was him, held up a finger for him to wait, and finished her thought in the form of several more slashes across lines of dialogue and a scrawled word in the margin he could read from eight feet away and upside down. It read, PP and NO!!

"PP?" he asked.

"Purple prose," she snapped. "This clown has a big future—as an elevator operator or doorman." She laid the red pencil in the gutter of the script and closed it. Then she took a last drag of her cigarette and stubbed it out in the overflowing ashtray. She stood and said, "I need to stretch my legs." She grabbed her cigarettes and a matchbook and walked into the hallway.

They proceeded together to the exterior doors and as he pushed one of them open and held it for her, he said, "Six thousand wealthy Jews were rounded up in Paris, and they're going to be sent to concentration camps."

Hal and Renie were outside now, and she looked up at him, a quizzical expression on her face. She seemed to be waiting for more, and when he didn't elaborate, she said, "It's horrible. It's been happening everywhere in Europe."

"We have to do something," said Wallis. "We have to fight."

"Absolutely," said Renie.

"All those people in your play who come to Rick's," said Hal, "they're all in the same position. Nazis pounded on their doors, and they managed to be one step ahead." He walked along First Street with Renie in the low California sun, and yet he was a continent away. "It's all simply—" he struggled for the words, "—very, very important."

They had reached the park bench by the Wardrobe Department. She sat on the green-enameled bench; he sat beside her. The studio hummed even on New Year's Eve. Crews scurried about, actors moved carefully in costume, and a green-uniformed messenger pedaled past on a bicycle.

"What brought all this on?" she asked him.

"A news report on the radio." They were quiet a while, and

then he said, "Oh, I need to change the title of your script." She turned to him and waited. "Let's call it *Casablanca*."

She took out a cigarette and lit it. "*Casablanca*," she repeated.

"Yes, like *Algiers*," said Wallis.

"Clever," she said. "Original."

He sometimes couldn't tell when she was kidding. He was pretty sure this time she was. "Okay with you?" he asked. "*Casablanca*?"

She turned away from him and spat out a bit of tobacco. "*Casablanca* works for me—as long as we make a perfect picture."

Hal said, "It might not be a perfect picture, but it must be an important picture." A Civil War caisson with a howitzer hitched to it was towed past—a prop from *Yankee Doodle Dandy*. He watched it clatter along. "We need a writer," he said. "What did you think of Nathan's list? You know who we should give it to."

She stretched her arms over her head. "Yeah, but they're still doing rewrites for Cagney. They probably won't be finished for another couple of weeks, and you can't wait that long to get started on your—on our picture." She thought for a moment. "Here's what we'll do. I'll send copies of the script to everyone on Paul's list and tell them to send their reactions back by memo. Then you'll know who has a feel for the material. In the meantime, you better start thinking about casting."

"Bogart," said Wallis. "I owe it to him."

"Good. The writer can tailor it to Bogart," said Renie.

She finished her cigarette, arose from the bench, gave another stretch, and dropped the cigarette butt to the pavement where she could press it flat with her shoe. "Break's over. I'm about to fire a hack writer as my last official act of 1941."

"Anybody I know?" asked Wallis.

"Nope. That's my job, boss, to keep the bad ones away from you. And this guy will never be heard from again."

They reached the Writers Building, and he opened the door mainly to watch her walk through it. "Happy New Year," he said to Renie.

"That's the plan," she responded, sashaying down the hall, and Hal walked back to the Administration Building to order one more memo from Paul that would be issued to all departments: "The story that we recently purchased entitled 'Everybody Comes to Rick's' will hereafter be known as *Casablanca*."

CHAPTER 12

Humphrey Bogart felt the boat tugging at her moorings as he lay with his head near a starboard porthole and attempted to lift himself out of dark dreams. He found himself on a set inside a soundstage. He knew the camera was rolling and he stood on his mark, sweating. He didn't know his lines and he couldn't move, and he knew everyone was waiting behind the lights. He snapped awake a moment and then went out again. This time Mayo hovered close by, very close. He could feel her menace and smell bourbon on her hot breath; did she hold a knife? He jerked away from her, and his forehead hit the bulkhead. Snapping to consciousness, he glanced across at the other small bunk against the port side of the hull and wondered if his wife had heard the thud. She was out cold, Humphrey Bogart's wife, the infamous Mayo Methot, lying on her stomach in pink pajamas, one arm dangling over the edge, knuckles on the floor. Oh God, what a curse this was. He only ever knew peace on the open sea, and he could never get there without his wife in tow because she didn't trust him, or couldn't stand her own company, or whatever the hell it was that kept Mayo glued to him every moment.

He felt like hell; his mouth tasted of something sour he must have burped up. Outside he could hear voices, and he craned his neck to peer out the glass of the porthole. Daylight drilled into him, and he squinted away, then looked again to see a couple of guys on the next boat over chattering. By the amount of light assaulting him, he thought it might be near eight in the morning. He needed to urinate and as soon as he began to move, his entire body ached, but he eased out of the bunk until his feet met the floor as gently as possible. More than anything he wanted to let his wife continue her slumber.

In slow motion he gathered his shirt, pants, and shoes and tiptoed to the head where he let loose a long, disturbingly brown stream and then splashed water on his face and brushed his teeth. Clothes on, he reached for cigarettes and a lighter and eased up the steps to the main deck of his thirty-eight-foot, diesel-powered boat dubbed *Sluggy*. A decent sea breeze, delicate and liberating, met his skin as *Sluggy* continued to buck at her mooring, one of dozens of boats parked in unison to represent a bit of the collective wealth of Southern California. On instinct he lit a cigarette and drew a vital hot jab of smoke into his lungs. He spotted Mary Baker back at the stern, sitting there prettily, legs crossed, gazing out at the hazy Pacific as the *Sluggy* swayed against the waves hitting the dock. The breeze knocked wisps of brown hair into her eyes, and she held it back with her hand and continued to look far off into the hazy blue distance. He had known her for fifteen years, since way back during his days on Broadway. Then she had moved out here and now served as his agent at the Sam Jaffe Agency on Sunset Boulevard. Mary's screenwriter husband, Mel, was with her to ring in the new year with the Bogarts; he must still be sacked out below.

"Sleep okay up in the sardine can?" Bogie asked. He offered Mary a cigarette, and she took one and borrowed his lighter.

"Oh sure," she answered, blowing a line of smoke into the

morning sea breeze. "Champagne puts me out." She was quiet a moment. "Happy New Year, pal."

He smiled, and it exhausted him. "We can only hope. Happy New Year, Mare."

The *Sluggy* wasn't exactly shipshape this morning; he counted three empty champagne bottles and a mostly gone bottle of bourbon, which his wife had seen to personally. He could remember only pieces of the revelry, as if lengths of film on the cutting-room floor. He remembered it had been pleasant enough at the big moment—midnight—but then he had said the wrong thing, this time not even trying to needle Mayo, and she had turned vile and began, "What the hell did you mean by that, big shot?"

He remembered at one point she stood an inch away from his face, and she was screaming, holding that bourbon bottle upside down by the neck. Didn't he push her away, and didn't she topple over with a thud? He recalled a thud that had sickened his stomach. Maybe that accounted for the taste of bile in his mouth all these hours later.

Standing on the deck in the light of day, eyes aching, he looked toward the horizon that had been fascinating Mary, its pale blue fading to brown. He said, "I wonder what part of the world has gone to hell since yesterday."

She stood, cigarette dangling from her lips. "Come on, let's go find a newspaper and see. Every once in a while, I smell coffee, and I'm buying."

They stepped down off *Sluggy* and walked along the planks of the dock to the Balboa Yacht Club's café. It was quiet, only a couple of people. She bought two cups of coffee and the *Times*, and they sat in a booth, waking up to learn that Manila continued to hold against the Jap hordes. She reported the news to him sentence by sentence, as she read page one.

Since long before Pearl Harbor, Bogart had been participating in Coast Guard patrols, during which he scanned the horizon for enemy activity. Now, as he peered out the window up into the velvety blue, he said, "Huh. I guess I'm getting used to the war. I haven't thought about Jap planes until this very minute."

She set the paper down and sipped her coffee. "Scary times."

In the café, people were coming and going, men mostly, but a few couples drifted by, and some paid the pair no mind while others did a double take when they saw the unmistakable face of Sam Spade. He felt the glances of the passersby and ignored them; he wanted nothing to do with snappy patter of moviegoers who thought they knew the real Humphrey Bogart because they had seen *The Roaring Twenties*.

Mary flipped back to the drama section of the *Times*, and he knew she was scanning for mentions of the battling Bogarts in Hedda Hopper's column or Jimmy Fidler's. He watched her pretty face, a girl-next-door kind of a face, with little lines around her eyes and her mouth, experience lines, and he had been thinking for years she favored the Warner actress Margaret Lindsay. Mary kept studying the drama pages with intensity until finally, with one last drag on the cigarette, her face relaxed and that meant all clear.

"*The Falcon*'s holding up well on the indie circuit," she said, analyzing a dense list of independent theaters and their playbills. She tamped out the stub of the cigarette and confided, "Minna says Hal says *Falcon* made a ton of money."

Minna Wallis was Hal's sister and one of the biggest agents in town, and with a sorority so small—two female talent agents in a field dominated by men—Minna and Mary tended to exchange trade secrets. And Bogart well knew that a backdoor pipeline to the executive producer at Warner Bros. was worth a fortune or two to a Warner contract player.

"If I'm making the studio so much money," said Bogart, "why don't they treat me better?" He felt himself begin to simmer. "You know what? Why don't we let my contract expire? Fuck Hal Wallis. Fuck every Warner brother, and every Warner sister, if there are any."

She looked up over the *Times* and her brown eyes grew weary. "We're not going to walk anywhere because they are treating you better, pal. They're putting you in better pictures with better scripts. Hal happens to like you. And so does Jerry Wald."

He felt himself turn down into a familiar dark corridor. "Hal has got no use for me, and Hal hates Mayo," he grumbled. He knew he was being a bastard; he took a deep breath and forced himself to back off. "Okay, okay," he sighed. "Where do we stand with the contract?" After *The Maltese Falcon*, Mary had approached Obringer about a renegotiation, and Obringer had been listening.

"We told the studio we want four thousand a week over the next seven years, and they're offering twenty-five hundred."

"That's bullshit," said Bogie. "Flynn gets something like six grand a week. And Davis, the same."

Mary nodded, all business now. "Flynn gave them *Robin Hood*, and Davis gave them *Jezebel* and *Dark Victory* and *The Letter*. You just moved up in weight class, and you need more wins under your belt."

How many women in this town would use a boxing analogy with Humphrey Bogart? He loved Mary even in the middle of a hangover, and it bothered him how the love he felt was lifting him back up from the depths. "Can you get me thirty-five hundred?" he asked.

"I think I can get you three thousand. And I can get you the ten radio jobs you want. Ten a year. Obringer said no problem to that." Bogart wanted the extra cash from the radio shows for upkeep on the *Sluggy*.

"All right," he said with another sigh; he was spent. "I just wish they would stop putting me in shit like *All Through the Night*."

"It's a good picture! We just went to see it and thought it a lot of fun!" She said this with such genteel enthusiasm that he gave up on any attempt to deflate her. She picked up the paper again and started scanning. "They can't all be *High Sierra*," she added in triumph.

He knew he was a pain in the ass when he was drunk and equally bad when hungover. Half the time when he was straight, he could feel more or less at peace and then he wouldn't allow himself to go on the attack. At this moment he felt the first hunger pangs, which meant the hangover had begun to ease its grip. "Mind if I gripe a little?" he asked.

She looked at him and smiled. "You haven't stopped griping since I've known you. But go right ahead; it's what I'm here for." There it was again; that sunny disposition, as if Mary Baker would burst into song any second.

He said, "It bothers me that I keep getting pictures George Raft turned down. It's as if all my wardrobe has George Raft's labels in it."

She dropped the paper on the tabletop, folded her hands on top of it, and met his gaze. "You want to know what I think?" she began.

He knew he was about to hear.

"What I honestly think?" she went on. "The biggest favor George Raft did you was to turn down *The Maltese Falcon* and then

All Through the Night. I read something in *Variety* about *All Through the Night* doing better than *The Maltese Falcon*. Better than a giant hit! So yeah, you can call these pictures shit, but it's money in the bank. You are money in the bank, my friend, and all you have to do is be a good boy and let me work out the contract, and pretty soon you'll get a big raise and another seven steady years at the finest studio around."

Bogart knew some drinking buddies and some guys he liked. But there was only one Mary Baker, who went so far back with him that they had become actual friends. It's the last thing in the world he expected, to have a real friend. A woman friend. A woman friend who could keep him under control. Mary Baker was Bogart's Clyde Beatty. He often envisioned himself the lion and Mary wielding the whip, and he knew the boundaries he dared not cross.

He looked into her brown eyes. "I'm sorry, Mare. I know I'm a pain in the ass. I wish I could tell you what I'm looking for out of life. Maybe I just want to take my boat and head straight out to sea, forever. I wish I could make one picture that meant something. One picture I was happy with and where I'd say, 'You see, Mary? That's an A picture, a prestige picture, with my name above the title.' But all the parts I get are gangsters and gumshoes. It's all my sorry old mug is good for."

She gave him a reassuring smile that indicated she hadn't taken this morning personally. She said, "You're my biggest client, and I'm not going to do anything against your interests. I have nightmares where Mayo sticks a knife in you the day before you sign that new deal. Sometimes I think that's the way it's going to end. Somebody's going to kill somebody."

He stared down at the coffee in his cup. He forced himself

not to mention that an hour earlier he had had that very dream. "Mayo just needs a job," he mumbled. "Why won't anybody call her for work?"

"I love Mayo, you know that. But have you checked her odometer lately? The booze is wrecking her. She'd get character parts except this is a small town and everybody knows she could blow up at any moment and ruin a day's shooting." Mary was looking at him hard. "She's not the only one they're talking about." Mary leaned forward and said quietly, "You've got to be very careful right now, pal. Matching Mayo drink for drink is bad for you. It all adds up and adds up. The camera sees it."

The conversation had worn him out. "Yeah, okay, Mare. Okay."

It was then that it hit him: It's very quiet. Too quiet. He forced himself into motion. "Say, listen, we better get back because she shouldn't wake up alone. Thanks for the talk, coach."

He asked the guy at the counter if he could buy a pot of coffee to take out, and who could say no to Sam Spade? It was added to his tab and with a pot of steaming coffee in hand, Bogart navigated his legs of rubber back to the *Sluggy* with Mary at his side. It was now 9:45 on a quiet, hungover Thursday morning, the first morning of 1942.

CHAPTER 13

Wallis walked into his office on Monday morning, January 12, full of joy at Loyd Wright's masterstroke: the piece in *Variety* about Wallis and Silverstone forming a partnership at UA. Jack Warner had been forced to capitulate after considering the prospect of having to deal with someone like Jerry Wald in Wallis's seat. Checkmate. Wallis buzzed for Paul Nathan to come in.

Nathan brought his leading-man good looks into the room, and Hal said, "Close the door." Nathan did as told, and Wallis motioned for him to sit in one of the chairs opposite the desk.

"What's up, skipper?" asked Nathan as he sat with pen and pad in hand to begin the morning's actions.

"This is off the record," Wallis said quietly. Paul nodded, *Of course*. Hal said, "The deal's done. I'm staying."

Nathan beamed, jumped to his feet, and reached out a hand to shake with Wallis over the broad desktop. "Oh thank God!" he exclaimed and then remembered the thin walls. He said in an urgent whisper, "You have no idea how terrified everyone has been. What a relief!"

"For me as well," said Wallis.

Nathan took a step back and sat down again, and said in a subdued voice, "And the terms? Can you tell me?"

Wallis nodded. "Five years as an independent producer, four

pictures a year, my choice, any property, any writer, any director, any stars. Loyd said they would hold out for six or eight pictures a year, but Loyd stuck to his guns, and they okayed four."

"That's fabulous. Which of the producers moves up to handle everything else?"

Hal gave a shrug. "That's Warner's problem. All I know is we sign the contract this afternoon, and as soon as we do, the chief is going to be gunning for me. You know how he is, and so I'm ordering you, put everything in writing. Leave nothing to chance—absolutely nothing. We're going to ride the wave, do you understand me? We're going to play by every rule and turn out great pictures. Great pictures. Because I will not give that man the satisfaction of worming his way out of this contract. As of this moment, the pressure is on me. And on you."

Paul smiled and nodded without another word, and the men set to work on the day's tasks.

Three hours later, Jack L. Warner sat at his desk watching Hal Wallis sign a thirty-five-page contract that would keep him at Warner Bros. Hal's mouthpiece Loyd Wright stood behind him like a gunsel, as if an assassin might burst into the room at any minute.

It occurred to Warner that everybody had to have a piece of the pie. Wallis made a good salary and enjoyed every privilege possible as production head of the best studio in the world—and none of that was good enough for Hal B. Fucking Wallis. Hal B. Fucking Wallis had made this grandstand play with Silverstone at UA and put the details on page five in *Variety*! Wallis had the mistaken impression he was running the studio, like the way he had just spent studio money on that play by some nobodies in New York, and the only reason Hal had bought it, suspected Jack, was because he was nailing the story broad, and so Hal bought it for her like some sort of diamond bracelet, this story he insisted on calling *Casablanca*. Jack was reminded that he couldn't let his guard down for a minute.

"Your turn, Chief," said a voice. It was Obringer, standing close beside Warner, holding out a pen. Hell, Jack didn't trust Obringer either. Trust a lawyer? Never. But today was all about Hal B. Wallis and getting the deal done and getting back to business with so many big pictures in production or pre-pro or the drawing board. Must keep the gears turning on every one, and down the line scores would be settled. On Jack's terms and nobody else's.

As he signed his name a flashbulb popped, and he became aware that one of his cameramen had snuck into the room. It was Bert Six, who usually took photos of stars and movie scenes. Six asked Warner for one more pen-in-hand shot of Wallis and Warner together.

"Sure, sure!" said Warner jovially. "So happy to keep Hal here in the family! How-are-ya Wallis, hardest workin' man in town! I see him lugging reels of film out of here at night, and I can only hope he's not selling it for the silver! Hal-be-mine Wallis."

Jack began to feel his skin couldn't contain him. He felt himself push back his chair and rise to his feet.

"Couple more, standing, shaking hands, Chief?" asked Six.

"Absolutely, absolutely," said Jack, smiling a million-dollar smile, a perfect smile. *It ought to be*, thought Jack, *for what these choppers cost me*. He took the hand of Wallis and put his other hand on Hal's shoulder. Jack could admit that Wallis was vital to the positive cash flow. He would never argue with the string of hits that Hal had produced. But loyalty was a two-way street, and it seemed Wallis didn't understand that part of the equation.

"I'm relieved to get this done," said Hal, "so I can get on the road in the morning."

The statement startled Warner. "What road?" he asked. "Road to where?"

"You remember, to Broadway to talk to Lillian Hellman about buying her play, *Watch on the Rhine*. I'm taking Casey Robinson and the boys."

The very thought of those Epsteins revolted Warner. "The boys," Jack sneered. "They're a couple of juvenile delinquents, and I don't want this studio paying their salaries to New York and back."

"It's expenses only, Chief," said Wallis.

"Yeah, well, keep those two out of the steakhouses!" Jack growled, and he wasn't kidding. He spun on his heel to Obringer. "Roy, I want a list of the expenses for those two schmucks on my desk the morning they're back here, okay?"

"I'll see to it," said Obringer.

"Let's have one more over here," encouraged Bert Six, "so we can see the portrait of Mrs. Warner."

Jack couldn't believe the idiot still man had thought of this and Jack hadn't. Ann would glory in seeing her portrait in the papers. "Great idea! Great idea!" Jack enthused, and he pulled Wallis into position still holding the producer's hand. Jack beamed a smile at the camera as they kept clasping hands.

Finally, the deal was done and everyone piled out of Jack's office. Alone, he stared at the portrait of Ann on the credenza for a long while, and then he reached for the phone. "Tell Abdul I'm going home," he barked into the receiver. Warner picked up his fedora, placed it on his head, and then, making eye contact with no one, he headed out. On the front drive of the Administration Building, his car awaited, and big, burly Abdul held the back door open. Jack didn't feel the need to say a word because Abdul Maljan knew Jack better than anyone in the world. Words were unnecessary with Abdul, who would take one look at the chief and understand what to do.

The door shut gently behind Warner, and Abdul drove him home, over to Laurel Canyon and down into Beverly Hills on a blazingly beautiful January afternoon, the sun low and golden on Sunset Boulevard. Abdul hung a right onto Benedict Canyon and a left on Angelo Drive to 1801. Only now did Jack begin to feel the tension loosen its grip, inside the gates of 1801, as the car eased up the long driveway where nothing could be seen but grass and trees and waterfalls and the fruits of Jack's labor, and then the driveway looped around to the left and pulled up before the gleaming white pillars of the front entrance of his mansion.

The car door opened, and Abdul the Turk stood at attention; Jack climbed out of the back seat and didn't even look at his friend as he strode between the pillars and inside the house. The grand entryway yawned open as he walked in, his heels clicking on the marble. He stood in the two-story-high receiving room and reminded himself that he had created all this—not Hal B. Wallis, but Jack Leonard Warner. Jack had crafted the empire. Jack had okayed every decision, and without Jack Warner, there would be no soundstages. Bette Davis would be a little hag scratching out a living on the stage. Errol Flynn would be in jail for killing somebody. Cagney would be God knew where, a pipsqueak picking fights. And the rest of them? Who the hell knew or cared because they were nobodies before Warner Bros., and they would soon enough go back to being nobodies after Warner Bros. For now, for this moment in the utter quiet, Jack felt peace here inside the walls of the castle.

He drifted over to the mantel, to Ann's portrait that had been painted by Dali and set into the wall. Gorgeous, sexy Ann. He gazed up into her serene beauty captured so magnificently and thought to himself, *Even you betrayed me, doll.* They all do, sooner or later. He thought about it all the time, every waking moment, his wife screwing a contract player right under his nose. The lovers had met up in Mexico City, which is where they were discovered. Jack knew his wife to be hot-blooded, and sure, she had been around. But with a contract player? And it wasn't even Flynn! He could see it with Flynn; hell, he had watched Ann and Errol flirt at the Christmas party and figured they'd sneak off and do the deed. But Eddie Albert? Jack wanted Albert dead and considered siccing Abdul on him, Abdul who had fought professionally under the name The Terrible Turk, but Jack was too smart for that because who knew if the evidence would lead back to the Warners—then the world would know why Eddie Albert had been beaten to a pulp and Ann would be embarrassed. No, Albert's death must be slow and tortured, and Jack would make sure Albert was blackballed by every studio in town.

Ann, well, Jack couldn't stay mad at Ann, even if she did spread her legs for somebody else. Obviously, Jack hadn't been paying enough attention or she never would have strayed with the likes of Albert. That was obvious now, and so Jack devoted every moment to pleasing his goddess; if she were getting enough attention, she would never have a reason to betray him again.

"Hello, darling," Ann said from the edges of the room, her voice echoing off the granite, and she walked in with a quiet smile like the one in the painting and kissed his cheek. She wore tennis whites today that showed off her magnificent, tanned skin and the toned legs that drove him wild.

"You look so trim! So lean!" he gushed, knowing she loved to hear it, longed to hear it, expected to hear it.

"Hello, Papa Jack," said Ann's shadow, Joy, also dressed in tennis white as she eased quietly in to kiss Jack's other cheek. Joy was seventeen and growing into a hot little number with dark skin, dark hair, and dark eyes just like her mother, pretty as a picture, and there was no one in the world who knew her and didn't like her. Sweet and innocent Joy.

"Out on the court? Who won?" Jack said happily without caring at all.

"Darling, we had a wonderful idea, and we wanted to tell you about it," Ann purred.

How he loved the sound of her voice. He loved everything about her, from her eyes to her toes, but that voice really got to him. "What is it, gorgeous? Every time you have an idea, it costs me twenty grand."

"It's not that kind of idea," she said with a flash of her dimples and a twinkle in those magnificent eyes. "It's about a script at the studio. I heard about it from a friend—this new story you're going to make."

Jack's defenses activated like RAF radar in the Battle of Britain. Who was this friend and was it a guy and was she balling him? And what story, anyway? "Where did you—"

"It's been retitled *Casablanca*," she cut in. "I heard about it at card club, and it gave me the most marvelous idea."

His blood ran colder. "Oh that thing. Wallis's new baby. Card club—you heard about it at card club?"

"I not only heard about it, I read it!" Ann said triumphantly. She reached inside her big gold bag and pulled out a script. Its blue cover complemented the vivid crimson of her fingernails.

There it was, "Everybody Comes to Rick's." Under the author names was a stamp that read in all capital letters, CASABLANCA. At the bottom of the cover, all capital letters pronounced, RETURN TO STENOGRAPHIC DEPT. Somebody had gotten this thing outside the studio walls, which was a big no-no, and now civilians were out there reading it. Jack laughed to himself, a hearty laugh, thinking how pissed off Hal the Bastard Wallis would be knowing his story was bouncing around Beverly Hills and God knows where else.

"That's fabulous, baby!" Jack enthused. "So, you read it, huh?" He couldn't help but laugh again.

She gave him the trademark Ann Warner cat-ate-the-canary smile, the one with a dimple on each side and a knowing gleam in the eye, which she usually flashed right before dropping to her knees. But now, with Joy right there, something about the smile frightened him. She could really turn the tables when she put her mind to it, and suddenly he got the feeling he was the fly and she was the spider.

"It's all about intrigue in North Africa," said Ann. "And there's a young Bulgarian couple who have fled Europe and they're at this club, Rick's, and they drive the whole plot. The girl is named Annina, and the prefect of police has his eye on her. He offers her an exit visa in exchange for sex, and—"

Her words jabbed into his brain like a hot dagger. "Wait, what? In exchange for sex? What the hell kind of material is Wallis buying with my money? We'll never get anything like that past the censors. Goddammit, visas for sex? What the hell!"

Joy's brown eyes grew wide like a doe in hunting season. She took a step back and swallowed hard.

"No, no, Chief, calm down," Ann said in a silken tone as she reached up and put a warm hand on his cheek. He felt himself settle at once because he loved it when she called him "Chief." How he loved it, this admission that he was a great man who had mastered a studio where everyone called him "Chief" and all feared him. "The thing about the prefect of police isn't important," said Ann. "What I want to talk about is the part of Annina, because I had this brilliant idea as I was reading the script."

Jack looked into Ann's dazzling, smiling face, and then he gave Joy a glance, poor frightened Joy. He was on guard now. "What's this idea you keep talking about?"

Ann's right hand continued to stroke his cheek, as if he were a house cat. "You know Joy has been taking drama lessons at the studio. And, well, she would be perfect for the part of Annina."

Suddenly the dawn broke, and Jack pieced the story together in about four seconds. "Oh, I get it," he began, removing her palm from his cheek. "I get it." He felt like Sherlock Holmes solving a crime. "You didn't get that script from card club; you got it from Sophie Rosenstein, the drama coach. Sophie put the bug in your ear about Joy and this part, not some broad playing bridge."

There it was again, the enigmatic smile that had launched a thousand erections. "Okay, okay," she sighed, "so it was a little white lie to protect Sophie, and yes, it was Sophie who thought of casting Joy. And who let me borrow the script. But she's your employee, and she's so excited at the thought of Joy in this part."

Jack looked at Joy and couldn't read what he saw. Was she a co-conspirator or not? She stood there as sweetly innocent as ever, but suddenly the full impact of the idea hit him, and he reacted on instinct. "No. No, no, no. It's out of the question. The Warners aren't actors—we're better than that. I don't want any actors in the family. No. Besides, they'll laugh me out of town for casting my own stepdaughter in a picture, or letting her be cast, because I'll not be involved in anything of the kind. No, no, no. Nepotism. Does the word mean anything to you? That's what Hedda and Louella will scream: nepotism! I'll be a laughingstock."

His arguments made perfect sense to any rational person, but as they hung in the air, every point he had just made, he could feel them begin to melt away under Ann's withering gaze. He knew if he relented and said yes, a superb experience awaited in their bedroom to cap the day. But every instinct continued to say no, no, and again, no!

He had to buy time, and so he turned to Joy the statue, standing under her mother's portrait by the fireplace. He took a step toward her. He couldn't remember a time when Joy had ever made him angry; she was always too busy trying to please her mother. She was a five-foot, five-inch carbon copy of Ann.

He looked at the fragile girl. "What do you think about all this, kitten?" he said in a measured tone. "Is this something you want to do? Something your heart is really set on?"

Joy considered the question; he could tell because she furrowed her perfect, unlined brow. She glanced at her mother, who returned the most intense look Ann Warner could muster. "I don't know, Papa Jack," said Joy. "I like my lessons very much. I don't know if I'm good enough, but I'm better than I used to be. Sophie says nice things every day, and I don't think she would say anything about me to Mother if she didn't think I could do it."

They had boxed him in. Jack could handle Davis or Cagney or Flynn, but little Joy his stepdaughter had just backed him into a corner. Ann continued to stare, promising delights. That smile. Those eyes.

He turned away toward the fireplace to clear his head just

for a moment. Without looking at either of them he said, "I can't lift a finger to help you. Joy, you'll have to go through the normal channels and take your chances."

He felt an explosion behind him. Ann rushed forward and grabbed him at the waist and kissed his ear. "That's wonderful, Chief. You're wonderful," she whispered. And while her hand had him at the belt buckle, she let it drift lower and rub his crotch without Joy seeing.

He pried himself away since Joy was so close by. "I don't even know who's directing this picture," he said uncomfortably. "I can't talk to Steve Trilling in Casting. You two are on your own." Now, he did turn to look at them both. Ann was radiant, beaming, ecstatic. Jack began to calculate the tricky course ahead: Ann would do anything for Jack to ensure that Joy landed this part. And Jack would let her, all the while asserting he had no control over casting. Joy probably stank as an actress anyway, but if by some hideous twist of fate they took her seriously, he could fix it so she didn't get hired. All this went through his head as Ann was embracing him from one side, and Joy had moved in and put her head on his other bicep. He put an arm around each of his beautiful women, smiled to himself, and thought, *Life is good.*

CHAPTER 14

In his office after the signing ceremony, Wallis reflected on the deal with the devil. He stared down at the contract resting in front of him on the desk that had been carefully crafted by Loyd Wright to protect the interests of Hal B. Wallis. But despite every safety feature built in, somewhere down the road, thought Wallis, this bargain would turn Faustian. He imagined the contract bursting into flames. He imagined himself bursting into flames. But he needed to be here at Warner Bros., close to the hand-chosen productions in his charge, and close to the new one that Renie loved so much for reasons he had yet to fully understand. He wanted to make Renie happy as much as she so clearly wanted to please him. He wanted her to be right that the setting in North Africa would prove timely down the road. And then it hit him: 6,000 Jews. Or was it 8,000. Or 10,000. I can't pick up a rifle; these pictures are my weapons.

Into the silence came a perfunctory knock on his doorframe, and Renie leaned her head in. "You ready for us, Hal?"

He shoved away a mental portrait of Jack Warner wearing horns and a goatee. "Sure, Renie. Come in."

She walked catlike across the long office floor. A meeting with Hal meant a dress and heels. It was nothing he ever requested, but she seemed to know what he would like to see. Behind her trailed two of her writers, Aeneas MacKenzie, who wore pince-nez and looked like a preacher, and behind him, Wally Kline, Hal's brother-in-law, suit rumpled as usual. Renie leaned against the side of Hal's desk and motioned for the writers to sit in the two chairs facing Wallis, who sat back and looked past Renie.

He said, "So, *Casablanca*. Renie's baby."

She turned to him. "It is my baby," she offered happily.

Hal forced his full attention to the writers. "You read the play and gave your thoughts. Two Americans meet up in French Morocco and rekindle their romance. That makes it an American story, despite the location, and you two are a natural for it. Look what you just pulled off with Custer and his wife." Hal paused, pulling out a memo from the stack. "And I liked what you had to say in your memo, Mac, about the possibilities of Rick finding a higher purpose in Morocco."

Wallis saw a surprising look of unhappiness on the face of the Scotsman MacKenzie. Mac said, "I've been thinking about it, Hal. We're just a little bit concerned about—" he paused, "—Renie's baby. The characters spend a lot of time thinking about—or having—sexual relations."

Kline added, "The remainder of the time, they sit around a nightclub and drink."

Wallis lit a cigarette. "It's a stage play. An adult stage play. Just do what you usually do and develop the story elements you need." Their unease aggravated him; clearly Wally had gotten to Mac and turned him negative, and it bothered Wallis. "This is why we pay you, to iron out such problems. You did it with Custer. Now do it with Rick Blaine." Wallis didn't feel he could make it any plainer than that. Brother-in-law or no, Renie's baby would now be the writers' baby.

"What about the war?" asked Kline.

"It's all about the war!" returned Wallis.

"But how do we approach it?" asked Kline. "Who knows how things will be in eight or nine months when this picture premieres? We're already losing. Hell, it might all be over in nine months."

"Now what the hell kind of attitude is that?" said Wallis. He clamped down on his anger and sat back. He thought about 6,000 of Paris's best and brightest. They were with him all the time now. "All those people who took the freedom trail and landed in Casablanca. The ones who are desperate for visas. I want you to think long and hard about those people. We need to use this story to show the resolve that exists in the free world." They both jotted notes as he spoke. Hal let them write for another minute to catch up, and then he said, "I'm in New York the rest of the week, but I want you to keep in close touch with Renie, and I mean every day, and inform her of your progress. I'd like an outline in two weeks at the outside, and a script three weeks after that. I'd like to be shooting in three months, in April. Okay with you?"

The writers now appeared to be terrified, which improved Wallis's mood. "Sure thing, Hal," said Kline.

"We'll give it our best shot," said MacKenzie.

Hal left the studio that evening with a stack of film cans— dailies from *Yankee Doodle Dandy* that he planned to review before packing for the trip. He worked until nine o'clock on the dailies and left a detailed list of notes for director Mike Curtiz and unit manager Al Alleborn. A studio messenger would pick up the film and notes in the morning. Then Hal retired to his bedroom where he found Louise on an evening-long mission to pack his suitcases.

In the morning he set off in the back of a studio car for Union

Station to meet up with the three finest writers at the studio, tall and refined Casey Robinson, who was, like Hal, a Republican, and the two frantic liberals, the Epsteins.

At the doors to the terminal, Army soldiers stood guard and eyed everyone going in and coming out. Inside the terminal, amidst the rush of people seeking trains, Wallis searched for his three companions. He couldn't spot any of them, but he did notice three reporters and two still cameramen lurking in the open, waiting. Hal felt a surge of pride that the press had tracked him down to talk about the new contract. He made a mental note to thank Bob Taplinger over in Publicity for arranging it. Oddly, the reporters seemed to take no notice of Hal. Then one of the photographers came to life as if someone had plugged him into a wall outlet. He pointed past Hal's shoulder and exclaimed, "There she is!" In a pack, the five press men jostled past Wallis; he turned to follow their course.

Walking out from the station's restaurant was blonde film star Carole Lombard, dressed to the nines. An older woman flanked her on the left, and a man who seemed familiar to Hal stood to her right. And walking with them were the Epsteins, cutting up with Lombard as only they could; she had one gloved hand hooked under the arm of each. Julie said something, and Carole screeched with laughter that echoed off the ceiling.

By the time Wallis drifted near the commotion, the reporters were scribbling madly on notepads. He could only watch the proceedings as a commoner and admire the beauty of Carole Lombard, the former Paramount star who had been working mainly freelance for some years with fair-to-middling results. Warners had signed her a few years back for a comedy that had bombed on release. The boys had worked on that one and had been Carole's pals who visited her dressing room, and Jack Warner blew his stack over it because Carole failed in the chief's eyes to pay proper homage—she was too busy hanging out with the schmuck writers.

Hal forced himself past the fact that the press people didn't even know he was there. Instead, he devoted these moments to an appreciation of the 110 pounds of prime female flesh standing ten feet away, working the press for all she was worth. Lombard was a stunner, dressed in a pink traveling suit over which she wore a deep brown sable cape tied at the neck. She had wrapped her hair in a pink turban, and she wore lipstick of deep crimson. The older lady, Carole's mother Hal speculated, was also adorned in fur.

"It's important that we support our president, now more than ever," said Lombard to the press. "And since I'm not working, I'm heading over to Indiana to sell war bonds and raise money for the effort. If, that is, anyone cares to come out and see me. I hear it's colder than shit over there right now."

"Can we quote you on that?" kidded a reporter.

"Hell, yes, you can quote me!" she enthused. And they scribbled away.

"How much do you figure you can collect, Carole?" a reporter asked.

"They tell me the goal is half a million," she responded. "Enough for some fighter planes to kick Goering's ass."

By now, tall, quiet Casey Robinson had drifted up to the spectacle. As Hal watched, Carole's topaz blue eyes locked with his.

"Ohmygod, Hal Wallis!" she screeched in high soprano. "Come to see me off!" She pushed through the crowd and wrapped her arms around Hal in a hug that meant it. She brought with her a cloud of Chanel No. 5, and with the embrace, Hal's wounds at not being noticed by the press were salved.

"Nice to see you, Carole," he said into her ear as she pressed a warm cheek to his.

"I'm surprised you'll still talk to me after that stinker we made," she said under her breath. "Where ya headed?"

"New York with these two," he said with a nod to the Epsteins, "and Casey here for some Broadway business."

"If you're in Indianapolis on Thursday, stop and give me a hundred bucks, will ya? You four might be all that show up."

"Tell you what. When I'm back home, Louise and I will buy a bond in your name. I promise."

"Deal, Mr. Wallis!" she said happily. When she hugged him a second time, she also planted a big kiss on his cheek. "There," she said with eyes fixed on the spot, "I gave you an autograph in lipstick. Don't you dare wash it off."

He laughed. "I won't wash it off, Carole."

Then she said suddenly to the older woman and the man, "Shit! Come on! Late for the choo-choo!" She brushed past Casey Robinson to hug the Epsteins. "Bye, boys! You be good for papa!" Then she looked one last time at Wallis and called, "Bye, Hal!"

Lombard turned to the reporters and raised two fingers like Churchill. "V for victory!" she shouted, and she and her companions trotted off and disappeared in the crowd, with only the perfume cloud remaining, like in the cartoons.

The reporters, however, had decided to remain with Wallis's group. "Where did you say you were going, Mr. Wallis?"

"New York for some studio business," he said.

"You just signed a new contract at the studio, isn't that right?"

Wallis took control. "I did, yes. I will head up Hal B. Wallis Productions and basically do the same job as before, serving as executive producer, but on just four pictures a year."

"Give us a preview. What kind of pictures are working on?"

"Well, *Yankee Doodle Dandy*, with Jimmy Cagney of course. And *Now, Voyager* is upcoming—that's Casey Robinson's script for Miss Bette Davis. And we recently bought another property, a wartime drama called *Casablanca*."

The reporters took furious notes while the photographers snapped a few photos. "And who's this traveling with you?"

"Well, Casey Robinson here and Julius and Philip Epstein."

The reporters turned to the boys. "And what are your roles?"

"I get Mr. Wallis's coffee," said Phil.

The reporters gave Julie a glance. "And I supply Mr. Wallis's broads," said Julie.

"They're Warner Bros. screenwriters!" snapped Wallis, and with that the reporters drifted away.

"This is studio business," he hissed at the boys, "and I didn't find that funny."

Julie shrugged and said, "They can't all be winners."

Hal started walking toward their platform and the group followed. Carole Lombard had boarded the Union Pacific *City of Los Angeles*, while Hal's party stepped onto the Santa Fe *Super Chief*.

Hal had packed a grip full of screenplays to review, old scripts that needed to be updated and remade and new stories in outline or script form. The miles clacked by until they reached Chicago and then arrived at New York's Grand Central Station and took taxis to the Algonquin on 44th Street.

The next day, Wallis and Robinson headed for lunch at Sardi's while the boys went off to the Lower East Side to visit their old haunts. Wallis could only hope they might stay out of trouble.

CHAPTER 15

At shortly after one in the afternoon of Friday, January 16, a taxi dropped Julie and Phil Epstein off at the corner of Bowery and East Houston. It seemed so odd to be here with a war on. How many sons of the Lower East Side had already gone off to fight in the name of uncles or aunts or grandparents sent to camps in Germany or Poland?

Snow had started to fall, and a gust of winter wind blowing along the street sandblasted their faces with a mixture of snow and grit. They started walking, huddled against the weather, and as usual they were arguing because, quite frankly thought Phil, Julie was being ridiculous.

"How can we not eat at Russ's?" Phil said to Julie.

"How can we not eat at Katz's?" said Julie in response.

"Look, we have one shot at this, one lunch, and it's got to be the herring at Russ's."

Julie reached out and snatched the hat off Phil and felt around his skull with a gloved hand. "Did you hit your head or something? Pastrami on rye at Katz's!"

Phil grabbed his hat, a tweed newsboy cap, back from his brother, dusted it off, and placed it on his head. He had to admit to himself, you couldn't go wrong with a Katz pastrami sandwich. At the same time, he couldn't allow Julie to be right. "You go ahead and eat at Katz's, ya putz. I'll be at Russ's, standing at the counter with the schmaltz herring."

By now they had reached Russ's on East Houston and stood staring at the sign in front. "Russ & Daughters," Julie read aloud. "You don't suppose the old man's dead?"

"You remember the daughters," said Phil. "They were pretty little girls. I imagine now they're pretty grown girls."

"Maybe," said Julie hopefully. He grew philosophical. "Be a shame if Mr. Russ is gone."

"Let's go in and see," said Phil, and that's how the argument ended, out of curiosity at how "& Daughters" had found its way onto the sign and if Joel Russ was alive or dead.

The bell above the door still jingled just as it had fifteen years earlier, and on the other side of the counter stood gaunt, bespectacled Mr. Russ, who said to the boys as they entered, "U-boats off Long Island! Can you believe it! They're laying mines and torpedoing ships, just like in the last war." The boys had expected warm remembrance at their sudden appearance after years away, but who could compete with U-boats? Mr. Russ frowned. "Where's your father? He hasn't been in lately."

"Our parents moved to Los Angeles, Mr. Russ, some years back," said Philip.

"Oh!" said Russ. "And why aren't you boys in the service?"

"I tried almost a year ago," said Phil. "They wouldn't take me. They thought I was a Communist."

Just then a young woman emerged from the back rooms of the store and stood dumbfounded for a second. They recognized Hattie Russ, who must have been sixteen the last time they saw her. "Oh my God, the Epstein boys!" Hattie called into the back, "Ida! Look who's here!" Ida Russ came rushing up from the back.

"Hello, ladies," said Julie.

Phil assessed that Hattie and Ida Russ were no longer pretty young girls; both had become pretty women, particularly Ida, who had filled out and still had a hint of Kay Francis in her face. The boys ordered the herring and then stood by the counter and ate off plates while keeping a running chatter going with Hattie and Ida.

"We see your names on the movie screen and can't believe we know you," said Hattie. "That *Four Daughters* picture with John Garfield—we cried, didn't we, Ida?"

"Cried our eyes out," said Ida.

"Julie wrote that one," said Phil. "I was working on something else."

Julie asked, "How did the name change come about—Russ & Daughters?"

"That's Dad looking to the future," said Ida. "When two of his brothers—our uncles—were sent away, it hit him hard."

"Sent away," said Julie. "You mean . . .?"

She nodded. Julie looked at Phil. The herring was as good as they remembered. Suddenly, it didn't matter.

"You know what's bugging me?" Phil murmured quietly to his brother.

"Of course, I do," said Julie. "*Casablanca* is bugging you and the fact we were not chosen to write it, even though we understand it has important things to say. The question is, do you know what's bugging me?"

"You mean the fact that there's a war on, and we're thirty-two years old and not doing anything about it," said Phil, who phrased it as a statement and not a question.

"Exactly."

Phil thought a moment. "There are lots of ways to serve. Writing war pictures is a way to serve. Making people laugh, keeping up their spirits."

"Which takes us back to what's bugging you," said Julie. "That picture."

"Well, what are we going to do about it?" said Phil.

"I think we overplayed it with Jerry Wald," Julie lamented. "It was so ham-handed that Hal got wise. Hal doesn't like to feel like people are scheming around him."

"Even though people are always scheming around him," said Phil. "Once he figured out what we were doing, he gave it to MacKenzie and Kline out of spite."

"But now we're in New York, and we've got Wallis all to ourselves for the next three days," said Julie. "We tried the sneaky approach; now let's try the up-front approach."

Phil nodded in agreement. "We've got a right to be interested."

After lunch and having solved the riddle of Mr. Russ, who was alive and had brought his three daughters in as partners in the business, the boys were back outside and walking south on Essex Street. The neighborhood had changed and no longer teemed with people and activity. There were no more horses at all; all the vehicles were mechanical, a fact that had driven their father out of the livery business, which was fine anyway because his health had started to go.

They turned left and headed into Seward Park, where they had spent a fair portion of their youth. At a particular spot, Phil thought back to the time he and Julie had been challenged by those unfortunately named Slutzsky brothers, two big bullies who thought they could push around the Epsteins. The four had arranged a meeting after school beside the pavilion.

"Remember the Slutzskys?" asked Phil.

"We kicked their asses," said Julie, who looked around and then pointed. "Right over there. Except, where's the pavilion? They tore it down!" Where it had stood was now a stately fountain.

Phil found it melancholy to be back; he still felt about twelve, even though he had a wife and two sons and a career. It was simple—neither twin wanted to grow up, ever, because they loved being kids. Being back, he could hear the clomping of horses' hooves on the pavement as wagons and freight trucks hauled along the streets at all hours. He could hear their mother's voice calling them home at dinnertime and smell their father, literally smell his approach, as they sat at the table and heard him climbing the stairs after a day at the livery stable. It was all so close at hand, even here in 1942 as motorized trucks, cars, and taxi cabs passed by and young kids wore long pants instead of knickers and paid no attention to the two adults.

For the boys, returning to the Lower East Side was like visiting tombs. They looked in on a few friends from the old days and then took a taxi up to the Algonquin Hotel and met up with Wallis and Robinson in time for dinner. Afterward, all walked west three blocks in time to see Paul Lukas and Lucile Watson in *Watch on the Rhine* at the Martin Beck Theatre on West 45th Street. At play's end, the four from Warner Bros. waited for Lillian Hellman and the play's director, Herman Shumlin, and had some drinks in a place across the street from the theater. At about eleven o'clock, Wallis stepped out with the others trailing. Wallis dug in his overcoat pocket and pulled out a slip of paper.

He said to the writers, "There's a club I want to check out." He read on the slip, "Café Society Uptown. There is a colored performer I'd like to get a look at for the part of the singer who plays the piano in *Casablanca*."

They started walking, heading east on 45th over to Fifth Avenue. Wallis said he liked to walk in the city; it inspired him. They turned left at Fifth and headed up toward Central Park. The night was clear and growing colder by the moment, and even approaching midnight the taxis zipped up and down Fifth Avenue. The Warner people passed St. Patrick's Cathedral at 50th and then a block past sat Tiffany & Co. They kept walking, turning right at 58th Street. In a couple of blocks, the men reached their destination, marked by a crowd of white people and Negros under a green awning that read Café Society.

Wallis and Robinson pushed their way in like a couple of fullbacks and the boys followed. They were led to a table on a balcony looking down on the action. Performing at the moment was the famous Hazel Scott, a beautiful, young colored woman backed up by six musicians. She wore an off-the-shoulder pink gown with pearls around her neck. Her hair was pulled back and tied with a pink ribbon. Lights trained on her from the rafters caught wafts of cigarette smoke and gave her the appearance of an angel floating in the clouds of heaven.

"Good, I wanted to see this girl," said Wallis.

Phil and Julie watched in amazement as Scott launched into Rachmaninoff's Prelude in C-sharp minor. So strong, so dramatic as she banged on the keys with authority. And then in a moment her fingers flashed into a light, boogie-woogie Rachmaninoff with such gentle dexterity that the mind couldn't keep up. Mesmerized, Phil looked over at Julie, whose mouth hung open.

In a moment Hazel Scott stood away from the piano and moved up before a microphone and began singing Gershwin's "The Girl I Love," but sang it as "The Man I Love," her voice sweet and perfect and pealing like a bell. At one point she looked up across sixty feet from the stage to the balcony and locked eyes with Phil Epstein, and he could feel himself melt from that distance.

"Whatever she wants, give it to her," called Phil to Hal.

When her set ended and the seismic applause began to subside, the din of 100 conversations bounced off the ceiling and walls of the club. Wallis handed the waiter his business card with the Warner Bros. shield on it and requested a meeting with Hazel Scott. As the card exchanged hands, Phil could see that Hal had already received new cards that read **Executive Producer, Hal B. Wallis Productions** beside the shield with its WB.

They sat taking in the atmosphere of the club. Smartly dressed waiters bobbed and weaved, holding trays high; patrons in evening attire filled every table, some of the customers exotic looking, reeking of money, and representing all skin colors. There were sparkling gowns, fur stoles, white tie and tails, and business suits. Over here, a huddled meeting over a small table—they looked like bankers; over there, an older gray-haired man and a young cherub in the shadowy corner.

In a few minutes, Phil felt movement above him at the entrance to the balcony. Hazel Scott made her way down the steps to the Wallis table. Behind her stood a mulatto who was every inch a Central Casting bouncer, his suit ill-fitting and his neck about nineteen inches.

Hazel wore a Hawaiian-print silk robe over her gown. Wallis's group stood, and Hal offered her a chair. She sat gracefully, and Phil plunked into the chair next to her and just dared to take her in. Her skin was a warm caramel color and her face sheer perfection. She wore the darkest crimson lipstick for dramatic effect. She was simply the most stunning creature Phil had ever laid eyes on, and he knew he should just sit quietly and not try to crack wise for fear of ruining the moment.

"I'm Hal Wallis from Warner Bros. Studio in Hollywood, Miss Scott," said Hal.

"So I gathered," she said saucily, holding up his business card. "Barney mentioned that you might be paying a visit." Barney Josephson owned the club; Phil knew that much.

"These are three of the studio's staff writers," said Hal. "Mr. Robinson, Mr. Epstein, and Mr. Epstein."

"My goodness," she said, taking in one twin and then the other. "You fellows look like trouble."

Phil smiled and shrugged his shoulders bashfully; Julie giggled under his breath.

Hal said, "I wondered if anyone from the studios has approached you about appearing in pictures."

Hazel smiled with the grace of a woman a generation older than her twenty or so years. "There have been some discussions," she said vaguely. Even her speaking voice was pitch-perfect.

"Oh?" said Wallis. "Anyone you'd care to name?"

"The Fox studio and representatives of Mr. Zanuck," she said, "and a couple of other inquiries."

Wallis took a beat and said, "And how do you feel about that, Miss Scott? About Hollywood, I mean."

She looked about her. "I feel as if I'm outnumbered here by you Warner Bros. gentlemen."

There followed a moment of awkward silence. She had set Wallis's business card on the table and now her hands, which Phil suddenly remembered had been ensured by Lloyds of London, fiddled with a Café Society matchbook. It was the only tell that the famous Hazel Scott might have been as nervous as the men sitting about her.

"Maybe you should tell me what you have in mind," said Scott, "because I have some very definite opinions about Hollywood that you might find to be a little unusual."

"For example?" asked Wallis. Standing behind Hazel Scott, the bodyguard, who sported a badly healed broken nose, stared straight ahead.

"Well, for example," said Scott, "I don't care for the way colored people are portrayed in pictures these days. They're slaves or servants and always the butt of jokes. I wouldn't play that kind of a part, and I wouldn't abide by any picture where that went on."

Phil could tell Wallis's mind was in high gear as Hazel challenged Hollywood's accepted code for Negro players. Not only must they be portrayed as clearly inferior to whites, but in any musical like the kind Zanuck produced at Fox, they must be used in standalone performances that could be cut out of the picture for distribution in the American South.

"The production I'm thinking about is nothing like that," said Wallis. "The part of the Negro is a very good one. It's a central part and it's written for a man right now. But we could change it to a woman."

Scott thought for another moment and then squared her shoulders. She sat up straight in her chair and picked up his business card and looked at it. "Maybe you had better consider whether I would be right for your picture, Mr. Wallis, because you might find me to be a bit of a problem child." As she arose, the men at the table snapped to. "And now I must prepare for my next set," she said, extending her hand to Wallis and then shaking hands with each writer in turn, a firm, warm handshake. "Thank you for your interest in me," she said and walked away with the bodyguard trailing behind.

It was almost two in the morning when they spilled out onto 58th Street to begin the walk back toward the Algonquin.

Without the boys exchanging a word or the merest glance, Julius engaged Casey Robinson in conversation and Phil moved in on Wallis.

"So, Hal," Phil began as nonchalantly as one could on a city street at two in the morning in twenty-five-degree weather, "Jerry Wald had showed us the *Casablanca* story the other week. We thought it was some slick shit. World of potential. We'd like a crack at it."

Wallis walked with his fedora pulled low and his hands in his pockets against the cold. He gave Phil a wry look that said he knew all about the programming of Jerry Wald. "You have to know I gave it to Kline and Mac, and I suspect you know why."

"What can I say? We're enthusiastic," Phil allowed. What else could he do? "Kline and Mac are good guys. But I know there are times you put more than one team on a script to see how it goes."

Wallis didn't answer immediately. They were approaching the corner of 55th and Sixth, and they had drifted close enough to the corner to hear the call of newsboys shouting headlines.

"Movie star in plane crash! Carole Lombard's airliner missing in Nevada! Read all about it!"

Phil felt his stomach fall out of his body and splat on the pavement like a raw egg. "Dear God," he murmured, staring at the newspaper headline. The Moviola in his brain rewound to that Monday morning—Christ, just the other morning! He and Julie had been sitting at the lunch counter in the restaurant at Union Station drinking coffee and trying to wake up when somebody had sneaked up behind them and reached around to put gloved hands over their two sets of eyes.

"Guess who?" said a woman's voice, pitched low like a gangster.

"Mae West, please," said Julius.

"Excuse him, he's got no class," said Phil. "Lana Turner."

The stranger took her hands away. "Yeah, well, fuck you. Both of you," she said. They spun on their counter stools to reveal the spectacular-looking Lombard.

It all played out in his mind in the middle of the night on blustery Sixth Avenue in New York City. He remembered how warm she was, how physically warm when they had embraced. He remembered he could smell her face powder and lip rouge. And now, somewhere in Nevada, Carole Lombard lay in a plane crash, and those other two nice people, and from the looks of the paper, many others. After that, nothing else on the New York junket was fun or funny. It had become cold, bleak January.

CHAPTER 16

Irene rushed about her apartment packing for two months at the Warner offices in New York. It was Monday morning, and she was thinking about Carole Lombard, who had died in a plane crash with her mother, an MGM press man, and a bunch of Army fliers. They had all died on TWA Flight 3, the same route Irene had taken two months earlier when she was rushing back to get her portrait taken.

She couldn't make sense of a world without Carole Lombard, who was the most alive person she had ever known. Irene remembered sitting at lunch in the Green Room with Carole one day during production of *Fools for Scandal*, something like four years earlier. Irene was the story editor even back then, and Carole was a big star fresh from *My Man Godfrey* who listened with great energy to everything Irene had to say about trying to make her way in a man's studio.

"Men in this town will always tell you what you aren't qualified to do," said Lombard. "But here's a thought: tell 'em to fuck off and then do whatever you want."

They had talked about a lot of things in that lunch, two women letting their hair down. Carole intended to be a director down the road—that was her big secret. And that was the day Irene first expressed the thought that she might like to be a producer. "That's the spirit!" Lombard returned. "We'll show 'em, you and me."

We'll show 'em, you and me.

Lombard's voice echoed as Irene sat in the back seat of the car that drove her to the studio. Carole had sold $2 million in war bonds in Indianapolis before dying on that plane and becoming the first Hollywood casualty of the war. *Who would have thought?* Irene mused with a shake of the head.

She turned her attention to the day ahead. Hal had asked her to route the *Casablanca* play and story outline to the studio's top directors to gauge their reactions. One packet went to William Keighley, director of studio hits including *The Man Who Came to Dinner.* A second went to up-and-comer Vincent Sherman, who had directed only six pictures to date, most recently the Bogart hit *All Through the Night.* The third found the desk of Michael Curtiz.

Hal was just back from New York and had scheduled a meeting with Keighley and Sherman to discuss their reaction to the play; Hal asked Irene to sit in. But first Hal wanted to meet with Kline and MacKenzie to find out what they developed in the way of a *Casablanca* script—Irene sat in on that one as well.

When they walked into Hal's office, neither writer looked happy after their first ten days on the job.

"We've been looking at the problems one by one," MacKenzie said as he slouched in one of the chairs before Wallis's desk. "We don't think Rick should ever have been married. We see him more as a loner, a man of mystery."

Kline looked like he had lost weight. "Yeah, if Rick was never married, then he isn't such a heel for running out on a wife and kid. He can't be an out-and-out heel or nobody will root for him."

"Losing your ideals is one thing," said Mac. "Losing your morals is another."

Wallis nodded and jotted some notes as Irene watched. She could tell that Hal was hungry for what they had to say. And he had expectations she could only hope her writers could meet.

Beads of sweat had formed on Kline's furrowed brow. "We agree the strong point is the rapport between Rick and Captain Rinaldo," said Kline. "Rinaldo is a cultured and polished man. We think Rick needs to be less stuck on the past, less bitter, and more an equal to Rinaldo through the first reel. They need to be less adversarial."

MacKenzie nodded. "Yeah. Rick is tough and all business—until the girl shows up at the first plot point. Only then do we see the cracks in his veneer."

"We have a lot of notes," said Kline. "Just no script pages yet."

The words took a moment to register in Irene's brain—*no script pages yet*. She watched Hal's anger rise. "Look, I'm going to need a script here in three or four weeks at the latest," Wallis told the writers. "In the meantime, yes, let me see your notes. What you're saying makes sense so far. I've got another meeting, so leave what you have here on my desk, and Renie and I will look at it."

He nodded toward the door, and the writers handed their notes to Hal and exited the room.

"They should be further along," Wallis grumbled as he shuffled through the pages of handwritten notes.

"I know they should," she responded. "Maybe it really is better suited to the boys."

A moment later, two men walked in and they were already talking shop. Bill Keighley was dressed in his usual uniform, a brown suit with a knitted sweater vest. He looked as if he were on his way to the track. Vincent Sherman was fifteen years younger and a jovial, outgoing guy, a former actor with a handsome face.

Wallis didn't waste time on small talk. He settled back in his chair and looked at the two men sitting opposite him. "I sent you each a story outline and stage play for our property *Casablanca*. I wanted Renie to hear what you think. She's the one who found the play, and she's heading back to New York in the morning."

Sherman gave Irene an indulgent smile and then nodded deferentially to his senior, Keighley. In the past several years, Bill Keighley had directed some popular gangster pictures with Cagney and Bogart and some adventure pictures with Flynn. Keighley looked at Irene, at the floor, at Wallis, and back at the floor. When he began speaking, it was to the carpet. "Well, I can say with certainty that I have mixed feelings about this concept. You can't film it as is; it's going to take an awful lot of work." He now met Wallis's gaze. "Who are you thinking of casting?"

"It's Bogart's picture," said Wallis, "with Ann Sheridan. That's as far as I've gotten with it."

"There are a lot of roles, important roles for the stock company," said Keighley. "You could populate the entire picture with Warner people or inexpensive character types. I could see Barton MacLane as the owner of that other bar. I think he'd be very effective. Allen Jenkins as the bartender at Rick's. You could save a few thousand that way, but you've still got the censorship problems, and this Negro fellow is another issue. You'll have to change him to a white boy."

Irene didn't like what she was hearing, not one bit. Barton MacLane as Martinez, owner of the Blue Parrot? Allen Jenkins as the Russian bartender, Sascha? It's almost as if Keighley saw this as a B picture. Wallis seemed equally nonplussed. He turned his attention to Vince Sherman, who had his fingers on the pulse of the under-forty market.

"Vince?" was all Wallis said.

Sherman smiled a guilty smile at Keighley and then stood and began pacing in an explosion of energy. "Don't get me wrong, Hal. Everything Bill says is right—this thing is junk. But it's . . . well, it's beautiful junk." He gave Irene a gesture that said, *Nice job finding this property.*

Then Sherman kept going. "They threw in everything and the kitchen sink—I mean the lights go out so the kids can escape, for chrissake! But the ingredients are all there for a great picture. The American expatriate with a mysterious past. The beautiful dame who comes back into his life. The rich newspaper guy Victor Laszlo who's a thorn in the side of the Germans. And, well, the Germans themselves. Menacing, dark, nipping at Victor's heels. And I think I'd take a different approach to casting. I'd shop around and get some Europeans in the character parts. You remember *Algiers*, right? It was all those offbeat actors that made *Algiers* interesting." He stopped and gave Irene a high-voltage glance. "Have you turned the boys loose on this one yet?" Then before she could answer, he was pacing the length of the office again. "Somebody's got to wring every last ounce of melodrama out of the script and get past the sex business. It's got to be either the boys or Casey Robinson, I think. Maybe bring Hellinger's sensibilities into it. Make it a man's picture. Somebody who's got the panache to really look this thing in the eye and wrestle it to the ground."

Irene was ready to have sex with Vince Sherman this very instant. He had just articulated in one long machine-gun burst everything she loved about the story, every possibility she had seen. She watched Sherman rein himself in and return to his seat. Vince had grown breathless and sheepish and lit a cigarette. "But I'll tell you," he said in summation, "if you need a director, I'm your guy."

Keighley let loose a good-natured laugh. "Maybe I'm getting too old for this business," he said with a sigh. "I just couldn't muster any enthusiasm for the material. I know you spent a nice sum for it, Hal, but *Casablanca* just isn't my cup of tea."

"You're not the only one who feels that way, Bill," said Wallis. "The opinions are very mixed."

Sherman now seemed embarrassed; he had shown his hand and upstaged a senior director.

"One more question, Vince," said Wallis. "What kind of visual look do you see?"

"*Algiers*," shrugged Sherman. "Crush the blacks, dark backgrounds, shadows, and a lot of foreground light. Let it rake across Bogart's face to reveal his character. It's not a pretty face, but it's an interesting face, and it loves the light."

Sherman should know; he had directed Bogart twice already, and this vision for *Casablanca* made sense to Irene, and it had to make sense to Hal as well. Vince Sherman's take had made the meeting worthwhile.

After the two directors had departed, Wallis sat in silence. Irene could feel a shift in his thinking because of all Sherman had said. It seemed to her that Hal took this picture a lot more seriously here at three in the afternoon than he had two hours earlier.

"I feel like I just got hit by a cement truck," said Hal finally.

"Yes," said Irene, "because Sherman understands. In fact, I think Sherman understands it better than I do. Everything he said sounded right." She paused. "Maybe the boys understand it that well too."

"Maybe so," said Wallis with a grim nod. "Maybe so."

CHAPTER 17

January yielded to February, and the boys breathed easier with Renie back in New York and out of their hair. That first Tuesday of the month, the phone rang in their office suite and Alice fielded the call. Julius heard her talking a moment but couldn't understand the words. Then he heard her holler, "Which one of you wants to talk to Frank Capra?"

Julie heard Philip bolt out of his chair and appear at his brother's door. "Shit, what does Capra want?" Phil whispered. "Think he wants rewrites to the *Arsenic* script?"

"Can't be," whispered Julie. "I think they wrapped."

"Then what?" said Phil. "Think we're in trouble?"

Julie calculated in his mind if the Epsteins could possibly be in trouble with Frank Capra. They had delivered a script that pleased the genius, and they had rewritten as ordered through the shooting of *Arsenic and Old Lace*. With production wrapped, he calculated that there was no way they were in trouble with Frank Capra.

"Let's find out," Julie whispered. Then loudly to Alice, "I'll take it!" Julie picked up the receiver and pushed a button. He had developed a strategy for dealing with situations like this one: Go on the offensive. "Frank, good morning! Julie here. How's *Arsenic and Old Lace*? How about Grant and his overacting? I mean, holy shit! Did he ever settle down?"

The boys had been on-set just enough through the autumn to come to the conclusion that either Capra couldn't direct comedy, or Cary Grant couldn't play it, or both. Julie and Phil had debated Capra's abilities; clearly Frank understood comedy because *It Happened One Night* had been sublime, beautifully underplayed by Gable and Colbert, neither with a reputation for comic timing. So, what the hell was going on with Grant, who seemed to be playing to the back row of the Fulton Theatre balcony? But then, Julie and Phil could only write the scripts; it was up to others to produce the pictures.

"Hello, Julie," said the voice of Capra in Julie's ear. "The picture is cutting together fine, just fine. I feel we're getting the performance we need from Cary, and I'll fix the, uh, the problems in post. I wonder if you can meet me in the executive dining room. I want to have a talk with you. Both of you."

Julius gave Phil a glance; Phil was trying to read his brother and the situation.

"You want us to meet you in the executive dining room," Julie broadcast to Phil, who shrugged his shoulders. Julie said, "Sure, we can do that, Frank. See you there in ten?"

"I'll be there," said Capra, and he hung up.

Ten minutes later, just short of eleven o'clock, Julie and Phil walked into the dining room next door to the commissary. They found Capra sitting at a table for four, waiting for them. The table was covered in linens, and coffee had just been poured for three. This room usually served only executives and brass, but Capra qualified to be in there; the boys on their own did not.

The Epsteins knew Frank Capra to be a quiet, odd little man. He had become accepted as a great filmmaker, but no one would know it to look at him. Everything about Capra was nondescript.

He wasn't handsome or polished or gregarious. His eye contact was scant. He could wear a dress shirt and a blazer but still look like he was down on his luck.

Now he stared into his coffee cup as he said, "Do you fellas love your country?"

Julie looked at Phil; Phil was looking at Julie. "Sure we do," said Julie.

"Come on," said Phil. "We're from the Lower East Side!" as if that was all the explanation Capra would need.

"I need to know," said Capra, "because I'm building a team. And it has to be a team of true-blue Americans. You see, I've joined the Army Signal Corps and—"

"Yeah, we saw that in the paper!" Julie cut in. "We think that's great; you're going to be an officer."

"Thank you," said Capra, and he paused. He had such trouble getting his thoughts to coalesce into words. He was always stumbling over his thoughts it seemed. "You see, here's the thing. General Marshall wants some short subjects that can speak to the hot-rodders—you know, these young kids who are enlisting or getting drafted. It's a series called 'Why We Fight.'"

"Fantastic idea, just fantastic," said Julie.

"And I'm going to need writers, you see," said Capra. "Naturally, I thought of you two. You would need to come to Washington, the two of you, and I've got some others in mind, and we'll meet with the brass and get some direction, and then you'll write scripts for 'Why We Fight.' What do you think—how does that sound?" Capra said, sputtering to a stop.

The boys didn't need much persuasion about this idea since they had already been talking about how to pitch in to the war effort. Phil said to Julie, "Just one thing—what if Hal puts us on

Casablanca? How could we be in Washington writing for the war and here writing for Hal?"

"If it's for the war, we gotta go," said Julie. "The war tops anything else."

"Even *Casablanca?*" Phil said to test his brother. Julie shrugged as if, case closed.

Phil said to Frank, "Is the front office okay with you taking studio writers to Washington?"

"Yeah," said Julie to Capra, "did you run this idea by the chief and Hal?"

"I did. I did. They said okay. They said they'd give me anything I need. But I've got to be honest with you; they weren't happy about it."

"How long would you need us in Washington?" asked Julius.

"A month, maybe," said Capra. "Six weeks at the outside to get things rolling."

Julie looked at Phil; his brother was in. "Unless something unexpected happens," Julie said to Capra, "you've got two writers. Just tell us when we're leaving for D.C."

"Probably a week or so? As soon as possible, actually. I'll keep you posted. My thanks to you both," said Capra, who stood to his feet, shook the hand of each, and left abruptly. The lunch crowd was just arriving, and the boys stood and headed next door to the commissary.

Phil led his brother to their usual places at the writers table, with Julie taking his turn on the end. The place was hopping, with pictures in full swing and swarms of actors and bit players making a great din as they came and went. To Phil, much more interesting than the actor goings-on were the hang-dog expressions of beleaguered colleagues Wally Kline and Aeneas MacKenzie, who sat adjacent to Julie looking like hell. They had been hacking away at *Casablanca* for three weeks now, and clearly, they weren't pleased with their progress. Or Wallis wasn't. Or everybody wasn't.

Phil leaned in close to be heard over the commotion of the day. "Come on, you guys, it can't be that bad," he began. Inside he was happy, and he could feel glee radiating from his brother at his shoulder. The writers table was full. Dick Macauley, Casey Robinson, Howard Koch, George Bilson, Buzz Bezzerides, Arthur Herman, Len Spigelgass. The gang was all here.

"It's flawed material," said MacKenzie, his voice sudden and angry, like a gunshot. Phil knew the feeling of being pressured to write a script for a concept you don't believe in and sitting cooped up too long.

"The defects are the defects," said Kline, equally psychotic. He had lost weight since the boys had left for New York, and dark circles ringed his eyes.

"How many pages have you got?" asked Phil.

"Fifty," said Mac, and looked at Kline. "Fifty?"

"Yeah, about that," said Wally. "Some of it's easy and comes right off the pages of the play. Tightening up the scenes between Rick and Rinaldo—that part's fine. But when the woman shows up, then where are we?"

"Screwed is what we are," spat MacKenzie. "Our hero goes to pieces like Dresden china over some two-bit trollop. And then they have sex!"

"In the play, Rick's supposed to have been married," said Kline. "But we changed that. He's got to be single; there can't be any ex-wife or any kid. And Rick and Lois can't hop into bed, for the love of God."

Both oppressed writers fell silent. "Have you showed your stuff to Hal?" asked Julie.

"We sent everything we have to Renie in New York," said Mac. "Hal wants to meet with us this afternoon."

"Yeah, 1:30," added Kline.

Phil and Julie silently remarked to each other that they didn't want anything bad to happen to these guys—they were fine fellows. The boys simply wanted a crack at this script. They wanted it so badly that their quest to write *Casablanca* had inspired a line they wrote into another script, for the new Flynn picture now called *Desperate Journey*. The director, Raoul Walsh, had called the Epsteins in because the script felt too flat, too earnest. It needed humor, and so the boys applied a few lines here and there as punctuation points in scenes.

In the tag of the picture, after Flynn and Ronnie Reagan had sabotaged half of Germany while on the run from Nazis, and after they had stolen a German bomber, mowed down scores of krauts, and escaped into the skies over the Fatherland, Julie had written a line for Flynn: "Now for Australia and a crack at those Japs!" He had written the line after daydreaming again about getting a crack at *Casablanca*—they had conquered *Yankee Doodle Dandy*; now for a crack at *Casablanca*. And they had laughed writing Flynn's line because it was pure, unadulterated hero shit. Imagine an action star actually uttering such a pompous line—I've conquered Germany and now I'm taking on Japan!

But then Raoul Walsh had said how much he loved that line and Walsh sent a memo around that congratulated the boys, and out of the blue even Jack Warner gave the Epsteins their due by saying how much he loved that line. And, speak of the devil, here came Flynn walking past carrying a tray full of food. He was dressed in a bomber jacket over a flight suit with fur-lined boots, and he scanned the room for a place to sit.

"Errol Flynn!" called Phil. "Come over here, my friend."

Flynn stopped in his tracks and assessed the situation, eyes raking the table full of writers. "Me, at the writers table?" he said in that famous voice. It was always surreal having anything to do with Flynn since they had seen his face twenty feet high so often.

Phil got up and grabbed a chair for Flynn, and the brothers pushed over to let the actor sit on the end.

"What's the gag?" asked Errol. He was a fantastic-looking male, but even in the four years Phil had been on the lot, Flynn had been aging, and fast. He was the same age as the boys, but hard living had rendered him gaunt, with gray skin and more lines on his face than his time on earth should reflect.

"No gag, Errol," said Julie. "You're one of us. We like you."

Flynn smirked and bit off half a hard-boiled egg. It was common knowledge on the lot: nobody knew if or when they could take an Epstein seriously, and Robin Hood was on his guard. "I'm one of you, huh?"

"We know you're a writer at heart," said Phil. "That stuff for *Photoplay*. And hell, you wrote a bestseller! Julie's never written a bestseller. I haven't." Phil scanned the table. "None of these clowns has written a goddamn bestseller. Faulkner has, but he's not here today."

Phil pointed a french fry at Errol Flynn and said, "I salute you, Errol, for your writing accomplishments."

"Goddamn! I didn't know you wrote a bestseller!" said Spigelgass. "Damn!"

"He did!" exclaimed Phil. "Yes, he did. What was it, 1937? *Beam Ends* it was called. I bought it in New York and I read it. I could not put that book down. The Great Barrier Reef and your boat, the, the—

"*Sirocco*," said Flynn, still wary, finishing his egg.

"That's it!" said Phil. "The *Sirocco*." Phil wasn't kidding. He had indeed read that book and couldn't believe the narrative voice of the actor.

Len Spigelgass said, "A goddamn bestseller, Errol? You had a ghostwriter, right? You didn't come up with all that shit by yourself. Level with us."

Flynn was holding a second egg by his mouth. "You know, I don't even know half you assholes, and I can't figure any of you out. If you're pulling my leg, I'll turn this table over and beat all of you to death with it. You motherfuckers."

Phil put up his hands to say, "Errol, Errol. We're dead serious. You're a god here. A writer."

Flynn regarded Phil for a moment with heavily lidded eyes. Then he finished the second egg and began sawing into the New York sirloin that accompanied the bowl of hard-boiled eggs and a second bowl heaped with oysters, with coffee to wash it down. It was as if he had decided all at once that he wasn't in the middle of an Epstein practical joke.

"All right, I'll level with you," said Flynn. "I had an editor at Longmans. But no ghostwriter." He said the last part with lethal emphasis. Then he took another hard-boiled egg in hand, salted this one, and popped it in his mouth. "I hear you fellas punched up my new script. I appreciate it. Some funny stuff."

"Now for Australia and a crack at those Japs," said Phil with a smile and nod.

Flynn kept on eating and stared blankly at Phil. "Is that in the script?"

"Yes, the last page!" said Phil, offended. "Now for Australia and a crack at those Japs. It's the tag of the picture!"

Flynn smirked again. "Listen, they tell me what pages we're gonna shoot, and then I read them. And they didn't tell me to read page 120." He was eating fast and downed the contents of his coffee cup. A passing waitress refilled the cup.

Julie said, "You've been around, Errol. Have you ever been to Morocco?"

Flynn thought a moment. Then he wagged his head as he ate. "Nope. Spain was the closest." He looked up. "Why?"

"New script these two are working on," Julius said, nodding toward Kline and MacKenzie. Flynn knew them all right, and it was clear by the look on his face that he felt he owed them for a good job on Custer. There was nothing better than a popular picture to elevate the status of a mere screenwriter in the eyes of the front office and of the star who benefited.

"What script are these two idiots working on?" said Flynn. He eyed the pair. "I'm not one to talk, but you fellas look terrible. What are you writing and who's it for?"

The stars were all the same. They competed with one another; each wanted to know every scrap of information about the goings-on of the others.

"It's set in French Morocco," said Phil. "About a guy who owns a nightclub in Casablanca. Something the size of the Troc. And if anybody would know about such things, about nightclubs in far-off places, I figured it would be you."

Flynn looked up toward the ceiling. "Well, let's see. I could tell you about a club in Rabaul where the girls were naked," he said as he flipped through the pages of his memory. "I could tell you about a club in Saigon where I saw a guy knife a guy." He thought some more and stabbed the air with his fork. "And there was a nightclub in Paris that was full of dykes. That's when I found out my wife swung both ways." He paused. "She was my wife at the time, but I imagine she still swings both ways." He paused again. "As for what it's like in a club in Morocco, if I were you, I would call Research."

Getting this much out of Flynn amazed Phil, who said with a nod toward Kline and MacKenzie, "Come on, Errol. Give these guys something to work with. Look at them. They're pitiful."

Because Phil had really read his stuff, Flynn seemed willing to play along, and Phil watched him apply his brain to the task.

Flynn said, "You know what I always find a bit funny? Here in America, everyone in a club is white. All the men wear suits or tuxes, and all the women wear gowns. Great masses of white people. But in a club in, say, Europe, you have all manner of characters. You have dark Spaniards, sultans in turbans, sheiks in robes, and the women . . ." Flynn smiled a vague smile. "Suffice to say, ladies away from the U.S. have a lot more skin to show." He looked about the table. "It's your loss, you pasty bastards. I doubt any of you has ever even gotten laid."

"I just want to say for the record," Buzz Bezzerides pronounced from the far end of the table, "that I have gotten laid."

"How much did she charge?" said Howard Koch. The table burst out in laughter. Even Flynn laughed.

Buzz exclaimed, "The first thing this big mute says in two years, and it's about me!"

"You leave that man alone!" said Flynn, pointing his fork directly at Koch. "Howard wrote *The Sea Hawk* and that picture earned me a three-week fucking vacation!"

"It was my pleasure, Errol, to bring some class to this studio," said Koch.

Flynn was in his element now. He pointed his fork at Koch again like Poseidon aiming his trident and bellowed, "Koch, did I ever buy you a woman for *The Sea Hawk*? If I didn't, I'm going to buy you a woman!"

"Errol, you did not buy me any women," Koch hollered over the din. "Not a one."

"Well, I'm going to," said Flynn. "I know a couple who would be perfect." He had eaten all the eggs. He had reduced his steak to white bones and now he was on to the oysters. He said, absently as he ate, "What is this picture set in a night club? Who's in it?"

"*Casablanca*, Errol," Phil reminded. "For Bogart and Sheridan."

Flynn held his cup and looked around for more coffee, but no waitress appeared. "Nobody tells me anything around here," Flynn groused. "Why didn't they offer this part to me? I could own a nightclub in Morocco better than Bogart could."

"Because the owner is an American with a mysterious past," said Julie. "That's Bogie's territory."

"Fuck Bogie," said Flynn. "Bogie's a prick."

"What's the matter, Errol? You don't care for Bogie?" called Buzz. Phil laughed to himself because Buzz liked to get the commissary riled up.

Flynn glared at Buzz. "Who the hell are you?" he called. To Phil he said, "Who the hell is this guy? I don't even know this guy! If this guy says anything to Bogart, I'll kick his ass and then have him fired off the lot."

"That's just Buzz Bezzerides," said Phil to Errol under his breath. "A while back Buzz took on the front office—and won."

Flynn gave a free pass of a glance to Buzz as he scraped up the last bits of food on his tray and then picked up the bone of his steak and snipped off bits of meat with his teeth. The stars could scarcely dawdle over lunch, and Flynn seemed determined to eat as much as his stomach could hold to keep himself going until quitting time.

"It's been a pleasure, gentlemen," Flynn said in a way that made all in earshot understand it hadn't been a pleasure at all.

Julie said, "Be mindful of those sinuses, Errol." Flynn had been using his sinuses to avoid work in recent weeks.

Errol's brown eyes sparkled with respect for humor wielded in such a way. "Fuck you, Epstein," he said pleasantly. "Whichever Epstein you are." And with that he glided away.

Phil glanced down at his wristwatch and said to Mac and Kline, "What time are you fellows supposed to meet with Wallis?"

"One-thirty," said Kline, who squinted at the clock over the front door. "Shit! Come on," he said to his partner, and off they went.

Phil and Julie cleaned up after themselves, stowed their dirty dishes and trays in the cafeteria's return area, strolled back to their office, and waited.

At 2:35 the phone rang. It was Paul Nathan. "Mr. Wallis wants to see you," he said. "Both of you. Bring notepads and pencils."

Phil thought they shouldn't seem too eager, so they strolled down the stairs, out of the Writers Building, and across the courtyard. They could only hope they knew what Wallis wanted to see them about. And that Wallis wouldn't fire them, or murder them, when he heard what Capra had offered in the way of jobs in Washington, D.C.

CHAPTER 18

Rochester, New York, was a world away from Hollywood, which, for a time, seemed a good thing to Ingrid Bergman. She had convinced herself that Rochester would make her happy: be a wife to her man Petter, be a mother to Pia, find fulfillment in the home supporting her husband until he completed his medical internship. In their five years of marriage, they had spent an aggregate of twelve months together, the rest of the time living apart while she acted and he attended university, so finally they could explore all that marriage had to offer. Ingrid had charged into this new adventure in Rochester with dreams of romance. The previous October they had rented a house with a pretty garden, and she had watched in delight as the leaves on the trees turned vivid colors like nothing she had ever seen from nature. Oh, those beautiful maples! The first dusting of snow came in November and as Christmas approached, it continued to snow. An inch here, three inches there. And ever so slowly she began to suspect, as she knitted sweaters and skirts for her three-year-old and prepared for a family Christmas, that just perhaps she had been tricked into a bourgeois American life that in no way suited her.

Ingrid's next-door neighbor was Dorothy "call me Dottie" Price, a woman of about thirty who stood barely five feet tall and had a voluptuous figure. Dottie was the mother of two girls and a boy, all under ten, and had a husband who worked at the Kodak plant, but the talk was he would be reassigned to defense work, and they'd have to move. About two weeks into Ingrid's stay in Rochester, Dottie came over to borrow a couple of eggs, and by Christmas she was visiting for half an hour or more a day. At first, Dottie had shown up at the door with her hair done and her makeup on, and Ingrid thought she was pretty, but since the early visits she had revealed herself to be what Americans called "frumpy," with no makeup some days and her hair tied back off her face.

"I still can't believe a movie star moved in next door," Dottie had said two days before Christmas. They had sat in Ingrid's kitchen and the *ostkaka*, Swedish cheesecake, sat between them on the table. Ingrid served her neighbor a piece. "Ohmygod, this is going straight to my hips," Dottie groaned before proceeding to eat the wedge in four bites. "That's okay, Walt likes hips," she added, and asked for another piece. "And you, you have to stay thin for the pictures, right? I mean, you're so tall and perfect."

With Petter at the hospital every day, Ingrid was grateful for someone to talk to, even an American frump. "I'm a big Swedish girl who towers over the men in Hollywood. It's quite embarrassing," she said.

"I can't figure out why you're here and not there," said Dottie, who spoke rapid-fire most of the time. "I mean, if I could leave Rochester, I'd do it in a minute and never look back."

"You don't like it here?" asked Ingrid as she ate the five-millimeter sliver of *ostkaka* she had allowed herself. She was determined to keep her figure no matter what and, oh, how she could put on the weight if she wasn't careful. She consumed the dessert in tiny, measured bites.

"Who could love it here?" groused Dottie. "Polar bears maybe.

All I've got is kids and housework. Kids and housework."

Ingrid had sensed in Dottie on this pre-Christmas visit a kinship that had eluded them earlier. "And what would you do if you didn't have kids and housework?" Ingrid asked.

"Don't laugh. I went to college for two years before I got knocked up ... er ... had my first. I wanted to be a librarian. You know, an MLS? A career girl. One night in the back seat of Walt's Hudson changed everything, and now here we are, a foot of snow outside and three kids I didn't want. Don't get me wrong; I love my kids. But this isn't the life for anybody with ambition."

Ingrid poured coffee for herself and Dottie, and then returned to her place at the table. Dottie lit a cigarette and took a deep drag and studied Ingrid through the smoke. "What's the matter? You look sad all of a sudden. Did I offend you? Ohmygod, I offended you. I'm sorry."

Ingrid couldn't help but say what she was thinking at that moment. "What you are feeling? I thought it was just me who was feeling it."

"About a career? Ambition? Ha! It's a man's world, and this life we're leading suits the men just fine."

Ingrid looked out the window a long moment. "For me it started with the snow," she said. "I grew angry with myself for allowing even the slightest feeling that I don't belong here, that every day here is a lost day. As if only half of me is alive." She looked Dottie in the eye. "I wanted to try to be a good wife, but I don't belong here."

"Then why don't you escape! You've got money, a career, a place in Hollywood! I never got anywhere but a back seat—you did it all. You're famous."

Pia trotted into the kitchen and reached up to stick her fingers in the cheesecake. Ingrid grabbed the child's hand just in time. "Oh no you don't," said Ingrid, who cut a piece of the dessert and forked it into Pia's mouth a tiny bite at a time. "Pia's happy here. She's got a mommy and a daddy, and it makes such a difference. I can see it. And I promised Petter I'd see him through his internship." She wiped Pia's mouth and added, "And the phone doesn't ring. There isn't any work for me in pictures right now anyway."

Dottie pondered Ingrid's situation. "If the phone isn't ringing, you must be worried," she said and smoked some more of her cigarette. That portion of the conversation had stuck with Ingrid as December had turned to January and the snows had deepened at about the same rate as the bond that developed between neighbors who were also prisoners.

David Selznick owned Ingrid's contract, and she had been relying on David to find her movie work. But he never called, and Ingrid's conversations with Dottie and Dottie's perspective on men had fueled a notion that Selznick was in fact Ingrid's jailer. She began to count all the perfectly fine offers from Hollywood studios for her services that Selznick had seen fit to turn down since she had last worked. Ten! Now here she was, with only Pia and Dottie for company in the ever-deepening snow.

Selznick had signed Ingrid at age eighteen in Stockholm after he had seen her in the Swedish film *Intermezzo*. He had kept her working steadily since then and along the way she had gained two companions: a husband, dental student Petter Lindström, and a daughter, Pia. Then came the great lull, with no parts offered that Selznick was willing to approve, and Ingrid made the fateful decision for Rochester, where Petter faced two years interning before certification in the United States.

Dottie became Ingrid's American sister and confidante. They

began to indulge in desserts, and Ingrid's weight ballooned. What did it matter, Ingrid thought; Selznick continued not to call. While Pia played with Dottie's kids, the mothers grew close.

One night at the beginning of February, Ingrid couldn't sleep. She didn't sleep all night long, she just lay in bed thinking. Petter had said at bedtime he had engaged a maid named Mabel to look after Pia. Ingrid had to admit, she didn't care much about anything anymore. She wasn't knitting or taking Pia for walks, but then how could she go for walks in two feet of snow? She remembered—when was it, a year ago?—David had told her about a part: *For Whom the Bell Tolls* by Ernest Hemingway, about the Spanish Civil War, where young Maria endures rape by the Fascists and then makes her way to the mountains to join resistance fighters. From the first instant she heard David describing the story, how Ingrid lusted for this skin to crawl into—Maria, raped, redeemed, and finding true love in romantic mountains. In a war! She had rushed from Hollywood to San Francisco in the summer to meet up with Hemingway and cement an alliance. She had enchanted the great novelist, the burly man, the adventurer Hemingway. In the days after, Hemingway stated that he wanted only Ingrid to be Maria just as he wanted only Gary Cooper as Robert Jordan, the American professor drawn to fight the Fascists. Ingrid felt certain she would play Maria, but David never called to say she had gotten the part—he had wanted her to get it, but there had been no word through all these long months about *For Whom the Bell Tolls*. There had been no word from Hollywood about anything, and this long night, Ingrid became convinced she would never work again.

"Happy Groundhog Day!" exclaimed Dottie the next morning as she charged past Ingrid into the kitchen. By now the women had dug a corridor in the snow from one house to the other.

"Happy what?" returned Ingrid as Dottie breathlessly stripped off her scarf and coat and mittens and settled in at the table while Ingrid closed the door.

"Oh, it's some Pennsylvania Dutch thing. If the groundhog sees his shadow, six more weeks of winter. If the groundhog doesn't see his shadow, spring has sprung! There's a groundhog here in New York too. I'm not sure which one takes precedence, the closest one or the more famous one."

Ingrid paused, trying to process or even imagine what she was hearing. "I'm sorry," she began. "I don't know your American customs. What is a groundhog?"

Dottie laughed. "You know, a woodchuck. A gopher. A beaver." She struggled some more. "It's a . . . a . . . groundhog! It's like a big, fat rat, two feet long!"

"Oh my God!" said Ingrid at the horrifying thought, but she wanted to be an American and so she must persevere. "And if this big rat sees its shadow, something? Where is the big rat when it judges its own shadow?"

Dottie plopped into her usual chair and lit a cigarette. "It's a ceremony, with men in top hats. They pull out the groundhog and look to see if there's a shadow." Dottie stopped and pondered. "Actually, it's pretty ridiculous when you stop and think about it."

She thought a moment and said with a knowing look, "Walt tried again last night, and I told him I'm on the rag. But I'm not on the rag, you know?" Ingrid sort of knew, but this was like the groundhog, and she was struggling to keep up.

"I just want him to leave me alone!" said Dottie. "I don't want any more kids, you know what I mean? Three is enough and the clock is running, and as soon as Bobby hits high school, I'm off to get my master's. No more kids!"

"Petter's the opposite," said Ingrid. "He's at work or studying. When he is home, he's an old woman, a nag, a fussbudget. Nothing I do is right." She shook her head and sighed. "I don't know why I never saw it."

Dottie finished her first cigarette and tapped it out. "Your guy doesn't seem like a lot of fun," she said, and Ingrid thought back to her long night. "I shouldn't say anything about your husband," Dottie offered in the silence. "He's awfully cute."

The statement drew Ingrid from her reverie. "No, no, it's not you. I'm thinking about everything. Life here. Isolation. David not calling me. Everything." She realized not only could she talk to Dottie—she had to talk to Dottie. "Petter is employing a maid. Someone named Mabel. He came home, and Pia hadn't eaten. I didn't realize. I was just sitting, not paying attention, just sitting and thinking, and he came home and saw Pia and began screaming at me. He screamed."

Dottie moved quickly to her knees in front of Ingrid and took both her hands. She said, "Listen, I've been thinking about this, and I have to tell you: You've got to get out. This place has driven me crazy, and I'm New York born and bred. For someone like you, it's just . . . it's just insane for you to be here. You need to get out. Go back to Hollywood and confront this David and get him to do something."

Dottie's hands squeezed Ingrid's, and the action shook loose a memory. "I was at MGM," said Ingrid. "David had agreed I should appear in *Dr. Jekyll and Mr. Hyde*, and they told me I would be playing the good-girl part, Dr. Jekyll's fiancée, and that suited David. And I hated that idea, simply hated it. 'What is that?' I asked them. 'It's a nothing part that anyone could play. Get a girl in off the street to play it.' I asked to switch parts with Lana Turner, who was supposed to play the barmaid, the bad girl. I said to let this Lana Turner play the ingénue role." Ingrid had plunged into such a vivid memory. She continued, "David had a fit! He had a fit, and he raged and said, 'You must be a certain type of girl always, a good girl.' And I stared him down. It was one time I gloried in being tall! I said, 'I must give life to the bad girl. I have to play an interesting character, because that is the art. The artist wants a challenge.' And you know what? He backed down. I played the barmaid, and it was such fun. It was so rewarding. And the notices were very good."

"Yes!" exclaimed Dottie. "That's because you are special, Ingrid. You know in your gut what's right for you. You know it deep inside, and you must listen to your gut."

Something about that word broke the spell, and the women looked into each other's eyes and both began to laugh. Gut. Their laughter broke the tension, and suddenly it didn't seem so terrible that David hadn't called or that Petter had hired a maid to look after Pia.

Later that very day, Groundhog Day, David called. David finally called. Just to hear his voice ended Ingrid's numb feeling. "How are you doing, my darling?" said David. "I think about you every day, and I ask for weather reports, and I know there is snow up to your hips."

"Just tell me you have good news, David. Tell me you have a part for me. I need the stage or the cameras. I need to work. I'm dying here."

"I know you are," said David through the long-distance hiss from California to New York. "I know you are. And you aren't to worry about what Paramount did. It's only one part, and there are other parts. Many other parts."

For the second time that day, she couldn't understand the words of an American. It didn't matter the language, the words confounded her. "What are you talking about, David? What did Paramount do?"

"Oh, my angel, I thought you must have heard. They announced Vera Zorina for the Hemingway picture."

The blackness closed in. She gripped the receiver in her hand. She pulled it away from her ear, this black thing, heavy, leaden. She carefully placed it in the cradle. For days after that, Ingrid sat numb. She watched as Mabel, a kindly Negro woman, washed, fed, and entertained Pia.

Ingrid dreamed of the warmth of the California sun. She dreamed of the golden mountains rising around Hollywood, the palm trees, the boulevards, the nightclubs. She wept at the thought of German ballerina Vera Zorina playing Maria instead of her. Zorina smiling out from magazine covers. Zorina in the clinches with Gary Cooper.

She avoided Petter, let Mabel care for Pia, and confided only in Dottie. By Valentine's Day, Ingrid had come to the conclusion that she must develop a plan to reclaim her career, somehow, despite a lack of prospects or a champion. She was better than this; she had to be.

CHAPTER 19

Wallis stared at an article in the *Times*: Wendell Willkie, who had lost to FDR in the presidential election of 1940, said, "When we talk of freedom and opportunity for all nations, the mocking paradoxes in our own society become so clear they can no longer be ignored." Willkie deplored what he called "race imperialism" and said that America must rise above beliefs espoused by the likes of Hitler—the races of men must be equal, said Willkie. With the newspaper still in his hands, Wallis heard Sally buzz him to say Irene Lee was on the line for their two o'clock meeting.

He picked up the phone. "Wallis."

Usually Renie gave a cheerful hello. Not today. Today, she began, "Well, I've read the latest from Kline and Mac. You are not going to be happy."

Wallis let those words sink in: he would not be happy with his writers' six weeks of work. He managed to say in a civil tone, "Walk me through it, will you?"

He heard the rustle of papers on her desk. "Let me see here—I took some notes. Okay, yes, I agree with their approach that Rick should be a bachelor," said Irene. "So Wally and Mac fixed that."

"Right," said Hal. "What else?"

"They also sharpened the relationship between Rick and the French police captain and that seems fine," said Renie. "They did a nice job of cutting down the endless back and forth in Act 1. But this is where they lost me. This idea to get rid of Sam the Rabbit because America isn't ready for a colored best friend . . ." Hal heard her pause to light a cigarette. "If we insist on keeping the character of Sam, they want to play it as comedy. That's the safe way out, of course. So that's the way they wrote it, as if it's a part for Clarence Muse."

"That's not the direction I want to take," said Wallis. "I thought I made that clear to them."

There was silence from Irene's end of the line. Then he heard her say, "I'm not sure I understand you."

Wallis said, "I want to keep the Negro, and he will not be comic relief."

Irene gave another pause. "You know what that's going to do to distribution. Overseas would be okay, but domestically, it's an issue. The South. And the chief—you know how the chief feels about such things."

Wallis picked up the newspaper. "Wendell Willkie just knocked me over the head. He's quoted in the *Times* talking about America claiming to be the beacon of freedom to the world, but if we look down on colored people—if we allow colored people to be second-class citizens—how are we any better than Hitler?"

Renie said, "I agree; with all my heart, I agree. But this is business. The studio does things a certain way. The chief does things a certain way."

Wallis stared at the article on the page. "Maybe it's time to do things a different way. Maybe it's time for Warner Bros. to proclaim that there's a war on, and we're all in this together."

"Just checking," said Renie, "that you are saying you want a Negro to be an ensemble player in our picture."

At times like this he knew he was right to trust Irene Lee, because she had the balls to question his thinking. Hal said, "What if the story is stronger with a Negro in such a part?"

"I don't know," said Irene. "Say more."

His thoughts coalesced. "Giving Rick a best friend who's colored says what Willkie is saying: we have to practice what we're preaching—all of our high ideals. Doesn't it?"

The phone line hissed in his ear as Renie grew silent. Finally, she said, "I love what you're describing. It touches me. It makes this picture so much more important." She paused again and said, "It also sounds like you have wisely given up on casting a woman for Sam."

"Did you go to Café Uptown and see her?" asked Hal about Hazel Scott.

"I did. I went last Friday, and I think you're crazy, Hal."

"Oh? This girl has all the talent in the world."

Irene sighed into the other end of the line, and then her voice raised an octave as she said, "I took one look at this girl up there on the stage with her ruby-red lipstick and the ribbon in her hair, her perfect chestnut shoulders exposed, and I burst into such a fit of laughter that I had to go to the powder room and put my face on all over again. I thought to myself, *What Thee Hell?*"

He was growing impatient. "Will you tell me what you're talking about?"

Renie said, "Before she had played a single note, my very first impression of Hazel Scott was, forget this goddamn *meshuga* idea, Hal Wallis!"

"But—" he started to say.

"If you are Rick Blaine stuck in Casablanca," Irene thundered, "and Hazel Scott is right within reach every day, working for you, this incredibly gorgeous and exotic woman, what the hell do you need Ann Sheridan for? In that scenario, Ann Sheridan is a couple of steps down from Hazel Scott!"

"But Rick and Sam are just pals," reasoned Wallis.

"You know that, and I know that, but the audience is going to wonder, 'Are these two healthy people having relations?' And it's going to distract them and torpedo you in the Bible Belt. Besides, I guarantee you, Hazel Scott will steal the picture. She's too good. If she's cast opposite Bogart, Hazel is going to render your star invisible in every scene they play together."

"All right, all right," Wallis said, worn out from the browbeating.

"Can we get back to the issue at hand?" said Renie. "Kline and MacKenzie ran themselves into a ditch at the first plot point: when Lois shows up at Rick's café and it's revealed she is the woman who wrecked Rick's life, your writers got stuck. In the play, Rick and Lois have relations that night. Kline and Mac didn't know how to get out of it. So they wrote it without the relations, and it's not terrible, but it must have hung them up for quite a while, because the script pages stop soon after."

Wallis's heart sank. "So then, where are we? We're set to roll camera in ten weeks and we don't have a script."

"We've got an Act 1," said Irene hopefully.

The sentence hit Hal sideways; in the back of his mind, he had already reached this crossroads. "I think it's time we sent a message to the Writers Building, and I want it to be loud and clear," said Wallis. "We took the wrong approach when we sent around the play for comment as if this were a democracy. Who the hell cares what the writers think? I should have bought the thing on your say-so and assigned it. End of story. But I didn't, and now I've got a mess to fix."

"Fix how?" asked Irene, her voice mixing in with the static on the line.

"A head must roll, and it's got to be Kline."

"Your own brother-in-law?" she croaked.

"That's exactly why it's got to be him. If I let Mac go, and Wally stayed, then they'd gossip about nepotism. Hell, fire them both and be done with it. I want it to be heard loud and clear that *Casablanca* is important. This script is important, to me personally and to you personally, so the writers need to know that." The line grew quiet again. "You still there, Renie?"

"Yes, I'm here, Hal. A little in shock, but here." She paused. "Do you want me to fire them long distance?"

"It's your job," Hal barked, but it irritated him that she was in New York and the task needed to be immediate and in person. "Unfortunately, you're there and I'm here, so I'll do it."

"When?"

"As soon as I hang up the phone," said Wallis. He took her silence as editorializing. "This is business, Renie. Sometimes the writers forget that. I'm going to remind them."

"It's fair," she said with a sigh. "It's just . . . sad. It's a shame one of my stories led to this."

"That's show business," Wallis said flatly.

She was quiet another moment and then said, "So isn't it time to turn the brothers loose on this thing? At least Kline and Mac gave them a couple of things to start with."

"Are the Epsteins done with Cohan?"

"It's the tail end of Cohan. Yes."

"Okay, I'll meet with those two after I finish with Kline and Mac."

"You haven't given me much to do here in New York."

"Send whatever Kline and MacKenzie gave you on the next plane," said Wallis. "And then, I guess, just sit there and look pretty."

"Always, boss. Always," said Renie, and then she added, "And will you please let go of this crazy idea that you want Hazel Scott in our picture? Time's too short to go down that road and then have to turn around and come back."

"I'll take it into consideration," said Wallis, who now felt oppressed at what he must do next. "Say goodbye, Renie," he sighed wearily into the phone.

"*Adieu*, Renie," she said on cue, and they hung up.

Wallis reached out and buzzed Paul Nathan's desk. "Paul, if Kline and MacKenzie are in their offices, could you tell them to come see me?"

Nathan acknowledged, and six minutes later the writers walked in and sat down as if they knew what was coming. "Irene and I met this morning about the material you turned in on *Casablanca*," Hal began. "I'm disappointed. Personally disappointed after what you did with Custer."

MacKenzie sat in one of the chairs facing Wallis's desk and said nothing. Kline said, "This is a tough one. If we had another month—"

"We don't have another month," Wallis snapped. "I'm going to have to take you off the payroll and go in another direction."

"You're firing us?" said Kline. MacKenzie's demeanor didn't change at all; he had come in the door sullen and remained sullen.

"I'm letting you go," said Wallis with a nod. "I appreciate your contributions and maybe down the road we'll work together again. But that's my decision. You can have today to clear out your offices, and I'll pay you through the week." Hal wondered sometimes if he were part reptile because he could feel the blood cool in his body at moments like this one. He didn't feel anything for these two except betrayal. And the look on his face must have been definitive because the writers got up, shook his hand, and exited the room.

After a silent moment alone, Wallis buzzed Nathan and asked him to come in. "I just fired those guys," said Wallis.

Nathan swayed a little. "Whoa," he murmured.

"Yeah," said Wallis. "Could you please see if there's any chance that the Epsteins are in their suite? If they are, ask them to come to my office."

Nathan said, "They're going to want to know if they're in trouble. They always ask. And if they know they're in trouble, they won't come over. Especially not if they know you're firing writers."

"No, they're not in trouble," said Wallis with another sigh.

Twenty minutes later, a knock at Wallis's half-opened door announced the arrival of the Epsteins. Julie walked in first and said, "So, just to be clear, we're not in trouble."

"Yeah," said Phil. "We heard about Mac and Kline."

Wallis glared. "Let that be a lesson to you. Both of you. You went on the stump for *Casablanca* and now you've got *Casablanca*. Renie and I want a script as soon as possible." Looking at them, Hal considered that perhaps fresh blood on the carpet had dampened their enthusiasm. "What, no smart-ass comments, Julie?"

Julie put out both hands in a gesture that said, *Don't shoot*.

"There's nothing funny about writers being fired," said Phil.

"No, there isn't," said Wallis. "I just want to impress upon everyone in your building how important *Casablanca* is to Irene and to me. It's very important."

Julie ventured, "Can we see what those guys came up with?"

"It's on its way by plane," said Wallis as he rooted around a desktop cluttered with memos, notes, and call sheets from multiple productions. He found the memo he wanted. "Here, listen to this. From MacKenzie to Nathan on the third of January about this story. 'Behind the action and its background is the possibility of an excellent theme—the idea that when people lose faith in their ideals, they are beaten before they begin to fight. That was what happened to France—and to Rick Blaine.'" Hal looked past the paper at the brothers. "When I first heard that, I liked this idea quite a lot, which is why I gave it to Mac and Kline in the first place."

Wallis set the memo down, leaned back in his chair, and closed his eyes, thinking about the idea of people losing faith in their ideals. He said, "Rick has run away from responsibility. He's hiding out in Casablanca and as the plot unfolds, he realizes he can't run anymore. All these poor innocents needing visas reconnects him to his American ideals. It's got to be about bigger issues than how he feels about some two-bit woman."

Phil said, "That's pretty much the play in a nutshell: Rick and a two-bit woman."

"That's exactly right, but our picture must do a lot more," said Wallis, pointing a finger at Phil for emphasis. "That's your job— find me the story that works."

Julie had seemed to mature by a decade in five minutes and was scribbling notes on his pad; Phil was not. Phil just watched Hal and listened to his brother scratch away. Phil said after a moment, "When you assigned the job to Kline and Mac, did they get this speech?"

Wallis picked up Mac's memo again. "I didn't think I needed to because Mac's the one who wrote about the theme of lost ideals. I thought all I had to say to those guys was, 'Follow this memo and write me a script,' and they'd go off and do it. But they didn't."

Phil said, "So, the way we see it, the inciting action is Ugarte leaving the visas with Rick. The first plot point is Lois arriving in Casablanca."

Hal nodded. "Sounds correct. Now, write me Acts 2 and 3."

Julie stopped scribbling and looked at Hal. "It's always helpful to know the cast and write to their personalities."

Wallis motioned to the wall at his left, where hung a bulletin board with a pinned index card bearing the name HUMPHREY BOGART and beside it a second index card reading ANN SHERIDAN.

"That's it?" Julie asked. "That's all we have to go on?"

"That's all I have to go on," said Wallis. "I need Europeans for Laszlo and Rinaldo, and a German for Strasser. And, of course, a colored actor for Sam."

"What about that hot number we met in New York? Hazel Scott?" asked Julie. "Is she in?"

Wallis thought back to the tongue-lashing just received from Renie. He tried to think of a time when Irene had been wrong about something important. Or something unimportant. Irene had brought the play to his attention and knew the story arc better than he did. If Irene thought Hazel Scott would be a mistake, then so be it—the goddess Athena had spoken. "I think it's going to be a male."

"But still colored?" asked Julie.

Phil said, "Any chance it'll end up being somebody like Mischa Auer or Alan Hale?"

"Nope," said Wallis. "Sam is colored, and Sam is Rick's loyal friend. That's the way we will play it."

Phil shrugged. "It isn't done, that's all. We might get boycotts.

People could stay away."

Wallis lit a cigarette. "Well, I'm trying it. It's my picture and I'm trying it." He took a long drag and said, "Write it that way—Sam is Rick's friend and confidant. You guys like to clown it up, but not with this character. This character, Sam, is the soul of discretion. Ultimately loyal. And he's played straight. Got it?"

"Got it," said Julie.

"Got it, Hal," echoed Phil.

"I want you to come to this office once a week so we can discuss the progress you've made. And about four weeks from now, I want the script to be complete. It can be rough, but I want it complete to fade-out."

Slouching in chairs across from him, the Epsteins didn't seem as happy as he thought they would be or should be. In fact, one looked at the other, and they began a strange form of nonverbal communication: they were arguing with each other without words. Then they turned their attention back to their boss.

"Thank you, Hal," said Phil. "Thank you for giving us this script."

"We're elated, really," said Julie. "The thing is—"

"Yes, Hal," said Phil, "there's a thing. A little problem. Not a big problem, but a problem."

"But we'll still write the script," said Julie. "Absolutely, we will still write it. We'll knock it out of the park. It won't be a single. It'll be over the wall."

Wallis forced himself to remain calm and said, "Will one of you please tell me something that makes sense."

The brothers looked at each other, and Wallis witnessed them culminate the argument via telepathy. Then they nodded agreement.

Phil the diplomat said, "The thing is, Frank Capra offered us a job writing his Army films in Washington. He said he had cleared it with you and the chief. And so we told Capra we'd do it."

Wallis was aware of Capra's assignment to the Signal Corps, and Frank had advised the front office he'd be recruiting writers, but Hal didn't expect a talent raid here at Warners. Wallis's thoughts kaleidoscoped—find another writer for *Casablanca*? Give it to Casey Robinson or Dick Macauley or Howard Koch? Hal had seventy-five writers at his beck and call, but the consensus was that the Epsteins were right for this one.

Phil went on, "We feel we have to find a way to serve, as corny as that sounds. We've got wives and kids, so we're not running off to enlist, but this is something we can do. He's calling his pictures 'Why We Fight.' It seems important, and well, we couldn't say no."

"Important," said Wallis aloud. Did they not understand that *Casablanca* was important? "I'm depending on you. Renie is depending on you."

Julie said, "If we end up going, on the train ride there and in the evenings at wherever we're staying, we'll be writing *Casablanca*. We've got some ideas already, and we agree with you about Bogart and Sheridan and the colored piano player."

Wallis didn't like Capra making an end run and rounding up his talent. He didn't like the boys accepting the job without asking Hal's advice first, but in his mind's eye, Hal could see Renie giving him one of those looks. He heard her say, "Don't you dare lose your temper, Hal Wallis. These are my boys."

The room was so quiet that the ticking of his desk clock filled the space. He looked at them; they looked expectantly at him.

"Okay, don't let me down," said Wallis amidst a sharp exhale. It killed him to say it; these two had hurt his pride and he wanted to let them have it. And he couldn't. He imagined Renie standing behind them, nodding approval. Renie, his quiet conscience.

"We won't," said Phil. "We won't let you down."

"You can count on us," said Julie.

"I want regular updates on your progress. You had better be sending me constant wires or calling me on the phone. And in exchange, when I cast a part, I'll let you know so you can pencil that actor into your draft."

"That's great, Hal, just great," said Phil, and the boys shot up as if their chairs had been electrically charged.

"We'll get on it right away," said Julie, and the Epsteins fled the room.

At the door Julius turned and pointed a finger at Wallis. "And in our spare time," said Julie, "we'll win the war."

CHAPTER 20

It was a quiet winter Monday morning at the Warner Bros. New York office, and Irene couldn't quite wake up, despite her third cup of coffee and corresponding cigarette. She had awakened at 3:30 thinking about an idea to be named associate producer on *Casablanca*. Hal hadn't assigned anyone, and why couldn't it be her? He had been open to the idea of this picture, and then Vince Sherman's enthusiasm, calling the story "beautiful junk," had really gotten Hal going. All she needed, she thought as she stared at the ceiling in the night, was the right opportunity to pitch herself as producer. It would have to be in person, next time she was back out there. Still sleepless, she had thought about the war, and the president's fireside chat to take place that evening. Roosevelt had asked all Americans to have a map of the world in front of them during the chat, and Irene still hadn't carved out time to find one. The war was always in view, everyone's view, this pressure on the heart no one could shake.

As she sat at her desk still trying to fully awaken, in mid-drag of a new Chesterfield, she heard, "Oh no!" A woman's voice. "Oh, dear God, no!" followed by uncontrollable sobbing. Irene shot from her desk chair, believing it to be the voice of Gladys Janowitz. Rushing down the hallway, Irene had reached a conclusion that, at once, must be true and yet must not be true.

She careened toward Gladys's desk, one of a formation of desks in a forty-by-eighty-foot open office. Irene pushed through a cluster of executives and secretaries to find Gladys leaning forward in her chair, arms wrapped tightly around herself, sobbing.

Irene knelt beside her friend. "Tell me, honey, tell me," she said, reaching out to embrace Gladys.

"It's Jack!" she screeched. "It's Jack! It's Jack!" Gladys was a plain girl who tried to match Irene style for style, and it never quite worked. Today she wore a purple dress like one Joan had worn in *The Women*. But, as usual, it seemed a little off, especially as she cried into it.

"It's okay, Gladys, it's okay," Irene soothed into Gladys's ear. Irene had already figured out the worst: Jack had been killed. She just didn't know the how or the where. She looked up to the sea of surrounding faces and motioned them away. She pulled a handkerchief out of her jacket pocket and handed it to Gladys. "It's okay, honey. Just cry it out. I'm here. I'm here."

Irene looked up to see Harry Warner standing over them. Harry was a grandfatherly sixty, with a kind face nothing like his younger brother, the evil Jack. Harry seemed a bundle of nerves, wanting to help, his body threatening to jerk into action, and yet he couldn't seem to decide what to do. Irene let out a breath and then, on instinct, she knew what to do. "Mr. Warner's here, Gladys. Mr. Warner." Irene said it slowly and deliberately.

Gladys gave a start and the energy in the room shifted. "Mr. Warner?" she gasped. It was everyone's instinct to revere Harry Warner, and Irene figured that hearing his name would help Gladys's rational mind kick into gear.

"Yes, honey, Mr. Warner's right here."

Gladys wrenched herself away from Irene. "I'm sorry," she

heaved. "I'm sorry, Mr. Warner." She wiped all the makeup off her face with one swipe of the handkerchief.

The boss of bosses looked about him and pulled up a chair to sit down. "Miss Janowitz is it?" he began, reading her nameplate. "You've had a terrible shock." It was half statement and half question.

"It's my brother," she choked. "In the navy. His ship ran aground. He was killed." She began to sob again. "My mother just called."

Mr. Warner was a good man; Irene knew that already. She saw the pain in his eyes and then tears in his eyes. He reached out and touched Gladys's shoulder. "Oh, my dear," he said. "My dear." He looked at Irene. "Does she have family close by, Miss Lee?"

"Yes," said Irene. "She lives in Brooklyn with her parents." Irene's mind careened back to the date she had had with Jack—when was it? November? Just three months back. That kiss; she had decided to teach the poor boy how to kiss. And in return he had told her about oil fields in the Caucasus and Libya and given her a vital clue about a story that became *Casablanca*.

"Get the address," said Warner. "I'll have my car out front in ten minutes to take her home."

"Yes, Mr. Warner," said Irene. "Thank you, thank you." He stood up and walked silently away.

Irene bundled Gladys up in her coat and gloves and wrapped a scarf over her hat; she held the girl close in the elevator and all the way to the curb, where she placed Gladys into the back seat of Mr. Harry Warner's limousine. She gave the driver the address in Brooklyn and watched the car drive off as a steady snow fell on Manhattan.

The day went by in a fog, until four o'clock when Irene realized she had forgotten to acquire a map of the world. The *New York Times* had provided a map in the Sunday edition, but she wanted a better map.

"Shit!" she muttered, remembering. She hurried into her coat and gloves and arranged a hat on her head, one like Joan had worn in *A Woman's Face*, and headed out to find a map of the world. Her plan was to go to Rand McNally on 52nd Street, but by now so many million city dwellers would have had the same idea. She ran the eight blocks in heels over wet pavement and splashed into the occasional puddle. As always, she imagined Nazis on every corner and then pushed the specters from her mind.

She arrived at Rand McNally at 4:50 to find the place packed. She pushed her way in the door into a crowd of maybe fifty, maybe eighty. She inched her way forward, submarining in some cases, which proved it could be an asset to be five-foot-nothing, and at 5:12, with store workers having given up on the idea of closing the doors, she reached the counter.

"I need a map of the world!" she barked.

"I need a map of the world!" the man next to her barked at the same instant.

The boy on the other side of the counter, who looked like a younger Eddie Quillen, shot a glance at Irene and then at the man and then at Irene again. Behind him, one rolled-up map rested in a bin against the wall. "There's one left," he cautioned, "and who the hell cares who gets it? I sure don't."

Irene thought back to the day she had just experienced. *Who the hell cares?* she asked herself. *The president's going to speak, and I care!* "I want that map!" she snapped at young Eddie. She hadn't looked at the man next to her; she didn't want to look at him. She was too tired and too angry, and she knew she was in for a scrap because New Yorkers, like pirates, always stood cutlasses at the ready for a fight.

"No, no, son, you give the map to the lady," said the man next to Irene, his voice gentle, with a southern lilt. "It's fine."

The words poured over her like warm honey, from her crown down over her body. That voice, so sincere. She turned to her right to behold the competition. Oh my God, he was tall and Jewish— she could have spotted it at a hundred yards. A tall Jewish boy in the snappiest suit, overcoat, and fedora she had ever seen in the city. And he was smiling the nicest smile.

"I'm sorry, miss," he said, reaching up to touch his hat brim and give a nod, "you take it. I'll use the map in the *Times*." Yes, the Jewish boy had a southern accent. She could swear he did.

She opened her mouth to speak, but no words came out. She tried again. "Thank you. That's very nice," she managed. She paid for the map and held the rolled document tightly in her fist as she made her way through the crowd and reached the door to 52nd Street with the young man walking close by. In the thirteen seconds it took to swim through the crowd, she knew she had to get away because this man seemed so perfect, he must be a crazed killer; such was her luck in the romance department. But he had stuck with her and out on the sidewalk, she breathed deeply in the cold February air after all those claustrophobic moments inside. He did the same.

Irene was vexed. Disconcerted. Unsettled. On reflex she fumbled in her purse until she had shoved a cigarette between her lips and lit a match against the winter breeze. She drew in deeply, the smoke hot in her lungs, and blew it out in a long line, the wind catching and scattering the cloud. She had spent years beside powerful executives, and world-class writers, and movie stars, but this Jewish boy had changed her molecules into wet noodles.

"Where else can a guy get a map in this town," he wondered aloud on the sidewalk of 52nd Street.

"You said you would use the map in the *Times*," she said, finding her voice.

"If necessary," said the young man, deep in thought. "But that map doesn't do the president justice. Or, at least, I don't think it does."

So, he wasn't just patriotic. He was also a fan of the president. Score more points for the well-dressed stranger because Irene simply didn't trust anyone who spoke badly of FDR, her god, especially now. "Listen, you were very gallant in there," she heard herself say, "and so, I'm willing to share my map with you."

He slipped a black leather glove on his right hand, and then a black leather glove on his left hand. Somehow, it was a very sexual thing, the way he did it, and she beat that thought straight out of her head. The last thing she needed was to feel what she was feeling at this moment.

"You mean, we'll cut that thing down the middle," said the southern stranger, alluding to the rolled-up map. "I'll take the eastern hemisphere, and you'll take the west?"

"Nooooo," Irene heard herself say, "I mean, we could find someplace to unroll the map and listen to the president together."

She shook her head to clear it. Had she just said what she thought she had said? That couldn't be right. But, yes, she was sure she had just more or less propositioned the stranger right there on 52nd Street. She took another nervous drag on her cigarette and stared down the endless, snowy urban corridor.

When she glanced back at the man, he was smiling. It wasn't a lecherous Hollywood smile. It was a knowing, civilized, respectful smile, or, at least, that's what she imagined in her suddenly fog-en-shrouded mind.

He folded his arms in front of him. "How about this," he said. "How about you let me take you to dinner at Sardi's—you know, so I can buy into the map—and then we will go to my apartment and listen to the speech." He unfolded his arms to hold a gloved finger in the air. "No funny business, mind you. I get up early. I'm a working man."

What. The. Actual. Hell? Irene thought those words at that cadence. Who in hell did this Jewish boy think he was, planning the evening of a Warner Bros. executive on a Manhattan sidewalk? It was the most outrageous thing she had ever heard!

"Okayyyy," she heard herself gush, felt herself smile, and hated herself for both. He walked ten feet to the curb and hailed a cab as if he owned the city.

Inside the cab he said, "What's your name, anyway?"

"Irene," she heard herself say. "Irene Lee."

"And what do you do, Miss Irene Lee?"

"I'm the story editor for Warner Bros."

He leaned away from her in the back seat of the cab, as if to check what he had just heard. "You mean, Warner Bros.–Warner Bros.? The movie studio? Cagney and Bogart and Flynn?"

"Yes, that Warner Bros.," she managed. "Not the other one."

They both laughed. "Well, I'll be a monkey's uncle," he said with that hint of a drawl. "I watch your pictures all the time. All the damn time. I just saw *The Maltese Falcon*. And that picture with Flynn on the aircraft carrier. What was it, *Dive Bomber*? I loved that one! I'm a Navy man, you know."

She snapped to attention; this boy really did know his Warner Bros. And he was a Navy man, like Jack Janowitz. They were turning left onto Sixth Avenue when she said, "How did you know Sardi's is my favorite restaurant?"

"I didn't," he said with a shrug. "It's my favorite restaurant."

Her mind swam, not to any specific place, but it took her along in a warm current as twilight melted into winter's night and the blocks of Sixth Avenue drifted by. As the cab turned right onto 44th Street she said, "What's your name?"

"Aaron. Aaron Diamond," he said. "I'm a buyer at Abraham & Straus."

"Buyer of what?"

He sighed. "Don't laugh: rugs."

"People need rugs," she heard herself say with a shrug in a voice that didn't seem to be her voice. The cab pulled up at Sardi's and Aaron paid the driver. This couldn't be happening; she must not allow this to happen, she thought, scolding herself. She forgot the rolled-up map in the cab, but Aaron rescued it at the last second and they went in to dinner.

She ordered her favorite, filet of sole with broccoli Hollandaise and then Boston cream pie for dessert. She smoked Chesterfields throughout, but Aaron didn't smoke. He ordered the breaded veal cutlet, à la Milanaise, with both coleslaw and fruit salad. A bold and sensible choice. Then, at about eight o'clock, they took a cab to his apartment up Fifth Avenue, which he said he shared with a roommate named Ira who was away.

Irene told Aaron about life at Warner Bros. working for men who struggled to respect her or simply didn't respect her at all. She mentioned the stories she had brought to the studio, including pretty much everything Bette Davis had done of late. Many had become million-dollar hits, and she went through the saga of the new property she had championed, which would be called

Casablanca, and the gamble it was, and her idea of being the first woman producer of her time. Or she could be let go August 1, if Jack Warner had his way. His threat was, she confided, never far from mind.

Aaron told her about his college days at the University of Chattanooga followed by a scholarship to Harvard Business School for graduate work, some years in the Naval Reserve, and his job at A&S.

The time flew until Irene glanced at her watch to see it was 9:50. "We can't keep the war waiting!" she said in alarm.

"It was nice not to think about it for a little while," said Aaron as he lifted the coffee table aside so she could unroll the three-foot-by-four-foot world map across the floor of his living room. She thought of Gladys and Jack and almost brought up what had happened but didn't have the will to do so.

There was no problem finding the president's fireside chat on the radio; every station on Aaron's floor-model RCA was broadcasting it. With the entire front of the radio cabinet serving as a speaker, when FDR said, "My fellow Americans, Washington's birthday is a most appropriate occasion for us to talk with each other about things as they are today; things as we know they shall be in the future," it sounded like the president sat five feet away. His voice went straight through her, at once both commanding and soothing. He always soothed in these fireside chats, no matter the topic.

He spoke first about the American Revolution, and how dire things looked for years with defeat after defeat—as dire as things look now, said the president. He said there were fifth columnists, rumormongers, and selfish men back in Revolutionary times who wanted to negotiate peace with the king of England, just as some in America wanted to negotiate with Hitler now. The president talked about the steadfastness of George Washington in these times and his refusal to lose. He talked about this new kind of war with its new weapons and its global scope involving every continent and every sea and air lane in the world. "That is why I have asked you to take out and spread before you a map of the earth," said the president to Irene and Aaron, "and to follow me in the references I shall make to the world-encircling battle lines of this war."

Roosevelt's voice sent tingles down Irene's spine, the same tingles she felt when she had first read "Everybody Comes to Rick's." The president pointed out the vast areas of China and Russia. He called attention to all-important islands—the British Isles, Australia, New Zealand, and the Dutch East Indies—and to places like India and Africa with their resources and raw materials. He said America must fight in such locations because the enemy was there—an enemy that sought to divide and conquer all countries like the United States standing in the way.

Beside her, Aaron sat on the floor with his back against the sofa, listening, all his concentration on the words of FDR and the map. He wasn't moving; he scarcely breathed as the president presented his case for sending aid to other countries and positioning American forces in far-flung corners of the world when many in the United States sought to provide only a "last-ditch defense" of U.S. borders. The American eagle, said the president, would never imitate an ostrich. "We prefer to maintain the eagle as it is," said FDR, "flying high and striking hard."

The president pointed out dots on the map in the Pacific Ocean, west of Hawaii, each one a tiny island that was vital to the defense of America, no matter how far away they seemed to be.

He mentioned Midway and Wake and Guam, and Aaron pointed each out on the map, maybe because he had been there while in the Navy, Irene wondered. Roosevelt coughed a smoker's cough every few sentences, making him even more genuine and fatherly. He called out the Philippines, Bataan, and Corregidor on the map and also Hawaii. He talked about the dastardly attack on Pearl Harbor and the rumors circulating that 1,000 American planes had been destroyed there, along with all the ships at anchor. None of that was true, said the president, citing this type of rumor and misinformation as an example of the danger of defeatism.

"We Americans have been compelled to yield ground, but we will regain it," said the president, his voice now strident. "We and the other united nations are committed to the destruction of the militarism of Japan and Germany. We are daily increasing our strength. Soon, we and not our enemies will have the offensive. We, not they, will win the final battle. And we, not they, will make the final peace."

When the fireside chat ended, neither Irene nor Aaron moved. They sat in perfect stillness as a big band program began. It all seemed so crushing, so overwhelming, this war. A world war for the very soul of the earth.

After a while, Aaron stirred, climbed to his feet, and snapped off the radio. He offered his hand to help her rise, a warm hand. She wrapped her scarf about her neck and slipped on her coat, hat, and gloves without a word, her mind a jumble of Pacific islands and eagles and scripts and bosses and poor, dead Jack Janowitz.

She picked up her purse and headed for the door. "Thank you for loaning me your map," said Aaron, who had rolled the item up and now handed it to her.

"Thank you for dinner and for loaning me your radio," said

Irene. She assumed a kiss was coming from the Southerner, the Harvard man, the snappy dresser. Instead, he put out his right hand and smiled, as if he had intercepted that thought in her head.

"Right," she said, clasping his hand with hers, "no funny business. You're a working man." It was a firm handshake both ways from people who were used to shaking hands.

"So are you, from what I hear," said Aaron.

"You're damn right I am," said Irene. "Goodnight, Mr. Diamond."

He hadn't yet released her hand, and he gazed down at her with a quizzical look. "This will probably be the oddest thing anyone asks you today," he said in that Tennessee drawl, "but will you marry me?"

The next thing she knew, she sat in the back of a cab heading for the West Side and wondering what the hell had just happened.

CHAPTER 21

True to their word, the boys gave their usual effort to *Casablanca* during the train trip from Los Angeles to Chicago and then on to Washington, D.C., just as if they were occupying their office suite at the studio, which meant for a solid few hours per day, they talked script. The other hours they read whatever big-city paper they could find in station stops. They were avoiding the front-page war stories because even with positive propaganda, the Allies were still getting their asses kicked. That left the sports pages, which was where they read about the casting of Gary Cooper as Lou Gehrig in *Pride of the Yankees*, which, the article announced, would be directed by Sam Wood for the Goldwyn Studios.

"What year was it you caught the Gehrig foul ball? One-handed!" said Phil. "And everybody chanted, 'Sign him up!'"

"Twenty-eight," said Julie at once. "They didn't sign me up though. The bastards." Julie thought a moment. "We could write that script, you know. The Gehrig script. We should call Goldwyn."

"We don't want to be anywhere near this picture," said Phil, staring at the article. "Gehrig bats left and throws left, and Cooper does neither. What if he throws like a sissy? I bet he does."

Julie stopped and thought about it. "Oh God. I bet he does too! There's no unseeing that once you see it. I'd lose all respect."

Phil closed and folded the newspaper and reached forward to

set it down, only to have Julie grab at it. Phil pulled it back.

"No! Maybe instead of violating our contract to go work for another studio, we should think about working on Renie's baby." Phil tossed a copy of the play and the bundle of Kline and Mac's notes instead of the newspaper in Julie's lap. "The inciting action of Ugarte's arrest has to involve murder."

"Why murder?" asked Julius.

"We want the audience to sympathize with Ugarte, right? So he murders some Nazis—"

"—which is how he got the letters of transit," Julie said sagely. "And that gives Strasser a very good reason to be in Casablanca and in the café for the arrest."

"Yep," said Phil. "Since Ugarte has already committed murder, he's more dangerous at the capture."

Julie snapped his fingers. "It becomes an action scene. And this thing needs action scenes." He pulled out his notepad and wrote furiously for a long time.

As he did, Phil picked up the play and turned some pages. When Julie stopped to sharpen his pencil on the little sharpener he pulled out of his pocket, Phil said, "You know who I'm not looking forward to writing?"

"Yeah, the part that's gonna kill this picture," said Julie, blowing shavings off his sharpened pencil onto the floor. Julie saw Phil looking at him to see if they were talking about the same thing. "Lois, the dame with no class and nothing going for her. Lois, the stock character from every bad play we ever saw."

"She's the worst of American womanhood," Phil grouched. "Anything we write for her is going to be crap and sound awful. It doesn't matter who plays her, even Sheridan. Lois is fickle. Unreliable. I hate her."

The brothers fell to silence. Julius stopped writing. Each sat back and watched the states go by. They recognized Pennsylvania by the mountain passes and tunnels, and then they were in the flatlands of Maryland, the grass pale green, the trees barren, and then the train glided into D.C. suburbs and finally, Union Station.

With the train stopped, they policed their sleeper car and stuffed odds and ends into a suitcase and briefcase apiece, already seeing themselves at the War Department consulting with officers before strategic maps and flirting with secretaries who brought them coffee. Phil strained to look out the window to see what military men might greet them as they stepped off the train.

"I wonder who's here to meet us," said Julie. "I'll bet you it's a major or a colonel at least."

"We're lucky if we get a captain," said Phil as they put on and buttoned their overcoats. "At least Frank will be here."

"But just imagine," said Julie, "sitting in meetings with General Marshall or the Secretary of War. Holy shit!"

"Yeah, General Marshall instead of Jack Warner," said Phil.

The boys carried their bags out of Union Station just after noon on Saturday, February 28. The sun shone warmer than Phil expected, temperatures in the forties. Dead ahead against blue skies rose the Capitol rotunda a good way down Delaware Avenue.

"We're really here," said Phil.

Julie looked all about him. Right, left, and back at Union Station. "Where's Frank?" he said, searching some more. "That's kind of strange. No Frank. No Army guys. No nobody."

"Face it," said Phil, "we're schmuck writers and have to make it alone in a cruel world."

Julie nodded in the direction of the Capitol, and the Epsteins set off down tree-lined Delaware Avenue, bags in hand. In the middle of a winter's weekend, there weren't many people around. A few walked dogs. A pair of lovers strolled hand in hand. Suddenly, Julius said, "I don't like the name Rinaldo. Our French guy's a smooth character; he needs a smooth name, and Rinaldo ain't it."

Phil noticed a robin hopping across the lawn nearby; Julie had stopped to get a better grip on his bags. "Hey look, a robin," Phil called back to Julie. "What's today, the 28th?" He looked back over his shoulder to say, "We'll be here for spring!"

He was stepping into the intersection with C Street at a go signal when he said it. Just then a blue blur zoomed up the wide, empty street from the west. Julie saw the gleam of a chrome grill and could barely say, "Look out!" He reached forward and grabbed his brother by the collar and gave a yank.

The blue four-door sedan sped past, and the brothers reeled backward in unison, catching their heels on the cement curb and falling onto their butts with twin sprawling thuds. Luggage scattered. Above them, their field of vision revealed a tangle of bare elm trees against a gray winter sky.

"Holy shit," Phil murmured, "they drive worse here than they do at home."

"Yeah, welcome to Washington," said Julie.

The brothers sat on the pavement, neither moving, and with nobody taking notice. A cop would have been helpful, but none appeared. Slowly they climbed to their feet and brushed themselves off. Phil could feel his heart thudding heavily in his chest.

"I bet that was a German spy," said Julie.

Phil removed his cap with one gloved hand and ran the other over his bald head. Both of his hands shook. "What the hell kind of car was that? I didn't hear it coming."

"Foreign," said Julie. "Pretty sure a Renault. Barney's got one at the studio. I think he calls it a Celtaboule. Something like that."

"Well, shit!" said Phil profoundly as he picked up his suitcase and briefcase. He was rattled; his brother was rattled. D.C. had lost its romance in the first fifteen minutes, and here they were, almost victims of murder. "What were we talking about?" Phil asked.

Julie searched his memory. "Oh, Rinaldo—we were saying we need a name that's smooth like the character."

Standing at the intersection, Phil looked east on C Street, down a long corridor that mixed stands of barren trees with nondescript gray buildings. In the sky, a twin-engine passenger plane, a DC-3, glided downward, right to left, and settled below the horizon. In a minute, another followed on the same trajectory. Phil's pulse had begun to settle down, and he took comfort in the possibility he might not die of a heart attack.

"Renault," said Julie to break the silence.

"Huh?" said Phil. Then it hit him. "Oh my God. Like the car that almost killed me."

"Ray-knowww," said Julie again, drawing it out. "And we'll keep it Louis, like the French kings."

They had both regrouped, picked up their bags, checked left, right, and left, and crossed C Street still heading toward the Capitol. "Louis Renault," Phil said to give the name a test drive. "So now it's got to be Jean Gabin."

"I believe he's in France," said Julie. "No, I think he came over."

"Doesn't matter, I think the odds are against it. How about Claude Rains?" Julie tossed the name off as if it were already a foregone conclusion.

"Claude Rains isn't French," Phil snapped.

"Noooo," said Julie, "but he's Claude Rains and we've written for him, and we've never written for Jean Gabin. Can't you see

Claude Rains as Rick's alter ego? Claude Rains is who burned-out Humphrey Bogart wishes he could be: self-assured, comfortable-in-his-own-skin Claude Rains."

Phil stopped walking and stared off for a moment. "Huh," was all he said in response, a very pregnant "huh" that pronounced the idea to be the most natural solution in the world. They had just cast Claude Rains in *Casablanca*. Not that they had the power to really cast anything, but Rains seemed to fit and so they would write the character for Claude.

In another moment they stood at the corner of Delaware and Constitution. Cresting a ridge across the street, as traffic motored by, lay the massive Capitol complex, of which they could see only a portion. It wasn't easy to impress Phil and Julie Epstein; now, despite the incident a block ago, they were impressed. They wanted to continue on and climb the Capitol steps, but a military checkpoint stood between the brothers and their destination, with Army guards in helmets and holding rifles walking the perimeter, which kept the boys rooted to the spot. But plenty of time to sightsee lay head, so they set to the task of hailing a cab. Once inside the vehicle, its heater blasting, Phil pulled out a slip of paper and asked the portly driver to take them to the Lee Sheraton Hotel at 15th and L Street Northwest.

In the back seat of the cab, they took in the sights heading west along Constitution Avenue. On the left, the National Gallery of Art; on the right, the National Archives. Another block and there was the Smithsonian on the left and beyond it, the Washington Monument. Scattered along the sidewalks, families of sightseers mixed in with military personnel; most of those in uniform wore the olive drab of the Army, and the men on duty sported helmets and carried rifles like the ones back at the Capitol. On a rooftop the boys spied an anti-aircraft gun and its crew, and it hit them: they had entered the nerve center of an America at war.

The car turned right from Constitution Avenue onto 15th Street and the driver instructed the boys to look to the left where lay a sprawling park. "There's the White House," he said and sure enough, they could clearly see the grand structure through the tangle of denuded trees. Phil revered FDR, as did most of Hollywood.

"Wonder if he's in there," Julie murmured.

In four short blocks the cab pulled up before an eight-story brick structure sitting on the right side of the street. A neon sign attached to the corner of the building read Lee Sheraton. They paid the driver, entered the hotel, and checked in. The clerk at the desk said, "We have some messages for you gentlemen," and handed Julius three telegrams.

Julie opened the first and read the contents aloud to his brother: "Have been talking to Robinson, stop. He says Lois should be European woman, stop. Agree this is the way to go so proceed accordingly, stop. Want to see results soon. Wallis."

"That son of a bitch!" snapped Phil under his breath.

"Who, Hal?"

"No, Casey Robinson. Haven't you been listening to the jungle drums? Robinson is balling that Russian woman—what's her name? Tamara something. He's angling to get her cast in *Casablanca*!" Phil pronounced the name Tamara as if it were the day after today. Tamara. Julius did remember hearing something about their fellow screenwriter Robinson being head over heels for some Russian gal, which didn't seem to thrill Casey Robinson's wife. But such was Hollywood.

"Toumanova." Julius pulled that name out of some dark corner of his mind, so yes, he had indeed been listening to the jungle drums after all. He remembered the odd pronunciation, Two-MON-oh-va.

"Yeah, that one," said Phil.

In the elevator going up to eight, the young, perilously thin operator in a bellman's cap and uniform asked the boys if this was their first trip to the nation's capital and tried to tell them that the cherry blossoms would soon be out.

"Do you realize what a break this is?" said Julie to Phil, ignoring the color commentary.

"Actually, yeah, I do," said Phil. "We're not stuck with Lois the tramp. This girl could be French, or Dutch, or Norwegian. British even. It's no longer an American and an American. It's American Rick and his American sensibilities and a European girl with those sensibilities. It changes everything."

"Everything," echoed Julius, and when the elevator stopped and the doors opened, they rushed to find their rooms, 801 and 803, adjoining, dumped their bags, opened the adjoining door, and Julie said, as if the dawn had just broken, "Of course they don't sleep together that first night at Rick's."

"No, because she's got class!" said Phil. "Hallelujah!"

Julius thought a moment. "She's got class. She's actually got class, which is why she needs to see him that first night when she comes back to the club after it's closed. She feels she has to face the guns and explain why she left him in Paris."

"But he's drunk," said Phil. "He's blind drunk because he can't deal with seeing her again."

"And he's not buying a word she says," Julius murmured as he pulled his pad from the briefcase, scrounged for a pencil, and started scribbling.

Phil paced the room from the window to the door, through

the door into the other room, and back again, deep in thought. After a long moment he said, "So she walks into the club that first evening with Laszlo, right after Ugarte's arrest. The fact that Rick sees her as soon as the commotion is over doubly blindsides the guy. Plot point one: Rick comes face-to-face with his lost love. He plays it cool, but it eats him up inside to see her."

"Yes, so after the club closes, he's sitting there by himself, drinking," said Julie. "We can take that straight out of the play. Sam says, 'Let's go fishing,' and all that. We need some business that cues the flashback and sets up their backstory. We're seeing it through Rick's eyes: happy days in Paris before the Germans march in."

Julie wrote it all down as Phil continued to pace. The rooms were surprisingly warm for the end of February; warm and stuffy—so stuffy Phil walked over and cracked a window. The distant hum of traffic below grew louder, but the sounds of humanity lent a hint of reassurance.

Phil was quiet a long time as he paced. He stopped suddenly and snapped his fingers, then pointed at his brother. "This is the only time Rick pities himself in the whole damn picture!" he exclaimed.

Julie nodded and wrote. "When he's drunk. I agree a hundred percent. The self-pity was killing this story, so we slam it all into this one sequence."

"Right. He's drunk and he's sad and he wallows in it. But then he gets organized."

"And she understands why he's bitter," said Julie, "and she does face the guns. And he's nasty. Boy, is he nasty. Drunk-nasty."

"Yeah, he asks her if she left him for Laszlo, or were there a lot of Laszlos in between. Maybe he doesn't really believe she's a tramp, but he wants to hurt her any way he can."

Phil paced into the other room and called, "She's got dignity, though. She stands there as the guns blaze away. She knows he has to get it out of his system. She owes him that."

"Question," said Julius in a way his brother understood—this was important.

Phil appeared in the frame of the adjoining door and waited. "Who does this Greta the European girl really love? Does she love Rick, or does she love Victor?"

"It has to be Rick," said Phil without hesitation.

"It has to be Victor," said Julie, "because she can't stay in Casablanca with Rick. The censors won't allow it. So she loves Victor."

Phil considered the argument. "Then you've got no conflict and no story. Certainly no love story."

Julie reviewed his notes. It had taken them a mere fifteen minutes to crack a code that had stumped Kline and MacKenzie and get into Act 2.

"Shit! This thing's practically written!"

"Except there's no love story," said Phil, "and it's supposed to be a love story."

Julie shrugged. "But now she's Greta the European and that's huge. Thank you, Casey Robinson and your wandering dick!"

There was a knock at the door. Three gentle knuckle raps against wood.

The boys reacted as if the cops had found their crap game. But no, thought Phil, it must be Capra.

"Who is it?" called Julie.

"House detective," came a voice.

Each looked at the other. Of course, they had nothing to hide, but Phil nodded toward the notes on his brother's lap. "Stash that!"

Julius shoved the notepad in his suitcase and slammed the lid as Phil went to the door and opened it.

Far from a house detective, the man standing there smiling when Phil opened the door was Len Spigelgass, one of the Warner Bros. writers. They hadn't seen him since that day he had poked the studio bear, Errol Flynn, about having a ghostwriter.

"Hello, boys," said Spigelgass as he strode in, hands in pockets. Len had a lot in common with the Epsteins; he was their age and hailed from Brooklyn, and his typewriter-for-hire had landed him at Universal writing a series of social comedies, which caught Renie's attention and led to a couple of scripts in Burbank—including Bogart's *All Through the Night*.

"Lenny!" said Julius. "What the hell are you doing here?" Spigelgass had about the friendliest face and most genuine smile in Hollywood.

"Hello to you too," he said as he wandered into the room.

"What are you working on?" asked Phil. Every writer always asked every other writer that question, half out of curiosity and half to compare dick sizes.

"Oh, I'm back on some crap at Universal," sighed Len, "and some crap at RKO. How about you guys?"

"Hal gave us *Casablanca*," said Julie.

Spigelgass spun on his heel. "No shit! The Bogart–Sheridan thing that got Mac and Kline fired?"

"That's the one," said Phil.

"Luck-ee," said Len, who ran his fingertip over the veneer of a chest of drawers against the wall, checking for dust. "I just wanted to see that you boys got settled in okay here at Fort Capra."

"Tell us what's going on," said Phil. "How long have you been here?"

"Long enough to see it's a mess," said Len. "The Signal Corps has already palmed Capra off to Special Services because nobody wants to deal with some Hollywood screwball. This is wartime and they think Frank's a phony. The top man, General Marshall, he likes Frank, no question about it. But between Marshall and Capra is a whole lotta brass, including some real assholes, which means we're pretty much sitting around twiddling our thumbs in a couple of closets over at the Library of Congress."

"Library of Congress?" said Phil, throwing up his hands. "We're not at the War Department?"

Lenny looked at Phil and burst into laughter.

Julius said, "How can we win the war from a closet in the Library of Congress?"

"Precisely," said Spigelgass. "So far, the most important military term I've learned is *snafu*."

After a moment, Phil said, "Which means what?"

"Situation Normal, All Fucked Up," said Len, "which I would say describes the Capra operation so far, from what I can see. Hell, I'm surprised they put us up in a hotel because there doesn't seem to be a budget for what we're doing."

"Lovely," said Julius.

"Then what are we doing?" asked Phil.

"Well, the group of us writers—we could all fit in a cab at first, and then a few more showed up, and now you guys—we sit in Army orientation courses on what it's like to be in the Army. It's like college all over again. Freshman year college where we sit around learning what recruits learn. And then we ride to the Library of Congress and sit at our desks and write scripts about it. You'll get to attend your first orientation class on Monday, I suspect."

"But there's got to be a plan, right?" said Phil. "Now that we're all here, we'll start in on scripts for 'Why We Fight.'"

Len rubbed a stubbly beard; it was obvious he had given his razor the day off. "Yeah, well, it's possible these are the scripts for 'Why We Fight.' I'm not really sure. But from what I can see, it's going to take a long time to get this operation off the ground. A very long time."

Phil felt himself deflating; he imagined Julie was experiencing the same sensation. "We don't have a very long time, Lenny," said Phil. "We've got a script to write for Renie and Hal, and they're not kidding around about it."

It was clear to Phil that Len Spigelgass had decided to laugh about the situation here in Washington because the alternative was to cry. He kept a sunny and ironic smile on his face as he sauntered over to the door. He turned back. "All I can say is, welcome to the war, boys," and he departed, pulling the door closed behind him with a gentle click.

CHAPTER 22

Paul Henreid sat in the executive offices of Universum Film-Aktien Gesellschaft, shortened to an easier UFA, which reigned as the most prestigious film studio in Germany, the place where directors Ernst Lubitsch and G.W. Pabst had earned their reputations, the place where hit pictures like *Metropolis* and *The Blue Angel* were made.

Paul Henreid was, as they say in America, cooling his heels, waiting hat in hand for his host to appear with contracts to sign. The twenty-six-year-old had traveled 425 miles from Vienna to the UFA Berlin studios just to sign his name—sign a contract with people whom he had never met. The office shone with elegance in the form of polished deco moldings and deco furniture of the latest design. On the desk in front of him, a vast model of executive power in cherry wood, sat stacks of scripts in one corner and on the other corner, an ornate gold-leaf base holding a fifteen-inch-tall flagpole with a red flag of the German Reich, a swastika at its center. The nameplate on the desk read Herr Heinz von Daniker, Production Executive.

Staring at the swastika turned Henreid's stomach, tied it into a knot, and gave him the urge to flee. He thought of his father, who had been knighted by Emperor Franz Josef I, but was a Jew who converted to Catholicism early in the twentieth century because of anti-Semitism in Europe. Until recently, Paul had been able to ignore the growing fascist-nationalist movement in Austria—until, that is, he met his girlfriend, Lisl, who had opened his eyes to the looming threats to his country and beyond.

Sitting in von Daniker's office, he stared at the Nazi flag on the desk, and suddenly the office door flew open and Herr von Daniker rushed in; behind him, a secretary in her middle years hurried on high heels to keep pace.

"Ah, Baron Henreid," said von Daniker, a stocky man of fifty-five who was graying at the temples and balding on top. He wore an expensive suit, and his secretary was blonde-haired, blue-eyed, and immaculate in every way. In fact, she was stunning. That thirty seconds, the grand entrance, the taking stock of his hosts, rattled Paul's brain.

"I'm sorry," Paul murmured.

Von Daniker had moved behind his desk. "I don't understand. You say you are sorry?"

"Yes. My father is Baron Henreid and he is in banking. I am but a mere actor and not a baron. I am sorry if you were misinformed."

"There is nothing mere about you, Paul," said von Daniker as he sat behind that grand desk and motioned for Paul to sit on a deco couch against the adjacent wall. "I saw you in Reinhardt's *Faust*—this tall, dashing Austrian with a regal bearing."

"Thank you for your kind assessment," said Paul, who really couldn't argue with a word of it.

The head of production opened a humidor and took out a five-inch cigar. He offered one to Paul; the guest politely demurred, so von Daniker sliced off the end of the cigar and lit it. He leaned back and took a dreamy puff.

"Cuban," he said. "I spend a fortune in shipping."

"I can only imagine," said Paul.

Von Daniker took another puff on the cigar, drawing in his cheeks. On exhale he said, "It must have been, oh, seven minutes watching you on the stage in *Faust*, eight minutes perhaps, before I knew that UFA must get you under contract." His secretary sat at a portable writing desk opposite the couch. "Do you remember that night, Annette?"

"I do recall it," said Annette in a cultured alto voice. "I had never seen you so taken with a young actor."

"And so we began tracking your progress on the stage in Vienna and made our overture. To be frank, sir, I had no confidence you would be interested. So many young actors have their, shall we say, ideals and look down their noses at work in the films."

Henreid had believed all his life in laying cards on the table. Honest, blunt, a craftsman in all things, this was what Paul offered the world. He had no trouble saying, "I too have my trepidations, sir. The stage is, to me, a pure form of art. An actor lays his soul bare on the stage, which is, I believe, what you reacted to in *Faust*."

"Why then did you agree to our terms?" asked von Daniker.

"Because I am also a practical man, with a fiancée named Lisl who would appreciate it if I could show a steady income."

"Bravo, Fräulein Lisl!" said von Daniker with a great laugh. He snapped his fingers once, and Annette stood, walked across the room, and handed Paul a set of papers with one hand and held out a fountain pen with the other. Paul set aside his hat and took papers and pen in hand.

"You initial each page here," Annette instructed, pointing to the spot with a varnished red nail, "and sign here on page three and here on page five."

Paul initialed where instructed and signed where instructed. She took the contract away, and Paul was left with another two-page document. The heading across the top of the page in heavy Gothic type read, National Socialist Actors' Guild of Germany. He scanned page one and then the remaining paragraph on page two above the blank space where he must sign.

"What's this?" he asked, although he knew well enough what it was.

"A mere formality," von Daniker shrugged, "that you will abide by the rules for performers working inside the Reich."

"I'm afraid it looks quite a bit more serious than that," said Paul, reading more closely. "I believe this document would in effect make me a Nazi." He raised his gaze to meet that of his host. Paul found it an uncomfortable moment. Von Daniker was still looking at him pleasantly, patiently; he did, however, carefully set his cigar on the edge of the ashtray at his left. Paul had been warned by his friend Georg not to "sell out" to the Germans, and Paul had dismissed the idea as so much dramatics. And now here he sat, uncomfortably. "I have nothing to do with politics," he told the production executive. "I am an actor."

"I agree; you are an actor and you will act. Politics need have nothing to do with it. But you must sign your name to this separate agreement." Paul sat unmoving. "If you do not sign, there will be no contract with the studio."

Paul felt a wave of relief. No, he would not sell out, and no, he would not lower himself to take work in films—not at this price. He had been looking for guidance from above, and this was clearly it. He arose and sniffed, "You could have told me this in Vienna and saved me a trip."

Von Daniker was clearly stunned. "I implore you, Herr Henreid: Don't do anything in haste. Talk this matter over with your fiancée and see how she feels about it. There is a great deal at stake!"

Paul smiled at the thought of telling Lisl that he almost became a Nazi. "Please rest assured she will feel exactly as I do," he snapped.

In a theatrical move that would have drawn an approving nod from Reinhardt, Paul grabbed his fedora, spun on his heel, and departed the studio without once looking back. Within days, Joseph Goebbels had added the name Paul Henreid to the growing roster of actors blacklisted by the Nazi Party.

From his vantage point in London four years later, the Austrian actor could only look back in awe at the series of events that had spirited him with his Lisl, whom he soon married, to Great Britain for a crash course in the English language. He picked up work in the British film *Goodbye, Mr. Chips* and then *Night Train to Munich* in which he played, ironically, a Nazi agent.

At the rooms he shared with Lisl in London, the phone rang one evening and Paul answered it.

"Mr. Henreid, my name is Lew Wasserman," said a distant voice on the line, a deep, commanding voice. A distinctly American voice with its severely rounded R's. "I'm representing MCA, a talent agency, and I'm calling from Hollywood, USA."

The name sounded Jewish, which put Paul at ease, and the American had put such emphasis on his location! "Yes, sir. How may I help you?"

"Well, we've seen your recent pictures—we were very impressed by *Night Train to Munich*," said Wasserman. "I wondered if you are represented by one of the Hollywood talent agencies."

"I am not. No," said Paul. "Should I be?"

The line hissed quietly for a moment. "Frankly," said the agent from more than 5,000 miles away, "there is a dearth of continental leading men over here. If you were to sign with MCA, I believe we could get you a lot of work in pictures."

Henreid knew from speaking with cast members on the film productions in which he had appeared that security for actors came in the form of long-term contracts with studios. He did not seek such a thing, but perhaps he needed such a thing. "Are you speaking of a studio contract, Mr. . . . Mr. . . ."

"Wasserman. Lew Wasserman. Yes, I am. We believe that, given your talent, we could find takers for a long-term contract."

"In America," said Paul, seeking to understand and thinking aloud. "In Hollywood?"

"Yessir," said the stock voice on the other end of the line—the stock American—the stock Jewish American. "That is exactly what I'm saying." God how he rounded his R's! Just like in a parody of Americans!

Paul and Lisl had grown accustomed to their vagabond life; uprooting meant nothing once they had left their beloved Austria. But now he heard the siren's call of stability, of safety. Imagine, to take Lisl to a place free of Nazis and their threat, if only for a time. He heard his voice saying, "All right, if you are willing to wire me 500 pounds, my wife and I will come to Hollywood. I will repay you from my first paycheck—if there is a paycheck."

"Fine, just fine," said Wasserman without hesitation. "More than fine. You have a deal."

Eight days later, after a blur of ship and plane travel, Paul walked into the Vine Street Brown Derby restaurant, a block south of Hollywood Boulevard. Inside the door stood a tall man in a suit and bow tie. His face was movie-star handsome, and he wore his abundant black hair combed back. His brown eyes were large and expressive.

"Hello, Paul. Lew Wasserman," said the young man, extending his hand. "I'm happy to meet you in person."

"My God, you are so young!" exclaimed the Austrian.

Wasserman laughed easily and directed Henreid to a red leather booth toward the back of the quiet dining room. Paul had loved watching Hollywood pictures in Europe. The walk through the establishment revealed Joan Bennett sitting in one booth and Robert Taylor and Barbara Stanwyck in another.

Once Henreid and Wasserman were seated, Paul said, "Now that I am here, what do you have to tell me?"

"You are very direct, sir!" exclaimed Wasserman.

"I once sat in a UFA office after traveling for two days on a train," said Paul. "I was about to sign a contract, only to be surprised to learn they required me to join the Nazi Party. Such an experience tends to make one direct. And wary of surprises from Greeks bearing gifts."

Wasserman shrank visibly in his side of the booth, perhaps at the thought that Henreid had matched wits with real Nazis. Paul found it charming—the American was mostly bluster, which Paul assumed was correct in a Hollywood agent.

"Here is what I think, Mr. Wasserman," said Paul. "I think that I am popular now, but I realize how many pictures are released here and how quickly my name and face will fade from memory."

"That's very practical," said the agent with a nod. "So, listen, I've gotten solid interest from RKO, a studio down the street from here. They're the people who produced the Astaire–Rogers musicals, so they have quite a bit of clout. In fact, they are thinking of using you in Ginger's next picture. What I need from you are the requirements you are seeking from the studio."

In his mind, Paul stepped back for a moment. He didn't seek to be here at all. He wanted Broadway and the legitimate theater, not Hollywood and the illegitimate theater. He had stopped in New York on his passage from Europe and dined with the great Helen Hayes. She had wanted him for a play, she confided, but alas, nothing was firmed up, and the actor knew that he had to eat. His wife had to eat. And now, here he was, in a restaurant named after a hat, in the land of make-believe—a land Paul Henreid didn't believe in at all!

He forced his mind back to the here and now. After dealing with Herr von Daniker at UFA, dealing with a Jew in Hollywood was easy work. "What terms do I seek?" said Paul. "It's simple, really. I would like to make a picture a year from May through August, which will leave me the remainder of the year to work on the stage. My first love is the stage."

Wasserman nodded earnestly, like an American. "What else?"

"Naturally, I will be the male lead in any picture I make here. And I will, how do you say, 'get the girl.'"

"Naturally," said Wasserman with great earnestness. "What about salary?"

Henreid took the measure of the man sitting across the table. He was an exceptional specimen: calm, positive, and clearly knew his business. Paul smiled and said, "You seem like a confident fellow; surprise me."

Forty-eight hours later, Paul signed with RKO Pictures at $75,000 per picture, and from a home base at the Beverly Hills Hotel, the Henreids explored the area known as Hollywood, from its nightclubs to its boulevards, from its palm trees to its jutting mountains. But wherever they went in this unbelievable Shangri-la, both husband and wife carried memories of UFA and Hitler's annexation of Austria in the Anschluss of 1938 and deportation of Jews into concentration camps. Despite the limitations of film work, every day he and Lisl felt fortunate to be so far away from the horror.

The project with Ginger Rogers fell through, but RKO put Paul to work on a picture called *Joan of Paris* with French sex goddess Michèle Morgan, also in her first American picture. The chemistry of Morgan and Henreid, two young Continentals, shimmered on-screen. He played the French pilot of a downed Allied air crew hiding out in Paris; Michèle was a barmaid working for the French Underground who makes the ultimate sacrifice to save the heroes. Upon release in January 1942, the inside-Hollywood newspaper *Variety* called the picture "a mild meller," but praised the lead players. "Miss Morgan and Henreid are definite assets to the Hollywood feature player group," raved *Variety*, "and both provide sincere and sensitive performances that will catch attention from paying customers and assist in buildups."

Catch attention they did; both Henreid and Morgan snagged the eye of Hal Wallis at Warner Bros. who picked up his phone soon after a private screening of *Joan of Paris* at the studio and got Lew Wasserman on the phone. Wallis had an idea that just couldn't wait.

CHAPTER 23

It had taken the remainder of the week for Irene to get over the shock of a marriage proposal from a man she had known for, she determined, five hours and one minute. She thought back to the way it had ended with director Ernst Lubitsch nine years earlier—Ernst had come by his nickname of the "horny Hun" honestly but was crazy-possessive. She thought about the way it had ended with beautiful Rouben Mamoulian, another director—she cheated on him after he had cheated on her. Then there were the men before and after, and the wrong turn down Sappho Street at Eva Le Gallienne's Dramatic School, and when adding it all up, she couldn't escape the fact she had rotten luck in relationships and always managed to attract the wrong ones. And she hadn't even attracted Aaron Diamond; they had met by chance and split a cab, split dinner, and split a map. She thought it a hundred times over this week: *He seemed so sane up to the very moment he asked me to marry him.* At which point she had said, "Oh my God, you're a lunatic!" and had fled his apartment.

By Friday morning, her head was on straight enough to call the Janowitz home to check on Gladys and her family. Gladys's mother, Mert, said that Jack's body had been recovered and would be coming home for burial. Irene's heart broke for these people, and after she set the phone down, she stared at it and wondered how many families were already going through this exercise and how much grief lay ahead for innocent people across the nation. All the boys killed at Pearl Harbor, and in the Philippines, and lost in the Atlantic as Jack had been.

She was still staring at the phone when it rang and gave her a start. On the second ring, she picked up the receiver. "Miss Lee."

"Howdy, neighbor," said a familiar voice. "Have you heard? Lois is no longer an American lowlife."

She sank back in her chair and felt herself smile. "That's the word on the street," she said to either Phil or Julie—she couldn't be sure which. "How's it going down there? Have you saved the world yet?"

"What is it, three hours by train? Come see for yourself."

Ah, Julius. It was more the way he said it than what he said.

"No time. But I'll see you when we're both back on the coast—if Capra ever lets you leave. How's the assignment going?"

"Well, it's going," said Julie, "but we haven't showed him anything we've written. And he hasn't asked to see. In fact, he hasn't given us any guidance at all. We're just doing what we want so far, writing pictures we'd like to watch. You know, war stuff—you're just a girl; you wouldn't understand."

Julie liked the game of poke-the-boss, but she didn't have the energy to play. Not today. "Well, I am little," said Irene, "but fierce."

There was a pause. "What's wrong, boss? You don't sound like yourself."

She shook her head to clear it and straightened in her chair. "Nah, I'm fine. Tell me about our script. How's it coming? Have you been talking to Hal?"

"It's going great!" said Julius. "Making Lois European broke the logjam and boom! We took Kline and Mac's notes and went to work here at the hotel. We tightened the opening in the club and now it pops. We figure Ugarte had to kill some Nazis to get the letters of transit, and that led us to the introduction of Strasser. Oh, and we changed Rinaldo's name to Renault."

"Wow!" said Irene, suddenly energized. She loved everything he blurted out and wished she had been taking notes.

"Yeah," said Julie, "we'll be sending some stuff to Hal in a couple days."

"That's my boys," she said, remembering why she loved these two miscreants.

"Phil sends hugs and kisses," said Julie.

"Hug and kiss him back," said Irene.

"Yuk," said Julie, who added, "See ya, boss," and waited for her to say bye before he hung up.

She set down the receiver and swiveled her chair to reach for one of the three scripts that represented the Friday slush pile, finally feeling as if the four cups of coffee from the last hour had begun to kick in. When the phone rang again, she knew it would be one of the Epsteins because they always forgot at least one thing they wanted to tell her when either of them called. It never failed and hadn't again.

She picked up the receiver and sighed, "What did you forget this time?"

The line was silent a moment; then the caller, a man, cleared his throat. "Uh, I'm looking for Miss Lee? Miss Irene Lee?"

Oh my God, she thought. The southern drawl, the voice like warm honey. It was him. The spark plugs in her brain fired all at once, and the result was an electric arc of impulses. Lubitsch, Mamoulian, Hal, Rand McNally, Sardi's, floor radio, crazed killer. She reached for her throat, to the cool, smooth strand of pearls she always touched for comfort in tense situations. Should she talk to him? Should she explain? Apologize? Call the cops? The void of silence was as wide as the Hudson River.

She heard herself say, "Hello, this is me."

"Hello, you," said Aaron Diamond. "I thought I should just tighten my belt like a big boy and give you a call and say thank you for a very nice evening listening to our president." Brief pause. "And so, that's what I'm doing."

What could she say to that? She was trying to decide when he added, "Oh, and I want to say in my own defense that I do not believe myself to be a lunatic."

"From what I know, lunatics never think they're lunatics," said Irene. "And, believe me, I read a lot." *Oh shit,* she thought, *I'm playing along. I'm flirting with this man again! Just stop it! Stop it right now!*

"Well, what I thought was," said Aaron, "I thought that, hey, it's Friday, and maybe Miss Lee would like to take in a movie, and I could clamp down on all my crazy impulses. Heck, I could even leave my murder weapons at home. There's a new war picture playing at the Rivoli over here in Brooklyn. It's not a Warner Bros. picture, but it's supposed to be pretty good, and so . . ." He paused, and she heard him let out a sudden breath. "Actually, what I need to tell you is . . . I'm sorry I ruined a nice evening."

By now she had wound the receiver cord tightly around her index finger and cut off the flow of blood. She realized what she had done and loosened it again and shook her hand and reached for a cigarette and lit it. She knew she couldn't give him the history of her junkyard of a love life as a way to explain the explosive reaction to his proposal, which might be considered, come to think of it, the reaction of a lunatic. Hmmm.

He was very gentlemanly at this awkward moment, with his apology hanging in the air. He didn't prod; he merely waited.

"I suppose it's possible we're both crazy, or neither of us is crazy," said Irene. "Time will tell. And maybe I'll go to a movie with you if, and only if, you promise not to ask me to marry you. Or anything of the kind." He remained quiet. "Just a movie," she added. "With no funny business."

He waited a little longer, as if to confirm that her response had reached its conclusion. "All right," he said in that wonderful drawl, "that'll be just grand. Can we say tomorrow evening?"

"That would be fine," said Irene. Something about his voice had a hypnotic effect, and she wondered if Rasputin also spoke in a caramel southern drawl.

"I'll pick you up at, say, six, and we can eat over here at Gage & Tollner and then see that picture *Joan of Paris*. With no funny business of any kind."

It was time to put up, shut up, or hang up. She took a drag of her cigarette and on exhale said, "Mr. Diamond, thank you for calling. I will see you in front of my building at six o'clock tomorrow," and she gave him her address on Central Park West.

"That will be fine. Thank you, Miss Lee. See you then."

They said goodbye and she hung up the phone and stared at it once more, mulling over three very different phone calls in the past hour. Only now did she realize how guilty she had felt running out on him the other night. Yes, that was it—she felt guilty, and he had, in his way, come to the rescue to alleviate that guilt. And in the next instant she chastised herself. Don't you do that, Irene. Don't you dare do that. He's no white knight, and you can't let your guard down for a minute. And that led to one more urgent thought: *Ohmygod, what am I going to wear?*

CHAPTER 24

By nine o'clock Wednesday night, March 10, the boys had written to the point where Victor and European-Lois walk into Rick's. They were exhausted. Julius looked solemnly at Phil and said, "We have got to agree that we'll never tell anybody about all the time we're putting into this piece of shit."

"Jack Warner must never know," said Phil. "No one can know."

"That's right," said Julie, "we have a reputation to uphold."

"Goldbrickers," agreed Phil, nodding.

The next morning, as Phil was tying his necktie in the adjoining room before heading over to the Library of Congress, Julie scribbled a note to Hal on Hotel Lee Sheraton stationery. Phil slipped on his tweed sport jacket and walked into the adjoining room to see Julie holding the note out for his brother's inspection.

Phil took it and read aloud, "Dear Hal, Here's the first batch. Will you please give them to our secretary, Alice Danziger, to type. She's the only one who can make out the handwriting. Will try to get back as soon as possible, but in any event will keep right on with the pages. While we handle the foreign situation here, you try to get a foreign girl for the part. Make sure she has big tits." Phil stopped reading and looked at his brother. "Nice touch." And then he read, "Love and kisses, Julie and Phil."

"Okay?" said Julie.

"Okay," said Phil.

In the lobby they handed off their package with the handwritten script pages and the note to a waiting Warner Bros. man from the regional office who would see it safely onto a DC-3 heading west. Then the pair took a cab down Massachusetts Avenue to 2nd Street and around the Capitol to the Library of Congress, where they headed into a third week as civilian writers for Army Special Services. Here in Washington they played it straight, reporting at nine and working a full day in the vast and magnificent Thomas Jefferson Building, looking at books and reading back issues of the *Post*, the *Times*, and the *Tribune* to research various topics in the series. They had already developed outlines for pictures about the fall of France, the Battle of Britain, and the fight for control of Russia, which was the one they decided to flesh out into a treatment; the most exciting one.

At about 9:20 on a Tuesday morning, the usually quiet, genial Frank Capra stood before the side-by-side desks of the boys in the Special Services writers room—a small meeting room upstairs in the Jefferson Building that Special Services had converted into workspace for the "Why We Fight" writing team.

"Just what the hell is this?" he demanded of them. He had headed straight for the Epsteins, although all seven writers sat at work. Capra held in hand what Phil recognized as the story treatment they had developed the previous Friday for the short subject about Russia's military stand against the Nazis.

"You don't like the treatment, Frank?" Phil asked.

"It's just an idea we fleshed out for an episode," Julius shrugged. "Sort of testing the waters."

Capra stepped back a foot as if he suddenly felt outnumbered. He held the eight stapled pages out in front of him. "I just don't know what this is," he stammered.

"Well, it's the story of Operation Barbarossa," said Julie. "You know, the German invasion of the Soviet Union?"

"Yes, from the Soviet perspective," added Phil. "It's about the bad guys attacking our ally on the Eastern Front." This was, thought Phil, pretty basic stuff. America had allies, and the Soviet Union was one of them, and the Germans were the enemy.

Capra seemed especially ill at ease. "Isn't it the story of bad people attacking other bad people? You're making the Russkies out to be some kind of heroes."

There followed a long, painful stretch of silence. Phil could feel the attention of the other writers at this watershed moment. Julius said, "We figured that 'Why We Fight' could use a segment about the Nazi rampage through the Ukraine and into Russia, murdering civilians and destroying whole towns. It's to show our boys another reason why we're fighting—you know, all those innocent people murdered."

Capra stood unmoving and apparently unswayed by simple facts.

Phil felt his face begin to flush. "Frank, they just stopped the Nazis dead in their tracks at the gates of Moscow! They were invaded and they turned the tables, which seems pretty goddamn heroic to me."

"And me," echoed Julie.

"I just don't think," Capra muttered, "I mean, we don't want to . . ." Suddenly, Capra seemed to become aware he had the rapt attention of his whole team. He said to the Epsteins quietly, "Well, I wonder if I can have a word with you boys out there in the hall."

Phil had been astonished, since becoming associated with Frank Capra this past month, at how little he represented the mystique of his own name: triple-Academy-Award-winning Best Director and visionary-filmmaker Capra. That Frank Capra. This man was not anything so lofty. This man seemed an actor hired to impersonate Capra but without benefit of a character sketch or time to rehearse. This man was so small and so unprepared for the assignment, that Phil was ready to leave town and knew Julius would happily go with him on the first train heading west.

In the hallway with its polished marble floor that gave the footsteps of passersby a solemn importance as each click echoed over and up and across, the three men huddled up.

"You know, I've been, er, it's not that, it's . . ." Frank began in his sputtering way. "We're going to have to take a pause, that's what it is. And I was thinking, I know you boys have a script out there you're working on for Wallis. You could go out and finish that script while we get things organized here. Special Services is giving us some space in one of their buildings across town. We won't be able to get in there for a while," stammered Capra. Phil noted the evasiveness in Frank's eyes. "So, I'm wondering how you feel about that," said Capra in summary. "How you feel about taking a pause."

What Phil could feel was his brother fidgeting next to him, and Phil received the frantic messages Julius sent on their twin-time secret wavelength. *Taking a pause*—those were the code words that would get them out of D.C. and headed back to the safety of the West Coast.

"You know what?" said Phil with tremendous enthusiasm. "Julius and I were thinking the same thing! We could go home and work on this script of Wallis's until you've homed in on your exact needs. And then we'll come straight back!"

But Phil knew and his brother knew that they wouldn't be

coming back. Whatever bullshit patriotic endeavor this was for Frank Capra, it was no place for an Epstein, and they didn't want to be any part of it.

"Beautiful," said Capra, a big, beaming smile on his face. "Perfect."

Philip could feel his brother bursting with happiness next to him.

"Okay then, Frank," said Phil. "We will pack up and hop on the train west in the morning! This has been such an honor. We can't even tell you." Phil pumped Capra's hand and then Julie did. And the top man stood there unawares at how he had been maneuvered into releasing the Epsteins from the worst assignment of their lives. The next morning, they fled Washington, D.C., after having sent a telegram to Wallis announcing the happy news: We're coming home!

CHAPTER 25

Hal Wallis was removing the index card labeled ANN SHER-IDAN from his bulletin board, but he was thinking about Irene Lee. He had never laid a lip on Renie, but lately, something about their association caused him to feel guilty. He only talked to her by phone from the office, never from home, and they were always talking about "their baby." He thought about this as he picked up the receiver and asked Sally to get Irene at her desk in New York.

"Irene Lee," said Renie's voice a moment later, and Wallis felt a surge of energy.

"So, I hear you're finally coming back," said Hal. Of all people, Paul Nathan told Hal he had heard Renie was returning to the coast.

"I am finally coming back," said Irene.

"How soon?"

"Next week, after I stop off in Pittsburgh to see the folks."

Wallis felt giddy at the prospect. "Let me know when you learn the arrival time, and I'll pick you up at the airport."

"No, I'm taking the train—no more air travel for me."

"Fine, Union Station then."

"Oh stop it," said Renie. "You have better things to do than pick up an underling at the train station. But I'll let you send a car, if you insist."

"We'll see," said Hal, and he forced his mind to business. Remember, Hal. Business. He said, "Listen, do you have a minute to talk about casting *Casablanca*?" Hal couldn't understand his own confusion with Renie's role in this picture and in his life. After all, why call her about casting when he should be calling the head of the Casting Department, Steve Trilling. Hal might as well admit it: he wanted to hear Irene's voice.

"Absolutely," said Irene. He could hear her chair creak, and then he heard her light a cigarette.

"First thing," said Hal, "I'm giving it to Mike Curtiz to direct. I thought about William Wyler, but he wasn't interested. I thought about Vince Sherman—"

"Who said beautiful things about our baby!" Irene gushed.

"I know he did," said Hal, "but Curtiz has the track record."

"You're the doctor," he heard her say from across the country.

Hal kept going. "Okay, so the leading lady. Lois is now European, as you know."

Irene said, "Right—Casey Robinson's brainstorm."

"Correct," said Wallis. "He fell in love with that Russian ballerina, so I've agreed to test the girl for our picture, and she's got no acting experience."

"Oy," said Irene.

"All in all, it's fine," Wallis sighed. "Lois was a real logjam and making her European delighted the Epsteins. So that's why I'm calling, trying to come up with who you think might be right for Lois as a European girl. Hedy Lamarr? Granted, she can't act at all, but she's got a world of European mystique. Then there's this French girl from the RKO picture *Joan of Paris*, Michèle Morgan. My God, the eyes on that one. If she walked into Rick's, it would surely knock Bogart's pins right out from under him."

Renie gasped into the phone. "I just saw *Joan of Paris*. My date said the same thing about Michèle Morgan, and I couldn't get even get mad about it. He's right that she's a stunner. Breathtaking."

Wallis's mind went on high alert. "So, a date," he tried to say casually. "Someone from inside the business?" It seemed logical if they were talking about talent.

"Yes," she said quickly and, it seemed to him, nervously, "the rug business. It's ridiculous—he's in the rug business! He's a big movie fan who loves Warner Bros. It's nothing, Hal. Just a couple of dates. You know me and men—it can't be anything."

She seemed to catch herself obsessing and fell to silence. And then she sighed. "I'm sorry," she said. "Yes, Michèle Morgan would be at the head of my list. Did you put out feelers? And about Hedy as well?"

"Trilling is making calls," said Wallis. He thought again about the subterfuge of involving Renie in Steve Trilling's business just so he would have an excuse to talk to her.

"If I were you," said Renie, "I would look into that big German who was in *Joan of Paris* with Morgan. The one who played the flier—he could do Victor Laszlo. What's his name, Henreid?"

"Yeah, Henreid. Paul Henreid," said Wallis. "I already talked to his agent, Lew Wasserman, and get this—this new guy will only play the lead! I asked about Henreid's availability for two of my pictures, including *Casablanca*, but he's not interested because neither is a starring part."

"So, screw him," said Renie, and she giggled, and then she fell silent again. After a moment she said, "Still, he's good, and we need somebody who's going to be right. Who's going to be perfect."

"We do," said Wallis.

"Let's not be too hasty on Henreid," said Renie, who had grown more subdued, "and let's not let Henreid be too hasty either, okay?"

"Okay, that's a deal," said Wallis. "Now, the French police captain. I want to see what you think. The boys changed his name to Renault and they're writing it for Claude Rains."

"Claude Rains for a Frenchman?" said Renie, thinking about it. "You know what? I can see that."

"Rains will cost us," said Hal, "but he's never let us down. He's always letter perfect."

Renie said, "The thing is, it sounds like the boys are making progress and the boys are happy with Claude, so why not give them Claude?"

Wallis was loath to give writers anything, except in this case after so long at square one, he could see the logic of it. "Yeah, let's give them Claude Rains, even though it will cost us $4,000 a week."

Wallis allowed a smile as he used his shoulder to clamp the receiver to his ear, pulled another card out of the drawer, and printed neatly, CLAUDE RAINS, CAPTAIN RENAULT. With satisfaction he pinned the card below the one reading HUMPHREY BOGART, RICK BLAINE. Two down, everyone else to go.

CHAPTER 26

The Yellow Cab proceeded across the Smithfield Street bridge and turned right. Rain had been pounding down since Irene hopped into the back seat of the cab at Pennsylvania Station. Nobody was out on the streets of downtown Pittsburgh given the slanting downpour and the wind, but she could see up the Mon River the mills belching smoke and fire, turning out steel for the war. The temperature seemed to be somewhere around thirty-five or forty and felt a lot worse in the wind even in those few seconds after she stepped outside.

She was thinking about Aaron. She didn't want to be thinking about him because Aaron Diamond couldn't be real. Sure, the second date had been better than the first, and true to his word, he had not proposed marriage, and the only funny business was a goodnight kiss in front of her building that was only funny in the ironic sense, because Aaron had taught her a thing or two about the French kiss the way she had taught Jack Janowitz a thing or two on that same spot facing Central Park. So now she knew he was hypnotic and likely a great lover. In other words, she could be sure that an iceberg lay dead ahead.

"How long you stayin'?" the driver called back.

"Huh?" she asked, shaken from her reverie.

"They say we're getting a snowstorm tonight. Maybe a foot of snow. Maybe more. Can you imagine, this late in winter?"

"Lovely," said Irene. "No, I'm just passing through. As a matter of fact, can you pick me up at that address I gave you on Hillsdale at a quarter of three?"

"Sure can, lady," said the driver as the cab lumbered up steep Hillsdale Avenue and stopped at 1670.

As Irene paid the driver, she said, "Remember, a quarter of three."

"Roger," nodded the cabbie, who likely had just seen a war picture. She stepped out of the car and rushed against the rain along twelve feet of immaculate brick walkway and up two steps to the protection of the porch. She almost reached up and knocked on the front door, she felt such a stranger, but she decided to open the door and enter. Warmth hit her the instant she passed the threshold and closed the door, which meant Daddy had just been down to tend the coal furnace.

He sat in his chair, where she knew she would find him, with the Sunday *Pittsburgh Press* in his lap, lit cigar resting in the ashtray on the arm of the chair, and he lowered the paper to see his daughter. "My God, Irene. What are you doing here?"

She wanted to linger in her sable wrap until Mother could see it, but it was so warm in the living room that she had to fight the urge to take it off. "There's another train west at 3:20, so I thought I'd stop and have lunch with you and Mother."

"My God! Irene!" exclaimed Leah Levine as she emerged from the kitchen wearing a housecoat that Irene recognized as new.

"That seems to be the general reaction," Irene said as she accepted her mother's embrace. "I just wanted to pop in and say hello." Mother instantly locked her eyes onto the fur wrap.

"What is this?" Mother asked, touching the fur delicately.

"Sable," said Irene. "A present to myself from myself in New York."

Mother pulled the wrap off her daughter's shoulders and hung it on the coat rack beside the door, and Irene recognized in the gesture, in Mother's expression, what she knew to be disapproval. Irene braced herself for what would come next. "When are you going to stop traipsing around the country? When are you going to get married and end all this foolishness?"

"Robert traipses around the country for all those concerts and recitals. Do you say the same thing to him?"

Daddy called over from his chair, "Stop it right now, both of you. Come over here and sit with me, Irene. How have you been? What's new at the studio?"

She pulled up a folding chair and sat next to him. "As a matter of fact, I think I found the one, Daddy."

He deemed this statement important enough that he closed the financial section, folded it carefully, and set it on top of the other eight sections resting on his lap. "The one what?" he said, picking up his cigar and clamping it between his teeth. "The one man?"

"The one story, silly," said Irene, "although I did meet a guy in New York. We'll see about that—I have my doubts—but I'm talking about the movie we're lining up now for Humphrey Bogart." Mother had moved to sit on the sofa opposite Irene. "I sort of made Hal Wallis buy this story for $20,000 because I had such a strong feeling about it, and now my writers are working on the screenplay."

There—she had managed to mention a star her parents would have seen recently at the theater on Potomac Avenue, along with Wallis's name, also important, the sum spent on the intellectual property, and the fact she had writers working for her, all in a single sentence. Daddy was an attorney for the Duquesne Light Company, so sums mattered to him. He pondered her convoluted sentence.

"We just saw that picture *The Maltese Falcon*," said Daddy. "There was your boss's name right at the front, Hal B. Wallis, and I wondered when the picture ended if one of your writers had done the script. It was very good. I looked for your name in the credits, but I didn't see it."

"I'm the power behind the throne, Daddy," said Irene as she riveted her attention on Mother. "And none of my writers wrote that one. That was written by Walter Huston's son, John. Hal loved John's screenplay and didn't think it needed any work at all. It was a remake you know, of an old picture."

"I saw the old picture," said Daddy, nodding. "This one was better." Irene could feel Mother's boredom growing by the second. Daddy said, "And you're going back to Hollywood?"

"Oh yes. This new screenplay—*Casablanca*—needs to be finished and it needs to be perfect, and so I'll be driving the troops pretty hard."

"You hear that, Leah?" said Daddy. "Our daughter has troops. How many troops do you have these days?"

"Seventy-five writers," said Irene with bursting pride. "Somewhere around there. And another dozen readers."

"And you are their boss," he said, wagging his head, marveling at the very thought. "Little Irene Levine."

"I am their boss, yes," she returned. "Little Irene Lee." She thought of mentioning her ambition to produce the picture, but she didn't want to jinx it.

"And who's the boy you met?" Mother interjected into the

awkward silence that followed. "Is it serious?"

"I don't think so," Irene returned. Then she thought about Aaron. "Maybe." Goddammit, this couldn't be serious. None of it was according to plan. She heard herself say, "His name is Aaron Diamond and he's a buyer for A&S, a department store in Brooklyn. He's from Tennessee." She flashed back to that day at Rand McNally and the map and Sardi's and his apartment and to *Joan of Paris* in Brooklyn. *Damn!* she thought to herself. *Am I stuck on this guy? I can't be stuck on this guy!*

"Aaron," said Mother. "A Jewish boy."

Irene felt her life flowing down a stream, like every other girl's life flowed down a stream, and along the banks were marriage and motherhood. *Damn!* she thought again. "He's nonpracticing," Irene snapped, knowing that would cut Mother to the quick.

"Well, if you're going back to Hollywood, that's the wrong direction," said Mother. "If he's in New York, you should be in New York and not rushing off to the other side of the world."

"Robert's out there on the other side of the world," said Irene, "and that doesn't seem to bother you."

"And he tells me you never get together even though he says you live only ten miles apart—wherever Glendale is. He's doing so well!" Irene fumed that "doing so well" in Mother's eyes meant he played violin for the MGM orchestra, just an anonymous musician in an orchestra that nobody ever saw. Robert was just a violin and nobody's boss, but Robert's career meant something and Irene's didn't. And that was the memory she took from a three-hour visit to rainy Pittsburgh. She stewed about it for 2,200 miles, until the *Super Chief* finally pulled in at Union Station in Los Angeles.

As she lugged a giant suitcase in one hand and a vanity case in the other up the aisle of the sleeper car, a porter stopped her.

"You oughtn't to be carrying that all by yourself, little lady," he said paternally. "I'll take it for you."

"No thanks," she said with a cold smile. "You'd be surprised what I can do all by myself."

She navigated the suitcase down the steps of the railcar and out through the terminal. At the curb she stepped into bright California warmth and there Hal Wallis awaited. Not a car sent by Hal Wallis, but the big man himself who hurried out of the driver's side when he saw tiny Irene with her bags and a purse on her arm. Hal looked thinner than she remembered him from three months earlier, and tan, healthy, and prosperous. He wore a crisp dress shirt with an ascot on top and dress pants on the bottom, with a jacket and no fedora. Sunglasses completed his look, and any woman there would have envied Irene being picked up by such a successful-looking businessman in a shiny Packard who effortlessly tossed forty pounds of suitcase into the back seat.

"How was the trip?" he asked her when both had settled in the car and he pulled away from the curb.

"Oh the usual," she replied. "The stop in Pittsburgh was a mistake."

She looked over at Wallis, who shook his head and said nothing, but it was clear he understood.

She felt an urgent need to change the conversation. "So, what's new at the studio?"

"Well, the big news is they made the chief a lieutenant colonel in the Air Corps to make pictures for the war."

"Oh for the love of God," she muttered, trying to come to grips. Jack Warner in a military uniform? The idea terrified her. "Oh my good God, Hal. Oh my good God! Such a monster that will unleash! Like Dracula and the Wolf Man combined into one!"

"I know," said Hal. "I know allllll about it. Let's talk about our baby instead."

She laughed. "What did my boys send you while I was on the train?"

"Nothing," said Wallis as he jogged right onto North Hoover. "They said I could have a script in the morning."

"A script at long last," said Irene as she took out a Chesterfield and lit it at a stop light. Now that the Epsteins were involved, she had felt the pressure shift. She knew they could bang out a script, but could they make it all work? "Where does it stand with the European girl?" she asked.

"Nowhere," said Hal. "RKO wants fifty-five grand for Michèle Morgan for a picture, which is a lot. Maybe too much."

Irene thought about Hal's process of casting and about the Epsteins. "Phil and Julie need to know who they're writing it for. It's not fair to leave them hanging."

"I'm doing what I can," said Hal as he turned left onto Santa Monica Boulevard. "It could be Morgan—French, or Toumanova—Russian. Or Ingrid—Swedish. Or Zorina—German. Who the hell knows?"

"The question is, when will you know, Hal? Because until you know, the boys are going to be in the dark, and they won't be able to give you what you need."

"Stop looking out for them," Hal snapped. "Start looking out for me."

Renie almost reached out her hand and laid it on his leg to calm him. It was an impulse; she knew it was the wrong impulse. "I'm always looking out for you, Hal. You know that. You and I are in *Casablanca* together. Really, it's the two of us against the world."

It was true. It was too true. She circled all the way back to

Warner's threat that he wouldn't renew her contract when it expired August 1. She had never told Hal about that incident because she didn't want him fighting her battles. She wondered if now was the opening she had been awaiting to talk about becoming a producer.

"In fact, I was thinking about who's going to associate produce *Casablanca*—"

"Don't change the subject," said Hal. He was turning right onto North Highland. "I'd like you to put Howard Koch on the script."

"You'd like what?" she shot back. "Replace the boys?"

"No, not replace," said Hal. "Add to. I was thinking about what Koch did for Flynn with *The Sea Hawk*. He managed to make a story that was set in 1585 parallel Hitler, for chrissake! If you take everything the Epsteins are doing, which seems to be right on the mark, and add the perspective of Koch and his ideals …"

Irene knew Howard Koch to be a teddy bear. A big-old, pipe-smoking teddy bear. "The problem is," said Irene, "I don't know where Koch is. He's off the payroll; he may be fishing on some damn river in South Dakota for all I know."

"I asked around," said Wallis. "I think he's in Palm Springs. So, if the boys turn over the script tomorrow like they promised, then you and I read it, and Curtiz reads it, and we make Koch read it, and then we all meet on Friday morning—it's already on the calendar. We could bring Koch into that meeting so everybody gets going in the same direction. You know?"

Irene did know and as usual had to hand it to Hal for following his instincts in the pursuit of success. "If Howard really is in Palm Springs, I'll give him a call," said Irene. By now the subject had drifted too far from who would associate produce *Casablanca*, and anyway, Wallis had turned right onto Franklin and now pulled into a parking spot at the Havenhurst, the four-story white stucco building where Irene kept an apartment. They climbed out of the car and with a grunt, Hal hoisted her suitcase from the back seat. She took her other bag in hand, and they entered the building, clomping over the Italian tile floor to the elevator. She pushed the button and when the car arrived, the operator made sure the doors were opened and awaited their entrance.

Hal said, "How are things otherwise? How's this new guy?" Irene recognized the question for a sophisticated code. He always seemed to be fishing around for some sort of loneliness quotient in her for whatever reason.

"He's fine," she responded.

"Well, tell Uncle Hal all about it," he tried to kid.

"His name is Aaron and he works for A&S."

"The Brooklyn place? What is he, a tie salesman? No, I remember: he's in rugs."

"Yes," said Irene, "at the moment he is a buyer of rugs for A&S."

"Aha," said Hal. "A rug salesman wouldn't really be your speed, now, would it?"

In all these years in circumstances like this, when they were alone together someplace other than the office, she felt herself walking along a narrow path set into a steep mountainside, and when she walked along, the path would threaten to crumble under her feet. It had been this way with Hal for years. And here, heading up to her apartment that had been closed up for three months, she felt herself easing along the narrow path once more.

"This guy's got some things going for him," she allowed.

"Oh, handsome like Errol Flynn?" asked Hal. She knew he was fishing, but what the hell, let him fish.

"Handsome enough," said Irene. She braced herself for the elevator's customary sudden stop at the fourth floor. The boy opened the door and stood back as the pair stepped out of the elevator, and she led Hal, who lugged her suitcase, to apartment 402 where she inserted her key and opened the door. The room smelled stale, the air still, and she pushed a button in the switching on a wall sconce that let off an orange glow like firelight.

"Where can I set this monster?" he asked her as he leaned right to balance the suitcase on his left.

She pointed him down the hallway. "Last door down. Just set it on the bed, please." She didn't know why she felt as if she needed to be on guard. This was Hal. But because it was Hal and because of the precipice, she was on guard and stayed by the opened door until he returned, and in the meantime, she fished through her purse for a quarter. He emerged from her bedroom empty-handed and at the door he struggled to regain his breath. She held out the quarter. "Here you go, boy. Thanks for managing my grip."

He laughed his easy Hal Wallis laugh as she placed the quarter in his palm. But in the next instant he set it on the telephone stand and said, "You know what? You may be needing this if *Casablanca* turns out to be a stinker."

"No! It's going to be a beautiful picture," she told him. "A perfect picture."

He walked past her and out the door, then stopped and turned. "Thank God you're back, Renie," he said. "Now whaddya say we get this script straightened out?"

"You got it, boss," she replied. "I can't wait to see what the Epsteins came up with. I know it's going to be gangbusters. Meantime, I'll see about tracking down Howard Koch." He nodded and she closed the door. Welcome back to Hollywood.

CHAPTER 27

It was the first Thursday in April, and Jack L. Warner stood before the full-length mirror in the washroom of his office in the Administration Building and admired himself this way and that. Head on, one-quarter turn, half turn, and three-quarters turn, over the shoulder. Any which way he looked, the Warner Bros. costume designers had nailed it. The Army uniform had been tailored just for him and he looked magnificent. He thought to himself, *I'm going to get laid tonight like I never got laid before.* He leaned in close to look at the circular patch of the 8th Air Force below his left shoulder; a big gold 8 with gold wings on either side on a field of royal blue, with a five-pointed white star inside the lower circle of the 8. My God, was he official now. Gen. Hap Arnold had commissioned Jack and now he was in uniform. Here he stood in his washroom on the happiest morning of his life wishing Errol Flynn could see him now, or Bette Davis, or Hal Wallis, or any of the sons of bitches who had ever mocked him behind his back.

A rapping on the closed washroom door startled him. He took a deep breath to clear his mind, then barked, "Yeah? What is it?"

"You've got a visitor, Chief," said the voice of Bill Schaefer, Jack's secretary. "It's George Raft."

"Raft? What the hell," Jack grumbled. He picked up the officer's cap that accompanied the uniform and placed it on his head.

He stepped to the washroom door and opened it with a flourish.

Mousy little Bill Schaefer waited in Jack's office adjoining the washroom, mouth agape, seeing his boss in uniform. "Wow, you look fantastic, Chief!" he said breathlessly.

"Colonel," corrected J.L. "You'll address me as Colonel."

"Yes sir, Colonel!" Schaefer fumbled. "Shall I, uh, shall I send Raft in?"

"In five minutes, Bill," said Lt. Col. Jack Warner calmly. "Let George cool his heels for five minutes, then send him in."

"Got it," said Schaefer, who turned toward the outer door to Jack's office, then turned back. "Got it, Colonel!" said Schaefer with a bow, as if Warner were King George. He rushed out, clicking the door shut behind him.

Alone now, Warner looked down at himself and brushed his palms over the uniform, the fresh khaki wool, the leather belt and strap, the pleated trousers. He ran his fingertips over the gold oak pins on each corner of his collar. Goddamn, he loved this. *General Arnold has tapped me to serve in his Air Corps; Jack Warner, nobody else at the studio but me, and I'm going to make the most of it.*

He must order a dress sword and a .45 with holster, he thought to himself, and then his uniform would be complete. And a riding crop—he would need Schaefer to call Props.

Oh! George Raft, he suddenly remembered, and he moved swiftly behind his desk and stood at attention. He thought better of wearing his cap indoors, reached up, removed it, and tucked it under his arm. Then he stood, waiting, at attention. A minute. Two minutes.

Finally, he heard the knob on the door turn and an arm appeared with George Raft attached to it. Raft wore a brown suit tailored within an inch of its life and strutted into the room like he owned it. He had been a dancer; he moved like one.

Raft froze when he saw Lt. Col. Jack Warner staring at him from behind the big mahogany desk. Raft held there in the middle of the room, his eyes scanning the colonel up and down and back up again. George Raft, the gangster with connections, seemed genuinely impressed. More than that, he seemed in awe.

Raft's lips began to move, but no sounds came from his throat. Then he forced out, "Chief, I'm . . . I'm speechless."

"Colonel," Jack corrected. "From now on address me as Colonel Warner, U.S. Army Air Forces."

Raft grew ghostly pale in seconds. "Right, Colonel Warner! Yes, sir!" And he smiled suddenly, one of those George Raft devious smiles, and he seemed to stand at attention without making it obvious.

The colonel led Raft over to the corner of the room where two chairs sat with a small circular table. Less than three months earlier he had sat here with Hal Wallis to sign that contract, but Jack was a civilian then and now things would be different.

"Have a seat, George," said the colonel. "Have a seat and tell me what's going on."

They each settled into a chair at the table. Jack sat back, gave the bottom of his jacket another tug to make his uniform taut, and waited.

"Well, Colonel," Raft fidgeted, "I finished a picture a couple months ago at Universal. Thanks, by the way, for arranging the loan-out."

"My pleasure," said Warner. Actually, it wasn't a pleasure at all. He had loaned Raft out to get him the hell off the lot because he kept turning down pictures or causing trouble.

"But I haven't made any pictures toward my Warner contract

since *Manpower*, and I thought it was time I got back to work. I thought I had something going at MGM with Norma Shearer, but it fell through."

There were players under contract that Warner actually liked on a personal level. Flynn, for one, was so goddamn charming you couldn't help but like him. Dennis Morgan—you had to like Dennis Morgan whether you liked him or not. But Warner found nothing to like about George Raft. Sure, he could admire Raft's success with women; in fact, he was nailing Betty Grable these days among others, but in general, Raft was trouble.

"So, you want me to put you back to work," said Warner.

"Yes, Colonel, I would appreciate that."

"Let's review, shall we?" said the colonel. "About a year ago, you kept goading poor Eddie G. Robinson into fights on the set."

"Robinson goaded me, the little prick!" Raft shot back.

Warner painted a smile on his face that said, *You just made my point.*

"Okay, right," said George with a sigh. "I started that beef and I apologized."

"Then there's the matter of all the scripts you've turned down since then. I'll leave the details to others, but off the top of my head I can think of *High Sierra*—"

"Whoa," said Raft, "I'm the first to admit that was a fine script, but I just couldn't play a killer. Not with what the press has been saying about me." Raft had been victimized by rumors about underworld connections.

"Okay," said Warner, "say I give you a free pass about *High Sierra*. What about *The Maltese Falcon*, *All Through the Night*, and *Juke Girl*?" He paused. "You can tell me if there isn't a kernel of truth in what I'm saying, George. What I, Colonel Warner, am saying about the kernel of truth is, for chrissake, we didn't hire you to pick and choose what pictures you feel like making; we signed you to make the pictures we need you to make!"

Raft didn't just play a tough customer; Raft was a tough customer. He sat opposite Warner and maintained piercing eye contact. "Those were not A pictures. Not a one of them. Sure that *Falcon* picture hit it big, but who could have predicted lightning would strike?"

Warner opened his mouth to come back at Raft, but George cut him off. "That's why I'm here, Colonel, because of my contract and because I'm feeling bad that I've not been working. But now a part has come to my attention. It's a picture I'd really like to make, if you'll give me your blessing."

Jack began to wonder if maybe Raft didn't have a point, if maybe Wallis was intentionally sabotaging Raft by feeding him inferior parts. It was a Wallis kind of thing to do. The colonel took a deep breath, settled back, and tugged at his jacket one more time.

"Oh? And what picture is that?" he said, a little distracted.

"*Casablanca*, the one you're getting ready to make. The Rick part would be wonderful."

Colonel Warner sat back, hearing yet again about Wallis's pet project. Bile rose in Jack's throat and he swallowed it down. "Oh, so you've heard about *Casablanca*, have you?"

"Yes, I've heard about it and, frankly, I'm hurt," said Raft. "I'm hurt that you didn't bring this idea to me. It's exactly what I've been looking for. You give me Claire Trevor, and we'll rewrite the history of this town. We'll make *Casablanca* a picture for the ages."

"Claire Trevor," repeated Warner. He had no problem hiring Claire Trevor, who was a fine actress and a babe. In fact, he'd bang her in a minute. No, wait; he did bang her in a minute, Warner remembered. It was back when she was working at the studio in '38, was it? But that was neither here nor there, and Ann didn't need to know anything about Claire Trevor. Whom Jack nailed was none of his wife's business.

"So if I give you Claire Trevor, you'll give me a hit?" said Warner to Raft.

"Absolutely, Colonel!"

Warner rose to his feet suddenly, on impulse. When he did so, George Raft shot out of his chair and snapped to attention so fast he nearly knocked the chair over. Jack loved this! The uniform made all the difference.

"Tell you what, George. I'll bring this idea to Hal's attention. You instead of Bogart for *Casablanca*. I think it's a very interesting dynamic, and I can't wait to hear what Wallis thinks of it." Jack already knew what Wallis would think of it; it would aggravate the hell out of Wallis, which was perfect. But maybe, just maybe, Raft had indeed been a victim here and deserved a look as the Rick character.

"All I ask is, give me a chance, Colonel. You won't be sorry." Raft said it with sincerity and thrust out his hand. Warner clasped the hand firmly and gave Raft a smile meant to thaw the chill between them. George added a smart salute. Warner peeled off a quick return salute. George Raft really did understand the protocol here, and all the rest of the goddamn actors could take a lesson.

As he ushered Raft out of his office, Warner said, "I'll do what I can for you, George." And the odd thing was, Jack really would. George Raft had changed the colonel's opinion of him in one short meeting.

Five minutes later, Jack rang for Bill Schaefer. As the colonel paced in his office in his crisp uniform, he dictated a memo to

Schaefer, "To Mr. Hal Wallis. What do you think of using Raft in *Casablanca*? He knows we are going to make this and is starting a campaign for it. Jack."

Jack laughed to himself—let Hal and his bitch Irene chew on that for a while, Raft inserting himself into the dream picture. That reminded Jack—Irene Lee's time was running out at the studio.

Warner laughed aloud, and then laughed some more. George Raft in *Casablanca*; that would be beautiful. And just maybe, Raft would do a better job of it than Bogart. After the thought wore out its welcome, Jack returned to his washroom and went back to staring at himself in uniform from every angle.

CHAPTER 28

The afternoon of the first Thursday in April, Renie circulated mimeographed copies of a partial *Casablanca* script just completed by the Epsteins. It was bradded in a blue cover marked ACT 1 TEMP, sixty-five pages in all that covered the first third of the story and concluded with Rick sitting alone in his closed club drinking after the shock of seeing Lois again. Lois, the lover who had jilted him in Paris; Lois, who was now on the arm of Victor Laszlo, the Czech newspaper publisher. Hal spent Thursday evening reading the new script, making notes in the margins, and fuming because it was only one act of three and not the complete script he expected.

At nine that night the phone rang at Hal's house, and Louise took the call. She motioned Hal over and handed him the receiver. "It's Paul Nathan," she said.

"Yes, Paul?" said Wallis.

"Can you meet me in Projection Room 5 first thing in the morning. Say at nine? I've got an idea to run by you."

"Let's say 9:30," Hal returned, "and I'll see you there."

The next morning, Hal stopped in his office first to look at memos about his productions from various corners of the lot and there saw the memo from Warner about Raft. The first thing he thought was, *No way in hell.* The second thing that came to mind was how much he hated Warner and his baiting. The chief knew damn well that Wallis thought Raft was trouble and couldn't risk him on a picture as important as *Casablanca*. Hal pounded down First Street toward Projection Room 5 fuming over that goddamn memo. From forty yards away Hal saw Nathan pacing back and forth in the spring sunshine and smoking a cigarette.

"Good morning, skipper," offered Nathan.

"Goddamn George Raft," said Wallis by way of greeting. "George Raft. Warner sent me a memo that asked what do I think about using George Nothing's-Good-Enough-For-Me Raft in *Casablanca*." Wallis stormed past Nathan into Projection Room 5. "Goddamn George Raft tries to get in the middle of my picture. And Warner lets him."

Nathan followed Hal inside. "Well, he can't do that. Neither of them can do that under your contract. It's that simple. You cast your own pictures."

Wallis stood inside the quiet projection room, all boilers lit. "I'll tell you, Paul," Wallis ranted, pacing up and down the center aisle of the projection room, "if it were up to me, I'd bar George Raft from this lot. I watched him go after Eddie Robinson, who's the nicest guy in the world. That was enough for me."

Wallis stopped long enough to give Nathan a glance and couldn't quite interpret the look he saw on his assistant's face, except he looked worried.

"He's baiting you, skipper," said Nathan. "You know he is. The chief doesn't want you to succeed."

"Even if he sabotages his own pictures?" asked Wallis.

"Even if," Nathan said with a nod. "If you give yourself a heart attack, or let him give you one, he wins. You lose, and he wins."

These words stopped Wallis cold, stopped him in his tracks.

He stared at Paul Nathan, panting, desperately angry. Then, by the second, Hal forced himself to calm down. After a moment, he drew in a deep breath and let it out. Then he gave Nathan a grateful smile and patted his shoulder. He said, "All right, Paul, what's the emergency? Why did you call me over?"

"Sit down, skipper," said Nathan. "I have an idea to run by you."

Wallis dutifully took his customary seat in Room 5, two in on the first row on the left, where the controls were. "We're supposed to meet with the Epsteins at ten," Wallis stated, looking at his watch.

"I know we are," said Paul as he sat down two seats beyond Wallis on the left and gave a motion with his arm to Sid, the projectionist, to roll 'em. The screen lit up and it was obviously a daily from their picture underway, *Now, Voyager*, an uncut piece of film, this one a master two-shot of Bette Davis and Paul Henreid, who had been convinced by Wasserman that working at Warner Bros. with Davis would be a smart move. Henreid had come up with a bit of business: lighting two cigarettes at once and giving one to Bette. It seemed so offhanded but so significant.

Wallis nodded; he knew this piece of film well; he'd watched it four times already. Henreid took one of the lighted cigarettes and handed it to Davis, who put it in her lips and took a drag.

Nathan said, "Is that not the most sensational thing you ever saw?"

"Yeah, it's pretty good," said Wallis. "They called me over to the set because Rapper didn't want to do the scene that way—it was Henreid's idea and Bette loved it. Rapper hated it, so he called me in for a tie-breaking opinion. I said yes, let's try it. And then I saw—it works. In fact, they want to repeat it in a key scene later."

Wallis watched Nathan sink in his seat. "Shit," he said.

"What?" asked Wallis.

Nathan motioned toward the screen and said, "I thought I was bringing you a great idea."

The scene continued to run, but Wallis seemed to disconnect from the rushes and said to Nathan, "What great idea did you have?"

Nathan said, "Well, that we should sign Henreid to a long-term studio contract, and put him in *Casablanca* first thing, you know, as Victor Laszlo?"

Wallis stared at Nathan to assess the statement, and then at the screen where Henreid dominated in perfect lighting, smiling down at Bette Davis.

"A couple of things," said Wallis as the scene continued. "First of all, I thought we agreed Henreid would never take the Laszlo part because it's too small. Wasserman wouldn't let him take it, and Henreid wouldn't want it. Second of all, Trilling thinks Paul Henreid is a ham, and I agree. He's so full of himself I can't stand it. Do we really want to be saddled with a ham for seven years?"

It was obvious Hal had left Nathan speechless, because Paul's mouth hung open as if thinking of twenty different responses at once. Finally, he settled on, "Lighting the two cigarettes and giving one to Davis—this is more than a bit of business with cigarettes—that move's going to get past the censors and put a tiny bit of sex in the picture. And we need to sign the guy who dreamed it up. And if he signs, then we appoint him as Victor Laszlo and solve that problem for you and *Casablanca*."

For Wallis, it was another of those moments, like with Vince Sherman. He trusted Nathan and could see how invested Paul was in his idea. And odds were, he was right.

Hal said, "Henreid is so conceited. I mean, look at him! And there aren't enough lines in *Casablanca* to make him happy."

Nathan threw up his hands. "We're meeting with the Epsteins in ten minutes. You can tell them to write more lines! He lit two cigarettes and gave one to Bette Davis! It's sensational. And if we don't sign him and put him into *Casablanca*, I swear, you're gonna regret it."

The scene ended and the screen flickered to white. Wallis sat staring at images that now played only in his mind. Hal thought back to how many times Paul Nathan had gone out on a limb; in fact, Nathan had never gone out on a limb like this with anyone, for anyone.

"When Rapper called me over to the set, I only saw a bit of business," Wallis said thoughtfully. "That's what I okayed—a bit of business."

Nathan shook his head no. Finding shtick, bits of business as they called it, that happened every day. But Hal now understood that the two cigarettes wasn't just that. It was imaginative film-making.

"Henreid for a studio contract," said Wallis, pondering. "Henreid as Victor Laszlo."

"Absolutely, skipper. One hundred percent to both," said Nathan.

Wallis glanced at his watch and hurried out of the projection room toward the Administration Building with Nathan trailing. He pulled a piece of paper from his side pocket; the George Raft memo. "We have to attend to this right now," said Wallis. "I know if I said anything about George Raft to Curtiz, he'd say, 'Fuck George Raft.'"

Nathan and Wallis walked into the Administration Building

and thundered up the stairs to Hal's office. Nathan asked Sally to send a stenographer in. When a young woman entered, obviously new and very nervous, Hal paced and dictated: "Wallis to Warner. Dear Jack, I have thought over very carefully the matter of George Raft in *Casablanca* and feel that he should not be in this picture. Bogart is ideal for it, and it is being written for him, and I think we should forget Raft for this property." He barked at the stenographer, "Send that off at once."

"Yes, sir, Mr. Wallis," she stammered, and arose in a burst.

But Hal reconsidered in a second, putting out his hand. "No! Give me that memo. I want to think about it some more before I respond to Mr. Warner. That's all. You can go."

When they were alone, Nathan said an incredulous, "You're thinking of casting Raft in this picture?"

"Hell, no," said Wallis. "But you said he's baiting me, so I'm not going to dignify it with a response. We can just let him stew about it for a while."

Nathan smiled a satisfied smile. "Right, skipper," he said.

"Let's get in there," said Wallis to Nathan.

Wallis grabbed his one-third of an Epstein script and headed into the second-floor boardroom to find Renie already in there, sitting at the conference table with the blue-covered Epstein script before her. She wore a pink dress under a white sweater, with pearls around her neck. Her reading glasses were low on her nose and had a silver chain draped on both sides that went behind her neck. She had the script open and was reading, or trying to.

Mike Curtiz sat on the table beside her like a bird of prey looking down at a bunny rabbit. They were chatting about God only knew what—but Renie seemed utterly calm and comfortable, as if the bunny rabbit held a snub-nosed .38 in her lap.

"Hi ya, Renie," said Wallis, as if to ask if the prey needed any help with vulture removal.

"Morning, Hal!" she enthused.

Wallis took his place at the head of the table with Nathan at his right hand as Howard Koch walked in, all six-foot-thirteen of him. Koch was a skyscraper of a man, all up and down with almost nothing sideways.

"Did you read it?" Irene asked Howard.

The professorial Koch was settling in next to her, arranging his yellow notepad and his pencils, and beside them he set the script. He smiled a self-effacing Koch smile, fumbled in his pockets, found his pipe, and lit it. "Of course I read it, Renie. Twice."

"That's my boy," she purred and reached out to pat his leg.

The Epsteins walked in next. Phil moved straight to diminutive Irene and gave her a kiss on the forehead. No greeting, just a big Phil smile and a kiss. Julie pretended not to notice as he sat down next to Nathan. Then he said to Irene, "He only kissed your forehead because your ass is already seated."

"Nice to see you, too, Julie," she replied sweetly.

"You must forgive my brother," said Phil. "He's an asshole." Koch and Curtiz laughed.

"It takes all kinds, my friend," said Lee. How Wallis admired his little tiger Renie. She never seemed rattled. Never let one of the men get the better of her.

The group all had found seats, and Wallis folded his hands in front of him on the tabletop and looked at the twins sitting to his left at the far end of the table. They seemed to be making paper airplanes in their minds. Wallis had learned over time that, to the Epsteins, this kind of meeting was fun, and it was clear the moment wasn't too big for them.

"I have to say, I'm pretty happy with what you boys have delivered here," Wallis told them. "I've made a great many notes, but we'll get to that." Hal looked over to his right. "Renie, what did you think?"

She took the glasses off her nose, and the chain let them drape over her chest. She seemed to be searching for the right words. "I thought the play offered possibilities," she said. "And this—" she tapped the script, "—this is what I thought it could become." She looked at the Epsteins. "Wonderful job, boys. A great start."

Curtiz had positioned himself in his chair at the corner of the table adjacent to Wallis, of course. Hal and Mike were allied by circumstance. Hal turned that way. "What did you think, Mike?"

Curtiz shrugged. "Still pretty rough. Too much talk. Only one act," was all the Hungarian said. Curtiz never made any apologies for thinking that, quite often, words got in the way.

Wallis looked to his right, past Irene. "I've asked Howard to come into the project for the sake of perspective. I know you all understand—he's got strengths we need to use on this." Wallis leaned back in his chair. "What did you think, Howard?"

Koch puffed on his pipe, the tobacco sweet and fragrant. He nodded thoughtfully and looked across the table at the Epsteins. "I think it's wonderful. You establish Rick; you establish his club. You establish Ugarte, who then provides perspective on Rick. You establish the danger and then there's action with Ugarte's arrest. All good."

Renie said, "The opening montage that sets up the city and the desperation of the people fleeing the Nazis—brilliant. You nailed it, guys. I love the line, the 'customary roundup of refugees and liberals' when the couriers are murdered. It's as if Julie signed his name. And then a little later, Renault says to Strasser, to impress him, that his men 'are rounding up twice the usual number of suspects.' I said to myself, 'That's my boys!' Nobody uses irony like you two."

"Let's not get ahead of ourselves," said Wallis. "There are whole pages we'll need to cut because the key is, this picture needs to move." He snapped his fingers rapid-fire. "Move, move, and keep moving."

Wallis said to Julie and Phil, "I've got some notes here. Some questions." He flipped over one page of his notepad and then a second, and set it before him. "Okay, first question: Why is Richard Blaine in Casablanca? Why didn't he return to America when war broke out in Europe? Sixty-some pages here and you never get around to answering that question." Hal sat unmoving, looking at the brothers.

The Epsteins regarded one another and seemed to be speaking without speaking. Then Julius said, "We've been trying to come up with the answer to why is Rick in Casablanca, and we have no idea. Nothing we came up with worked. He's just . . . there. We decided we'll figure it out later."

Wallis digested the response, then returned his attention to his notes. "Why is Lois still Lois in this script? I thought we decided she would be European."

"It's just a name," said Phil. "We left it Lois because we have no idea what to call her. What country is she from? We don't know that yet, and it makes a difference. When we write her stuff, we're calling her Greta, you know, like Garbo. We figure you can't go wrong with Greta."

Wallis nodded; he was focusing on his written questions. "And the young couple, the Vierecks, what happened to them? They hardly appear in Act 1 at all."

Phil said, "Because they get in the way of the story."

"We don't need these kids," said Julie. "Renault wants to nail the girl, and that's his character as drawn. But this story is a love triangle between adults and doesn't need kids in the way. So, we figure we'll put the children in Act 2, and then we plan to resolve that storyline also in Act 2. We're getting rid of that crap with the lights going out so Rick can stash the kids, like in the play. We won't need it."

Wallis sat quietly, taking a moment to digest the explanation. He considered all Julius had said and the way he had said it. He nodded, jotted on his pad, and returned to his questions. Suddenly, he said, "Oh, by the way, I want you to build up Victor Laszlo's part. Nathan and I were talking, and I think we're going to go after Paul Henreid for Victor. We're talking about signing him long term, but I already know he's going to count his lines before he'll agree. And I'll bet Wasserman will want a co-star credit."

Hal could see Nathan practically dancing a jig in his chair. Hal forced himself to remain stone-faced.

Phil took in the information and gave Wallis a nod. "There's more we could do with Laszlo, sure. He's one-third of the triangle."

Renie said to the brothers, "Why don't you guys work on building Victor up in Act 2 and let Howard give him some more lines in Act 1. You need to plow ahead and not stop for anything." She turned to her left. "All right with you, Howard?"

"Sure," Koch replied, pipe clamped in his teeth, and made some notes.

Wallis said to the boys, "Tell me what you've done with Rick and the Frenchman. You call him Renault now. Explain their relationship."

"Easy," said Phil. "They're equals. Alter egos."

Wallis stared at Phil. "I don't get you," he said.

Julius said, "In the play, they're antagonists, but we asked ourselves, is this right? They're really two sides of the same coin. It works better if each has a code that they live by."

"Right, there's a code," said Phil. "Rick and Renault abide by a code that they both understand."

Wallis jotted more notes. He gave a glance to Nathan to see what he thought. Paul gave a slight shrug of the shoulders. "Makes sense," Nathan forced himself to say aloud.

Wallis said to the Epsteins, "Just so I understand: Rick and Renault are not enemies."

"Oh hell no," said Phil. "Rick and Renault can't function without each other. That's why they're friends. Casablanca is a cutthroat place and life is cheap, and they need each other."

Hal nodded. "Okay, I'll buy that. Fine. But what's this here—this line where Renault asks Rick what brought him to Casablanca and he says the waters?" Wallis was looking at the script now, reading. "'Waters? What waters? We are in the desert!' And Rick says, 'I was misinformed.'" Nathan let out a spasm of a laugh, and Renie laughed along.

Wallis leveled his gaze at the brothers. "I thought you didn't want comic relief in this picture."

Julius raised a finger in the air, like Warren William as Perry Mason. "No! We agreed that Sam couldn't serve as comic relief, but this story needs some laughs. These people are cooking in a Nazi stew, and that's pretty heavy going."

Curtiz had been flipping through the script. "What is this stew? What is this? A bunch of talking? Where is the action? Who want a bunch of talk?"

"It is a bunch of talk, and we can't do anything about that," said Julie. "What we can give you is Ugarte, killer of Nazis, who is hunted down in Rick's club in the first reel. You should play that for all it's worth—it's just two minutes of shoot-'em-up, and the rest of it is up to you, making all these refugees important."

Wallis was haunted anew: six thousand of the best and brightest in Paris. Eight thousand. Ten thousand.

"Refugees," said Curtiz, latching onto the word. "Yes, I have been thinking about the idea of these refugees."

"They're Jews, but of course we don't call them Jews," said Phil. "A lot of Free French, Bulgarians, Germans, Norwegians, Russians—desperate fugitives in all shapes and sizes, and each has a story to tell about the Nazis. Getting away from the Nazis."

Curtiz gazed out the window and said, "I know many such people." Wallis liked Curtiz, who could be quiet and thoughtful, or lecherous, or out-of-control frantic. Now Mike just stared out the window and said quietly, "So many actors run from Europe. I can stand here and name twenty, thirty, forty." He looked at Wallis. "I hire these people to make picture real."

Wallis knew when to let the reins on Mike go slack so he could run at full gallop. Like what Hal had just done with Nathan regarding Henreid's two cigarettes. Hal said, "Do it, Mike. We can't bust the budget, but I like the idea, the authenticity. Actually, I love it." Hal couldn't save the Paris Jews, but he could represent them.

Wallis settled back and focused his gaze on the Epsteins. "Okay, boys. The heat's on. I want Act 2, and it better be good."

Julie laughed aloud; Phil was smiling. "As if we'd give you anything else," said Phil.

CHAPTER 29

The news shocked America: Bataan in the Philippines had fallen to the Japanese. The defenders had held out day after day, month after month. But they had proven human after all and they had capitulated, and would Australia be invaded next? And then what? Such a nightmare. Irene could feel the weight of it in Projection Room 5 where she sat with Hal, Steve Trilling from Casting, and Paul Nathan as the test of RKO actress Michèle Morgan unspooled.

Irene loved the fact she could sit in on casting decisions—hell, in many ways she was already a producer, which she would point out to Wallis at the key moment. This morning, Irene found Morgan to be a delight, small and vulnerable, with big eyes that lit up the screen like diamonds. Her English was exceptional. The scene used for Morgan's screen test showed Lois visiting Rick, played by Warner contract player John Ridgely, for the letters of transit. When pleading with him doesn't work, Morgan pulls a gun.

They watched the test through once, then Hal ordered it respooled for a second run. Irene found herself liking Michèle Morgan even more the second time through. This was a woman who could make any man lose his head.

"How old is this girl?" asked Wallis without his eyes leaving the screen.

Trilling shuffled through Morgan's paperwork in the darkened projection room. "She turned twenty-two in February."

"I love her," said Renie as she watched the close-ups. "Those eyes!"

"I know," Wallis murmured. "She's wonderful. She could play it."

They watched Morgan pull a gun out of her purse and evoke sympathy just by holding the weapon. "All right," she said in little more than a whisper, her French accent delightful—it could be detected but just barely so. "I tried to reason with you. I tried everything. Now I want those letters. Get them for me."

Trilling's voice broke the spell that had captured Lee. "I see a lot of nerves," said Trilling. "She would have to settle down."

"I don't see it," said Hal. "The nerves work for the scene."

They watched the test play to its conclusion. Ridgely showed the letters. The actors exchanged lines until she dropped the gun and collapsed into his arms. "Richard, I tried to stay away. I thought I would never see you again, that you were out of my life. The day you left Paris, if you knew what I went through. If you knew how much I loved you, how much I still love you." Clinch. Kiss. The lights came up.

Paul Nathan leaned forward in his seat and shouted at the screen, "You're hired, baby doll!"

"Absolutely," echoed Renie. "She's a winner."

Wallis interlocked his fingers and held them by his lips. "I love her for this part. She's perfect."

"More perfect than Selznick's girl, Bergman?" Trilling asked in a tone meant to corral the others.

Irene could see what Trilling was trying to do—counter the fact that Wallis seemed to be experiencing Michèle Morgan in his soul.

"I can't wait forever for Selznick to make up his mind," said Hal.

Trilling said, "I've been checking around and Selznick doesn't have a lot of choices for Bergman. I'm told we can get her for twenty-five grand. This Morgan girl will cost us fifty-five. I talked to Charlie Feldman, and there's no way to negotiate. It's an iron-clad RKO contract for fifty-five grand, or we don't get her."

Wallis said, "They're crazy to charge that for this kid. They'll kill her career."

Irene's frustration grew by the second at what she was hearing. The test they had just watched was sheer perfection! "How can you say no to Michèle Morgan?" Irene asked. "My God, we love her! She's perfect!"

"I do love her," said Wallis, staring at the white screen.

"I definitely love her," added Nathan.

Wallis said, "A French girl is what we need—this French girl. She works for the story. She's vulnerable; she's mysterious. She's got it all."

Irene's stomach had knotted up. "Well?" she said.

Wallis arose. "This is a business, Renie, and we can't blow the budget because RKO pays its talent stupidly."

Irene and the others also stood. She said, "We need a leading lady. We need this leading lady!"

Wallis continued to gaze at the white screen as if Michèle Morgan still graced it. "I'd love to hire that girl, but we can't pay fifty-five." He said to Trilling and Nathan, "I believe we're going to have to settle for Bergman, so get on the horn to Selznick and get the terms. But it better be twenty-five, and if he tries to stick you up, tell him . . ."

When Wallis paused, Trilling waited and when he heard

nothing, he said, "Tell him . . .?"

"Tell him whatever. Tell him we're thinking of Vera Zorina—that'll get him. Tell him Wallis loves French girls, and tell him that Hal fell in love with Michèle Morgan."

Nathan gave a chuckle. Trilling said, "Right, skipper," and they walked out of Projection Room 5 into the warm April sun.

Two hundred yards away in what was referred to as the "upper ward" of the Writers Building, Alice sat at her desk and watched as Phil and Julie sparred over the naming of the character formerly known as Lois Meredith. The space of the two small offices and antechamber was thirty-by-twelve feet in total, and so over the course of months, it got awfully chummy in there.

"What's wrong with Greta?" Julie snapped. "It worked for Garbo!"

"It worked too well for Garbo," Phil reasoned. "When people hear Greta, they're going to be distracted thinking of Garbo. So I don't think it's a good idea."

"Astrid," said Julius. "How about Astrid?"

"Astrid's not bad," said Phil, and he pointed at Alice. "Write that one down, will you?" Alice did as instructed and now her list had a total of one name on it.

"How about Brigitte?" said Julie.

Phil said, "They're going to hire Bergman and what's Bergman, a Fin?"

"Ingrid Bergman is Swedish, I believe," said Alice.

"How about Lili?" said Phil.

"Eh," groused Julie. "Write it down." Alice did. Then Julie said, "We had an Aunt Leah. How about Leah?"

"Isn't that Hebrew?" asked Alice.

"Oh yeah," said Julie.

"Emma's nice," said Phil. "I always liked the name Emma." He turned to Julie, who gave his head a *comme ci comme ça* swivel as if to allow it without saying anything, so Alice wrote it down. "Eva, how about Eva?" said Phil.

"The world's got an Eva already," said Julie. "Eva Braun, so no thank you."

Alice started thinking about her own family tree. "Elsa," she blurted out.

Julie and Phil both stopped and considered. "Sounds too German to me."

"Then how about Ilsa," Alice said with a shrug. She watched her bosses for a reaction; they locked eyes and started their thing, that communication thing. Then Phil nodded and rushed over to the bookshelf where they kept a set of World Book Encyclopedias. He pulled a blue hard-covered volume out and dropped it on Alice's desktop. It was the S volume.

"How about opening to the map of Sweden and find us a last name," said Phil.

"A last name?" she asked.

"Yeah, a town name, for Ilsa."

She opened the book as instructed and found a list of cities in Sweden and their coordinates that preceded the page with the map. She ran her finger down the long list and any name that didn't have funny symbols over it, she said aloud. "Boden. Eda. Falun. Flem."

"Ilsa Flem," said Julie. "Perfect!"

"Julita," Alice went on, "Kolback, Kumla, Lund, Lundby, Mora—"

"Wait a minute," said Phil. "Lund. Ilsa Lund?" He looked at

Julie, who made a face that said he didn't hate it. Phil turned to Alice and pronounced it again, carefully. "Ilsa Lund."

Moments like this made Alice feel a part of something, like more than a secretary. When one of them asked for her opinion, they really wanted to know what she thought. They had already worked with her idea for the character's first name and now here she sat about to participate in the last name as well. Ilsa Lund. Alice shrugged her shoulders and nodded. Ilsa Lund had a nice ring to it.

"Say it aloud," Phil ordered.

"Ilsa Lund," said Alice. Phil kept staring at her and so she said again, slower this time, "Ilsa . . . Lund."

Phil stood quietly a moment, his brown eyes on her as he internalized the name. Then he said, quietly, "Wow."

As usual, Julie wasn't so introspective. "Now Bergman had better get this part," he grumbled, "or we'll have to start all over. And that was exhausting."

CHAPTER 30

Neither Wallis nor Warner made it a point to visit each other's office. Once upon a time, they had made small talk and chatted about horses and cars, back when Jack was something of a regular guy. But then Jack had gone Hollywood, around the time he met Ann. During the past couple of years, the second floor of the Administration Building had become Europe with the two overlords engaging in their own *sitzkrieg* along their own Maginot Line. Wallis felt he could come to work on a given day seeing Warner only in the Green Room or when they passed in the hall, and even that was too much. Almost all communication had been carried out via memo, like the memo about George Raft for the role of Rick. So it was with equal parts surprise and distress that Hal looked up from making notes in his copy of the play *Watch on the Rhine* to see Jack Warner open Hal's door without knocking and enter, closing it behind him.

Jack was dressed in his colonel's uniform and held a riding crop, which only served to churn Hal's stomach. Warner walked quietly into the room and approached the chairs facing Wallis's desk. He did not sit down. Instead, he put the riding crop behind his back and held it in both hands. He was playing general, but Wallis had to force himself not to smile at the comic-opera result.

It occurred to Hal to offer a greeting or to say something,

anything, but the moment was too odd, so he waited as Warner surveyed the window treatments, the mementos on bookcases, the framed photos, the plaque with the Thalberg Award given to Wallis by the Motion Picture Academy in 1939, and the Emerson quote. Warner took it all in as if a visitor to a museum or a potential home buyer.

"I don't understand," said Warner, finally.

Wallis was frozen in place, holding a hand in the *Watch on the Rhine* script. "You don't understand what, Colonel?" said Hal, mindful of how Warner wanted to be addressed these days.

"I don't understand why you're so interested in this *Casablanca* picture when you already have a full roster. You have *Now, Voyager*, and Flynn's picture, and *Air Force*, and *Watch on the Rhine*. Suddenly, you're spending my money on this *Casablanca*. I don't understand." Jack's paranoia would seep out sometimes; if left to his own devices, he'd begin to imagine all sorts of things. "It's that little girl's doing, isn't it? Listen, it's none of my business if you two are playing around, but I draw the line when you, or she, or the two of you spend my money. In fact, I'd like to have a conversation with you one of these days about replacing her."

Playing around with Renie? Replace Renie? Wallis knew better than to take the bait. Instead, he reached for an envelope, used it as a bookmark, and carefully closed the script. He leaned back in his chair, letting some seconds pass, took a breath, and said, "Miss Lee routed the story to one of the readers, who gave it a recommendation. Wald read it and liked it, and so did some others. Only then did I purchase the play. In fact, I sent you a memo about it, and you said if I felt so sure, I should go ahead. I'm planning to shoot most of it on one soundstage, on one set. It will not be a big-budget picture. And I'm using Bogart, a contract player."

"And not Raft, who needs to get some work on his contract," said Warner. "George came to my office and I sent you a memo about it, and you didn't respond."

"I simply won't use George Raft in this picture. No. Maybe your other producers can find something for Raft, but not me."

"And you couldn't lower yourself to put that in writing to me. You couldn't answer my question."

"Oh, I would have. I will. I just haven't done it yet." Wallis congratulated himself on the decision to hold the return memo; it had indeed pissed off the chief.

Warner could have been posing for a portrait, he stood so still. "My sources tell me you won't fill out the cast with contract players. Alan Hale, Tobias, and so on. That's the cost-efficient way to go."

"It doesn't feel right to me, not for this. I want to be careful casting this picture."

"Which is going to cost me money when you go out and get Otto Preminger for the Nazi or Jean Gabin for the newspaper guy."

Wallis wondered where the hell Warner was getting his information—it was all accurate. "I'll use a contract director, Curtiz. I'll use Rains, who's moderately priced and always perfect. I'll use Max Steiner for the music, also under contract. I already turned down Michèle Morgan for the female lead because RKO wants too much for her, even though she'd be perfect; I think I can get Bergman for half the price. I'm as careful as ever spending the studio's money."

"What about that darkie in the cast," said Warner. He pointed the riding crop at Wallis. "That is bad business, putting a darkie in an important role, and you know why. I do not like that."

"The world is changing," said Wallis, locking eyes with the chief, "and I for one want to be leading that change, and not fearful of it or worried what the Old South thinks and the two or five or ten cretins who might get up and walk out of the picture."

Wallis had resisted the urge to feel trapped or attacked or uncomfortable; instead, he had counterattacked.

Warner returned the riding crop to its place behind his back. "I don't like that little story editor calling the shots around here. I don't like those two schmuck brothers getting paid week after week when half the time they don't even come to work. Six weeks I've been paying them to write *Casablanca*, and there's no final script."

"Believe me, I'm as unhappy about that fact as you are, but they're making progress."

"And now you've added Howard Koch to it, and so we're paying three writers and there's no script. And the worst thing of all is half the creative people in this company think your picture is smut that can never be shot! And that really pisses me off, Hal, if we go down this road another couple of months and then cancel the picture and have nothing to show for it. What am I supposed to say to my brother about all this?"

As careful as Hal was being, he could feel himself getting hot, as if somebody had turned the thermostat way up. But if this were one of those chess games that Bogart was so fond of playing, Warner had just moved his queen badly by mentioning New York-based Harry Warner, the studio boss of bosses.

Wallis looked up to his left at the Emerson quote for strength. He said, "Well, I would say this to Harry. I would say, 'The executive who produced *Captain Blood*, *Robin Hood*, *The Roaring Twenties*, *Dark Victory*, *The Sea Hawk*, *Sergeant York*, and, oh, a dozen or two other big pictures, is working on a new one he thinks is going to make just as much money.' And, hearing this, I'll bet Harry will smile, and nod, and all will be well."

Warner glared at Wallis another moment; Wallis maintained the riveting eye contact, challenging the bully. Hal knew that the colonel, as he was loath to think of him, was finding no weakness in his rival.

Warner turned slowly and walked out of the office the way he had come in, silently. Wallis watched the visitor go out as he had watched him come in, silently.

At times like this, Hal wondered about the chief's sanity, just as he wondered how long this relationship between the two men could possibly hold together because he despised Jack L. Warner, and it was clear the feeling was mutual.

CHAPTER 31

Julius pulled up to the curb along Washington Boulevard in Culver City and cut the motor, then sat motionless. Beside him, Phil wasn't exactly bolting from the car.

"Why us?" Phil wondered aloud.

"Hal says we have to explain the story because we're the only ones who understand it," said Julie.

"You understand the story?" said Phil without looking at his brother. "That's good. Maybe you can explain it to me before we try to explain it to him." He nodded to his right, where a sprawling white building looking like Mount Vernon loomed up. Across the eaves were the words SELZNICK INTERNATIONAL PICTURES in all capital letters. All the world knew what the Selznick studio looked like because it was the first thing people saw when they sat through *Gone With the Wind*—which everyone in the world had. Today it was a quiet place. Very quiet. Too quiet. Nobody went into or out of the big building because Selznick wasn't making any pictures. He had burned out on his masterpiece and then on the one he had made after called *Rebecca*.

"We know Act 1 and that will do, so let's get this over with," said Julie and he forced himself out of the car. He grabbed his briefcase from the back seat. A white frame bungalow flanked each side of the big Mount Vernon building; Julie had been given instructions to go to the white bungalow at far left of the property. He and Phil walked to a screen door of the bungalow and entered. A pretty young brunette sitting behind a desk greeted them. They removed their hats.

"Good morning. Julius and Philip Epstein to see Mr. Selznick."

She glanced down at a list and made a check mark. Then she rose from her desk and walked a memorable twenty feet to a set of closed double doors and rapped lightly twice.

She opened the door a foot and leaned forward to say, "Mr. Epstein and Mr. Epstein are here to see you." As she did, Julie got a nice view of leg. He was smiling when she turned back. "Go right in, gentlemen," she said in a musical sort of way. Julie had the fleeting thought to let Phil go in alone while he kept this little beauty company. Then he felt Phil clamp a hand on his elbow and tug him along into the next room.

The room they entered was surprisingly large and done in white, with crown molding and a big bay window with curtains. In front of the window sat a large cherry wood desk and behind the desk sat the big man, hunched over a bowl of tomato soup, with what looked like a sliced turkey sandwich sitting on a plate beside it.

"How you boys doing?" said David Selznick. "I hope you don't mind. I was starving."

Julius felt his stomach go into a spasm and wanted to grab that sandwich and devour it in a bite. "No, that's fine, David," he said with a smile.

"How's Jack doing?" asked the big man without eye contact.

"We couldn't rightly say," Phil answered. "We stay as far away from Jack as possible."

Selznick was a doughy-looking man of indistinguishable age—forty maybe—with a square face, wire-bristle hair, and glasses. He looked as if he hadn't exercised a day in his life, except his eating muscles. He picked up half the turkey sandwich, opened wide, and took a bite. A big bite.

"Wise policy," he said with mouth full. "So they sent over Act 1 of this script; Wallis wants me to think about loaning Ingrid for it. I haven't had a chance to look. Some play, right?"

"It's our first cut turning the play into a picture," said Julius, who was unsettled by watching this man eat.

"Why should I give Ingrid to Wallis to be in this picture?" said Selznick. "My Ingrid is a very valuable commodity. A brilliant young star."

Julius looked at Phil; Phil was looking at Julius. What the hell did they care if Ingrid was in the picture? Julius thought this task—trying to procure talent for Hal Wallis—the most thankless assignment yet at Warner Bros., which was saying something. Julie decided not to answer the question; it wasn't his question to answer. Phil must have come to the same conclusion because he stood in silence as well.

Selznick took notice of the lack of a response. He set down what remained of the sandwich and wiped his hands and mouth on a white linen napkin. "I'm sorry, I'm sorry." He motioned to the couch opposite his desk. "Have a seat, fellas. You work directly for Wallis, right? Wallis and that hot little number who picks his stories."

"Irene Lee," said Phil with an artificial smile as the brothers moved back to seats on a big, finely upholstered green couch against the wall. The couch felt like sitting on a cloud.

"Right, right. Irene," said Selznick. "You boys, I just saw your names on a picture. *The Man Who Came to Dinner*, wasn't it? A fine, fine picture."

Julius nodded. "One of our adaptations, yes. We're hacks, but that one was okay."

"Julie's the hack," Phil corrected. "I balance us out."

Selznick was watching the matched pair, suddenly enjoying them, and he laughed easily. "So, you're here about this *Casablanca* picture that's getting some buzz about casting. Boil the plot down for me. Where does my Ingrid fit in?"

Julius hadn't known what to expect from David O. Selznick the pill popper, who was notorious for staying up two or three days at a stretch making *Gone With the Wind*, but here he sat like a normal person, a businessman on his home field, and waited.

Phil said, "The story's set in Vichy-controlled Morocco in 1941. Refugees are pouring in from Europe, hoping to fly out to Lisbon and then to America, but it's impossible to get a visa. Refugees pack the place. There's a café run by an American ex-pat named Rick who lucks into some exit visas that everyone wants."

As easily as they had snagged Selznick's attention, they lost it again and he went back to his soup; it must have been cold already, but he spooned it up. "Exit visas. The plot device. Got it," he said between slurps.

Phil hesitated; Julius could feel his brother's aggravation growing. "Yeah," said Phil. "There are refugees, and French police, and German and Italian military who all go to this café for its atmosphere—and it's a place where visas are bought and sold. There's a piano player and a band. Then a newspaper publisher from Czechoslovakia comes to town and he expects to get one of the visas that Rick has, and the Germans want to capture this guy, but the city is under control of the Vichy French, so the Germans are cooling their heels."

Selznick had finished his soup. He pushed the bowl aside, sat back, and folded his hands behind his head, revealing an un-exercised torso under a dress shirt and suspenders. He didn't say anything, but he seemed to be processing all he had heard so far. When no one was talking, the room grew uncomfortably quiet. At this moment Julius realized that their office suite in the Writers Building really wasn't so bad. He longed to be there right now.

"I haven't heard a word about the female lead—the one you want my Ingrid for."

Phil said, "Your Ingrid would be the girl who arrives with the newspaper guy, Victor, who the Germans are after. And it turns out this girl—named Ilsa Lund—is the lost love of Rick the café owner. They had had an affair in Paris."

Hands still behind his head, leaning way back in his chair, Selznick said, "Doesn't sound like much of a part. Pretty passive stuff. Ingrid likes the parts to be juicy. She's a nut about that stuff."

Julius sought to end Phil's pain, and his own, and get the hell back to Burbank. "We haven't worked it all out yet, David. What we do know is it's a lot of shit like *Algiers*. Shadows, criminals, guys in fezzes, mystery women. A lot like that. Personally, *Algiers* didn't do anything for me, but it sure did a lot for Hedy Lamarr."

Selznick made a sound in his throat, a sort of "Huh," revealing that one of the Epsteins had finally gotten through. David contin-ued to lean way back and stared at the ceiling. "*Algiers* didn't make any money," he said as much to himself and the ceiling as to his guests.

"No, but that's not the point," said Julius. "It showed Lamarr to advantage, that's all I'm saying. They lit her well and shot her well, and *Algiers* made her into somebody, and she ended up at

MGM." Julie arose from the world's most comfortable couch. "So that's what we've got so far. If it's Ingrid, we'll write it for Ingrid. If it's somebody else, we'll write it for whoever that is. I hear they're looking at some other girls—"

Selznick plopped forward in his chair. "Other girls? What other girls?"

Julius said, "Well, I heard Hal was talking about Hedy, if he can get her from Mayer."

"He won't," said Selznick with a snicker, and Selznick should know because he was Louis B. Mayer's son-in-law. "Who else?"

Julie couldn't think of any other names from the rumor mill. He looked at his brother.

"Michèle Morgan, the French girl, I heard," said Phil. "That was in the trades, and I know for a fact Hal loves her."

"I saw that in *Variety*, but I didn't believe it," said Selznick. "I thought that was Wallis trying to scare me."

Phil followed his brother's lead and rose to his feet from the cloud-couch. "I don't think so. After Morgan's screen test Renie said—"

"The hot little number who picks Hal's stories," Julie interjected by way of subtitles.

Phil gave Julie a glance that said, *Touché*. "Right, Renie was enraptured by this French girl, and Hal loved her too. He said so."

"Michèle Morgan," Selznick murmured. "I'm not sure I like this."

Julie imagined this as a boxing match, and after a couple of rounds of harmless sparring, the boys had landed some punches and might just win on a decision. Selznick had become so distracted by the idea of others being considered for Ilsa that the remainder of his sandwich sat forgotten on the desk.

The boys stared at an unsettled David Selznick, the Hyperion of Culver City, and Julius decided this hadn't been a fool's errand after all. They could go back to Burbank carrying a pile of political capital. They could tell Hal Wallis that Selznick only pretended not to care if his Ingrid got a part in *Casablanca*. In truth he was bluffing and cared a lot, but he had showed his cards and somehow or other, if Hal decided he wanted Bergman, he would get her.

"We've got to get back to the studio," said Julius to break a long and uncomfortable silence. Selznick's face reflected wheels turning, and he looked up at his visitors.

"Huh? Oh right. Thanks for stopping in, fellas." Selznick arose for the first time, all smiles, and shook the hand of each Epstein. "Really, the best of luck with your script. If you happen to see Hal, ask him to give me a call, will you?"

"If we see him, we will," said Julius in triumph. And the boys left Culver City's god of light to his thoughts, troubled as those thoughts seemed to be.

Three thousand miles to the east, Ingrid Bergman continued to live an agonizing reality in Siberia, New York. By the time February had become March, she loathed Rochester and Selznick equally, the former a prison and the latter its jailer. Fate mocked her. She was twenty-six, at her peak, and wasting away, while Hollywood cranked out one quality picture after another without her. Selznick kept saying yes, there were parts, but they just weren't the right parts for Ingrid. He had a persona in his mind that she must represent—certainly not a trampy barmaid as in *Dr. Jekyll*; never again that—and none of the scripts he was seeing reflected the image he had in his mind for "his Ingrid."

And then, sweet revenge. In desperation, longing for civilization, she had escaped the snows of upstate on a secret trip to New York City. There she met with one of the biggest agents in Hollywood, Charles Feldman of Feldman-Blum. On the spot, Ingrid signed a Feldman-Blum contract, and Charlie promised to represent her personally. She had gained protection, legal representation, and one of the best-connected specialists in the motion picture business.

March had become April. The snow had melted; the rains had come. Now it was Feldman who didn't call, and her initial elation evaporated. Again, she felt herself pulled down a long, narrowing stairway deep into the cellar of her mind. She began to wonder what she had done to deserve this fate, to be so close to career success and yet so far away. She lived to act, to paint vivid portraits on the screen, and here in endlessly dreary Rochester, she felt she would shrivel up, starved of the one thing in life that had ever filled her soul.

And then, two weeks into April the phone finally rang. She jumped a foot in the air hearing it, and her hands shook when she picked up the receiver.

"Hello?" Her own voice sounded so hollow, so weak.

"Ingrid, my darling." It was David.

"David! David, is that you?" May God forgive her—she was ecstatic to hear that voice. Much too ecstatic, but she didn't care.

"Ingrid, my angel, there's a part here that might be good for you. I'm checking it out and need to get on the phone with Hal Wallis."

"What part?" she asked. "At what studio?"

"It's at Warner Bros., you know over in Burbank. Something called *Casablanca*, and it sounds very promising. Woman of mystery part. They've got a designer there named Orry-Kelly who can put you in fabulous gowns. You sit tight and I'll see about the details."

She thought of civilization, of Hollywood, of a glamorous part. "You must get it for me," she said, out of breath. "Please, David. I must get out of this place. I need to work!"

"I know, darling, I know. But you leave it to me. I'll talk to Wallis and learn more about the part and call you back. Don't worry about a thing."

After they hung up, Ingrid sat beside the phone, staring, replaying the conversation in her mind. *Don't worry about a thing,* he had said; the words echoed over and over. Don't worry about a thing. She wondered if David O. Selznick had ever really known her or cared in the least. Or if her instinct had been right, and he had been revealed as nothing but a flesh peddler. She picked up the phone and called Charlie Feldman and told him about the conversation.

"Very interesting," said Charlie over a phone line that seemed every one of the 3,000 miles separating the two parties. "Very interesting. I was certain Wallis had cast Michèle Morgan in that part. I guess I was wrong."

The name of the hot young French actress shot through Ingrid's body like a bullet. "What should I do, Charlie?" she asked.

"Give me a day. I am going to call around and get the lay of the land. I know some people at Warner Bros. I'll get to the bottom of it. Sit tight and I'll be back in touch tomorrow."

Now, new words echoed in her mind. *Sit tight. Tomorrow.* The only problem was that tomorrow seemed forever away.

CHAPTER 32

It was 7:30 on an April evening when the phone rang on Council Street. Dooley Wilson had sat in his easy chair most of the day, worrying. It was his nature and among the best of his talents, worrying. He had appeared in exactly three pictures on his Paramount contract, three pictures in four months, which seemed reasonable. But the parts—oh, the parts—a porter and two butlers, although the role in *Night in New Orleans* had at least afforded some lines to learn and reactions to enact, granted the reactions of a menial Negro saying, "Yes, boss" and "No, boss" and "Sure, boss." Where, exactly, was all this going, this Paramount contract?

It was far too easy for Orson Welles to promise to Dooley that big things lay ahead for Negros in Hollywood, but then Welles was nowhere to be found when Dooley actually hit town. Dooley wondered how long he would be willing to pursue a career in Hollywood when he could be making more money drumming in bands or maybe getting another part on Broadway. How foolish he had been to entertain the idea of buying a house out here for Estelle. He turned the situation over in his mind all day, like a plow turning up the soil in his native Texas. He'd plow a row and then turn around and go the other way so he could grind himself some more about the stupid move out here and the pipe dream of a house for his wife.

When the phone rang, he was still sitting in his easy chair, and he watched Estelle rise from the couch and take the call. She held out the receiver and whispered, "It's for you."

Dooley ambled out of his chair and over to the phone, feeling his fifty-seven years and then some. "Dooley Wilson speaking."

"Hey, Dooley, it's Ben Carter," said the voice of Hollywood's most prominent agent for colored actors. "So listen, Warner Bros. has a part, and I'd like to send you over there. The picture is called *Casablanca*."

Casablanca? That name rang a bell and Dooley remembered: somebody had said the colored part in *Casablanca* had already been offered. "I thought Clarence Muse had that part."

There was a pause on the other end of the line. "Who said so?"

"I don't remember. Maybe Noble Johnson told me on the set of that picture at Paramount?"

"Well, that might not be accurate information because Clarence can rub some people the wrong way," said Carter, "and Hal Wallis over there at Warner Bros., he has some thin white skin. So let me send you over some test pages for this part." Dooley heard the shuffling of papers. "Sam is the part. Sam the Rabbit. They can give you a test in Burbank on Thursday at ten in the morning."

"Is Sam a butler," Dooley asked, "or a porter? Which is it?"

In his ear there was a longer pause. "What kind of question is that?" Carter snapped.

The agent's anger confused Dooley. In his mind there was a distinction. A porter was indifferent to whom he served; a butler had a personal stake in his employer, whether a man or a family. "What do you mean?" said Dooley. "Either it's a butler or a porter, and there's a difference in how I will approach the part. I'm just asking."

"You know, Dooley," said Carter with unveiled impatience, "there are people working hard to get Negros better parts in pictures. Paul Robeson's working, and the NAACP, and Bill Robinson—even some white politicians. And we've got to be ready. Each of us. All of us."

Dooley felt the blood rush into his face. He had no idea he had asked the wrong question. "I'm sorry, Ben. I'm sorry," he said.

"Listen, Dooley," Carter hissed. "You listen to me. I've been out here a lotta years, and I understand what you're feeling. Three pictures and always a menial. And all the colored folk you're working with are playing the same kind of roles. I hear that. I get it. But this part might be different. I'm looking at these pages, and it feels . . . it feels different to me. So you keep an open mind and be ready."

"Yes, sir, ten in the morning on Thursday," Dooley stammered. "I'll check out the bus schedule and—"

"No, you don't have to worry about getting there," said Carter. "They'll be sending a car for you. They'll pick you up at nine. You got that? Nine on Thursday morning. Be ready and know your lines."

For a moment, Dooley wondered if he had nodded off in his easy chair and if he were dreaming. But the next morning a courier knocked on the door with a nine-by-twelve-inch manila envelope bearing the Warner Bros. shield and the notice: From the Office of Steve Trilling. The typed address read Mr. Dooley Wilson, 2842 Council Street, and inside he found four pages of script reflecting Scene 105 INTERIOR RICK'S.

Dooley carried the script to his chair, slipped on his glasses, and sat down to read: "The customers have all gone. The house lights are out. Rick sits at a table. There is a jigger glass of bourbon on the table directly in front of him—and another glass empty on the table before an empty chair. Near at hand is a bottle from which this one drink, exactly, has been poured. Rick just sits, staring at the drink. His face is entirely expressionless. Sam comes in. He stands hesitantly before Rick."

Printed handwriting in the margins reads: "Sam is the piano player at Rick's Café and Rick's friend."

Dooley read through the scene. Rick is drunk and agonizing over a woman. Sam is worried and engages Rick in conversation. The dialogue plays out a few words at a time; Rick's lines longer, and Sam's retorts crisp. Dooley read through it over and over, for hours. Then he asked Estelle to read Rick and she held the script in hand and Sam enacted his part from memory. When he stumbled, she cued him and by Wednesday afternoon, he had it cold.

Thursday morning a limousine pulled up on Council Street at nine sharp. Dooley put on his fedora, kissed Estelle goodbye, and opened the front door.

"Dooley," she called. He turned back, and she handed him the script pages and his reading glasses, both of which he was about to leave behind. She smiled reassuringly, reached up to kiss him again, this time on the cheek, and said, "Break a leg."

He stepped out into the damp April morning feeling the love of a good woman. His good woman. The driver wore a dark uniform with a black cap. Under the cap, his hair was gray, and his expression blank.

"Good morning," said Dooley.

"Sir," said the driver with a small bow as he held the rear passenger door open. Dooley had spent a lifetime feeling the coldness from a white person that he now felt this instant, but he slid in and the door closed behind him and then it was quiet. The driver got in and headed west on Beverly Boulevard all the way to North Highland, where he made a right and drove up past the boulevards: Melrose, then Santa Monica, Sunset, and Hollywood. They proceeded up to Cahuenga Boulevard, where Dooley had never been, into the jagged hills, and turned onto Barham. In a moment the Warner Bros. Studios loomed up on the right, and Dooley took it all in, this gleaming Olympos of filmmaking on a hazy April morning.

Inside the gate the car took him to a soundstage. Dooley had enjoyed the ride very much, and the scenery, and took in sprawling Warner Bros. in its tropical splendor. He felt his heart beating slow and easy. He knew the part and would say the lines any way the director wanted. Then he would go home. Maybe the phone would ring; maybe it would not.

The driver exited the car, then walked around to hold Dooley's door open. A young man came out the door of the soundstage. He wore dress pants and a shirt and tie, with the sleeves of a blue sweater tied about his neck. "This way, Mr. Wilson," said the young man without introducing himself.

Dooley followed blue-sweater man to a set that looked like some sort of library. There was a table with a single chair, and beside it an upright piano and stool. A camera set on a dolly faced the staging, and a very short, older man sat looking in the eyepiece. A tall man stood beside the camera, studying a script. It was all very stark.

"Mr. Curtiz?" said Blue Sweater. The tall man turned, and Blue Sweater held out a hand vaguely as an introduction to Dooley Wilson, then turned and departed.

"Dooley Wilson, I am Michael Curtiz," said the tall man with a heavy accent. From Dooley's years on the continent, he knew the accent was eastern European. "You will test with Mr. John Ridgely who will portray Rick. Do you need something? Water?"

"No, no sir," said Dooley quietly, observing the reverence a soundstage deserved.

"Okay," said Curtiz, with Dooley still trying to pinpoint that accent. "The picture is *Casablanca* and Rick is café owner. You are his singing piano player. Rick has just seen girl who broke his heart. He is alone now late at night and drinking. You worry for him. You want to give him cheer. Halfway into scene you go to piano, there. Sit down. Begin to play. Any questions?"

Dooley processed the direction: give him cheer, but do so as one in servitude. To the performer, it seemed a small target to hit; Dooley gave the director a glance and saw him staring. "Questions? No, not a one," said Dooley with a shrug.

"Okay," said Curtiz. He turned and called, "John, you ready?"

A tall, lean man in a business suit emerged from the shadows and sat down at a table. He laid his script pages on the table surface. "John Ridgely, Dooley Wilson," said Curtiz. Ridgely nodded vaguely to Wilson with the barest of eye contact.

The lights came up and Dooley watched the actor named John seem to absorb the script. He slumped a little in his chair as he got in character. Curtiz said, "Sam stand beside Rick. We play scene."

Curtiz walked to the director's chair beside the camera and sat. He said, "Roll camera."

The cameraman pushed a button; in two seconds he said, "Speed," and Dooley could hear the faintest of whirring sounds in the silence.

A sound assistant held a slate before the camera lens. "Wilson test, Scene 105," said the assistant, and clapped the slate.

"Action," said Curtiz.

Dooley looked down at the back of the actor playing Rick. "Boss?" he said tentatively. The actor ignored him. Dooley moved to stand beside the actor. "Boss?" he said again.

"Yeah," said the actor.

"You goin' to bed, boss?"

John the actor picked up a prop bottle and pretended to fill his glass. "Not right now," he grumbled.

Dooley remembered the direction in the script. He moved in closer to see the condition of his boss. Dooley thought it odd—he could swear he smelled real liquor on John the actor. In Dooley's mind was the direction, cheer him up. "You plannin' on goin' to bed in the near future?" he said brightly, kiddingly.

"No," growled John the actor without looking up.

"You ever goin' to bed?" Dooley inquired, drawing out the word bed.

"No."

Dooley shrugged and gave the kidding one more try, per the script: "That's fine. I ain't sleepy neither."

John pushed the prop bottle in Dooley's direction. "Good. Have a drink."

"No, not me," Dooley-as-Sam responded.

"Fine. Don't have a drink," snapped John-as-Rick.

Now the scene moved into deeper waters; what did the writers have in mind? Dooley had been asking himself this question for two days. Did the writers really intend to make Sam sort of an equal to his white boss, which was what the script seemed to imply? But this couldn't be; he had been wondering if the director would provide any clues, but he hadn't, and Dooley wasn't about to risk the inquiry. He plowed ahead, remembering the porter and the butlers in pictures he had just finished.

"Boss, let's get out of here. Please boss, let's just get in the car and go."

"She's coming back. I know she's coming back," said John flatly. He wasn't exactly helping the job-seeker out.

Dooley brought his energy level up to compensate. "Boss, we'll take the car and drive all night. We'll get drunk. We'll go fishin' and stay away until she's gone."

John the actor now brought his face around to give Dooley a glance. "Shut up and go home, will yuh?" he said without force.

The script direction told Dooley to be stubborn as Sam replied, "No, sir. I'm stayin' right here." He tiptoed around John the actor to the piano and sat down gingerly. He pretended to finger the keys on the closed keyboard cover as he stared directly into the lights trained on the stage. He sat there blinded.

"They grab Ugarte and she walks in. That's the way it goes. One in, one out," recited John-as-Rick. He paused and then said, "Sam, if it's December in Casablanca, what time is it in New York?"

"Uhhh, my watch stopped," Dooley replied. He had chuckled to himself at the unexpectedness of this line on his first read of the script.

"I bet they're asleep in New York. I bet they're asleep all over America." John the actor paused and then said with the pain of a seasoned performer, "Of all the clubs in all the cities in the world, she walks into mine." He had really gotten into it. After another pause, "What's that you're playing?"

Dooley-as-Sam shrugged as he mock-fingered the keys and said cheerfully, "Oh, just a little somethin' of my own."

"Well, stop it," said John-as-Rick. "You know what I want to hear."

"No, I don't," said Dooley.

"You played it for her, and you can play it for me."

"Well, I don't think I can remember it—"

John-as-Rick cut in with, "If she can stand it, I can. Play it!"

Dooley upped his energy one more time. "Yes, boss," he said, and fingered the keys one more time.

Then the Rick actor knocked over a glass and slumped in his chair. Dooley scrambled to support him. He pulled Ridgely to his feet. "C'mon, boss. We goin' upstairs." Dooley led the actor a few steps. "You'll feel better tomorrow, boss. Jes' let time pass by, like de song say."

"Annnnnnd cut!" said Curtiz.

In an instant the lights blinding Dooley switched off and his eyes saw only several black spots. He blinked some life back into them as the actor he had been holding by the arm pulled himself free. By the time Dooley could see anything at all, John the actor had left the stage and the director stood before him.

"Good, Mr. Dooley," said Curtiz, who was all business. There was clatter around them as the crew knocked down the lights and removed the piano, which gave a clear indication they weren't seeing any more Sams today and certainly didn't want another run-through with Dooley. The director patted Dooley on the arm. "Car take you back now. We call agent after decision."

"You're very kind, sir. Thank you," said Dooley. The director motioned Dooley out the way he had come in, and now Blue Sweater was nowhere to be seen. So Dooley picked his way around the corner and out into the steam of an April morning.

The next day, Friday, Wallis sat with Paul Nathan and Renie in Projection Room 5 looking at Dooley Wilson's test. They watched it through once, and Hal asked for a second viewing.

"Can this boy play the piano?" said Hal as the projectionist re-wound and respooled the film. Nathan held Wilson's resume and scanned it.

"Drums. No piano listed, skipper."

"Mmmm," said Wallis, going over in his mind what he had just seen. "He's older than I thought he would be."

"I like him," said Renie. "He's got a nice presence."

Hal leaned back to look at Irene two seats over. "You liked this test?" Renie shrugged in the affirmative. "But does he have the range?" said Wallis, thinking aloud. "Why did Mike have him interpret it that way? What's with the bouncy manner? It's as if Sam doesn't understand how much his friend is hurting. That's the whole point of the scene—he does understand. It's killing him to see his friend in so much pain. We need a colored actor who can do that."

Nathan was silent a moment and then said, "I don't think that's fair to Wilson. I think he would play it any way he's told, but he's always been directed a certain way. And you're describing a different way. That would have to come from the director, and for whatever reason, that's not what Mike chose to do."

Wallis needed a Sam; after all the speculating on Hazel Scott, after figuring he would get Clarence Muse but then second-guess-ing the caricature performance that Muse was bound to bring, Hal knew he needed to settle this and move on. "You think Wilson can handle this part the way the boys wrote it?"

Hal looked over at Nathan. Paul was studying Wilson's long and varied resume. "Oh heck yeah," he said without any reflection at all. "He's got the chops."

Hal was aware of Renie and her opinion in favor of Wilson. The lights went down and the test began a second time. The Epsteins had finessed this scene so nicely, giving Sam great lines, beautiful lines. Poetic lines as he deals with his friend in pain and rolls with him through the waves.

Wallis watched and listened as Sam said almost merrily, "Boss, we'll take the car and drive all night. We'll get drunk. We'll go fishin' and stay away until she's gone."

"Dammit, Mike, why did you play it that way," Wallis said aloud so the others could hear. Hal picked up the speaking tube on the arm of his seat. "Okay, you can cut it, Vince," he said to the projectionist, and the film stopped in mid-sentence. The lights came up.

Hal said to Paul and Renie, "If Wilson can handle that line, about driving all night and such, if he can deliver the sentiment, the concern, the pleading, he can do the rest. I'm not worried about the rest. But Mike blew it, and now we have to guess."

Hal put out his hand for the actor's resume, which Paul handed over. Right there Hal read: twenty weeks on Broadway with *Cabin in the Sky*. He thought about Paul's rapid response to his question, can Dooley Wilson play this role the way it needs to be played? He thought about Renie's immediate approval of what she had seen.

At long last, Wallis turned to Irene for a final opinion. "You're in favor?" asked Hal.

She was ready. "Sam's character is built around that line about driving all night. This ain't Stepin Fetchit. He's a wise friend who's been through the ringer with Rick, and I feel this actor is right for it."

"Even though Mike blew the direction?" said Wallis.

"Even though," Renie responded. The way she said it sealed the deal.

Wallis drew in a breath and said, "Okay then."

"You're hiring Wilson?" asked Nathan.

"Has Muse been tested?" Hal responded. "There was talk of it, but I've lost track."

"I'll ask Mike, but I'm thinking he hasn't."

"This guy, this Dooley Wilson, is new at Paramount and he'll come cheaper."

"True," said Nathan. "Muse is MGM and he'll cost us. And he's been around. This guy's fresh."

"That's what I like the most of all," said Renie, "the fact that I've never seen this actor before. No preconceptions."

Wallis heard Emerson in his head: *Do not be too timid or squeamish in your actions.* "Okay, let's cast Wilson." He handed the resume back to Nathan and looked at both his confederates. "On your say-so, he'll get the part."

Nathan laughed. "Oh, thanks a million, skipper."

"It's going to work," said Renie.

CHAPTER 33

"I can't believe you're finally taking me to Ciro's," Frances grumbled as she sat beside Julie in the Buick sedan. "It only took two years and a separation."

"I've been busy," said Julie as he navigated a brightly illuminated Sunset Boulevard. "Besides, I hate black tie. So does Phil."

The more diplomatic brother sat in the back seat with Lillian and thought about how much he had dreaded this attempt by Julie and Frances to reconcile after their three-month separation. "I don't hate black tie," Phil countered as he tried to convey to his brother to play nice.

In the back seat, Phil gave his wife the best smile he could under the circumstances and saw how tense she was. Neither Phil nor Lillian wanted trouble—they had agreed on that as they dressed before Julie and Frances picked them up—and yet, if there was one thing Phil and Lillian could suspect about this foursome at Ciro's, it was trouble.

"Are you going to pay us one ounce of attention tonight?" Lillian asked her husband in the back seat and her brother-in-law up front. With the blackouts lifted and so many men in uniform, the boulevard pulsed with a bold heartbeat at each club entrance.

Phil took his wife's gloved hand. "We will make sparkling conversation," he said. "We'll dance."

They were driving up the Strip, and Phil looked at the now-closed Trocadero on the right, and then the busy Mocambo another block up. Ahead on the left stood Ciro's, lights blazing. Julie drove on by and then waited for a quiet moment and hung a delicate U to pull in at the curb for the valet to take the car. Frances climbed out of the front seat while Lillian and Phil slid out of the back. The ladies were dressed elegantly, each in a fur stole about her shoulders over an ankle-length gown, Lillian in black and Frances in silver.

"I wonder who's here tonight," said Lillian, scanning the comers and goers.

"Lana's got to be here," said Frances. "She's always here with somebody or other."

Phil shot Lillian a glance; she shrugged. It sounded like Frances knew Ciro's pretty well—for a woman who didn't know Ciro's. But then Frances had had a fair amount of time on her hands once Julie moved to his own apartment four years and two kids into their marriage. They had been a mismatch from the beginning, the beautiful up-and-coming actress Frances Sage and upstart Warner writer Julie Epstein. Lillian hooked her gloved hand in at Phil's elbow as a tether so she wouldn't be jostled away by a growing crowd of autograph seekers mixing in with would-be diners.

The art deco entrance to Ciro's resembled Grand Central Station with people passing in and out at eight on a Thursday evening. Everyone looked great, but then the most beautiful stars in all the heavens should look the part. A foursome in conversation at the curb included the fashion designer Oleg Cassini and his wife Gene Tierney, who were laughing it up with George Montgomery and Hedy Lamarr. Charlie Chaplin and Paulette Goddard were walking in ahead of the four Epsteins as Olivia de Havilland and

Buzz Meredith walked past heading out.

"Hello, Epsteins!" Livvie said with a broad smile as she passed the boys. She gave Phil's left arm a squeeze, and he felt Lillian tighten her grip on his right. Boa constrictor tight.

"I wonder what happened between Livvie and John Huston," Phil said into Lillian's ear as he turned in time to see Meredith's arm encircle Livvie's waist in a loving manner.

The newcomers climbed eight steps to the entrance and passed through the front doors, where a deafening din of at least 300 people struggling to be heard in the yawning space just about bowled them over. Above eye level hung a blue haze of cigarette smoke, and the place was warm, too warm, the bodies-of-all-those-people warm. Julie addressed the maître d', who studied his seating plan, and the two couples were led through a gauntlet of humanity, tables and tables and more tables, around the dance floor, to a place in the farthest corner, diagonally opposite the entrance.

The husbands held chairs for their wives, and all were handed brown Ciro's menus. When Frances realized the spot to which they had been assigned or, rather, exiled, she said, "You have got to be kidding me." She glared at Julie. "This has to be one of your practical jokes." She said it loud enough to be heard in any din.

"I sort of . . . forgot to call until yesterday," said Julie in what was, for him, a pathetic tone.

The truth was that the boys spent every waking moment on *Casablanca*, figuring out this and that and the other thing to make the script work as a story where it had never worked before. Now they had reached the part where the young Bulgarian couple drove the action, where Rick suddenly wanted to come to their aid and the lights went out and the young couple vanished before Renault's eyes. The boys knew such a cheap old bit of business wouldn't work with audiences grown suddenly more sophisticated by war, so they had spent days tinkering and rearranging to find something that would. But Julie had decided to try to make peace with Frances and thought maybe Ciro's would do it. Phil wondered if maybe Julie had sabotaged his own plan by forgetting to make the reservations.

Phil forced himself to concentrate on the list of hors d'oeuvres. Seafood à la Russe. Easy enough. The other three studied as if an exam would follow; Lillian had slipped on her reading glasses, in which she looked sexy and adorable but felt horribly self-conscious, and she must have made her choice because off they came again. In a flash, she had slipped the glasses into her beaded handbag.

A waitress appeared. She was brunette, beautiful, and about twenty. She wore a black dress so brief that her garter belt and black hose were exposed above black patent high-heeled pumps. "Can I get y'all a cocktail to start off?" she asked in a drawl that might have been Kentucky or West Virginia—another hopeful actress just off the bus. The four ordered drinks, and Phil sensed danger when Frances ordered a double. They chose appetizers, and the waitress tottered off in her heels as if she knew what she was doing.

"We need some business for the gambling den," Julie blurted out.

Frances grimaced. "Oh no, shop talk? Julie, you promised!"

"I just want to put the thought in Phil's mind so we don't forget," Julie told her. "Some business at the blackjack table or roulette wheel, to give the club flavor."

Lillian was half listening. She laughed and touched Phil's arm. "Remember that time in Palm Springs when we were playing roulette and I kept losing?"

"Yes!" said Phil. "You started to cry."

"I couldn't help it; champagne makes me sad," said Lillian. "And losing makes me sad."

Phil said, "Finally the croupier said out the corner of his mouth, 'Put your chips on 22.' And you did."

"And I won!" Lillian shrieked happily. "And then the croupier said to me, 'Now get out and never come back!'" Lillian giggled at the memory, a giggle like music, which was the first quality Phil had fallen in love with. He admired her now, a big mushy admiration that took all his concentration. When he returned to earth, Julie was glaring at him.

"What?" said Phil to his brother.

"You idiot," said Julie, "that's a good bit of business! There's a couple, and the woman is a whiner, and keeps complaining she's losing, and Emil the croupier gets so fed up with her he goes to Rick, and Rick says to let her win and tell her never to come back."

Lillian grinned at Phil saucily. "I should go on the payroll," she said with a wink.

"You would be a welcome change," said Phil. "Much easier to take than some people."

The waitress brought their drinks. As she set each down, Julie assessed the brunette's limbs in detail not quite as subtly as he intended. Phil shot him a glance that Julie was too busy to see. Frances didn't miss any of it; as soon as her double scotch and soda hit the table, she downed half of it.

The foursome returned attention to the menus and ordered entrees. Phil and Lillian both had the prime rib, and as the other two ordered, Phil felt something rub his calf. He put his hand down and felt Lillian's stockinged foot—she had removed her shoe and was playing footsie with him. She winked again; Phil thought it to be her thank you for not eyeing up the waitress.

Sammy Kaye's orchestra busily worked to set up on the stage; the atmosphere would be getting even livelier in a little while. The number of patrons continued to increase, and the crowd ebbed and flowed around the Epstein table. Waters would part—Phil could see Betty Grable and George Raft. Then the waters closed. Then there, Carole Landis with Cesar Romero. Then, gone.

The hors d'oeuvres arrived and more drinks. Maybe fifteen yards away Phil caught sight of Sydney Greenstreet at a table near the dance floor. There was no way to mistake Greenstreet, who must have weighed in at 275 on a frame of maybe five-nine. Phil strained to see who was sitting with him. Then he realized, holy shit, Peter Lorre! The ladies with them must have been wives; they did not quite resemble the waitress or random starlets.

"Julie!" said Phil urgently. Julie didn't hear him; he was leaning in with Frances. Phil slouched down in his chair and kicked his brother under the table.

"What!" growled Julie. Phil didn't try to speak over the roar; he merely nodded to the table off to the right. Julie's eyes followed the other twin's signal beacon and feasted upon Casper Gutman sitting with Joel Cairo. A smile washed over Julie's face.

Phil saw his brother mouth, "That's beautiful."

"We gotta write them in!" Phil shouted across the table. Julie cocked his ear. "How can we not write them in?" Phil shouted louder.

Julie threw up his hands, as if to say, in what roles? There weren't parts worthy of a Lorre or a Greenstreet in *Casablanca*, just a bunch of small secondary characters with a line or two. Phil gave his brother a sideways nod, which meant consultation, and the Epsteins got up from their chairs. Phil reached down and took

Lillian's hand—she had removed her gloves—and kissed her palm to signal, *I'll be back.* Then he rushed after his brother, around the dance floor and toward the exit. They needed more moves than Mae West to get there, but finally they reached the lobby and then the fresh air of Sunset Boulevard. The relative silence assaulted Phil's ears; he continued to hear the roar of the crowd inside, like water rushing over Niagara Falls. When Julie spoke, Phil's brain began to make sense of normal conversation.

"I grant you, those guys are brilliant," said Julie. "But where would we put them? You gonna make one the maître d' and the other the bartender?"

"I was thinking of Ugarte and Martinez," said Phil.

"Nope," said Julius instantly. "They both vanish in the first reel! They're throwaways! What, ten lines for Ugarte and five for Martinez?"

A convertible pulled up at the curb; from behind the steering wheel and wearing a white jacket, trousers, and shirt with ascot stepped Errol Flynn. Errol seemed to be a little smashed and had trouble finding the hand of the attendant so he could turn over his keys. There was a handsome kid with him who seemed about twenty-one, with dark hair and eyes. Flynn and the kid walked toward the brothers deep in their casting conversation by the curved glass of the Ciro's entrance.

On approach, Flynn smirked and said, "Well, well, if it isn't the studio wiseguys."

"Errol," said Julius warily in greeting because everybody knew that Flynn could be a nasty drunk.

"Well, well," Flynn murmured again, slowly. Then he pulled the kid forward by the neck. "This is Helmut, just signed by the studio. He's in my new picture and he's going to be a great star, mark my words." The kid shook each brother's hand.

Flynn had pronounced the name HEL-moot, with reverence. "He's a fucking hero out of the Austrian resistance. You should hear the stories."

"Dantine," inserted the kid quickly, nervously, as DON-teen.

Phil said, "I'd like to hear your stories. We can use them in our scripts."

"He means steal 'em," said Julie.

The comment took a moment to register with Flynn, but then he laughed his easy laugh. It was a genuine laugh, writer to writer. He clamped a hand on Julie's shoulder and squeezed. "I don't care what anybody says, these fellas are all right," said Flynn to his friend. "And they're mean doubles players. Watch out for this one," he added, jabbing Julie in the chest of his white shirt. "He's a poacher."

To get a tennis compliment out of Errol Flynn, well, Phil considered maybe the boys should head home now and call the evening a win. Instead, he offered as the two men passed, "Be careful, it's loud in there."

"After the next round of drinks, we'll make it louder," said Flynn, and he stumbled up the steps with Dantine where the entrance to Ciro's swallowed them whole.

In a flash Julie was back in their argument. "Wallis will never pay salaries for Lorre and Greenstreet for throwaway parts."

"Ugarte drives the whole picture!" said Phil. "We could build Martinez up for Greenstreet. Give him another couple scenes."

"It's casting against type," said Julie, "Greenstreet in a part like that."

"Exactly why it's perfect!" said Phil.

Julius stared up Sunset Boulevard into the headlights of oncoming cars that had just passed through the intersection with Laurel Canyon. It had turned into quite a lovely April evening, with a gentle breeze from the west. Phil deferred to Julie on matters like this; Julie was and always had been the senior brother, first to write for a living and first to get hired at Warner Bros. So whatever Julie decided now would be the way it would be.

"We can write it any way we want," said Julie with a shrug, "and they'll cast who they cast."

"But I'd sure like to write it for those two," said Phil.

Julie stared off a moment longer. "I wonder what they would think about it," he said, and headed back inside at once. Phil knew what this meant; Julie was going to go to their table and ask. He hurried inside after his brother. They ducked and dodged through the throng just as the Sammy Kaye orchestra opened its set. Phil realized there was no point talking to the *Maltese Falcon* duo now; Julie must have felt the same way because he veered off toward the corner and the wives.

The boys returned to their table to find that Frances and Lillian were sitting close to each other, and one would point at a patron and speak into the other's ear, and they would confer and giggle. Phil knew what this meant—they were playing a game Frances had made up called "Would You Nail?" It wasn't much of a game; Frances or Lillian would point out a man and then say whether she would sleep with him, and the other would agree or disagree. At the moment, they were assessing Don Ameche and next, John Carroll. They found it a great way to kill time in Hollywood clubs while their husbands discussed work or conferred with colleagues or actors. It always happened and the girls had obviously realized that tonight would be no different.

To wait out the moments until the band finished, Phil asked

Lillian to dance and Julie grudgingly asked Frances. The dance floor was so crowded Phil and Lillian could do little more than inch to the right and inch to the left, but Lillian enjoyed the attention and snuggled close to Phil despite the heat of all those bodies.

Phil backed into somebody and out the corner of his eye saw an Army uniform. He turned and saw Jimmy Stewart smiling down at him, his arm around the waist of Dinah Shore. "Watch it, fella," Stewart said with a wink.

Finally, Phil recognized "Swing and Sway," the best-known Sammy Kaye tune, which likely signaled the end of their set. The herd of dancers had thinned by now, and Phil and Lillian could dance a foxtrot and enjoy it.

Heading back toward their corner exile, Phil saw that the ladies accompanying Greenstreet and Lorre weren't at their table. Phil headed straight over, and the actors looked up as one to see him standing there. Sydney Greenstreet's great girth had been lessened by a black tux; Lorre looked almost childlike in contrast. "May I join you a moment?" Phil asked.

"I know this gentleman," said Lorre to Greenstreet. Lorre looked up again to see Julie slide into the other vacant seat. "Yes, yes! These two are writers at Warner Bros."

Phil figured they had only a moment with the actors. He said to Greenstreet, "I'm Phil Epstein and this is my brother, Julius."

"Brothers!" Sydney Greenstreet exclaimed in a gruff tone, looking from Phil to Julie and back to Phil. "Egad, who would have thought it?" And then he gave a great guffaw.

"We have a quick question for both of you," said Phil. "A question that's strictly off the record."

"Of course, sir," said Greenstreet, who talked in bursts, like the characters he played. Lorre said nothing, just sat there with chin in hand, his sad moon-eyes fixed on Phil.

"We're writing a picture for Wallis. It's an important picture to Hal, and Bogart is to star. It's got two roles that we think would be great for both of you—against type. The catch is, they're small parts. One is the mysterious operator who sets the story in motion—which we're thinking we could write for you, Peter. And another part that's only in Act 1 at present, a shady nightclub owner. But maybe we could build it up a bit. That one would be for you, Sydney."

"Ah," Greenstreet mused, "the shady characters are always more interesting, I find."

"Wait a minute," said Lorre, "you said my part would be mysterious. Would it also be shady? It must be shady—in fact, it must be shadier than Sydney's."

Phil could see Greenstreet's fondness for Lorre by the way he looked down at him, smiling happily, and the way his body shook in amusement just listening to his friend speak.

Phil said to Lorre, "The plot is set in French Morocco, where refugees from Hitler gather seeking passage to Lisbon and the U.S. You deal in visas for these people and among your shadier dealings, you murder two Nazi couriers and steal some special visas that drive the plot of the whole picture."

Lorre thought about it. "Excellent, excellent," he said.

"Our question is," said Julie, "if a part is small, would you consider playing it? We don't want to tailor the script to each of you if you wouldn't even consider agreeing to it."

The actors looked at each other and Lorre nodded in deference to Greenstreet. Sydney said, "I like to make my mark on a picture. I am fortunate that the parts I've taken so far have been prominent. I am grateful to Warner Bros. for that. But I assure you, I do not count lines. I count quality."

Lorre lit a cigarette and sat silent, as if pondering all that the brothers had said. There was a sadness about Lorre, his eyes, his posture, thought Phil, and it seemed pretty obvious he had had a lot to drink.

"Quality is a rare, rare thing here," said the small man. "I spent five years imprisoned at Columbia Pictures; there, all notions of quality were beaten out of me. Then I come to Warner Bros. and make something wonderful like *The Maltese Falcon* with this fellow," he touched the giant's forearm, "and I see there can be hope." Lorre was known from one end of town to the other as a prankster, but he sat now with heart on sleeve. "Characterization is the most important thing to me." He paused. "Well, characterization and drugs."

It was an odd thing to say; Phil wondered, was he kidding? Then Lorre leaned forward toward the brothers and put his elbows on the table to say, "If you write me a good character, I will make him mine and be grateful." He dragged on his cigarette and added, "With no counting of lines."

The spouses of the two actors returned and Phil and Julie jumped up at once. Greenstreet and Lorre stood as well. Greenstreet introduced his wife Dorothy, a matronly woman with a dazzling smile, and Peter introduced Celia, whose sharp European features likely meant she was a character actress—or should have been one. The Epsteins held chairs for the ladies to sit and then took their leave.

When their husbands had moved within earshot, Frances said to Lillian, "Honest to God, I don't know what we would do without each other." Lillian was sawing into the prime rib; Frances attacked French lamb chops.

"You said it, sister," replied Lillian in a tone softened by food.

Phil sat down and said to Lillian, "What would we do without you? This very evening you saved Act 2 with that story about the roulette wheel."

Phil realized as he looked down at the prime rib just how hungry he was. And he knew he had better eat up because in a couple more hours they would be back at the script with new elements in place, including the roulette wheel gag and dialogue tailored to Peter Lorre and Sydney Greenstreet.

CHAPTER 34

Irene sat thinking that even if she hadn't finished two gin and tonics and ordered a third, she would still consider her companion, Conrad Veidt, to be the sexiest man she had ever seen. From his great height to his sharp features to an urbanity no American man could match and superb blue eyes that evoked the most vivid summer's day, Veidt was simply a dream, so much of a dream that Irene had already melted into the leather Brown Derby seat. Every time they made eye contact, she heard a raft of violins playing music she couldn't quite identify. She only knew that if this man made any reference to meeting later that evening, or any evening, she would say yes, and yes, and yes again. Sure, Aaron had managed to muscle his way into the picture, but she still fought against anything developing there. Career. Career. Focus on career. But Connie Veidt was a different matter; Irene was ready to become a notch on Conrad Veidt's Luger whenever he wished.

Irene stabbed carefully into each element of the Cobb salad before her so as not to embarrass herself with food flying this way or that or missing her mouth. One simply had to get the Cobb salad at the Vine Street Derby. As she speared a quartered hard-boiled egg, she said, "I just loved *A Woman's Face*. Loved. Anything with Crawford. I simply adore her."

"Ah, Joan," said Veidt wistfully, with a sparkle in his delicious

eyes seeming to hint that he knew Joan Crawford not just professionally but also biblically. *Choan.* That's the way he pronounced it.
Choan. "We had so much fun on that picture."

He was so dreamy she couldn't stand it. She set down her fork
and leaned forward. "You were deliciously eeeevil in that one." She
could hear her voice purring and she didn't care. His blue eyes
were pools and she wanted to strip off her clothes and dive into
them. And there was no doubt he was enjoying her attention.

Veidt said, "Joan and I joked that I was 'Lucifer in a tuxedo' in
that part. Oh, that scene in the attic—she was so wonderful in that
scene because she just stood there impassively while I revealed my
true nature. I said things like, 'The world belongs to the devil,' and
such." He laughed happily, remembering. "Such moments of truth
for an actor, of pure characterization, are so rare. I credit Mr. Cu-
kor for giving me that, and Joan, of course. Joan might have stolen
that scene from me if she'd wanted to. It was her picture, and there
were so many instances when she might have upstaged me. But
she remained quiet and still in that attic scene, and her face invited
me to seize the moment. It was an act of pure generosity and I love
her for it." His voice and his eyes revealed the passion he poured
into his craft; Irene's pulse raced.

Sitting next to her in the booth, Hal Wallis didn't just nudge
her; he kicked her in the ankle with his heel so hard that she grunted. Hal cleared his throat. *Oh that's right, dammit,* she thought to
herself. *Hal's here.*

"So, Connie, speaking of characterization," said Wallis in what
Irene considered a shameless attempt to make the business lunch,
in fact, a lunch about business instead of a prelude to passion,
"we've got this part we'd like you to consider. We start shooting in
about a month."

Veidt had been cutting a bite of his breaded veal cutlet but paused and said, "Do I get three guesses what this part entails?" Oh, the way he delivered that line. It wasn't three, it was *sree*. Sree guesses. She swooned anew.

"All right, I confess, it's another Nazi," said Hal. "I know you did one for us a few months ago with Bogie."

"My dear Hal, it's all Metro lets me do!"

"And you don't mind?" Irene asked. She didn't care about the answer; she merely needed to feel his gaze and hear him speak.

Veidt set both knife and fork down on his plate so gently that neither made a sound. "My stars no, I don't mind!" He reached out for his wine goblet and took a sip. Pinot Noir. Then he set the glass gently on the linen. "I will grant you that if you were to cast me in a romantic comedy, I would be delighted. But I happened to have been born in Berlin, and my wife happens to be Jewish. I did not want the National Socialists to come to power. I did not choose that a madness should grip my country and yet it happened. And so, you see, due to circumstances beyond my control, I have become a voice of truth who can show the free world what a Nazi is all about, for I know him all too well. He is a fanatic who is gullible and all too readily believes lies. He is the worst of humanity and must be exposed." Veidt sat back in the booth. "Many of my friends are dead or missing. Half my wife's family is gone. I feel what I am doing is important."

Irene couldn't think of another thing to say; Hal also seemed to be rendered speechless. They had picked the perfect time and place for their meeting, as the Derby was quiet, with only distant chatter and the occasional clinking of a plate.

With a satisfied smile Connie took another sip of wine, then picked up his knife and fork. "I didn't mean to spoil our delightful lunch. It's just that I so miss the old Germany. I fear that when the madness ends, there will be nothing left at all—either we will all be enslaved, or my homeland will be destroyed. Neither eventuality appeals to me, but of all outcomes, this corrupted Germany must be crushed, and so, bring me your villainous role. I am ready."

Irene was halfway into her third gin and tonic; she leaned forward and said, "You will be so perrrrrfect for this part." However she said it, Wallis kicked her again and she grunted again.

Veidt tilted his head back and laughed. He touched his lips with his napkin. He leaned forward over the table so their faces were mere inches apart and his eyes drilled into hers. "Tell me more."

She thought to herself, *Easy, Irene. You're a professional and this is business.* She drew in a quick breath and said, "Three of our best writers are working on the script. Major Strasser—that's you—the boys just gave you a promotion from captain—you have come to Casablanca to nab Victor Laszlo, a newspaper publisher who has spoken out against the Nazis."

"Ah, *Casablanca*," said Veidt. He said it so elegantly that the strange music began to play again in Irene's mind. "I've been hearing about this picture. In fact, who was I speaking with . . .?" He tapped his temple with a long and graceful finger. "Peter Lorre, that was it. Peter told me about it." He took a bite of veal and then stopped short. "Did you say the script is not yet completed, and you wish to be shooting in a month?"

"Guilty on both counts," said Wallis. "It's a stage play that Renie, uh, Irene found, and the subject is so timely that I moved it to a fast track—the fighting in North Africa, the refugees fleeing Europe. Now the production has taken on a life of its own. I've got some of the players lined up, and we are developing a schedule, all very much on the fly."

Irene said, "And when it came time to think about Major Strasser, naturally we thought of Hollywood's favorite bad guy."

"How charming," said Connie, who was no longer making any attempt to camouflage the fact that he was flirting. His eyes had locked on hers, and she was grateful to be seated so she didn't faint and drop to the floor.

Veidt was giving his full attention to Irene but managed to say to Wallis, "So you will be shooting *Casablanca* . . . when?"

"We'll roll cameras, I hope, on May 11," said Hal. "We would probably need you to be available for a couple of weeks in June if it's possible, and if we can work something out with MGM. So, if you can keep your calendar clear . . ."

Veidt pulled out a pen and took in hand the matchbook sitting atop Irene's Chesterfields. "You may rely upon it," he said, jotting down the dates. He realized he had taken her matches. "Oh I'm sorry, Miss Lee."

"Renie," she said. "Everyone calls me Renie."

"Charming," sighed Connie Veidt as he once again gazed into her eyes. "Simply charming."

CHAPTER 35

It seemed to Alice that her bosses, the Epstein brothers, intimidated Howard Koch. Granted, Mr. Koch towered over them by more than half a foot, and he had written the radio play "The War of the Worlds," which half the nation thought was real at Halloween 1938, and screenplays for *The Sea Hawk* and *The Letter* in 1940. Even with all that, she thought that Mr. Koch working with Julie and Phil resembled the way a high school freshman tried to deal with two seniors.

Koch sat leaning forward in the chair beside Alice's desk holding the blue-covered script, with the brothers in their desk chairs by the doors to each office. "And a little later," said Howard, "when Ugarte says to Rick, 'Too bad about those two German couriers, wasn't it?' indicating to Rick that Ugarte had killed them, Rick shrugs and says, 'They got a lucky break. Yesterday they were just two German clerks; today they're the Honored Dead,' that is really good stuff. I don't know how you guys do that." The brothers didn't seem flattered by the statement; in fact, they had no reaction at all, so Koch pressed on. "This is your script, I realize, and I'm the new guy, but Renie's put me on the hot seat."

"We're all on the hot seat, professor," said Julie.

"Okay, then, here goes," said Koch. "I'm just not seeing in Act 1 any sense of nobility in Rick. He's a tough, cynical American, granted. But where is any hint of the kind of self-sacrifice he's got to make at the end?"

Phil said, "We figure he grows into doing the right thing, you know, because of circumstances."

Howard said, "I think there's a danger it's going to come off as stagy if it's not established early."

"How early?" said Julie.

Koch said, "Well, in that first conversation between Rick and Renault, here on page five, what if Renault were to give Rick's backstory there, the intelligence that's been gathered?" Koch pulled out some handwritten papers that had been folded in half and tucked in his script. "I tried some things—see what you think. Renault could say Rick was in Ethiopia and in the Spanish Civil War, but on the losing side both times. This would give him a history of fighting Fascism without us coming out and saying he's anti-German."

Koch looked up and awaited a reaction. The brothers turned the idea over in their minds. "That's pretty good," said Phil, who looked at Julie and received an acknowledging shrug.

Howard pressed on. "Now that Lois is European, Rick is the only U.S.-born American in the story, so he's got to represent everything we stand for."

"Wait a minute," said Julie. "Aren't you a Communist?"

Koch said, "Oh, I've been a lot of things, but I think I understand what the American audience wants to believe about itself. You know, all that God-fearing, apple-pie, flag-waving shit? Americans are the greatest. Americans do the right thing. That's got to be the definition of Rick Blaine by fade-out."

Phil took a moment to roll up his sleeves. "So, in Ethiopia and Spain, Rick was on the right side, even though it was the losing side, because Americans do the right thing." He looked at his brother and added, "Why didn't we think of that?"

Julie shrugged. "We would have, eventually."

Phil said, "But Julie, we don't have until eventually to get this thing done." He turned back to Koch and said, "What else?"

"Oh, there's lots," said Howard. "Victor Laszlo needs to be more than a rich newspaper publisher who prints anti-Nazi columns. Let's make him a resistance leader."

The brothers ruminated. "So, he's sort of like—" Phil began and paused.

"—de Gaulle?" Julie concluded.

"Yes, exactly," said Koch. "Think Charles de Gaulle, driven from his own country and fighting the Nazis through his inspiring words from any available haven."

"Oooh, my dad will love that," Alice blurted out.

"Your dad?" asked Phil.

"My dad is big on de Gaulle since those speeches on the BBC," said Alice. She remembered sitting with her father listening to de Gaulle on the radio as he attempted to rally the French troops after Dunkirk—was that almost two years ago already? "I love the idea of making Laszlo like de Gaulle," she ventured.

"Shit," said Julie. Alice knew him well enough to understand just how impressed Julie was at the new ideas. Alice watched as Koch grew more comfortable in his new role by the second.

"Now let's talk about Captain Renault, the child molester," said Koch as he leafed through the script. "You've left an awful lot of his lechery in here. You know it's never going to get through the Breen Office."

Julie said, "You've got to throw a lot at the censor so a little bit might survive."

Koch shook his head. "I like sex as much as the next guy." He paused and looked at Alice. "Excuse me, Miss Danziger," and she was thrilled to see a hint of flirtatiousness in his eyes. "But, fellas, this is an A picture, a platform to say important things."

"But we like Renault," said Julie. "It's a running gag that all he thinks about is sex."

"Hilarious," Howard said with a nod. Alice was amazed how he had relaxed in just a few minutes working with the Epsteins. "But we don't want to get distracted. A little goes a long way. Granted, you need Renault to be interested in Annina to drive the plot."

"We're working on that now," said Phil. "How to get the kids out of the story and out of Casablanca so we can focus on the love triangle in the final act."

"Oh, just so you know," said Julie, "we're writing Ugarte for Peter Lorre and Martinez for Greenstreet."

"Does Wallis know this?"

Phil said, "We told him that's what we were doing, and he told us there were no guarantees—salaries and schedules and such. Still, we've gotta write it for somebody."

Koch nodded, then opened the script again. "I had a couple of ideas for the Martinez character, the black marketer."

"I want to change his name to Ferrari," said Julius.

"Since when?" said Phil.

"Since I saw the name in the paper a half hour ago. He's some Italian guy attached to auto racing over there. Ferrari. I like that name."

"Alice, can you make that change?" said Phil.

"Sure can, boss," she said.

Phil said to Howard, "What's your other idea?"

"Martinez—Ferrari—the guy doesn't have much to do in Act 1. But I thought in the bit where he comes in to buy Rick's place and Rick says no, he could offer to buy Sam. But since Rick is an enlightened American—"

"I get it," Julie cut in. "The American does not like the idea of buying and selling human beings, especially colored human beings."

"Exactly, and Ferrari offers to buy Sam from Rick, and Rick could say, 'I don't buy and sell people.'" Koch kept flipping through Act 1 and said, "And here, when Rick bars the slimy gambler from entering the gaming room, he's just a stock Englishman who writes bad checks. How about we make him a representative of Deutsche Bank?"

"As I live and breathe!" said a female voice from outside the office, in the hallway. "They're here! Both of them! Before lunch! In the office!" Alice looked up and there stood Miss Lee, the bosses' boss. Today she wore a blue print dress under an off-white jacket with the sleeves rolled up, looking like she had stepped out of *The Front Page*. She glided into the room all smiles, cup of coffee in one hand and cigarette in the other.

"They're here all right, and they've got company," said Alice, "so guess who hasn't gotten a thing done."

Miss Lee took in the brothers and their guest. "Is everybody playing nice?" she asked Alice. Opinions on Irene Lee among the secretaries and typists varied; some figured she had slept her way into management. Some admired her pluck, or her style, or both. To Alice, Lee remained a mystery—how had this tiny woman managed to stay alive in such dangerous waters? Why did she want to buck the stares and the comments when she so clearly didn't fit? She was David against a hundred Goliaths, which made

Alice root for Miss Lee every day.

"It's been smooth sailing," said Alice. "No meanness. No practical jokes."

As Lee stood next to the seated Howard, he remembered his manners and jumped to his feet to offer her the chair. She sat delicately, rested her cigarette in the ashtray, and crossed her legs. "Howard, if you get a sudden memo saying you're in trouble and Mr. Warner wants to see you, suspect these two. Or if you get a phone call supposedly from Mr. Warner's secretary or Mr. Wallis's secretary instructing you to do something outlandish, make sure it isn't the voice of this one," and she nodded toward Alice.

"They make me do these things!" said Alice. "I don't want to do them. But they threaten to hide my car keys or replace my toothpaste with Preparation H. Awful things. And I know they'll do it!"

Phil said, as if to change the subject, "Howard's got some great ideas for Act 1. Stuff we never would have thought of."

"That is exactly what I want to hear," said Miss Lee.

"Here's one for you guys," said Koch to the Epsteins and Irene. "I was thinking that Rick and Renault could play a chess game throughout the course of the picture. Something that symbolizes the intrigue of the city and the characters. In fact, they could be playing chess in that first scene we talked about, when Renault says he knows all about Rick's ventures on the losing side."

"Mr. Koch," said Julius, "I invite you to write a chess game into the script, so I can have the satisfaction of scratching the chess game out of the script."

"What's wrong with a chess game?" said Lee.

"It's straight out of drawing room melodrama," said Phil.

"Yeah, there's nothing like reaching out from the screen to

beat your audience over the head with a metaphor," said Julie.

"But you liked my other ideas," said Koch.

"Because your other ideas were pretty good," said Phil.

"It sounds like I came in and interrupted some sort of amazing chemistry," said Miss Lee, and she arose and stamped her cigarette out in the ashtray on Alice's desk. "Play nice, children," she called over her shoulder as she headed for the door.

"Okay, one more and then I'll go," said Howard. The boys waited. "After Ugarte's arrest, Victor and Lois walk in. I'm feeling like we need someone from the resistance movement to greet Laszlo, our de Gaulle character, and quietly inform him that the man he had come to meet for exit visas, Ugarte, has been arrested. We need to establish that he's already a celebrity, and there's a vast underground network he's leading."

"I like it," said Phil.

Julius jumped to his feet and said, "Up until the very moment a chess game breaks out, I'm with you, Howard."

CHAPTER 36

Joy Page reasoned that if she became an actress on salary at Warner Bros., she might be able to escape Papa Jack Warner's estate at 1801 Angelo and find a quiet life on her own, away from Mother, Papa Jack, and their ever-uglier arguments. Drama coach Sophie Rosenstein became a central part of Joy's plan; Sophie had excellent connections inside the studio, and when the writers completed Act 2, Sophie obtained a copy of the script at once and went over it with Joy. Annina Vierek had become Annina Brandel, and Annina's part in Act 2 was large but not too large. Sophie led Joy through the dialogue hour after hour, until Joy would beg for a break. Papa Jack grew increasingly grumpy at the idea of Joy trying out for the part, which led to big arguments with Mother and the slamming of doors, and then apologies, and the process would start all over again. Through it all, Joy never revealed to Sophie the reason she wanted to become an actress: to escape from Mother. As the saying went, loose lips sank ships.

Monday, May 4, found Joy at drama school onstage as Annina, with a tall, young actor named Ray Montgomery playing Rick. There were no other students today because Joy's screen test was scheduled for Wednesday after school at four, and Sophie wanted to give Joy one last rehearsal. Standing onstage reciting lines after a long day at Beverly Hills High, with the countdown on to the screen test, Joy cracked. She began to sob without understanding why. A tidal wave of sadness descended upon her all at once, and with Ray Montgomery wearing a frightened expression as he looked at her, Joy wept and couldn't seem to stop.

Sophie rushed onto the stage. "What's wrong, dear?" she demanded, grasping Joy by the shoulders and giving her a shake.

Joy could only weep and feel raw pain, as if someone dear to her had died.

"I'm sorry," the very tall, handsome Ray said to her in his most gentle voice. "I'm sorry if I did something wrong." Joy looked up at him through a sea of tears. Sophie led the girl off the stage and into the wings to a prop couch that the actors used between scenes.

Joy rested her head on one arm of the couch and gazed out at the stage and the empty seats of the theater.

Sophie said nothing. She just sat and waited.

Joy's head felt stuffed with cotton. Sophie handed her a handkerchief and she blew her nose. "Mother pressures me every day about this part," Joy heard her voice say in the big empty space of the studio. "Papa Jack is furious that I want to act. They fight about me and about everything. I don't know. I just don't know."

Sophie said, "What do you want, dear? Do you know what you want?"

Joy felt herself laugh. Nobody ever asked that question. They just told her what she should or shouldn't do, what she should or shouldn't feel. "I'll do anything to get away from them. I'll do anything to escape."

Sophie gave a half-chuckle. She said, "You are like Annina in a way. She is willing to do anything to get out of Casablanca, even sleep with the police captain. And you'll do anything to get away from home," Sophie paused, "even act." Joy looked at her in alarm.

Sophie said, "It's okay, sweetheart. It's just that you don't have the bug like all the others around here. I know you're forcing yourself."

"My secret is out," said Joy. She felt relief course through her and straightened on the couch. "I am Annina, and I'll do anything to get away from 1801, from Mother and Papa Jack. If I can get this part, maybe I can afford an apartment. Maybe I will find peace. And quiet." And then reality crushed down. "But Wednesday is the test. I'm not ready. And if I fail, I won't ever get away from them. I'll be trapped in 1801 forever."

"Listen to me," said Sophie. "You are good enough for this part. And if you connect your own situation to Annina's and use what you are feeling, you will be even better."

Ray had been hanging around the edges of the scenery. He stepped forward silently, and Joy realized what he had witnessed. "Ray, I am sorry," she called out across the span of thirty feet. "You were so nice to agree to read with me today."

Ray drifted closer. "You scared me pretty good," he allowed. Then he said, "Are we all through, Mrs. Rosenstein?"

Sophie turned her attention back to Joy. "I don't know, are we?"

Joy felt a mess; she knew she must look one as well. But she also knew this was her one chance to connect what she suffered inside with the character she would be enacting in the screen test. Joy arose from the couch and said to Ray, "Can you give me five minutes to get myself together? I would love to run through the scene with you one more time."

"Sure," said Ray. "Why not?"

Joy did pull herself together and even rationalized that Annina wouldn't look her best under the pressures she felt in Casablanca. Joy couldn't get over the realization that she was Annina, trapped in her own hell, with bayonets at her back. Energized by this information, she poured her heart out to Rick, played by Ray. They did a read-through and blocked it out together, and then worked on their reactions to each other until by the third run-through, Joy began to feel Annina melting into her. They were one.

Two days passed. She didn't sleep much at all Tuesday night. Wednesday, she went to school and the limousine picked her up afterward, schoolbooks in hand, and raced her to the studio.

With Curtiz directing, Joy aced the screen test. She would remember thinking halfway through, *You are doing it. You are good.* And yet she had stayed in the moment and finished her lines, and then she heard Curtiz say, "Cut!" It was abrupt, so abrupt that she felt her psyche slam on the brakes. She realized she had been outside her own body—such a strange feeling.

The limousine drove her down to Beverly Hills and back inside the prison walls of 1801. She gathered up her schoolbooks from the leather seat of the car and stepped onto the cobblestones of the drive. Inside the front door Mother awaited, like a cat awaiting a mouse.

"Well," said Ann Warner, "were you wonderful? Did you make me proud?"

Joy laughed to herself. During the test she had thought only of making Sophie proud—Sophie, who proved more maternal to Joy in these few months than Mother had in a lifetime. But Mother would believe what she wanted to believe at any rate. "I think I did very well," said Joy.

"That's good," said Mother. "You simply must get this part."

CHAPTER 37

Spring had sprung in Rochester when Ingrid Bergman got the call making it official: she finally had a picture assignment, playing the role of Ilsa Lund in *Casablanca*. After getting this news, Ingrid devoted one more lunchtime to Dottie, celebrating with *ostkaka*, then embarked on a crash diet, and packed up for the train west, Pia and Mabel in tow. She kissed Petter goodbye until they would be reunited after production. In her mind, she didn't want to be reminded of Rochester, New York, ever again.

Nine days later she parked her car at the Warner Bros. studio for wardrobe tests. They had sent a girl out to take measurements as soon as Ingrid hit town. As a star, she could drive through the gate and on to the Wardrobe Department and park right in front. She was no longer a Rochester *hausfrau*. She had returned to the world in which she belonged. Inside Wardrobe a rack of clothes on rollers was wheeled in. Not many clothes. Not enough clothes, it seemed to Ingrid, for a feature film.

"Where are the others?" Ingrid asked of the woman who had rolled in the rack. Ingrid dragged each garment along the long rod. Blouses, skirts, jackets, a traveling suit. Hats rested on the wireframe shelf above the rack. But where were the evening clothes David Selznick had mentioned—the glamorous outfits of a European woman of mystery, as Ilsa Lund was supposed to be?

"This is it, Miss Bergman," answered the woman, looking at a list on a clipboard.

Just then, two men swept into the room. One was handsome and young, with scripts in hand, the other plain and middle-aged. This older man wore a gray business suit and smiled broadly, thrusting out his hand. "Hal Wallis, Ingrid. It's a pleasure to finally meet you." As she shook his hand, Wallis said, "This is my assistant, Paul Nathan. We're thrilled to get this far—wardrobe tests!"

She loved the idea that the executive producer would seek her out, the powerful Hal Wallis, and she also felt attracted at once to the handsome Nathan as they shook hands. "I'm so grateful for this part," said Ingrid. "It's wonderful to be back. You have no idea."

"Rochester, wasn't it?" said Wallis. "I've been to upstate New York. Beautiful country, but in winter, you can have it."

Ingrid shoved the memories aside and turned to the wardrobe rack. "I'm most curious about my clothes for the picture. Most curious. Where are the gowns? I've heard so much about Orry-Kelly, and I can't wait to see what he's designed for me."

Wallis hesitated, and Nathan said, "We had some issues with the new regulations. No silk. No unnecessary zippers. As little wasted material as possible. War-related, you know?"

"All very true," said Wallis. "We aren't allowed to build new sets. We've got to reuse everything possible. The Paris train station that's in the script, that'll be reused from a picture we're shooting now. Lumber, nails—everything's in short supply."

Ingrid tried to process all that the men were telling her. This was not the Hollywood she remembered, the richest place on earth, the place where dreams came true, especially hers. Why should the government care if her blouse was silk? She reached out and rubbed the material of one of the garments; it was cotton.

Cotton! How would cotton look on-screen? She would not shine in cotton. She couldn't for a moment imagine a UFA production allowing such measures to interfere in this way. It was madness.

Still touching the fabric, she heard herself say in a faraway voice, "Does Charlie Feldman know about this?"

Out the corner of her eye, she saw Wallis and Nathan exchange glances. "The rules apply to everyone," said Nathan, "on every production."

She felt herself growing impatient. She turned squarely to the men. "And the gowns? Where are the gowns?"

"Paul and I were discussing it," said Hal, "and I thought, are Ilsa Lund and Victor Laszlo not refugees who have fled from the Nazis more than once? If that's the case, where did the gowns come from? Did the escapees leave Czechoslovakia and France with trunks filled with clothes? No. They grabbed what they could and they fled, and there are no gowns because Ilsa left them behind. She sacrificed her gowns for the cause."

Ingrid kept scraping the hangers of clothes along the rod on the rack. The upshot seemed to be there were no gowns for *Casablanca*. She knew on instinct that she dared not be angry—Selznick had presented her with no other pictures to make; *Casablanca* was it. And yet she felt herself boiling, nonetheless.

"Then who is this character," she said testily, "this Ilsa, who dresses like a peasant and follows some man through Europe? Why should this part interest me—or the audience, for that matter? What cause is it that would make me give up even the clothes off my back?"

She wondered at once if she had made a tactical error, for Wallis and Nathan both studied her with what seemed to be offense. She had reminded herself often between New York and California that she must not allude to the fact that she had worked for the Germans, and she had heard Herr Goebbels, and she didn't really have a problem with whatever the Nazis were after because it simply didn't concern her. Her mother was German and she knew the Germans to be a fine people. She also understood, intellectually anyway, that no one in America would follow this line of logic now that war had been declared. She was, so to speak, in Rome and when in Rome . . .

"What cause would make you give up the clothes off your back?" Wallis repeated. His voice had grown flat. "Freedom is the cause. Liberty. Not just for you and me, but for all people. Especially Jews and others who are being murdered right now in Europe and in the Far East."

Concentration camps. Murder. Ingrid felt horrified by her own shortsightedness. "Of course, of course," she said in almost a whisper.

"We are at war, Ingrid," said Wallis, looking her dead in the eye. "We are at war for the soul of the entire planet. Every picture we make is keeping that thought front and center, including *Casablanca*."

"Especially *Casablanca*," added Nathan.

Such a blunder she had made. She knew it now, from looking into their faces, and feeling the shock and hostility pouring off them. "Forgive me, please, gentlemen," she said softly. "I have had many difficult months and a long journey to get here. If the character requires these clothes, then that is fine. I want only to interpret a fine character. Do you have a script for me?"

Nathan held out a script for her and said, "This is new as of yesterday."

"It's rough, Ingrid," said Wallis. "I would only look at the first two acts; we are still working on your character, and Act 3 is something of a mess right now."

"And what can you tell me of Ilsa?" she asked.

Wallis considered the question. He said, "Ilsa is a complex woman. She is in love with two men."

Nathan added, "She's torn between the men throughout, but haunted by Rick and what they had in Paris. A wild love affair."

The way Nathan said it, Ingrid felt herself engage. "In love with two men; that could be interesting to play. As long as she's not a victim. As long as she's not a mannequin in cotton who stands around pining for one man or the other."

Wallis said, "Your character is vital to the action. You appear at plot point one and spin the story on its head. Later you pull a gun on Rick and demand visas to get you and your husband out of Casablanca. And I'm having my writers give you more to do. More scenes. Better scenes."

"And who wins my heart in the end?" asked Ingrid.

Wallis smiled, but she thought it a bitter look on his face. "We are wrestling with that," he said. But he quickly added, "Wrestling is an American word. We are working on the script to decide why Ilsa must leave Casablanca with Victor, no matter how she feels about Rick. Our censors insist that this married woman must leave with her husband, but that becomes difficult because the love story is Ilsa and Rick, the American she must leave behind."

"In love with an American and married to a Czechoslovakian, whom she idolizes," said Bergman."

"Yes, exactly," said Wallis.

"Interesting," said Ingrid. "Very interesting."

"When you read this," said Wallis, rapping her copy of the script with his knuckle, "you will see two very strong acts. Making

Act 3 plausible is the challenge I've given to our story department."

"One good thing about a script that is not yet final," said Ingrid. "You can tailor the lines to the actress. Ilsa must be interesting. Ilsa must be memorable. I want a part I can sink my teeth into. Can you do that much for me? Clothes? Unimportant, if the character is worth playing."

"My writers are doing all they can with it," said Wallis.

"Well, then, get out the whip," said Ingrid with a smile meant to soften the words, "and make them do more."

CHAPTER 38

Irene kept a running score of her remaining time at the studio. If the chief had his way, she thought as she sat in the boardroom, she would be gone in nine weeks. An Epstein sat on either side of Irene, and across the table sat, left to right, Curtiz, Koch, and Nathan as all prepared to review Acts 2 and 3 delivered by the boys and Act 1 polished by Howie, an exercise complicated by the fact the Epsteins were removing some of Howie's additions and Howie kept insisting some of the Epstein humor had to go.

Hal walked in and took his usual spot at the head of the table. "I've never seen anything like this," he said by way of hello. "My leading lady is being fitted for wardrobe, and I'm having to tap-dance around the fact there's no final script."

"I wouldn't show her our Act 3," said Phil. "Act 3 is rough."

Wallis looked at Phil. "I can't wait any longer—we shoot next Monday."

Koch lit his pipe and said, "The script can't be finished by then." He said it matter-of-factly, as if oblivious to the stress of the executive producer, or of the story editor, or of his fellow writers. Or was Howard delighting in their stress? Whichever it was, Irene wished he hadn't said what he had said.

"That's why we're here, Howard," Wallis said testily, "because we have to shoot and I want agreement on some things."

"Fine with me," said Julius, with an edge.

"And me," added Phil.

The silence of the group, knowing that cameras would roll in mere days, was a vast, still pool. Irene decided a little perspective at this moment couldn't hurt, and so she put her hands together, took a deep breath, and dove in: "For the most part, I think we are in a great place. The characters are so goddamn strong and well defined from going over and over the scenes and motivations. I love the idea of Laszlo as a resistance leader like de Gaulle. I love all the new stuff to build up Henreid's part, and all the new lines for Greenstreet and Veidt."

Wallis listened, hands folded on the tabletop. When Irene ran out of words, Hal continued to listen, awaiting more, awaiting someone else to jump in. No one else did. "I agree, Renie," said Wallis, finally. But he stopped there, abruptly so, and the room grew quiet again. He pulled out a memo and looked at Koch. "Let's talk about the memo you sent me, this new scene you want to add, Howard. You want to stage the underground meeting and give Henreid a speech to his followers."

Koch said, "Yes, we need that speech. We need to see Victor in action—like de Gaulle on the BBC."

"Bullshit," said Julie. "We allude to the meeting of the underground. We don't need to see it, because we talk about it. We know all we need to know about Laszlo. We can't give him a big speech at the start of Act 3."

Phil said, "And Henreid already has the 'Marseillaise' scene, and that's plenty enough to establish his leadership."

Koch adjusted his lanky frame in his chair. He sat back and puffed on his pipe. "Granted, but Victor's speech reminds us what we're all fighting for: good against evil."

Into the ensuing silence, Wallis interjected, "While I am certain that Henreid would love such a scene, and yes, it's an important message, I think there's a danger of tipping the picture in Henreid's favor." Hal paused without looking at anyone in the room. Instead, he looked at his clenched fingers as he added, "And the last thing we need is Henreid's head getting any bigger."

Curtiz said, "Bogie not be happy we give Laszlo speech."

Hal nodded gravely. "The action of Act 3 is to resolve the love triangle."

"And staging the underground meeting would mean adding another set to build and a couple days of shooting," said Nathan. "A budget-buster."

"Case closed," said Julie with an undertone of glee.

"I'll trade you," said Koch to the group. "Give me the underground meeting and let's ditch the Paris flashback sequence."

"No!" barked Curtiz. "We need to see happy times for couple! Paris sequence make all happy! Must stay in script."

"Good," said Julie, tapping the tabletop with his knuckles as he said it. "Let's move on."

Irene could feel Howard's frustration over losing the battle, and she needed to keep him in the game. "All your points are valid, Howie," she allowed. "But let's talk about your stroke of genius, using the business the boys put in about the woman winning roulette on 22 to resolve the story of the Bulgarian kids."

"Yeah," said Julie. "We feel like chumps for not thinking of that ourselves." For all the egos Irene had to wrangle in the Writers Building, she knew her writers were awfully good. She watched Howard brighten.

"The kids win enough to escape, and Rick saves Annina from Renault," said Nathan. "It's poetic."

"The way I shoot that, there won't be dry seat in house," assured Curtiz with reverence.

The room erupted in laughter. Mike's face grew red at not knowing what he had said wrong, that the expression was a dry eye in the house, not a dry seat, but God love him, Irene thought. These guys needed a laugh and the tension broke like an August thunderstorm. Wallis pulled out his handkerchief and swiped at tears, then blew his nose. "I guess we can hope there's not a dry seat in the house," Hal said.

"Or not," said Phil.

They laughed some more. Hal wiped his face again and said, "Now that we all feel better, let's feel worse again." He pulled out a set of papers. "I've gotten reaction from Breen on Acts 1 and 2."

"Shit," Julie muttered.

Irene knew the government censors must see and approve the script, of course, and the writers were used to this step in the process. Wallis looked down the list of demanded changes and deletions. "Mr. Epstein," said Wallis, "Mr. Julius Epstein, Mr. Breen seems to have noticed the disgusting lines you give to Renault about illicit sex with young women."

"Listen, we all know my brother is a pervert," said Phil. "We also know a little spice is good for the soup. And painting Louis as a corrupt official who preys on women becomes important at the end when he does the honorable thing and sides with Rick."

Wallis let this statement sink in a moment; Irene could see it was resonating. She said, "Phil's right, it's important to see Renault grow into a hero. When the couple wins at roulette and Louis sees that Rick has tricked him, he accepts it with grace. Maybe we can salvage enough of the sex lines to keep it interesting."

Wallis said, "Agreed. Let's try." Hearing that, Julie smiled as

Hal said, "Now we come to the biggest issue."

"The ending," said Nathan.

Irene felt her stomach drop.

"Ugh," said Phil.

"The way this is written at present, the ending troubles me," said Wallis. "It's troubled me since the play came in the door." He turned his attention to Irene as he said, "It still troubles me because it doesn't work. Rick is in his club with Ilsa. Victor comes in. Ilsa announces she's staying with Rick."

Hal opened the script to the pages in question. "She says to Victor, 'I hate to tell you this way, but I'm not going with you. I'm staying here with Rick. I love Rick.' How can Ingrid play that? She wouldn't play that because it's not true to the woman who has a resistance-hero husband. She can't leave her husband for the bar owner—it's wrong for the characters. It emasculates Victor. It makes Ilsa two-faced and weak. And even the inference that Rick would go along with it makes him a villain."

Irene felt the air drain from the room. Julie leaned forward, his head in his hands. Usually, he'd be doing that for a laugh, but the horrifying reality was, he meant it. "Yeah, it stinks," he admitted. "It's a play that ended with the hero tossing his gun on the table and giving up. It's what we've had to work with all along."

"We haven't figured it out," added Phil with a sigh. "The only thing we know for sure is that Renault is going to side with Rick at the payoff. It's natural the way the characters have evolved."

Irene couldn't bear the angst. "I'm the one who brought the play to Hal. I always felt there was an answer. And I knew I had the best writers in the world, and they'd find it."

"Fine. Give it to those guys," said Julie.

Hal continued to stare at the script opened on the table before him. "Everybody's standing around in the club. Ilsa tells Victor she's staying with Rick. Then Rick tells her to get out. 'Go with Victor,' he tells her. It's like watching a train derail."

Howard said, "All three sides of the love triangle look bad. Victor says, 'If I had any pride, I'd leave you here, but you're still my wife, so what the hell, let's go.' And she leaves with him? Then into that static moment, Strasser walks in. He wrestles with Rick, who shoots him in the back. In a picture that's supposed to be about ideals, he fills Strasser with lead from behind?"

Wallis nodded. "Renie and I have talked this over. We think it's time to bring in a fresh set of eyes."

Irene jumped in as she saw her three writers begin to panic. "Yes, we sent the script over to Casey Robinson. He's got the time and said he'd compile some notes."

"The mighty Casey," murmured Phil.

"Casey at the bat," added Julie. They didn't sound bitter; they sounded like weary versions of their smart-aleck selves.

"Robinson's not coming on to rewrite the script," Wallis assured, "because a lot of what we have now is stout. I want him to make the love triangle work, which might lead us to an ending." Hal looked at the Epsteins. "In the meantime, give me a better Act 3."

"Better how?" Julie asked. "We need more from you and Mike than 'make it better.'"

Wallis said, "Okay, how about, make it better or else?"

"Renault need change of heart," said Curtiz, drawing every eye in the room. He nodded toward Phil and added, "This one say Renault side with Rick at picture close. Need to work up to that."

"That's a good point, Mike," said Wallis. "And the staginess of the last reel playing out in Rick's. Maybe we should take it outside, set it somewhere else, open up the play some more. We've been staring at the walls of Rick's for a long time. How about a change of venue?" He stood abruptly, declared, "Improve Act 3," and walked out of the room.

The next morning, in the same boardroom, Irene sat in the same seat as yesterday, with Casey Robinson across from her. She had slept badly after awakening with a start, realizing she was out of time to pitch her idea to Hal about getting a screen credit for associate producer. She lay there thinking of a half dozen ways to broach the subject, and none of them seemed to work. In a nightmare, her mother had appeared and stated that Irene was fired from her job at Warner Bros. And Irene was on her knees naked in front of her mother as Leah Levine proclaimed, "Give up, Irene. You're not your brother and you never will be." It was a vivid dream in Natalie Kalmus Technicolor, and it had stuck in Irene's mind throughout the morning.

They waited for Hal in silence as Casey wrote notes at a furious pace on a yellow legal pad. She couldn't imagine what he was writing, but words flew out of his pencil so fast that he could scarcely turn from one page to the next. Robinson was, from Irene's point of view, a mountain of a man; it would take all day to climb to the peak. He had to be nearly a foot and a half taller than she. He was distinguished, fortyish, with big blue eyes and a full head of wavy gray hair. He wore snappy suits and always smelled of cologne. Just the right amount of cologne: a hint. Some men just wanted to knock you over with their cologne and render you unconscious, but Casey wore it just right. He sported probably the biggest ego on the lot fueled by the fact he was the only scenarist who had signed a ten-year contract, but as a Libra, he didn't flaunt the ego and might even admit he was wrong about something. And he had the writing credits to back up his high opinion of himself, including an Oscar nomination for *Captain Blood* and big successes ever since.

As he kept on writing and Irene kept on assessing him, she remarked to herself that Casey had slimmed down in recent months, leading her to assume he was having lots of sex with his Russian ballerina girlfriend, Toumanova. It mustn't be easy to keep up in the sack with a world-class dancer, Irene reasoned, but it seemed pretty obvious that Casey was having a hell of a time trying.

Robinson's copy of the script had already been dog-eared and marked with paper clips. He had scribbled notes on the cover page and marked various spots with slips of paper. There was no doubt that the mighty Casey was indeed at the bat.

Hal entered the room and sat at the head of the table as usual, and Irene noted how awful he looked—as if he hadn't slept either. Robinson stopped writing just as if a professor had said during a blue-book exam, *Pencils down.*

"Well," said Wallis, "what did you think?"

"Do you want a Miniature Review, like in *Variety*?" Casey began with a smile. "If so, then I would say, slick setup, excellent humor—the boys really hit the mark. But—"

"Yeah," Wallis grumbled. "But."

"But the love story is so bad. The love story is going to sink you, and that ending! I just couldn't make sense of the ending, with Rick tricking Victor and then tricking Louis, and Ilsa wanting to stay with Rick but he orders her to go. So she leaves with her humiliated husband and then Rick empties a magazine of lead into Strasser's back. Your hero is a back-shooter who doesn't get the girl. The humiliated man gets the girl." Robinson sat back in his chair and folded his arms casually over his chest, bringing his right ankle up to rest on his left knee. Everything he did was elegant. "By my calculation," Robinson concluded, "all the characters end up miserable. Fade out a million bucks in the red."

Irene watched Hal rub a spot through his tie, just below his breastbone. She suspected he was growing an ulcer in there. She said hopefully, "I thought the boys and Howard did a nice job warming up the Ilsa character. Of course, your suggestion was key, Casey—changing her from American to European."

"Yes, but—" said Robinson.

"Again with the buts," groaned Wallis.

"I don't care for Rick," said Robinson, "and even if she's European, and the boys have warmed her up, I don't care for Ilsa. He's a masochist and she's a sadist, and in the end they both get what they deserve: unhappiness."

"And the camera rolls next Monday," said Hal. "So what the hell do you suggest?"

"Well, toughen up the hero and soften the girl," said Robinson.

"In four days," said Wallis.

Robinson shifted in his seat, calmly, elegantly. His tone said, *Let's be reasonable.* "You're not shooting all of it in four days, Hal. I've made pages and pages of notes of things to rewrite and tighten. Sam the piano player, for example. Great character—I'm urging you to get rid of the rabbit business. That gag worked in the play to have him play 'Run, Rabbit, Run,' but it gets in the way in the picture. Not to mention it's demeaning. So Sam's a vital player who can help to reveal the true nature of Rick and of Ilsa. Maybe each character talks separately to Sam. The scenes of Rick and Louis are fine pretty much as-is, and the Nazi is the Nazi."

Wallis kept rubbing his sternum through his necktie until he finally realized he was doing it and stopped. He turned to Irene. "What do you say, Renie? Can you work with Casey and coordinate it with the boys and Howard?"

"Sure can," she said, trying to hit a mark that was upbeat without going overboard into burlesque. She had that sixth sense going, that jingly feeling at the base of her spine when higher truth was revealed. Casey had just rung that bell somehow, and she saw it as a sign from above to make her move.

Wallis got up to exit the room; she said a rushed, "Hal, can I have another minute of your time?" Robinson didn't need an invitation to leave; he was tactful enough to walk out and close the door behind him, leaving Irene alone with Wallis. He returned to his seat and waited.

Irene's heart pounded. Her mouth grew desert-dry. "I had an idea," she began. "I was hoping to get your approval on it."

Wallis seemed wrung out. "Sure, Renie. I'll do what I can."

This wasn't the perfect time, she realized, but there never seemed to be a perfect time. "I've been with this script every step of the way so far. Story development, casting. I was hoping . . ." She paused; she had his full attention. "I was hoping maybe you'd let me get my feet wet with production when the shooting starts."

He gave her a curious look. "Production?"

"Yes. I'd like to try it out. I'm hoping you'll consider giving me a job as associate producer of *Casablanca*."

It took another moment for the words to come together for him; his face had changed. It was the face of a stranger; an angry stranger.

"You want to be a producer?" he said in a tone that indicated she had somehow betrayed him. He looked down at the stack of papers in front of him, then back at her. "You want to be a producer. Your job isn't good enough for you? Is that it?"

"I love this job," she said. In her mind, the building had begun to crumble around her, as if in an earthquake. "That's just it, I love it so much. Every aspect of it, and I thought—"

By now he had begun shaking his head. "No. Just, no. Don't mention this idea ever again. Not to me, or to anyone in this studio." He got up; he walked out. She was left alone to deal with the rubble.

CHAPTER 39

Jack Warner had not tired of wearing his uniform to the studio every day; he loved that everyone addressed him as Colonel Warner, including Hal Wallis with his big contract and delusions of grandeur. The colonel faced an immediate problem, unfortunately, which demanded something he didn't want to contemplate: he needed to speak with Wallis personally, face-to-face, which he hadn't done since that day he had visited Hal's office to express his displeasure with the rising costs of *Casablanca*, a picture he didn't believe in. Jack sat at his desk and considered the things he would rather do than ask Wallis for a favor. Chewing glass and jumping out of an airplane without a parachute, for instance, but he was in a bind, a genuine bind, because Ann wanted Joy to be cast in Wallis's picture and Jack wanted no such thing. Her screen test was already in the can, and so Jack couldn't put this chore off any longer. On the third try he managed to lean forward and place his right index finger on a button and press it.

"Yes, Colonel?" came a voice on the intercom. It was Bill Schaefer. But just this instant a commotion out the window caught Warner's attention, and he jumped from his seat to look outside. There, on the tennis court directly below his window, on Jack's grass tennis court, a doubles match had begun, and he felt his head burn red-hot. The goddamn Epstein brothers were on his tennis court playing doubles against Flynn and that German kid Dantine. Jack looked at his watch. It was 10:30 in the morning, and why wasn't Flynn shooting, and why weren't the writers writing?

"Son of a bitch!" he growled into the windowpane.

"Colonel?" said the voice of Bill Schaefer on the intercom. But Warner kept glaring out the window to watch the game in progress. If any of those bastards tore up the tennis court, he'd fire their asses. But all four knew what they were doing—if it hadn't been his court or his time, he would have enjoyed watching the match because Flynn was just about the best in town and the Epsteins had won doubles tournaments at the West Side Club.

"Colonel?" said Schaefer, in person now. "Chief?" he said again, by way of prodding.

Jack spun on his heel. "I want those sonsofbitches off my tennis court," he snapped. Schaefer tip-toed across the room to the window and watched for a moment.

"That's Flynn," he said to Warner.

"I know it's Flynn!" Jack shouted.

"It's in his contract; he can use the court," said Schaefer.

"Well, those schmuck writers don't have it in their contract," said Warner.

"But if they're Flynn's guests . . ." said Schaefer, letting the remainder of the thought hang in the air.

Warner forced himself away from the window. "Fine," he said to calm himself down. "Fine," he said again. He had been told by Dr. Ryan, his personal physician, that he had better rein in his temper or he might just keel over with a heart attack, and it was moments like this that set him off. "Fine!" he said a third time, after hearing Ryan's voice in his head.

"Fine?" repeated Schaefer.

Warner wiped the slate clean with a wave of his hand. "Listen, I need a moment with Wallis in his office. Can you see if he's available for a chat? A chitty-chat?"

It was clear that Schaefer couldn't believe his ears. "You," he said slowly, "you want a chat with Mr. Wallis." Schaefer pondered some more. "In his office?"

The words as said by Schaefer hit Warner like a slap across the face. "No!"

"No?" asked Schaefer.

"No, tell you what. Get Obringer in here. I want to know exactly what's in Wallis's contract. Tell Roy to bring the contract. I want to know how I can get some things I want."

One look at Schaefer showed he didn't understand, but then Bill was clueless anyway, so no matter. Warner gave a quick little wave in the air to scoot Schaefer out of the room and summon Obringer. Seconds crawled by into a minute and then two minutes, with Warner hearing tennis rackets hitting balls in the distance, until finally Roy Obringer, a big, strapping guy in a dark suit, appeared in the doorway. He always wore dark suits. Jack imagined Obringer woke up in a dark suit and showered in a dark suit.

"You wanted to see this, Colonel?" asked Obringer as he strode into the room holding a manila file folder bulging with pages.

"Shut the door," snapped Warner. Obringer did as ordered.

Warner sat down at his little round table in the corner and motioned for the lawyer to follow.

"I want to know what's in there about Wallis hiring actors."

Obringer was a good deal sharper than Schaefer and opened the folder without hesitation; in seconds he found the contract language and read aloud, "Mr. Wallis has first call and right to use the services of any director, actor or actress, writer, unit manager, cameraman, and administrative assistants who are under contract with the company who are not otherwise actually engaged in other productions at the time Wallis may need them."

Warner forced himself to remain silent during the oration while needing to scream throughout. "Aha," he said when the lawyer fell silent. "What if it's an actor not under contract? What if it's a minor?"

Roy assessed Warner and the questions. "You mean your stepdaughter?"

"Yes, Joy. Yes."

Obringer carefully closed the folder and set it on the table as he formulated a response. "As her legal guardian, I imagine, yes, you could forbid her from working at the studio. Then it wouldn't be a matter of Mr. Wallis or his contract. It would be a matter of the law."

These were the words Jack wanted to hear, but his frustration boiled over. "Shit! I can't. Ann would kill me. Ann would rip the house to shreds and then she would kill me." Warner forced himself to think of Dr. Ryan again. "Motherfucking Hal Wallis," he muttered.

"I should tell you," said Obringer, who hesitated then added, "Mr. Wallis has asked me to draw up a contract for Miss Page at $100 per week for four weeks."

"So he is gonna use her."

"That's his intention. Yes."

Outside his picture window, Jack could hear the doubles match and the calls of the men on the court: "Take it!" and "I got it!" and "Good shot!" and "Shit!" But he wrenched his gaze over to the framed photo on the credenza—the portrait of sexy, impossible Ann.

"Oh, the price of pussy," he said under his breath, but loud enough for his companion to hear. Then, louder, "I want Wallis to pick somebody else. It's got to be his idea so I can say to those crazy broads, sorry, I tried, but he said no."

"The only thing I can advise," said Obringer as he arose, "is to ask Mr. Wallis as a personal favor." The attorney departed, and Jack fumed for a moment, then got up and buzzed Schaefer to come in again.

With bile rising in his throat, he watched Bill appear at the door and said, "See if Wallis is in his office." And then Jack corrected himself. "See if Mr. Wallis is in his office and can spare a moment."

Bill scurried off and came back in less than a minute. "He's in his office and he's alone. He's got ten minutes before his next meeting."

Warner nodded. He straightened his uniform for the umpteenth time, drew in a deep breath, and walked past Schaefer, out his door, down the hall, and up to the edge of Wallis's domain. He raised his fist to knock when he saw Hal at his desk but thought better of it and simply walked in. On seeing Warner, Wallis stood as if in deference to the uniform.

"Good morning, Colonel," said Wallis with an annoying pleasantness. "What's up?"

Warner reached behind him and closed Hal's door. He didn't need anyone overhearing. "I'm wondering if you can do me a personal favor."

Wallis's ever-present veneer seemed to crack just a little at hearing such a sentence from the mouth of Jack L. Warner. "I'll try to help if I can," said Wallis.

"My stepdaughter tested for your picture."

"I know. I saw the test. She's excellent. You should be very proud of her."

The words stung, but Warner pushed on. "My wife wants Joy to get the part, but it does me no good to see that kid in the picture business."

Wallis seemed confused. "What's wrong with the picture business?"

"For you or me, nothing. But for that kid, everything. It's beneath her. It's beneath any Warner to get into acting. She's all wrong for that kind of life, so I'm asking you as a favor: find somebody else."

"It's a little late for that," said Wallis, reaching down to shuffle through the papers on his desk. "I've already asked Obringer to get a contract together for Joy because she's perfect. She's dark. She's exotic. And, frankly, she's different. I want faces that are fresh, and Joy's got that—a fresh face. Exactly what this picture needs. I'm sorry, genuinely sorry, because she's family. Had I known a couple of months ago . . ."

Warner felt his temples throbbing with every heartbeat. "Even if I come to you hat in hand and ask."

Wallis said, "If I had the luxury of time, yes, I would absolutely find somebody else. But we're shooting in three days, and she knows the part."

This is what you get for playing nice, Jack thought as he turned to leave.

Wallis said, as if to help, "I'll get her in here and closed out as fast as I can."

Warner forced a nod and again stepped toward the door.

"And, Colonel?" said Wallis in a quiet voice. "I think we need to call a truce."

"What are you talking about?" said Warner.

Hal rose to his feet and slid hands in pockets. "The way it's been. It's bad for business that we don't talk like we used to. I think there are things we need to say—about *Casablanca*, for example."

"What's to say? Your little story editor convinced you to buy it, and that reminds me—her contract is up August 1, and I want to bring somebody new in. I've got a couple of men in mind."

Wallis's mouth fell open. "Replace Irene Lee? Why, in God's name?"

Warner felt on firm ground. "The *Casablanca* debacle, for one thing. This picture can't help but fail because after insisting we buy the play, she can't get her writers to make it work. I don't like to lose money, especially on this scale, because of some broad with no head for business."

Hal seemed in pain; he didn't seem angry, he seemed wounded. He turned away toward the window and said, "Can I ask you something, Chief?"

"You can ask," said Warner.

"When was the last picture I gave you that ended up in the red?"

Warner searched his memory. "I can't recall offhand, but I'll bet Paul Muni starred."

Hal turned back, a smile on his lips. "I'll bet you're right," he said. "I think my track record allows me to say *Casablanca* might be something extraordinary. It's a picture the world needs right now, and we are going to give it to them—if only we can work out Act 3."

Jack remembered the old days when they could shoot the breeze for half an hour at a time. This was that Hal Wallis, and he was looking at Warner expectantly.

"All right," said Jack, "I'm a gambling man. I will give you some more time to work out your script, and I'll be the first to congratulate you if the picture works out and we make money."

Wallis smiled, but that smile faded when Warner added, "But if it doesn't work out, Miss Lee will be replaced on August 1. That's the terms of the truce."

He put out his hand, as if daring Wallis to shake. Hal took it; they had a deal.

CHAPTER 40

Dooley Wilson found the Warner Bros. studio to be a world apart from Paramount. He was accustomed to taking the streetcar part of the way to the Paramount lot and going shanks' mare the rest. But Warner Bros. sent a car that drove him in style over the peaks from Los Angeles into the San Fernando Valley. On this first day of production, he reported to Makeup and Wardrobe and then was led down to Stage 12A, where the French café was ready. At least twenty men prepared equipment, and a cluster of men and women riffled through script pages, the air electric at the kickoff of a new picture. He had never been in on a picture from the beginning; he would just come in for a few days here and there. This felt different. He allowed the possibility that this could be the one—he and Estelle might finally get that house. And just as fast, he shoved the thought out of his head as bad luck.

The set of La Belle Aurore, a Parisian café, looked authentic enough. There were a half-dozen tables, each with a checkered cloth covering, a piano sat in the center of the set, and odd wall angles closed in around it, as if the various parts of the restaurant had been added over centuries. A low, beamed ceiling completed the authentic effect. As he stood taking it all in, another Negro approached, a welcome friendly face. "Eliot, I heard you'd be here. It's wonderful to see you." Dooley shook hands with Eliot Carpenter, piano player and band leader with whom Dooley had played drums many times in New York.

Only now did the giant camera get wheeled into view. It must have weighed 300 pounds the way the men were muscling it. The camera faced the set and then a second piano was rolled in near the camera. "I'll be doing the playing," said Elliot. "You know the song, right? 'As Time Goes By'?"

"Oh sure, I been singing it for a week, getting ready. And listening to the piano on a record album and practicing the hand movements."

A tall man with dark hair, an athletic build, and friendly face approached. He held a binder in his hand. "Dooley Wilson, I'm Hugh McMullen, the dialogue director. I'll need to borrow you for a few minutes so we can go over your lines and delivery." This man sounded like a teacher, with crispness in his voice and words.

"Yes sir, sure thing," said Dooley. They walked over to camp chairs lining the edge of the set.

The teacher said, "Now, I've gone over all this with Mike and he agrees with my approach." McMullen paused, collecting his thoughts. "Bear with me here. Sam is Rick's friend. You, Sam, look out for Rick. Always, you are looking out for Rick." He paused, studying Dooley carefully. "We want you to underplay that. Mr. Wallis loves your calmness. You are the anchor for Rick. You've seen a lot in your life all over the world. You use what you've learned to protect your friend. Can you do that for me?"

Wilson laughed to himself, then said aloud, "I have seen a lot in my life. All over the world. I played in French cafés much like this one that you've built here. A dozen of them."

"Really," said McMullen, genuinely impressed. "Then bring it all to bear. Okay, give me your first line in Scene 118. Hugh opened his script. "Rick says, 'Henri wants us to finish this bottle and then three more. He says he'll water his garden with champagne before he lets the Germans drink any of it.'"

Hugh McMullen looked up, anticipating Dooley's line. Dooley couldn't quite decide what it meant to underplay. He took a breath and said, "This sorta takes the sting outta bein' occupied, don't it, Mister Rick?"

The dialogue director winced. He didn't make eye contact, and Dooley felt foolish for missing the direction. But then it became clear that McMullen was processing what he had just heard. "That's Sam played as comic relief," he said carefully. "Now think about this: Sam has no intention of touching the champagne. He doesn't want to be seen as a spoilsport, so he's just playing along to please Rick." McMullen took a moment to look Dooley in the eye. "And consider this: Sam doesn't care for champagne. Do you see what I mean? Sam, in fact, is his own man. A very thoughtful man. Try that." He cued Dooley again.

"This sort of takes the sting out of being occupied, doesn't it, Mister Rick?" The delivery felt different to Dooley. It was slower, quieter. Suddenly it was something he might have said to Estelle or to any friend.

"Yes, better," said McMullen. "The script is written as Negro slang, and I wish it weren't. Play it like it isn't Negro slang and let's see how that goes." He flipped two pages of the script. "Now, Scene 120. Rick says to Ilsa, 'Here, drink up. We'll never finish the other three.'" McMullen looked at and nodded to Dooley.

Dooley knew the lines, but this delivery—he hadn't practiced anything like this: "Dem Germans'll be here mighty soon. They'll come lookin' for you. There's a price on your head."

The dialogue man wasn't pleased. He was wincing again. "Less of a pronouncement. More of an observation, and a warning. Take your time with it. And, quieter." Dooley said the line again, slower, quieter. McMullen nodded his approval. "Yes. Practice it just like that. Remember what I said. Unlearn everything they told you at Paramount. Underplay. Got it?"

Dooley did get it; he couldn't believe it, but he got it. The dialogue man rushed off to speak with Humphrey Bogart, who huddled with Curtiz. Then a tall woman with the face of an angel and light brown hair floated into the conversation with the men. Dooley sort of gasped. He knew he was gawking, which one dared not do on a movie set—a colored man gawking at a white woman—but he searched his memory and all the places he had been to think of a more beautiful white woman. None came to mind. With nothing else to do for the moment, he kept on looking.

But then he noticed another conversation. Three crew members were working frantically twenty feet away. One man wore headphones while another man held the microphone on a ten-foot boom. Usually, the boom was just above the frame of the camera, but the boom operator kept bumping into the beam of the ceiling above the piano.

The conference between the four people, the director, stars, and dialogue man, proceeded for a solid fifteen minutes. All the while, the sound people scurried and whispered and sweated.

A fifth man, older, full of energy, joined the main conference of actors and director and then turned and hollered, "Places everybody! Let's try one!"

Dooley knew the tall, angry director, Mr. Curtiz, from his screen test. Curtiz barked where he wanted the marks for his actors to be placed. "I say, 'Action one,' piano start playing, Sam start singing. Sam here (sitting at the piano). Ilsa here (standing on the far side of the piano). Rick position one (at the bar). Position two (fifteen feet away, beside Ilsa at the piano). Quickly!"

Dooley hurried to the piano bench. "Sam play song and sing. I say, 'Action two,' Rick take bottle from bar, walk to piano. Camera follow. Pour champagne, say lines. We cut. Ready!"

"Quiet please! Quiet on the set!" yelled a voice. The same voice, after about five seconds, called, "Lights!" Artificial daylight from sun arcs poured in through all the windows of the café and Dooley felt himself bathed in its warmth. But he could also hear a certain pitch from the lights. A middle A that he wasn't used to hearing on a movie set.

"Camera," said the director, who had grown quiet now.

"Speed," said the cameraman.

A sound assistant appeared and held his slate before the lens. "Scene 118, take 1," he said and snapped the slate.

"All right, make movies now!" said the director in such a way that Dooley couldn't tell whether he was having fun or not. "Action one," called the director. Over his shoulder, Dooley could begin to hear Eliot playing "As Time Goes By" on the piano. Dooley mimicked playing along and after a bar he sang softly in accompaniment.

"Action two!" whispered the director. Dooley could hear Bogart's heels moving on the floor behind him and then Rick, holding a bottle of champagne, made his way around the piano to stand beside the lovely woman.

"Henri wants us to finish this bottle and then three more," said Bogart cheerfully as he poured champagne into three glasses sitting atop the piano. "He says he'll water his garden with champagne before he lets the Germans drink any of it."

The piano playing off camera stopped, which was Dooley's

cue. "This sort of takes the sting outta being occupied, doesn't it, Mister Rick?"

"You said it!" said Rick happily. He turned to the woman as they both held glasses of champagne. "Here's good luck to you," said Bogart, and they sipped their champagne.

A cue was heard off-camera—both stars look to the window in alarm at pretend German cannons. "Cut!" said Curtiz. "Back to first position! We do again!" And they did. After the second take, which had gone identically to the first, Bogart set down his glass.

"Mike! Hugh!" called Bogart. Dooley watched the director and dialogue director approach hurriedly. Bogart said, "That line stinks. 'Here's good luck to you'? What the hell is that? I wouldn't say that to anybody, ever, especially not a girl I'm supposed to be in love with."

"I can get Koch down here to change it," said McMullen.

"Koch don't know," growled Bogart. "It's a toast. So something that's a toast. Here's looking at you. Something like that."

"Kid," said the woman with a smile as she looked at Bogart. "You called me 'kid' a little while ago without even realizing. I liked it." The pretty lady had a lovely voice and how her eyes sparkled.

"Yeah, 'Here's looking at you, kid,'" said Bogart. "Yeah. Exactly."

"Script girl, change!" shouted Curtiz. "Back to one!" Scene 118, take 3 went well enough that Curtiz ordered it printed. After the take, Bogart set the champagne glass down on top of Sam's piano.

"That's nice delivery there, fella," Bogart said to Wilson, who arose from the piano bench in deference. "And a sweet singing voice."

"Dooley. Dooley Wilson," he said and reached for Bogart's extended hand to shake. "And thank you. Thank you very much."

"Good to know ya," said Bogart, the grip of his handshake

firm. Some white folk wouldn't shake a colored man's hand, and it reassured Dooley that the star wasn't like that.

Bogart turned away and called to Curtiz, "Are we breaking for lunch, or what?"

"You take thirty minutes—no more!" the director barked.

"See you in forty-five," said Bogart, and he walked off without another word to Dooley, who stuck close to Eliot all the way to the commissary. They chose a table next to a conclave of studio writers, where suddenly a bald man pointed at Dooley as he was about to take a bite of his tuna sandwich.

The bald man exclaimed, "It's Sam!" And another bald man sitting next to him turned and revealed he was identical to the first. Dooley didn't take the bite of his sandwich; he placed the sandwich carefully on his plate out of courtesy.

The identical men dragged their chairs over so they were flanking Dooley on either side. "I'm Julius and this is Phil, my brother," said the man on Dooley's right.

Dooley half-rose to his feet and shook the hand of each man, then introduced Eliot Carpenter.

"We wrote all your lines," said the man on Dooley's left, now identified as Phil. "Aren't they good?"

"Well, yes," said Dooley carefully. "It's very fine writing."

"He even sounds like himself!" Julius exclaimed.

"You've been inside our heads for three months," said Phil, "so we feel like we know you." He studied the tabletop. "Where's your script? What are you guys shooting today?"

"Paris scenes in the café," said Dooley. "'This sort of takes the sting outta being occupied, doesn't it, Mister Rick?'"

"Ohmygod, you're perfect!" said Phil.

"Did they tell you about the little problem we have?" Julius asked. "The script they gave you only has a bum Act 3. The ending stinks."

These frantic white fellows bewildered Dooley. "No, I hadn't heard anything about that," he said diplomatically. All he wanted to do now was eat his sandwich and get back to the set because the clock was ticking and the director was, well, frightening. Finally, he took a big bite with the writers on either side of him watching and then continued to eat purposefully until finally Julius stood and dragged his chair to the writers table and Phil followed.

"Back to the salt mine," said Phil.

"Us too," said Dooley, wiping his mouth with a napkin and rising to his feet. Eliot had finished eating as well. Dooley said, "See ya around," to the brothers. "Good luck finishing your script." He watched Julius shoot a friendly finger at him from the writers table, and the colored men walked outside the commissary with the sun directly overhead and beating down. It was hot today and Dooley began to perspire at once.

On the walk back to Stage 12A, Eliot caught Dooley up on the fact that the pretty lady was a Swedish actress named Ingrid Bergman. When they returned to the set, Curtiz had Bergman and Bogart stand beside a darkened window. They were rehearsing.

"With the whole world crumbling, we pick this time to fall in love," Ingrid was saying, her voice hollow on the vast soundstage.

Curtiz hovered over them and listened as they exchanged a few more lines. "Good," he said. "Then clinch, then booms. Pickup now."

"Was that cannon fire or just my heart pounding?" said Ingrid.

"That was the new German 77. And judging by the sound, about thirty-five miles away."

"Boom," said Curtiz, studying the script and providing sound effects. "Now you sit." The couple sat at a table with champagne glasses. "Boom," said the director again.

Bogart said, "And a little closer every minute. Here. Here. Drink up. We'll never finish the other three."

Dooley piped up automatically from his spot as a spectator of this rehearsal. "Dem Germans will be here mighty soon. They'll come lookin' for you. There's a price on your head." Curtiz gave a clenched fist toward Dooley as if to say, *Good going!*

Bogart said smoothly, "I left a note in my apartment. They'll know where to find me."

Curtiz looked about him to see the crew standing and watching. "Good, lunch bums back," he said. "No more rehearsal. We shoot one." The sun arcs came up and streamed in the windows, and there in Dooley's ear was that middle A hum again.

"Scene 120 apple, take 1," said the sound boy before he snapped the slate. Curtiz called action.

"With the whole world crumbling, we pick this time to fall in love," said Ingrid-as-Ilsa.

"Yeah, pretty bad timing," said Rick with a chuckle identical to rehearsal. "Where were you, say, ten years ago?"

She thought a moment. "Ten years ago? Let's see—"

Dooley's line was coming up and he argued with himself over how to underplay it when suddenly, "Cut!" called an urgent voice. Dooley looked about him because it wasn't the director's voice. To his surprise, Dooley saw Bogart and Bergman react the same way—what had they done wrong? Who had called cut?

After a gulf of silence, except for the middle A hum in his ear, Dooley heard the director scream from his chair, "What the fuck! Who call cut?"

"Over here, Mike." The soundman waved his hand in the air

at his audio set fifteen feet away. He was wearing headphones and turning dials. "I've got a hum from the lights. It's mixing in with the voices."

The director shot up to his feet from behind the camera and zoomed to the soundman's station. "Scheid, you goddamn motherfucker! You don't ever call cut. Ever!"

"I've got a hum," said Scheid, to which Dooley wanted to add, "Yes, it's a hum in middle A." But he knew better than to move a muscle.

"Fucking hum!" screamed Curtiz. "To hell with you! To hell with you!" he raged. At which point, soundman Scheid whipped off his headphones and slammed them down on the console.

"To hell with you, Mike! There's a hum from the arc lights and it's bouncing off the ceiling and I'm picking it up in my headset. I can't do anything because we can't position the boom because the ceiling is too low. So what am I supposed to do? Let you roll a few hundred feet of film on a busted take?"

"How you not see this hum, you sound bastard?" raged Curtiz.

"You ordered the lights up and there it was," said Scheid. "It was fine until the lights went up. I debated on whether to mention it before lunch. It's an issue."

As they went back and forth, Dooley turned away and let them rage. His field of vision sitting at the piano included only the two principals—Bogart and Bergman—and he couldn't quite believe it, but Bogart had hidden his mouth with his hand, and Dooley could see that he found it funny. His shoulders were heaving. Dooley made a mental note: anybody who found such a scene comedic had something wrong with him. This was business, and a lot of money was being lost by the minute while these two men argued. Meanwhile, the tall lady, Miss Bergman, stood there with wide, frightened eyes, and Dooley felt bad that she must hear such language and see such anger.

Curtiz and his soundman agreed to try the scene again and let it play through without interruption. So they shot it a second time, and then a third, with everyone on edge throughout. At six o'clock they broke for the day, with Dooley happy that he hadn't flubbed a single line.

As the first day of shooting progressed, Irene had been summoned to Projection Room 5 by Wallis. She hadn't seen him since he shot down her idea to produce, but she had come up with a list of rationalizations why he had done it. Numbers one through five were: Warner would never allow it, so she couldn't hold a grudge against Hal. When Zeus threw a thunderbolt, one didn't ask questions. One ducked.

At Room 5, she found Hal and Paul Nathan waiting. Hal said, "Mike started shooting today and I wanted to step in and watch, but the *Miniver* picture came in and I want us to look at it." Hal had received a print of *Mrs. Miniver* sent over by Metro as a courtesy. Hal said he thought *Miniver* important because of its *au courant* look at wartime topics, and because the word of mouth had been out of this world. He wondered aloud how MGM's director and writers would position the war within the narrative.

"If they've skunked us and done something new, I want to know about it," said Hal, "so we can adjust *Casablanca* accordingly."

Two hours and twenty minutes later, they stepped into the waning sunlight stunned to silence. The lot seemed somber: not much action, and the air had grown very still. Irene knew only one thing from this sneak peek. "I'm in love with Greer Garson," she blurted out as they stepped into the middle of First Street.

"Women don't fall in love with women," snapped Wallis.

"Oh, don't they?" she shot back, arching an eyebrow.

"I have to agree," said Nathan. "Garson was incredible. We need to get her in here to do a picture, but they'll never let her go after this."

Wallis was pale, his face drawn, the way people get when they're standing in front of the casket of a loved one. "I thought I knew MGM product," he murmured. "But from start to finish, *Miniver* is honest and understated. With a sock payoff."

"The way they wove the war into their storyline was poetic," said Irene as she patted her pockets looking for cigarettes, pulled out a pack from her jacket pocket, and lit one. She thought about Garson again. "That's all there is to it; I've got to meet this woman."

"I thought you wanted to be Joan Crawford," said Hal.

"Until today I did," said Irene. "But Garson, oh my God."

Wallis motioned for one of the cigarettes from her pack and also her matches. "The question is," he said, lighting up, "what do we need to do to adjust our script based on everything we just saw out of *Miniver*? They put the war sometimes in the background, sometimes front and center. Their characters had to adjust to the changing circumstances of war."

Nathan said, "The *Miniver* package says to me we're right on target, skipper. Rick and Ilsa see the Germans march on Paris, and there are no heroics. They simply get out of the way, like when Mrs. Miniver has to deal with a Nazi flier in her kitchen. She makes this deal with herself to just get through it because her children are upstairs asleep. It's a practical decision. She doesn't slug him with a frying pan. She does what he tells her. When he faints, she doesn't want to touch his gun. She hides the gun rather than hold him prisoner. I loved that."

Wallis thought some more. "When the Minivers walked into their home after the air battle, half of it was in rubble. It was as if they didn't even take notice."

Irene nodded. "Personal sacrifice," she said, and when the men looked at her, she added, "for the common good. That struck me too. These people aren't about to let the Germans win. Not on any level."

Wallis nodded a long while, checking his own thinking. "Yes. I agree. Does our script hit that mark? That's what I want to know."

Nathan said, "Maybe. It's a different kind of story."

Irene felt such disquiet in her stomach; she thought her writers alone could produce the kind of brilliance in a wartime picture that she had just seen in *Mrs. Miniver*.

Nathan said, "What now, skipper?"

"Clear enough," said Wallis. "Tomorrow morning I want the Epsteins and Koch to get themselves over here and watch this picture. Then I want them to sit down and rewrite Act 3 so it matches *Miniver*'s class."

Irene said, "Getting Julie and Phil over here to watch a movie in a projection room—easy. They like to sit around and do nothing. But, come on, Hal. The Metro writers caught lightning in a bottle. You can't tell my boys to match that. It isn't fair."

"Who the hell wants fair at this point?" said Wallis. "The word is perfect. I want perfect like *Miniver* did perfect, and if I don't get it, I'll take blood instead." And he stormed off.

"What the hell has gotten into him?" she asked.

"No idea," returned Nathan, "but the chief went into his office to see him the other day, and this is how he's been ever since."

CHAPTER 41

A schnauzer sat alert at the bedside of her master, Humphrey Bogart, as he slipped on his shirt and pants. "You don't believe all this crap about the new 'romantic' Bogie, do ya, girl?" he asked the dog, who didn't as much as shrug. She merely wagged her tail, alert for any sign of affection. But a notion had been eating at Bogie; Bob Taplinger and his Warner publicity hounds had determined to make Bogart into a ladies man, and the star wanted nothing to do with it. He looked in the bedroom mirror as he tied his tie and saw what there was to see. He knew for certain that no young girl the likes of Ingrid Bergman would ever give a second look to a Humphrey Bogart, let alone sleep with him—unless the Epstein brothers happened to write it that way. But now, reporters from the insufferable movie rags and even some legitimate papers were lining up to interview Bogart about his approach to wooing women. And then his wife would be scouring each magazine and newspaper for intelligence about her husband's love life. He hadn't nicknamed her Sluggy for nothing—her little fists of steel could fly at any moment; he had even honored her by naming the boat *Sluggy*.

He could hear her downstairs banging around; she was up already and on the prowl. He could also hear the clinking of bottle against glass, which meant that breakfast was bourbon. There were some mornings when she wouldn't drink her breakfast, but they were becoming less frequent.

Bogie glanced at his watch to see it was 6:10. Mary Baker would arrive at 6:30 to drive him to the studio, which was part of the agreement she and Bogie had made: Mary agreed to assess Sluggy's condition each morning in an effort to prevent her from causing mischief.

He spent these quiet predawn moments going over his lines, although he knew them well enough after three full run-throughs the day before as Curtiz and Scheid had had their knock-down–drag-out over the sound quality on Stage 12A. It was hilarious the way the two old pros had gone at it on day one, and there at ringside was thunderstruck Ingrid Bergman witnessing it all, getting her first taste of life at Warner Bros.

Bogie grabbed his suit jacket. "Come on, girl," he said to the schnauzer, and they headed downstairs in the Spanish-style hacienda that meandered over a steep hill above the Sunset Strip and offered impressive views of Los Angeles. The dog reached the first floor without a care, although Bogie was wary.

Sluggy sat on the couch in the darkened living room, tumbler in one hand, bottle in the other. "So, going to work with your new whore, are you?" she said as if learning to pronounce words in English for the first time. She said the word "work" with a spin of nastiness, just to push his buttons.

"Not that it matters to you, dear, but Ingrid, the lady in question, has got no use for me," said Bogart. "We sat there yesterday with nothing to talk about. Hell, I'm practically twice her age. And she's practically twice my height. And if you want to know the truth, it bugs me. I feel like a runt next to her. And she's a kid. Just a kid. So lay off me and lay off her, will you?"

"Yeah? Just a poor wittle kid? Well, I bet she's got a hole between her legs and that's all you ever cared about. I know you. I know what you're thinking." Sluggy had an unfocused stare about her, the one that often led to violence. He felt himself shift forward to the balls of his feet in case she lashed out all of a sudden. On occasions when Bogie drank as much as she did, he often couldn't react in time when she threw a bottle or swung a deadly weapon. But now she did neither. She just occupied the couch like a sack of dirty laundry.

This morning he was sober. Mostly sober anyway, since he had stopped drinking sometime around midnight. He looked at this pathetic excuse of a human and mused that she represented dirty laundry in more ways than one. She could kill his career if she worked at it—kill it in its tracks after he had finally gotten someplace. He said, "What are you gonna do today, sit here and drink? Sit here and brood all day? Get out of the damn house. Get some fresh air. Take a walk along the Strip. Do anything but sit."

She smiled coldly. "Oh, I got plans. See if I don't."

He felt a chill run along his back, which served as his trouble-detector when it came to Sluggy and her stunts. Since the first words out of her mouth this morning concerned Bergman, it seemed pretty obvious where Sluggy would decide to strike. "Stay away from the studio," he said, jabbing a finger in her direction. "Stay away. When I get there, I'm going to tell them at every gate to bar you. Every gate, goddammit. You won't set foot inside that studio."

The doorbell chimed, signaling the arrival of Mary Baker, but the last thing he felt he could do was leave Sluggy like this. She had a lethal quality about her, and if she weren't a drunk, she could find work as a professional killer; he was convinced of it. She had stabbed him in the back with a kitchen knife that one time and broken enough bottles over his head to cause brain damage. Now she leaned forward suddenly. He flinched, which made her laugh. She struggled to focus as she looked up at him standing before her. "See? I knew you had something to hide. Couple days on the job and you're slipping it to the new girl." She sank back onto the couch with a thud. "Bogie don't waste any time. Well, don't you worry. I'll get in. I can get into any studio annnnnytime I want. I've worked at all of 'em. I have ways, you'll see."

"Listen, baby, Mary's here and I gotta go," he said in a gentler tone. Sometimes that worked, sometimes it didn't. "Just take it easy, will you? Eat something. Eat some breakfast. Get some sleep. You want me to run you a bath? I'll run you a bath right now—how about it? I'll put some bread in the toaster. How about some toast?"

The dog stared at the front door across the hallway and began to bark. Between barks, Bogart heard a faint rapping at the door. That would be Mary checking to see if everyone was alive and to clean up the blood if there was blood. Sluggy stared off at nothing. "Sure, some toast," she said so vaguely that he didn't know if she was mocking him.

"Okay, coming right up," said Bogart, rushing to the kitchen. He shushed the dog and then detoured at the run to the front door, unlatched it, and called, "Come on in!"

Inside the kitchen, he stumbled over the poor dog as she waited by her bowl, which prompted him to look down and see that the bowl was empty. He began to consider the implications of arriving late at the studio, which was now inevitable. He pulled a can of Ken-L Ration out of the cupboard and muscled it with the opener. He spooned half of it into the dog's bowl on the floor, then pulled half a loaf of bread out of the ice box, sliced off two pieces, and dropped them in the toaster. By now, Mary had wandered in, and he looked up from his chores to see her pretty face full of concern.

"Bad night?" she asked.

"Nah, no worse than usual," said Bogart. "This is good, getting something into Sluggy's stomach. But she's holding a bottle and I've got to get it away from her. That'll be dicey."

"Let me go," said Mary. "We can't risk your face on the first week."

He knew that if Sluggy came up swinging, she could kill Mary. "No, you butter the toast when it pops, and grab some orange juice. I'll get the bottle."

He tiptoed into the darkened living room and found his wife with eyes open but slack, almost as if the left and right were looking at different points in the room. The empty glass had fallen out of her hand onto the carpet. She held the bottle, which was about a quarter full, against her stomach. He eased his way over and lifted the bottle out of her hand as gently as if it held nitroglycerin. It was so quiet in the room that he could hear the rattle in her breathing. He took the bottle of bourbon to the kitchen and held it over the sink.

"I hate to do this," he said to Mary, and he poured the contents down the drain.

The dog had cleaned her bowl by the time Bogie and Mary returned to Sluggy in the living room. Bogie sat beside her on the couch and put his arm around her to bring her head forward. "Come on, baby, let's eat some toast," he said. She roused herself and grunted. She didn't seem to miss the bottle or the tumbler that she had been holding. He brought the slice of toast up and touched it to her lips. Her mouth opened and he shoved the corner in. She bit down on it and began to chew. "There! That's my baby," he said gently. It wasn't until he urged some orange juice past her lips that she came to. She focused on him, took the small plate he had been holding, and began to eat the toast on her own. She didn't say anything, but it was obvious she had been hungry.

She picked up the glass of juice in a remarkably steady hand, considering. "Awww, did you make me a screwdriver, baby?" she said and bumped his knee with hers in a flirty way. He laughed, and her eyes began to come to life; there was a glint and she gave him a "let's fuck" wink.

"Not at 6:30 in the morning I didn't make you a screwdriver," he said with a smile. This was the Sluggy he could relate to and kid around with. Five years earlier, this had been the girl he loved: savvy, sexy, funny Mayo Methot.

"I promise I'm being a good boy, baby," he said with all the sincerity he could muster. "I promise you. Will you make yourself some coffee and take a shower. And then get the dog out for some fresh air, will you? And don't forget to feed her." Knowing the conversation concerned her, the schnauzer jumped up on the couch and rested her paws and front end in Sluggy's lap.

Sluggy finished one piece of toast and tore into the other, holding the plate higher so the dog didn't poach. The orange juice was soon gone, and Sluggy had grown reasonably alert, even now noticing that Mary stood watching.

"Where'd you come from?" asked Sluggy.

"And a good morning to you too," Mary said with a smile. "I'm your husband's driver, remember? You listen to him, will you, Mayo? Make some coffee and get some fresh air. That's an order." Mary glanced at her watch. "Come on, pal. We gotta go."

He kissed Sluggy on the forehead, scratched the dog behind the ear, and headed toward the door with Mary trailing behind.

"Break a leg," Sluggy called after him. "As a matter of fact, break both." He stopped breathing and looked back; she was smiling. It was a joke. He felt himself sigh in relief, then hurried outside to face the day.

How happy Ingrid was, and how unhappy. She felt joy to be back in Hollywood with Pia and Mabel; ecstasy to be wanted, to be cast, to have a character to inhabit and breathe life into and interpret with all the human frailties and foibles that a screenwriter could dream up. She felt guilty for not missing Petter more than she did. In fact, of those left behind in Rochester, she found herself missing Dottie more than she missed her own husband, and only now did Ingrid understand the deep level at which the two women had connected. But she had Pia to return to every evening for a connection to family, and Mabel to see to Pia's every need.

More than anything, Ingrid found herself already looking past this picture to the one she would never make, *For Whom the Bell Tolls*, which would be rolling soon over at Paramount with Vera Zorina and not Ingrid Berman as the female lead. Why, oh why was she so haunted by this part and so troubled by the fact she had not been chosen?

Ingrid reported for hair and makeup at 7:30 as ordered on day two of *Casablanca*. She seated herself in the makeup chair, and a girl named Peggy reached out to work on her, paused, threw up her hands, and just stared. "Just some lipstick, please," said Ingrid.

"I'll be damned," said Peggy, who caught herself, aware that this was said within earshot of a star. "Oh excuse me. But, I'll be damned." The makeup supervisor came over, inspected Ingrid, combed out her hair, and applied something from a pump bottle to make the hair shine.

The makeup supervisor said to Peggy, "You're right to not put any makeup on her. Just stay close and powder down the shine through the day."

"Yes, ma'am," said Peggy.

When Ingrid walked from the morning sunshine into the temporarily dark cavern of Stage 12A and the set for the French restaurant called La Belle Aurore, she dreaded what she would find there. Would Curtiz and the other man continue their horrid argument? Would there be a killing on the set? Asking herself these questions, she couldn't quite believe her eyes as she progressed from bright sun to darkness to a lit set. The two men who had been at each other's throats the previous day were laughing together. She managed to overhear Curtiz say the words, "I am sorry." She heard that plainly. The soundman named Fanny or Franny or something said, "Okay, Mike." And all the furor of the day before was forgotten! They had been lethally angry with each other!

Michael Curtiz turned away from the soundman with merriment in his eyes. The first thing he then saw was Ingrid standing there holding her script. "Ingrid, my darling! You know what you are? You are my Christmas Baby, the answer to my prayers. So beautiful, so perfect!"

Ingrid thought to herself that as far as she was concerned, no man could go wrong praising her beauty. But the script troubled her, or rather, the lack of a script troubled her. "You are very kind, Michael. But I have a question. When will the script be marked final? The Act 3 in this version is awful, and I need to know when and how it's corrected—who I will finish the story with and why. How can I know how to play the scenes we're shooting today, or any day, until I see the final script?"

He was taller than she, but not by much. She felt that their nearness in height gave her an advantage over some ingenue he could tower over. He stared at her, saying nothing. Then he took her by the hand and said, "Come over here, Christmas Baby. I tell you something."

He led her over to the line of camp chairs. As luck would have it, the one with his name labeled on the back sat next to the one with her name on the back. Each took a seat. "Actually, I tell you two things, my baby. First thing is, script is not done. Writers working on it this minute. But no matter because you do not make this Ilsa girl complicated. This is ingenue role. You play what public wants to see you play, *n'est-ce pas?* Mysterious Swede everyone fall in love with but never figure out."

Ingrid could not believe that a director the stature of Curtiz would tell her something so outlandish. "No." That was her impulse and her response. She caught her breath and then said, "No, no, no, no, no. I will play a human, not some painting from some museum. Ilsa must be interesting. Why do these men love her? I need a completed script to know that. We'll shoot a scene in a minute, Rick and Ilsa professing their love as the Germans march on Paris. What makes them love? What is their story, their beginning-to-end story?"

"Not to worry. Ilsa want Rick but leave with Victor. Some censor thing where married girl stay with husband always."

"Okay, fine, Ilsa will leave Casablanca with Victor," she said. "But how and why?"

He stared blankly for a moment, then shook his head. "You not so much Christmas Baby right now."

"Good, because I don't feel like one," she responded. She realized that Humphrey Bogart had walked into range and stood listening to the conversation. He unbuckled the belt around his trousers, adjusted it, and then walked forward.

He said to Ingrid, "The way I see it, in what we're playing today, you're a mystery. Rick's lines are asking, 'Who are you? Where do you come from? Where were you ten years ago?' Rick doesn't really know you, and he's saying he doesn't know why he loves you. He just does. You know there's more to your story, but for whatever reason, you don't want him to know what it is. Can't we play it that way?"

She gazed into Bogart's brown eyes and felt that for the first time they were communicating. What he was saying at least made some sense; what Curtiz was telling her made none. Bogart added, "It's like we're playing poker and not showing each other what's in our hands, just raising and calling. And my guy Rick is saying, 'I call, kid. What's in your hand?'"

She felt charmed by him. She wasn't a child, but he had called her kid for a second time. She composed her thoughts for a moment, with the two men looking at her. "I can play it that way today, yes. But at some point, I need to know what drives Ilsa. Her passions, her likes, her dislikes. I need that from these writers. I'm telling you, at some point I'm going to need to know."

"They're the best we got, the Epsteins and Koch," said Bogart. "If anybody can find it for you, it's these guys."

Curtiz turned abruptly. "We must shoot!" he yelled to the crew working to set and light the café.

So confusing, all of it. The director called her darling and Christmas Baby one moment and screamed at crew the next. The leading man rather than the director was offering advice on interpreting her character. And there was no finished script! Yes, she was back in Hollywood where she had longed to be, but for what? How could all this confusion lead to anything but disaster?

With the writers viewing *Mrs. Miniver* in Room 5, Hal sat fuming in Projection Room 3 with Renie and Nathan watching rushes from the first day of *Casablanca*. Wallis and Curtiz had decided to begin shooting with the last setup in the flashback sequence because they were able to get three of the actors in one place at one time—Bogart, Bergman, and Wilson—and because this little part of the script had been deemed final by Wallis and the four writers involved. But as the actor portraying Sam simulated playing the song "As Time Goes By," a buzzing could be heard on the audio track. The buzzing was throughout, on all the takes from the entire day. Hal seethed as he watched the dailies.

"Was the sound guy drunk or what?" Wallis snapped.

"It was Fran Scheid," said Nathan, "who's usually great. But he said the ceiling on the set was too low, and he couldn't get a boom mic close enough. And the sun arcs were making noise that bounced off the low ceiling, and Curtiz was at Franny's throat, and voilà."

"But the height of the damn ceiling wasn't exactly a surprise to the sound mixer," Wallis grumbled. "A whole day lost."

"Not entirely lost," said Renie as the dailies played on. "Look at those three." Hal watched the trio of actors, with Sam sitting at the piano and Bogart and Bergman standing with him. "They're very good together. I think this is going to work—which is a big, fat positive, sound or no sound."

"Thank you, Pollyanna," said Wallis, who covered his ears from the swarm of bees on the audio track.

Nathan said, "What should they do, loop in their dialogue?"

"They're reshooting this morning," said Wallis, "and it better go fast."

They watched some more and Renie said, "Bergman glows. Look at her, Hal. She glows."

Wallis saw it all right. He thought back to months of hand-wringing over a European leading lady and could at least take comfort in the fact that, yes, they had gotten this decision right.

CHAPTER 42

Because Peter Lorre felt genuine friendship for Bogart, on Lorre's sixth day making *Casablanca*, he resisted the urge to take morphine before he reported to the set. Oh, how he needed it, because today he would be shooting the capture scene of his character, Ugarte.

In the next moment, he reconsidered the decision. Okay, he thought, maybe for Bogart's sake, he wouldn't take too much morphine; he would only use enough to calm his nerves. One half of a pill. There, down the hatch. Ever since the two crazy brothers had approached him and Greenstreet at Ciro's, Peter had felt an allegiance to this production, God help him. No, the part wasn't large, and no, he wouldn't get to work with dear Sydney, but Ugarte was wonderful, and dark, doomed, mysterious, and deadly. Ugarte was the cold-blooded killer of Nazis! Lorre would have no opportunity to kill them in real life, but he could kill them here at Warner Bros., off-camera unfortunately, and that would have to do for the time being.

He sat in his dressing room down the row from that of Bette Davis and grew nostalgic for the Europe of old. Morphine did that to him sometimes, made him sad and wistful, and then bitter that Hitler's thugs had driven him away from the continent. He belonged there with Bertolt Brecht and Fritz Lang, but both of them had been chased away to Hollywood as well, and now all must endure this place and these times.

Concentrate, he ordered himself. *Think of the sequence to come. Ugarte deserves your full attention as they corner him.* Peter studied the new blue pages of Scene 62 that described Ugarte's run of luck at the roulette wheel until two French police approach him from behind. The rewrite was a big improvement over the original scene in the bound script. There a cop had grabbed his wrist as he reached for winnings—a clichéd move, Peter had thought. Now, thanks to the rewrite, the police would not touch him; instead, he would be given an important moment to display a range of emotions.

He heard a knock at the door. "Mr. Lorre. They're ready on Stage 8A."

"I'll be right along," he called back.

He stood, steadied himself, and slipped on his white dinner jacket, then moved to the full-length mirror to appraise Ugarte. He looked into his eyes to make sure they were clear. No problem, he thought. He smoothed his hair, straightened his bow tie, and headed out into the blazing sunshine of June. The walk to Stage 8A made him grow wistful again—another part in another picture come and gone.

Inside the soundstage, he found the camera and lights trained on the roulette table in the gambling room of the Rick's set. Lorre saw Curtiz conferring with Arthur Edeson, the sad-sack cinematographer and a man so tiny that even Peter Lorre looked down at him. Curtiz was the best straight man in the world—Lorre had cut the end off a distracted Mike's lit cigarette three times this week, much to Bogart's delight. It didn't seem like there would be time for practical jokes today.

Extras were already seated around the roulette wheel, and Marcel Dalio waited as the croupier. He was another one Peter knew from Europe, a great actor there forced to bit parts here.

When Curtiz saw Lorre waiting, he said, without a hello or any greeting at all, "Did you see change to script? Policeman not take your wrist. Time now for you to give me reaction when you see two big scary police. Then you say, 'Will you allow me to cash my chips?' Give me sadness, fear, desperation. All underneath."

Lorre was touched by this last-minute opportunity to offer his talent to the camera. "The script change is wonderful, Mike," he managed to say. He watched Curtiz return his attention to Edeson, but the director looked back.

"Maybe next time you leave my cigarette alone, eh?"

Lorre smiled with embarrassment as some of the crew laughed.

"We must shoot!" said Curtiz, always impatient, always on the charge. He pointed out Lorre's mark by the roulette table, then shouted to Dalio and the twenty or so well-dressed extras sitting in the background, "Remember what I tell you! You play roulette but give careful glances to what goes on here with Ugarte and police. You hate police, fear for Ugarte. If I see one of you look into camera, I kill you. Then fire you."

In the rehearsal, the actors playing police stood behind Peter. One said, "You will come with us, M'sieur Ugarte," causing Peter to turn toward the camera for whatever look he could dream up. And as they had finished setting up the lights, he imagined what he would feel if he were still in Germany and the Nazis had come for him. He would have been, at best, confined to a concentration camp. But Ugarte had killed German couriers, so he would face torture, followed by execution. So, when Peter turned to camera, his expression reflected the doom of a man condemned. He knew he could express it in his eyes, with no other movement necessary. Then his line, "Allow me to cash my chips?" was said shyly, pitifully. How could the arresting officer refuse? And those players in the background giving him their glances would reveal the pathos of the moment. Bravo, Curtiz, for directing them that way.

They shot it quickly and moved on to the short, locked-down scene at the cashier's booth—another blue, rewritten page. "Pretty lucky, huh?" says Ugarte, his hands full of chips, as he bravely reaches the cashier. "Two thousand, please," he says. Then, with cash in hand, he sizes up the situation—he has been buying time to look for a means of escape out of Rick's. The previous version had him shooting a policeman here at the window, but Curtiz wanted the action to be drawn out, much to Peter's delight. As Ugarte walks away from the cashier, he suddenly bolts out of the camera's frame.

The third setup was angle-on-the-door as Ugarte flies past other policemen and pulls the door closed behind him. Then the fourth, Ugarte, pistol in hand, firing shots at the door as the police open it, squibs going off at points in the wooden door hit by Ugarte's bullets.

They broke for lunch. Bogart had been watching, and as the foreground and background players herded off the set toward the commissary, Bogie said to Lorre, "Come on to my dressing room. What do you want to eat? I'll have somebody bring it over."

"Lamb chops, please, and coffee," said Lorre without hesitation. Bogart asked a runner to go for it, and the two men headed up the avenue between soundstages. They said nothing as they navigated busy First Street, the sun high and hot overhead. Inside Bogart's dressing room, Lorre collapsed on the couch inside the door and kicked off his shoes. He gave a glance to Bogie's low coffee table, where a chess game was in progress. No players, but a chess board with pieces all over, and a few off to the side.

"Still playing chess by mail, I see," said Lorre.

Bogart turned to see a collapsed Peter—in Ugarte's wardrobe from the picture. "Hey, the jacket!" scolded Bogie.

"Oh yeah," said Lorre, forcing himself back up, his joints beginning to ache as the morphine loosened its grip. He removed his jacket and gave it to Bogart, who placed it carefully on the back of the chair at his makeup table. Then Peter returned to the couch and collapsed again.

"And the answer is yes, I'm still playing chess by mail. And don't you touch that board, you sonofabitch."

The implication insulted Lorre. "Any five-year-old could rearrange chess pieces. I pride myself on more creativity than that." He lit a cigarette and stared at the ceiling. "How's Mayo?" he asked.

The couch was L-shaped and Bogart settled in on a spot adjacent to his friend. "Mayo's Mayo," he said with a shrug of his shoulders. "And these days, a little more so." He paused. "How's Celia?"

"Still a bitch," said Lorre. "She doesn't like me taking dope. She says it's bad for me."

"Everybody needs a little somethin'," said Bogart, sounding like Bogart.

He gave his watch a glance and snapped on the floor radio. "There's a big sea battle going on in the Pacific," he said. "I gotta hear the score."

In a moment a newsman read, "Two and perhaps three Japanese aircraft carriers and all their planes and eleven or twelve other enemy warships have been damaged in the great naval and air battle going away off tiny Midway Island in the Pacific. Admiral

Chester W. Nimitz, commander of the U.S. Pacific Fleet, reports that our own losses have been light."

Bogart snapped the radio off again. "Fuck you, Japan," he enthused. "There, that made my day. Payback."

None of the news penetrated Lorre's brain. "The Pacific—who cares? Nothing can save Hungary or my people."

Neither of them liked to talk shop, so Peter was surprised when after a moment his friend said, "You were good on this one. Real good. You look at the lines in the script and Ugarte's nothin'. A walk-on. You made him somethin'."

"It's those writers, the twins. When they sat at our table that night at Ciro's, I thought you had put them up to it. But it wasn't a gag."

"Where you going next?" Bogart asked. He seemed sad, maybe because he was losing a friend from the production and he didn't have many.

"Columbia," said Lorre, exhausted to even say the name. "Some shit about the boogie man."

Bogart stopped what he was doing. "You're kiddin'," he said.

Peter slowly turned his head to the right to glare at his friend. They were quiet for a bit, and a knock on the door announced the arrival of food. A waitress set a covered tray on the low table by the couch. She uncovered it and departed quickly as Peter forced himself into a sitting position and considered taking another half a pill. He wanted to sand the edges off his tension before the final scene. He wanted a smooth and memorable exit for his friend Bogie's picture.

As usual, Bogart wasn't eating except to pick some boiled carrots off the plate with his fingers and pop them in his mouth as Peter sawed into the lamb chops and ate greedily. Bogie went over to his kitchenette, reached up into the cupboard, and took down a bottle of vodka, half full, and two glasses. He poured two inches of vodka into each glass and held one out for Peter to take. It was as if he had read Lorre's mind about the pill. Vodka wasn't morphine, but vodka could do in a pinch.

"Here's to Ugarte," said Bogart, "and to boogie men."

"You're a prick," said Lorre, and they each downed their shots in one smooth gulp. Peter poured and downed a second before they departed and found the walk back to the soundstage very pleasant. His stomach was full and his head felt a little detached from his body—and reality. This time the camera had been placed at a corner of the bar, and all the crew was present and waiting.

When Curtiz saw his actors arrive, he said, "Ah! Lunch bums back!" Lorre didn't dare say anything but expected Bogart to toss off a *Back you, Mike.* None was forthcoming. Was Bogie losing his touch? Or was he simply being deferential to Peter's last couple of hours on the picture? Peter didn't know, so he remained mute. Scene 65 had no blue-page substitutions. It was as written in the script: Ugarte runs to Rick, pistol in hand, and begs for help.

"Now, lunch bums," said Mike, "we finish only action sequence in picture. Rick back to camera, Ugarte run up, beg for help. Police close in."

From ten feet away, Curtiz jabbed his riding crop in Lorre's direction and said, "Peter, this time, you fight like tiger for camera. Desperate. End of your life near. Fight. Plead. Desperate. Police grab you, fight them! Fight like tiger. They drag you away."

He waved the riding crop in Bogart's direction. "Rick knows score. No way out. Rick would help, if help possible. Bogie, give me brilliant take!" He retreated to his chair beside the camera.

"Position one, Ugarte out of sight around corner, Rick back

to camera. Ugarte rush to camera; Rick push Ugarte into wall for cut-in."

Lee Katz, the assistant director, called, "Ready on the set!" A bell rang. Lorre headed to position one.

A prop man handed him the pistol he had used that morning. "No ammo," a voice said into Lorre's ear.

"Places and quiet!" screamed Curtiz to shush chatter from extras in groups around the soundstage who had relaxed during lunch and now threatened the integrity of his shot. In an instant the place fell to total silence. Peter reached within himself, to a deep, dark place. He thought of Brownshirts marching through Berlin streets. He thought of people he knew who were now in camps—if they hadn't been killed. A makeup man rushed up and assessed his sweating forehead. It was right for the moment, so he left it but pulled some strands of hair loose to fall over his forehead. Lorre barely noticed. He began to breathe deeply and let it out. Inhale, exhale. He must be breathless in his desperation.

"Camera," Lorre heard Curtiz say.

"We have speed," he heard. The voice of little Arthur Edeson. A sound assistant slated the take.

"Ready, Ugarte?" called Curtiz from around the corner. "And action!"

Lorre ran around the corner and into the view of the camera, gun in hand, and fixed his eyes on his old friend Bogie. "Rick! Rick! Help me!"

Bogart grabbed him, his face cold. "Don't be a fool! You can't get away!"

Lorre released the tiger. "Hide me! Do something! You must help me, Rick." By now the extras dressed as policemen had grabbed Peter from both sides. "Do something!" cried Peter as he felt the extras muscle him out of frame.

He took a good jostling before Curtiz yelled, "Cut!"

Peter struggled for breath. He swiped at tears that surprised him. "Makeup," he called so the man could blot him.

"One take," Curtiz observed. "Not bad for lunch bums. We print that one. Now safety."

They did it again in the coverage shot, and then Curtiz moved in for an over-the-shoulder close-up of Bogart holding Peter at the wall. Lorre knew that Mike was cutting in the camera again, giving the editor only what he wanted to be used, and Peter had heard that this habit made Hal Wallis furious. Peter loved the very thought of it, so he gave the close-up his all. "Hide me! Do something! You must help me, Rick!"

In the next two hours, the group of athletic extras dressed as police muscled Ugarte across the crowded dining room of Rick's and out the door. Several takes from different angles, and reaction shots of Rick watching.

By 5:30 that afternoon, Lorre sat in his camp chair exhausted. Sweaty, bumped and bruised, and done with the picture. He was closed out in only six days of work. Bogie walked up, sat beside him, and slapped him above the knee.

"That wasn't bad," said Bogart.

Lorre had his handkerchief out and swiped it across his brow. The white cloth was stained from hours of flesh-colored pat downs. "I gave you what I have," said Peter. "Now you're on your own."

Bogart laughed his easy laugh, but it was short-lived. "I can't tell if the thing's going to be any good, or if it's just a crock of shit."

Lorre lit a cigarette and melted into the canvas back of the chair. Every muscle in his body, and he knew there weren't many, ached, but now he could look forward to a nice pill dead ahead.

"Well, at least the boogie man script they sent me is final. Yours isn't. I'd worry."

"Yeah," said Bogart in summation, sadly, and he stood. "Meet me at the Cock 'n Bull around eight?"

"Sure," Lorre shrugged, "if Mayo lets you out." Lorre thought another moment. "Or you could bring her along. I bet I can get her to break a bottle over your head in—" he reasoned it out in his weary mind, "—ten minutes."

"Sadistic little bastard," said Bogie, who started to walk away.

"Take a steam afterward?" called Lorre. They both had made it a practice to sweat out the booze together at the Finlandia Baths down from the Cock 'n Bull.

"Of course," said Bogie, "unless Mayo breaks that bottle over my head."

CHAPTER 43

Claude Rains had a fondness for Warner Bros. going back seven or eight years to the time he had first set foot there. Since then, he had made umpteen pictures on the lot with never a dull moment, and he thought the place so familiar that it seemed just yesterday he had last been here. He laughed to himself—oh, it *was* yesterday when he had finished up as Dr. Jaquith in *Now, Voyager*. Today he would begin as Renault of the French police, and it required mental gymnastics to exorcise the one character and conjure up the other while learning enough lines to get through the day.

Instead of looking at the *Casablanca* script, he read the *Times* with its headline screaming JAP PLANES BOMB ALASKA NAVY BASE, which meant the war was getting closer every day. Thoughts of the cataclysm of another world war always evoked for Rains the Great War when, as a British officer, he had been gassed at the battle at Vimy Ridge on the French coastline. One never quite got over being gassed in battle, and yet he couldn't complain about how things had worked out. He had a wife (his fourth), a daughter (his first), and a farm in Pennsylvania sprawling across 320 acres. He didn't know any other actor who brought seed catalogs onto the set; he wished he did. Some found him comical, and he long ago decided he didn't care. At the thought of all those jokes about Farmer Rains, he opened his flask to take a deep, soothing swig of vodka, which couldn't be detected on the breath, then stepped out of the limousine that had conveyed him to the studio. He emerged from Wardrobe and Makeup before 8:15, script in hand, in a French police captain's uniform, with an applied moustache and a kepi that he had learned in the service to wear at a rakish angle.

"Mr. Rains!" a voice called to him as he began heading in the general direction of Stage 8A. He turned to see a petite young woman, very pretty, hurrying toward him. She was dressed in a tailored brown suit that set off her large and striking eyes. She put out her hand and showed off a formidable grip in greeting. He knew he had seen this girl around the lot, and he had wondered at various times if he would one day marry her, for he found her exactly his type.

"I'm Irene Lee, the studio's story editor," said the pretty girl.

"Ah, Miss Lee," said Rains with a small bow and touch of his hat brim.

She opened her arm in the direction of the soundstage and said, "I thought maybe we could chat about your character for a moment." They began strolling ever so slowly down Avenue B.

"I'm all yours," said Rains, and the way it had come out of him made him chuckle.

She gave a flirtatious smile. "That is exactly in character. Exactly right," she said.

"Ah, Captain Renault, debaucher of virgins," sighed Rains. "I was surprised to see so many wonderfully naughty lines. He's a man after my own heart." As they walked along ever so slowly, he could sense distress from her. "Do you expect some sort of problem with this character the way it's written?"

"Why do you ask that?" said Miss Lee in a tone of suspicion.

"Well, because I've worked here how many times, and yet we have never spoken before."

She flashed that flirtatious smile again, and with it, an expression that admitted, *You caught me*. She reached up to touch the pearls around her neck. "*Casablanca* is sort of my baby," she allowed, "and Renault is very nuanced. I want to make sure you don't play it—"

"I believe the American term is 'creepy.'"

They laughed together. "Yes, not that," she said, and she took out a cigarette and lit it, then offered him one. They paused, and he held the script under his arm so he could put his hands out to shield her match from the morning breeze. She said, "The script you're holding doesn't have a final Act 3 in it—"

"I had heard that!" he interrupted. "Most curious."

"So, for all you know, Renault could be revealed as a villain and die before fade-out, and I want to assure you that's not the case. Renault is going to save Rick at the end. Or at least that's the plan once we figure out how."

What a strange way to run a studio, he thought to himself. He was used to blue pages signaling changes to a script during production, but never before had he received a script at the start of a job with a notation cautioning that Act 3 was not final.

"I'm happy to know I'm going to live," said Rains with a smile.

"That's why I had to track you down," she said, "because nobody else can give you the inside story at this point and ask you to go easy on the lines about the girls you're after."

"I can see that. Delivery is everything on some of those lines."

"Yes!" she said with passion. "Yes," she said again as they arrived at the soundstage door. She reached out her hand, and as she clasped his said, "Thank you." Then once more, "Thank you."

She turned to walk away, and he gave her an up-and-down assessment. "Anytime," he said, practicing Renault. "Any. Time."

He tossed aside the cigarette butt and entered the busy soundstage. The first person he saw was the director, blustering about. "Bonjour, General le Curtiz!" bellowed Rains. Oh, that Mike was a blusterer, all right. Claude could now smile at memories of the way Errol Flynn chafed under the Curtiz whip. "Iron Mike," Flynn called him, among other less kind things.

Rains beheld the maestro in riding pants and knee-high boots, holding a riding crop, as if about to set off with the hounds. Such a fraud Curtiz was, such a bully. But to a little man, and Rains was indeed a little man of five-four, Michael Curtiz was a tempest in a teapot. And Claude could laugh at him and with him, and Curtiz knew it, so Mike had never given Rains the slightest problem.

"Ah! Claude!" called Curtiz in return. "Now all is well!"

Rains found Rick's Café Americain a sight to behold, with its Moroccan accents and dozens of actors and bit players milling about. Unit manager Al Alleborn, whom Claude knew all too well from so many pictures here, led him into the middle of the melee.

"Of course you know Bogie, don't you?" said Alleborn.

"Actually no," said Claude, "unless you count three viewings of *The Maltese Falcon*." The men shook hands, and Claude added, "Homework, you see."

Bogart's handshake was stout but not as impressive as Miss Lee's. Claude saw something in Bogart's eyes he hadn't expected, and Bogart seemed to recognize it as well: a boozer spotted another boozer. Rains felt it as an unexpected bond.

"Meet later, make movies now!" was the way Curtiz reined in his people. He ushered the two actors to a setup representing the exterior of Rick's Café. "You know this," said Curtiz. "Outside Rick's. Scene 48, first Renault. You both see plane to Lisbon go overhead."

"I know it indeed," said Rains, because he had memorized the scene.

"Rick put Yvonne in cab, then walk back here," said Curtiz. "You are waiting, Louis." The director looked about him and spied a push broom leaning against a ladder. He took the broom in hand and held it high. "Sight line here as plane go over. You look here, see plane. Get it?"

Claude said he did get it; Bogart agreed, both understanding the plane would be added in a separate over-the-shoulder process shot. Rains took a seat at the chosen exterior table outside the facade of Rick's and rehearsed the scene with Bogart, with the director watching every sound and every move. Flawless. All knew it at once, so Curtiz ordered a camera setup and lighting and a take.

Thirty minutes later the slate snapped, and the two actors would be ratcheting up their performance levels. Curtiz called action for Bogart to walk toward Rains.

"Hello, Rick," said Rains-as-Renault.

"Hello, Louis."

"How extravagant you are, throwing away women like that. Someday, they may be scarce." Bogart sat down at the table with him. Claude added, his manner merry, "You know, I think now I shall pay a call on Yvonne—maybe get her on the rebound, eh?" In his mind he hoped the delivery would please Miss Lee.

Bogart planted himself in the seat near Rains and said, "When it comes to women, you're a true democrat." The delivery astonished Rains the actor. He didn't know Bogart from Adam, but it was as if he did know him from centuries together.

"Plane go overhead!" Curtiz shouted. "Cue Renault!"

Claude waited a beat and then looked at the spot where the push broom had been held. "The plane to Lisbon," he said and looked over at Rick. "You would like to be on it?"

Bogart gave a nonchalant nothing of an action. "Why, what's in Lisbon?" he asked. Claude thought it extraordinary, such skill in a Hollywood actor, to toss off a line in such a brilliant way.

Claude as Renault said, "The clipper to America." After a good, long beat with Bogart sitting there, Rains said, "I have often speculated on why you do not return to America. Did you abscond with the church funds? Did you run off with a senator's wife? I should like to think you killed a man. It's the romantic in me."

Claude watched Bogart look after the imaginary plane that had just flown over. Such skill in this man, thought Rains. "It was a combination of all three," Bogart quipped.

Rains knew to remain still—the action was on Bogart. "And what in heaven's name brought you to Casablanca?"

"My health," said Bogart. "I came to Casablanca for the waters."

The response motivated Claude forward in his chair. "Waters? What waters? We are in the desert."

"I was misinformed," said Bogart so coolly Rains restrained his smile at his companion's delivery.

Another actor appeared. "Excuse me, M'sieur Rick," he began. Rains heard Curtiz bellow, "And—cut!"

Bogart leaned forward toward Rains and said, "Holy hell! Where have you been all my life?"

Claude could only laugh, and ask himself, where indeed? He had had such chemistry before on this lot, most notably with Basil Rathbone on *Robin Hood*, where the characters felt vital and connected, by design in the script and by circumstance. And he had felt it with Bette Davis on *Now, Voyager*, and here it was again, unexpectedly, after only an hour, with this stranger Bogart. Curtiz repositioned the camera and they played the scene again, with the same result. Claude thought of Bogart as a gangster in pictures he had seen here and there, and of course he had studied Sam Spade. But the range and the intuitive nature of this actor enthralled him.

When Curtiz was satisfied with what he had gotten and ordered the takes printed, Rains looked at Bogart and said, "We're going to do all right." And Bogart took a drag on his cigarette and nodded, his eyes half-lidded against the smoke.

CHAPTER 44

Julius was sorry he had ever seen a play entitled "Everybody Comes to Rick's" and doubly regretful that he and Phil had so arrogantly gone after it. They had now invested four months into writing the screenplay, the past two supported by Howard Koch, and then Casey Robinson had come aboard, but all the work by all these people indicated just how bad the story had been in the first place. Julie and Phil could knock out a script in a couple of months, tops; the adaptation of *The Man Who Came to Dinner* had taken just seven weeks and been a smash hit. But *Casablanca* was a process that never ended, and, it seemed, never would end.

Wallis had developed a new practice: whatever was being shot the next day fell under his scrutiny, and Hal would tinker with dialogue and stage direction. He would send marked-up pages over to the Epsteins, and they would have to solve the day's problems that Wallis caused so Alice could type up new pages on blue paper. But now, suddenly, Hal had started to intercept the blue pages and make changes to the changes.

"Aw, come on," said Phil the first time blue pages that had been marked up by Wallis came back to the Epsteins' offices. It was a scene with Rick, Renault, and Strasser, the "I'm a drunkard" scene, which they had thought was perfect.

Outraged, they walked the edits downstairs to Renie, who

gave the blue pages a glance and said, "Yeah, Hal and I went over the scene, and he had some ideas that made sense, so we did some fine-tuning."

"But we're never going to be done at this rate, going over his changes and your changes."

Renie said, "What can I tell you—it's the scene where Rick's history is revealed, and so it has to be right. Every line has to be perfect."

"We thought it was perfect," said Julie.

Phil's frustration spilled over. "This is crazy!" he blurted out, and pivoted, and pivoted back. "Whose side are you on?" he raved at Renie.

She slid her glasses up on her head and looked at him with a sideways tilt that inquired, *Do you know who you're talking to?* Julie watched Phil wither under her gaze and put out his hands; Phil had never been the beneficiary of a killer's instinct.

"I'm sorry, Renie. I'm sorry. It's just that every day we spend grinding the gears on these rewrites keeps us from cracking the code of Act 3. For every step forward, there's a step back."

"Listen, we're all in the hot seat here," said Renie. "Maybe all three of us made the biggest mistake of our careers. Maybe all three of us will be following Mac and Kline out the door."

"You think it's that bad?" asked Julie.

"Oh yeah. I know Hal and I like Hal, but he's not kidding when he says business is business, and that makes us all expendable anytime he chooses. Have you noticed how terrible he looks? He's on the hot seat too because the chief is watching. That's why Hal is up all night and half the day rewriting. Second-guessing."

Julie nodded at the logic of the explanation. "That's all fine," he said. "Just so long as you understand why we can't get Act 3, because we're forever refining the plot and the characters. Every single day we are going back to work on material we thought we had finished."

"Duly noted," said Renie. "Now get upstairs and keep going." On their way out the door, she added, "The Chinese curse has hit us—we have gotten what we wished for."

Julie and Phil trudged upstairs to work on changes to the rewritten "I'm a drunkard" scene, and later that day they handed the changes to Alice to type on a different colored paper. This time it was pink.

CHAPTER 45

Joy could scarcely hide her embarrassment as she slouched low in the back seat of the limousine that brought her through the gate with Mother beside her—Mother, wearing a fur about her neck and a maroon suit and jewelry. Joy could die. She could simply die. Why couldn't she just be allowed to ride in with Papa Jack today of all days? But no, Mother had insisted on coming in with her. "You're just seventeen," Mother had said an hour earlier, "and you know about movie sets. I've heard about that German boy in particular, that friend of Errol's. He's no good."

The car eased through the gate and Joy's heart pounded. On this her first day as an actress earning $100 a week, she allowed herself a mental glimpse of the apartment of her dreams, away from 1801. The car stopped fifty feet or more before the Wardrobe Department, where Joy was supposed to report. Joy could see eight or nine people waiting in a line at the front of the two-story building as the driver stepped around to open the rear passenger door. Mother said, "Now, don't embarrass me."

Her words were often worse than a slap in the face. "I won't, Mother," said Joy.

The people in the queue were older, in their thirties on up, some of them ancient, and they waited patiently. Joy headed for the back of the line, but Mother pounded toward the door. "Come along, Joy!" she commanded, and led Joy past the people in line and through the door into the Wardrobe Department. Joy followed, looking at the floor to avoid what she believed would be hostile stares.

At a counter, Mother stopped and said to the woman on the far side, "Joy Page as Annina Brandel."

In fifteen minutes, Joy was off to Makeup, and then down they walked to Stage 8A, through the humid heat of morning. Joy carried script in hand and wished for more moments to study Scene 161, which she would shoot today with Humphrey Bogart. She felt such excitement to have gotten this far, to have won the part, to be heading for the set to shoot a scene. But to be trailing behind Mother yet again, as she always had, literally walking in Mother's shadow, living Mother's dream of a screen career—these things had never appealed to Joy at all. She kept firmly in her mind: I will do this job, and then I will do other jobs, and the years will pass, and I will get my own apartment. And someday, I won't be in Mother's shadow any longer.

The pair stepped through the soundstage door. Inside, a crowd awaited, and it took a moment for Joy to adjust to the chaos of the Rick's Café set, a complex of interconnected rooms with open walls for camera movement. Dozens of technicians moved about, and the many extras milled as if at a morning cocktail party. With every set of people she passed, Joy heard a different language. She recognized French, German, and, she thought, Dutch.

The crowd moved aside as Ann Warner proceeded through it. She didn't have to push her way through; people just seemed to sense danger and back away. As the sea parted, there ahead was another unwelcome sight: Papa Jack dressed in his Army colonel's uniform chatting with the director, Michael Curtiz.

"Oh hello, dear!" said Papa Jack at the top of his voice on sight of his wife. Mother leaned over and offered her cheek for a kiss. They sure hadn't been chummy the previous evening. "Well, here we are, the big day!" proclaimed Papa Jack. "The bigger-than-big day!"

There were other men standing by Curtiz. Joy recognized Al Alleborn, the unit manager, and Lee Katz, the assistant director. Papa Jack moved forward and put his arm around Joy's waist and held her close. "This little girl is going to guarantee us a hit! Joy Ann Page, the new sensation of the year!" he said, swiping at the air as if painting a headline on a movie screen. "Now, I'm putting her in your hands, Mr. Curtiz. You take care of our little Joy; she's precious!"

He squeezed her waist again and Joy wished she had a shovel so she could dig a grave and throw herself into it. She tried her best to smile but could feel her face flushing crimson.

Curtiz looked down at her with a smile he probably thought was soothing, except it wasn't. "We take good care of you, Joy Page. We make you star," said the director.

She swallowed hard. "Thank you, Mr. Curtiz."

"Well, now, we're holding things up, dear," said Papa Jack. "Let's keep these people on schedule. Time is money! Let's get things moving!"

As Papa Jack released Joy's waist, Mother grabbed her at the elbow so hard it smarted. "I'll be right here, darling, if you need anything."

"Yes, Mother," Joy murmured and awaited release of the grip.

As gently as possible, Alleborn led Mrs. Ann Warner to a wait-ing chair by a wall of the soundstage. Papa Jack watched her go, and when she had reached a safe distance, he kissed Joy hard on the cheek and said, "Break a leg, kitten," and walked stridently away.

Joy turned to see Humphrey Bogart leaning against the bar of Rick's, taking a drag of his cigarette, watching her. With all the commotion of all those people surrounding them, why was he looking at her? She felt herself flush red again and wanted to flee when he straightened away from the bar and approached her.

"That was some performance," he said.

She didn't understand the statement and wondered if he was mocking her. "Performance?" she asked.

"Yeah, the loving parents. I'm not sure I bought it, but Jack—the colonel—signs my checks, so I guess I did." He took another drag of his cigarette and blew a line of smoke away from her. "That mother of yours," he added, "she scares the hell outta me. At all those parties, I stay as far away from Mrs. Warner as possible."

Joy leaned a little closer to him and whispered, "Me too."

Bogart's heavy-smoker laugh rumbled deep in his chest and forced him to cough. She laughed along with him and realized that the guy she had imagined would be so frightening instead seemed to understand her, and her mother, and her stepfather.

"So, today's the big day, huh?" he said in a friendly voice. "Scene 161." Over a ways in the middle of the set, a man dressed identically to Bogart sat at a table while the camera on a little truck sat pointing at him, and men fiddled with measurements and lights beside the camera.

The thought of her big day made Joy stiffen. "Yes, sir," she said.

"No, no, none of that 'sir' business. I'm 'Bogie' or 'hey, you' or anything but 'sir,' okay? I have a suspicion you and I have some things in common, and we're going to be pals."

It took her a moment to process the information. Was he making a pass? Was he mocking her again? "We have things in common?" she said finally, as if putting it out there: *You must forgive me, but I'm a stranger here. A babe in these woods.*

"Yeah, pretty sure we do. Maybe we'll talk sometime."

"Rehearsal! Rehearsal" called the voice of Lee Katz. She felt she had jumped a foot in the air on hearing it. "Rehearsal!" repeated the assistant director.

"Do you know your lines?" asked Bogart.

"I knew them this morning," she returned. She felt breakfast coming up the way it had gone down. "I don't know anything now. I think I'm going to be sick."

"Oh, no you don't," he said sternly. "You just say your lines and let Hugh—that's the dialogue guy over there—you let him help you. That's what he's here for, to help you." Bogart searched the room and nodded at a tall, handsome man with glasses over by the bar. "There he is. You march yourself right over and he'll take care of you."

She decided she couldn't be sick now and disappoint someone who had befriended her. "Thank you, Mr.—"

He gave her a raised eyebrow.

"Bogie," she said and hurried over to the man pointed out as the dialogue director.

"Hugh McMullen, Miss Page," he said, extending his hand. "Quite the debut, eh? Four pages with the star, but Sophie says you're perfect." McMullen flipped through the pages. "Easy back and forth for a while. Your character needs help. She's desperate, but she's also innocent and earnest. I would just play it that way. You're asking for help in the only way an eighteen-year-old girl can: honestly. Annina is an honest character who has accepted she will do everything she can to find happiness with her husband. So just say your lines and take your time with them."

"Okay, yes, sir."

"Mike will give you the stage direction, and you say your lines, and it all goes well. Knowing Mike, he will want to do it several times, at different focal lengths." He closed his script but kept a finger on the spot they'd be shooting. "Let's go see what Mike wants you to do." He walked her onto the set, where Curtiz was rubbing his chin, seeming to survey the position of all the tables.

Joy gave a glance to see what Mother was up to. She sat over near the wall in a chair that said on the back, MICHAEL CURTIZ, DIRECTOR. Of course, she would sit there of all places. She was leaning forward with her legs crossed, posed care-fully—she always posed for maximum effect, this time revealing a stockinged knee—and she was watching Joy. On the set, the lights that had been under adjustment went dark.

Joy returned her attention to Mr. Curtiz and awaited his in-structions. He stood on a spot and pointed down. "Position one," he said, looking at her. "I say 'Action,' you walk ten feet to ta-ble with Rick, stop there, position two. Rick sitting. Start lines. 'M'sieur Rick?' Then you stand until Rick offer you seat. Then keep going back and forth, easy little lines, JoyPage, then we cut before get hard. Okay? Okay."

He turned and then stopped and pointed at the floor. "Posi-tion one." It was obvious he meant stand here, now. She did, and then he walked the path he wanted her to walk, up to the table where Rick sat, and he pointed again. "Position two." She nodded. Then he walked around the all-important table occupied by Rick and stood beside the camera.

She waited with all these men around her, and the camera aimed at her. She found it terrifying and thrilling and exhilarating all at once. She thought again: *This is a means to an end. This is the beginning. I will get away from her and this is my first step.*

"Ready for rehearsal!" called Curtiz.

Joy walked back to position one, and there ahead at the table sat Humphrey Bogart, who was looking elsewhere. She was so grateful they had spoken because he didn't terrify her at this moment.

"Action!"

Joy moved from position one to position two beside the table. A boom mic floated into view and settled three feet above her head, which disquieted her. She pressed on.

"M'sieur Rick?"

He looked up at her. "Yes?"

"Could I speak to you, just for a moment?" So strange to be saying these lines here, after practicing so long and hard with Sophie and the other students and alone in her bedroom and in the pool house, also alone. Practice, practice, and more practice.

Bogart frowned and said sternly, "How did you get in here? You're underage."

"I came with Captain Renault."

He gave a bitter smirk. "I should have known." How easily all this came to Bogart, she thought in that flash of a second.

"My husband is with me too," she recited.

"He is?" said Bogart, and he searched to find the imaginary character Renault across the way. "Captain Renault is getting broad-minded." He nodded to the chair opposite him. "Sit down. Will you have a drink?"

She carefully sat in the chair. "No, thank you," she said of the drink. Beside her, she could feel the camera on its little truck glide in closer.

"Of course not," said Bogart. "Do you mind if I do?"

She said, "No." She watched Rick pour his drink, as the script said he would. And her line as he poured was, "M'sieur Rick, what sort of a man is Captain Renault?"

Bogart said easily, "Oh, he's just like any other man," but then he paused and added, "only more so."

She said, "No, I mean, is he trustworthy? Is his word—"

Bogart said, "Now, just a minute. Who told you to ask me that?"

Curtiz snapped, "Cut rehearsal!" The director put his chin in his hand and rubbed at it, pacing around silently, seemingly deep in thought, as if he were replaying each line in his mind. She was aware how quiet it was, how all eyes were on the director. Then he walked up to her as she sat waiting. He knelt down beside the table so he was between Joy and Bogie. He said, "Walk is good, stop good. Make every line softer. Boom mic pick up everything. This not stage, everything softer. And slow down. Much slower. Beat in each exchange. Not too long, just short beat, okay?"

Oh my God, she thought to herself, *I wasn't terrible!* "Okay, yes, Mr. Curtiz," she stammered, trying to remember everything he had just said. Softer. Much slower. Short beats.

He got up from a kneeling position and said, "We roll camera." And the army of technicians rushed to their essential duties, and the character actors and extras moved onto the set in a wave of activity. As Joy was about to stand and walk back to position one, Bogart reached out a hand and touched her wrist lightly.

"That was pretty good, Joy," he said over the commotion, as now the choreography of background players was attended to and the lights began to come up. "Just remember, acting is fun. We get to paint a portrait of a character. And they pay us to do it. Okay?"

As she stood, he added, "Remember, just relax and have fun."

"Yes . . . Bogie," she forced herself to say. After all, this man was more than twice her age, and she had just seen him bigger than life on the screen as Sam Spade. She walked back to position one considering what he had just advised. Only once in a great while in Sophie's class had Joy experienced what she would call a fun moment. Too often she just clamped down on her emotions as she had all her life, as trained by Mother. Behave perfectly. Don't make a mistake. Don't be embarrassing. She doubted she had any idea at all how to relax or have fun with much of anything.

After they had shot the scene once and then again, the crew expended furious energy to reset for close-ups, and the camera moved and the lights were adjusted. Through it all, Bogart seemed to be utterly calm. Joy couldn't understand it, but she could feel it, that calm, set against her tightly packed nerves. She searched about for her script pages; she didn't know where she had set them. Bogart watched for a second, then leaned back.

"Al?" he said as Alleborn rushed by and then stopped short at hearing his name. "Can I borrow your script?" Alleborn handed it over without hesitation, and Bogie offered it to Joy. She couldn't even speak, the gesture so astonished her. How did he know what she had been searching for?

She furiously opened the document and flipped to Scene 161 to study. She said, "Don't you need to memorize?"

He dragged on his cigarette. "Nah, I think I've got it."

She tried to focus on her lines. "We come from Bulgaria. Things are very bad there, M'sieur. The devil has the people by the throat. So Jan and I . . ."

But something Bogart said had stuck with her, and the way he had said it, about how he and Joy had things in common, and the way he seemed to understand Mother and Papa Jack just by observing for a moment or two—all these things seemed important.

"Can I ask you something?"

He had dropped the butt of his cigarette to the floor and leaned over to rub it out with his shoe. "Sure, ask away."

"What did you mean about having things in common?"

He laughed an ironic sort of laugh. "I'm not sure this is the place to talk about it." He was so mysterious but so—what was the word?—so kind. Yes, that was it, so kind and understanding. He seemed to understand everything about her.

"Please," she said.

His smile faded a bit, but he held it in place. "Your parents remind me of my parents. It seems like everything is about them, right? And your house—we lived in an apartment, but we had a summer house on a lake. Not as grand as Jack's palace on Angelo, certainly, but grand enough. The drive up to your place at 1801 always reminds me of that summer place I grew up in."

She couldn't believe what he was saying. She had never thought to connect Humphrey Bogart with a wealthy background or that someone like him could understand someone like her. But he seemed to. It seemed he could pull the thoughts right out of her head. And what he had told her begged another question. "Were you happy?"

Now he laughed another big laugh that rumbled in his chest, and he coughed. "Let me put it this way: I'm here, 3,000 miles from those places I grew up in. And it's not far enough."

And that led to a final question that she asked without pausing to process it. She leaned forward and whispered, "Was acting part of your escape plan?"

He lit another cigarette and said, "I was brought up to be lazy, and acting had late nights and no hard work—it was that or digging ditches. It wasn't a plan. It was just easy." The answer disappointed her because she wanted him to be like her, to really understand, maybe even to be her confederate.

He could read the disappointment on her face. He said, "It doesn't take a genius to see you want out of the mess you're in. And all I can say is, sock away some cash. Any amount you're able to." He looked past her and said, "Uh-oh, here comes trouble."

Mother walked up. "What are you two going on about?" she asked with what passed for a smile, although Joy knew there would be cross-examination later. Mother could also read Joy's mind if Joy wasn't careful. Maybe everyone could.

Bogart leaned back in his chair and stretched his arms. "We were talking about the finer points of performing for the camera," he said wearily. Joy realized this instant what a good actor he really was and that there were many kinds of acting. A person really acted all the time, whether for a camera or a mother.

Joy noticed that Curtiz had finished setting up his shot and the frantic activity had slowed. "Rehearse next setup," he called, giving Mother a glance meant to shoo her away. Joy loved it! She loved being among these people who could be a sort of shield and give her protection in the adult world that she hadn't considered could be there. Putting Joy before the camera had been Mother's great plan, Mother the failed actress, and what if the plan were to backfire? Joy felt a surge of excitement, of delicious irony!

Bogart seemed to notice the change in her. "I'll tell you something else," he began, "about this scene we're doing. You give me a lot to play. Here you come, this kid, and you present your case, and a lot of what you are telling Rick troubles him. His friend Louis is a rat who wants to sleep with you, and you're just a young girl. And you have dreams for your life, and Rick used to have dreams, but he doesn't anymore. And then the kicker: when you say, 'If someone loved you very much,' and that's a punch in Rick's gut. So your character does the talking, and mine does the reacting. It's good stuff, for both of us."

So much made sense now that hadn't earlier in the morning when she and Mother had been driven through the gate. She had already gotten such an education, and it wasn't even lunchtime! And Bogie had shown her that it's possible to get away. She can survive. She really was Annina, as Sophie had said. Rick was helping Annina escape to freedom, and Bogie was helping Joy.

His hands were resting on the table. She leaned forward, touched his jacket at the wrist, and said, "Thank you, M'sieur Rick."

CHAPTER 46

Irene had tiptoed into Stage 8 in time to catch the end of Bogart's scene with Joy Page. The skeptic in Irene doubted any ability in Page, but the girl had done okay, and all seemed to be going very well indeed. With the crew battening down the hatches to close out the day, Irene strolled outside, purse on her arm, and figured to call a car and head home. The heat of the pavement boiled up under her dress, and on instinct she headed for the shadows cast by the soundstages as she walked up Avenue B.

At the curb on First Street, waiting for his ride was Dooley Wilson. In a moment the limousine pulled up and the driver, Dennis, rushed out to open the door for Wilson.

Two of the laborers, carpenters judging by their attire, walked past and one called, "It's supposed to work the other way, boy!"

"Yeah! You should be opening the door for him," growled the other. The men glared another moment until they saw Irene walking up to Wilson, at which point they seemed to shrink visibly and walked off.

"I'm sorry for that," Irene said to Dooley. "I've never seen such behavior on this lot."

Wilson gave a chuckle. "Oh it's fine. This is a mighty nice place, and folks are treating me well. Very well."

A thought seized Irene, and she gave her watch a glance. She touched Dooley's arm and said, "Would you mind if I hitch a ride down to my apartment on Franklin?"

"It would be my pleasure," said Dooley, and with Dennis still holding the door open, Wilson motioned for Irene to slide in first. Dennis was often her driver, and he would know where to go, and so she relaxed to enjoy the ride. She didn't know how to approach a conversation with Dooley; the feeling seemed to be mutual.

After they had pulled out onto Barham, Dooley asked, to break the awkward silence, "What do you do at the studio?"

"I'm Irene Lee, the story editor. I find properties that would make a good movie, like *Casablanca*, and recommend that the studio buy them. Then I assign a writer—I'm the head of the department—and, I suppose you could say, I watch the magic happen."

He seemed to process all she had told him and then proclaimed in the gentlest of voices, "That's marvelous. Such an important job for . . ." His voice trailed off.

"Go ahead and say it. For a woman."

"For a lady, I would have said, but yes."

They shared a laugh and then fell silent again. At length he said, "You must do an awful lot of reading."

"I love to read. Always have. I used to read by flashlight under the covers in bed after my parents had ordered me to go to sleep. The Brontës, Dickens, Tolstoy—anything and everything."

She thought him an awkward man, so soft-spoken and deferential. He grew quiet and then said, "Do you mind if I ask you something? If you are the boss of the writers, the lady boss, maybe you can tell me."

"I'll certainly try," she said.

"How can a colored fella . . ." he said slowly and paused. "How can a colored fella with a piano be allowed to play the best friend of a club owner who's . . . well, who isn't colored? If you get my meaning."

She got his meaning all right, and in her mind instantly replayed every conversation in Hal's office and in the boardroom concerning the politics of this issue. Sam would be comic relief. Then maybe Sam would be a female. Then no, Sam would be a male and played straight, even if the South boycotted the picture. Through it all, every person involved, from Hal to the writers to Irene, believed in the sanctity of the character of Sam—not as written in the play, but as that role had evolved, as a statement about human dignity in a world gone mad.

She gave him a reassuring smile. "So, you're surprised at the way the character is written?"

"Oh very surprised, yes," he replied.

She decided there was a bit of Candide in Dooley Wilson. Voltaire's innocent hero saw the good in everyone. But just now, as she pondered his question, she saw something else. "You are Jesse Owens." She said it as a statement of fact.

He flashed her a look of great surprise, as if an electric current had zapped him. "No, no, no," he murmured.

"Yes, yes, yes," she said back with a smile. "Jesse Owens went to Berlin and ran some races. He wore his brown skin in Germany and proved what a pack of lies Hitler peddles over there and goes right on peddling."

"I'm . . ." he began and hesitated before he said, "I'm just an actor doing a job. Jesse Owens is a hero."

"A hero," said Irene, "and a symbol representing the fact we're all human beings, just a collection of atoms, and nobody's better and nobody's worse. And that is the essence of the relationship between Rick and Sam, two characters who don't see that skin color—or any other difference—matters. That, my friend, is a world I want to live in. It's something we want the world to see right now, something you can help the world to see."

He pondered her words. "Quite a lot of responsibility," he said softly, "for a fella who can't run a lick."

She laughed. "Okay, how about this: you can be Joe Louis knocking out Hitler's darling Max Schmelling in the first round. Same principle."

He straightened in his seat at that one and said with conviction, "I'll say this much: you are very kind to a worn-out old drummer!"

"I've seen the dailies," said Irene, "and you are a wonderful Sam. I'd love to have Sam as a best friend." The car had turned onto Franklin and eased to the curb before the Havenhurst.

"Thanks for allowing me to hitchhike," said Irene to Dooley.

"Oh, it was my pleasure, Miss Lee," he replied.

She waited for Dennis to walk around and open her door. "Dennis, can you pick me up at 8:30 tomorrow morning, please?"

"Of course, Miss Lee," said the driver. "See you then." He tipped his cap and turned.

She ducked down and waved to Dooley through the window; Dooley waved back, and the car zoomed off.

CHAPTER 47

For Michael Curtiz, it was Monday afternoon at the begin-ning of the fourth week on Stage 8A, the Rick's Café set. They were shooting the late-night scene with Rick drunk in the closed bar when Ilsa walks in for a tense reunion. After lunch the lights had needed to be reset, and Bogart slouched in his chair wearing a bemused expression. Dooley Wilson stood with hands in pockets beside Sam's piano, both of them watching Ingrid Bergman pace nervously. Ingrid had been mostly quiet about the lack of an Act 3 marked final, but now something had set her off.

"I don't understand," she said as she paced. "I don't understand why the third act isn't final. I've been here a month. A month! I'm supposed to play this scene with Rick, but I don't know how to play it. What does Ilsa feel for this man? She is married to Victor, but here she is with Rick. Where is Act 3 so I can understand the story of this character? Should I believe the Act 3 as it's now written?"

Mike fumed inside. He needed to shoot to stay on sched-ule, but Bergman was correct: The script should have been fin-ished by now; the script should have been finished a month back. Mike loved Ingrid's professionalism. My God, he loved her! Each Christmas, his wife would ask him what he wanted for a gift. Each year he would respond, "An actor who doesn't make me crazy."

And husband and wife would share a laugh because he had never met such a creature. Well, here she was, the most perfect actress he had ever directed or ever seen. But now he must shoot, and that meant getting Ingrid to move on and just play the scene as written.

"Christmas Baby," he began as gently as he could, "we shot the Paris scenes, so you know how Ilsa feel about Rick. Just say words on page."

Ingrid stopped pacing and turned to him as if he had just spoken blasphemy. "But they aren't just words on a page, Mr. Curtiz. They are tiny details in a portrait of this character. What does she feel? And how will I know that? I need to be able to step back and view the entire portrait."

Mike had no answer. Mike had only a schedule, and minute by minute, he was falling behind that schedule. He could see the sadist Bogart enjoying his predicament. He could see Dooley Wilson watching, waiting for him to make a decision. It was already two in the afternoon, with less than four hours to finish this scene, and Mike had told Al Alleborn the unit manager that he would indeed finish it today. There were only so many scenes they could shoot without the other actors—Henreid hadn't yet started on the picture—and this was just such a scene. Mike's patience was limited, even with Ingrid Bergman.

"Okay, look," he said suddenly, so suddenly that Ingrid gave a start. "Girl go into man's place late at night. Man drunk. Girl be scared. Play that, for chrissakes!"

She tilted her pretty head and squinted her pretty eyes. It was clear she didn't understand. "Play that," she repeated, her words tipped in ice. "Very well."

Mike felt his heart pounding. When he turned away from Ingrid, he stared into the face of an incredulous Al Alleborn, who put out both hands, palms up. Alleborn was Wallis's eyes and ears, and if Mike didn't shoot right now, right this minute, Wallis would be sending a memo at best or calling Mike into his office at worst.

Mike had worked it out with Edeson that the camera would shoot across the table where Rick sat, then rack focus to show Ilsa walking in the door in the far background. "We try rehearsal," said Mike. He positioned Ingrid by the door and Rick in his chair and called action.

She walked in toward foreground and stopped by the table, where Bogart sat. "Rick, I have to talk to you," she said.

He was playing it drunk. He slurred, "Oh. I saved my first drink to have with you. Here." And he reached for the bottle.

"No, Rick, not tonight," she responded.

"Now you sit," instructed Curtiz.

"Especially tonight," Bogart replied, pouring another drink.

"Please don't," she urged.

"Why did you have to come to Casablanca? There are other places."

She was leaning toward him. "I wouldn't have come if I had known that you were here. Believe me, Rick, that's the truth. I didn't know."

Curtiz watched Bogart lean back in his chair, thinking. "Funny about your voice, how it hasn't changed," said Bogie-as-Rick. "I can still hear it, 'Richard, dear, I'll go with you anyplace. We'll get on a train together and never stop.'"

Ingrid was fully in character, whether she knew that character or not. "Please don't," she begged. "Don't, Rick! I can understand how you feel."

Bogie was fully engaged, fully experiencing Rick. "Huh!" he said. "You understand how I feel. How long was it we had, honey?"

"I didn't count the days," she sighed, per the script.

He looked past her and said, "Well, I did. Every one of them. Mostly, I remember the last one. A wow finish. A guy standing on the station platform in the rain with a comical look on his face, because his insides had been kicked out."

Ingrid waited a long beat, to let the energy of his bitter words drain off. What an actress she was, thought Mike. Then she said, in a masterful change of tempo. "Can I tell you a story, Rick?"

"Has it got a wow finish?" he asked, looking at her with tortured eyes.

She looked at him sweetly. "I don't know the finish yet," she said, and then glared at Mike and shouted, "because the goddamn script hasn't been written, and I don't have Act 3!"

Bogart had been locked in his performance, and her alteration caught him between worlds. He just stared for a moment, and then erupted in a fit of laughter. "Oh my God," he bellowed, "that is rich!" And he went on laughing, clearly and utterly at Mike's expense, and what could the director do? His favorite actress had turned on him to make a point. She needed the script—the entire script, and she didn't have it, and that script was nowhere in sight. And from all Mike knew, it wouldn't be available anytime soon.

Bogart continued to guffaw, but Ingrid didn't. She glared at Mike and breathed deeply until Bogart's laughter became funny in itself and she began to giggle.

All Mike ever wanted in life was to make good pictures. Well, make good pictures and get laid. Two things. He couldn't control the output of the studio writers, but Bergman didn't seem interested in that practical fact. She was an actor, and this moment reminded him that all actors were crazy. He couldn't reason with them; he could only shout at them loud enough that they would do what he required. And yet, even after this outburst, he couldn't bring himself to raise his voice at Ingrid Bergman. Instead, he counted to ten in Hungarian, then breathed in deeply and exhaled in equal measure.

"Christmas Baby," he began, looking at her as she sat beside Bogart, "I do anything for you. I write script myself it make you happy. But you are great actress, and scene was perfect. Please, let me roll camera and just say all words again?"

She lifted off the chair efficiently and stood to her considerable height. "Of course," she replied, but then she paused and turned back. "But I have a stake in the arc of this story. I want to be believable. I want the character to work for Bogie," she alluded to Bogart and he nodded with either appreciation or bemusement—with this actor they were interchangeable, "for Bogie, for me, and for the audience." She shrugged her shoulders, no longer angry but rather, trying to communicate. "I just want it all to work."

Bogart had to call for the makeup crew to come put his face back together, and then he was ready for a take.

With the camera rolling, Mike led Bogart and Bergman through the two-and-a-half pages of dialogue, shooting the first page as a continuous two shot, and then the second page in over-the-shoulders and extreme close-ups both ways.

The actors were flawless, magnificent, and they finished twenty minutes early, allowing Mike to escape the studio and race the sun west to his ranch in Canoga Park. In large part because the scene had gone so well when the actors put their minds to it, he was able to leave the conflicts behind.

He asked Jim, his wrangler, to saddle the quarter horse Dakota, and Mike climbed into the saddle. He needed to ride, to give Dakota some exercise, and to go fast, very fast. He kicked the horse to a gallop and headed into the sagebrush hills.

As always, he thought about the picture he was making. He couldn't quite put his finger on exactly what he was feeling, except his instincts told him *Casablanca* was a good picture—so far, he believed, he was painting a beautiful canvas of this club in this place with these interesting people, and the two actors he had just left were simply superb. Mike had no idea Bogart had kept such talent hidden inside him. But so much would need to go perfectly for the good picture Mike had started to end as a good picture when he finished. These crazy writers, all four of them, would need to figure out the ending, and they couldn't write as fast as Mike could shoot.

As he rode at the gallop, he realized something else: something told him he might be losing Bergman, that she was frustrated to the point of checking out emotionally. If Mike lost Ingrid, Wallis wouldn't get what he wanted—Mike understood that Hal imagined he might obtain a perfect picture. And merely as an observer, Mike knew that Hal wanted to please Irene Lee. It was as if Hal wanted to make the perfect picture as a present to her.

Mike could only think such lucid thoughts when he sat in the saddle and he and the horse were one, and my God they were, he and Dakota—one beast with one mind on open prairie with the sun big and orange at the horizon. He let Dakota go and the horse strode up a long rise to a hill that overlooked the flat expanse of the San Fernando Valley all the way to the San Gabriels. The sun began to sink behind the far hills, and horse and rider panted from the trip. Mike felt good. Really good. He had gotten laid at lunch and going for a ride here to close out the day felt just as satisfying.

They started back toward home the way they had come but slowly and carefully now, descending over the uneven trail. He thought about what lay ahead this week—Lorre was closed out as Ugarte, and Claude Rains had joined the picture, but not Paul Henreid, who was ill. He must speak with Hal at once about the writers—the crazy brothers, Koch, Robinson. They had to deliver a final act or Christmas Baby might have some sort of breakdown and end up in hospital. By the time he reached the barn, it was twilight and he handed Dakota over to Jim for a good, long rubdown.

Inside the house, he heard Bess on the phone, her laugh hearty. When she saw Mike, she said, "Here, Szoka's on the phone and wants to talk to you."

Mike had been hoping Szoka Sakall would ring him up. They had been friends since childhood, and now Mike wanted Szoka for a part. More than that, Mike knew Szoka needed a part, but the proud Hungarian Sakall had been going back and forth with Hal Wallis about his salary, either two weeks or three guaranteed, and Mike had convinced Hal to give Szoka three weeks for the role of Carl the headwaiter.

Mike took the receiver from his wife and said in Hungarian, "Szoka, how are you? Did you get the script?"

"I got the script, yes, Mike," said the familiar, high voice, "but Carl the waiter—not so many lines. Anybody could play this little part."

Mike said, "Nobody but you, Szoka. You are perfect, and don't worry, I promise I get you more lines. Writers still working on Act 3, and I have some ideas to build up the part."

Szoka made a noise into the phone, a hemming and hawing noise, and then Mike could hear Szoka talking to his dog. Well, to his dog or his wife, Boszi—Mike wasn't sure which.

"Szoka! Listen, Szoka, many of our friends are on this picture.

Lots of wonderful actors from Europe who are playing, well, refugees from Europe who make it as far as Casablanca. Then they are stuck there waiting to get out. You won't believe how many I have rounded up."

"You give them all parts in your picture?" Szoka asked.

"My God yes!" said Curtiz. "The writers were talking about the story being full of refugees, and it was obvious. I said to Wallis, I know so many! Let me hire them and they give you authenticity! Truth! Ludwig Stossel, you remember him. And for his wife, Ilka Grüning. Curt Bois plays a pickpocket. Marcel Dalio is in it. Wolfgang Zilzer. Peter Lorre is already closed out of his role as an assassin of Nazis. There are a dozen more I could name, and they all get little bits of business."

"If you give me your word the part will be bigger," said Sakall, "I will be there."

"Thank you, thank you," said Mike. "See you soon, my friend."

Harriet the cook had prepared dinner, and Mike sat down to eat with Bess—roast beef, mashed potatoes, and summer squash. "How did it go today, Michael?" asked Bess. She was every inch the Hollywood matron, large and blonde and intelligent. She was no Gloria, the little brunette Mike had had for lunch, but neither was little Gloria a top Hollywood screenwriter. Bess was.

"Did you look at Scene 33 like I ask you to?" asked Mike. "That will be my first scene with Szoka, and I want it to be just right." Nobody knew that Bess was advising Mike on the characterizations in his picture, but she was, and he relied on her to interpret the nuances of American motivations that eluded him at best and bored him at worst.

"Yes, the scene with the banker," said Bess. "The boys did a marvelous job with that one, so you just make sure Carl is indifferent to the pretensions of the people at the table. One woman calls Rick snobbish. The man suggests Rick will be impressed by the fact he is an important Amsterdam banker. But Carl simply doesn't care, so make sure Szoka underplays it. Then he gets the punch line when he says the leading banker in Amsterdam is our pastry chef. Wonderful! Just wonderful writing," she enthused. "Just you make sure he plays it indifferently. Don't let him try to be funny—and Szoka will try. The words are funny, so he must play it straight. Quiet and straight."

Mike buttered a slice of bread as he hung on her words. "Yes, yes, I understand. Szoka, no bits of business."

"The next scene, on the other hand," said Bess, "that one play to the hilt. The German banker is outraged to be kept out of the gambling room. He simply won't have it!"

She was bellowing now, captivated by the script the Epsteins had delivered and the other writers had fine-tuned. Mike loved her enthusiasm and the pitch her voice would reach, big and booming, as much as he relied on her interpretations.

"And Rick is the cool gangster. No, no, Mr. German banker, you run along now." She sipped the goblet of Bordeaux that Harriet had just poured. "Marvelous," said Bess. "Those writers are simply marvelous."

But Mike thought, they may be marvelous, but they are slow. Much too slow. Something must be done.

The next morning, Curtiz awaited Wallis in the Warner parking lot. He knew what time Hal arrived. He knew Hal would have a cardboard box of film cans to lug into his office. So Curtiz leaned against the trunk of a palm tree at the edge of the lot, staked out the parking spot, smoked some cigarettes, and waited. Such a beautiful morning, the kind Curtiz had only ever experienced here in Hollywood, the sky a perfect blue without a cloud in sight, and the air crisp and clean. At 8:01, Wallis drove up in his Packard and parked, regular as a Swiss watch. With Hal leaning into the back seat to retrieve the inevitable box of film, Curtiz strode across the lot and said, "Hal! Good morning! So glad I run into you."

Wallis smacked his head on the doorframe at the sudden intrusion. He stood to his height outside the car, rubbing his crown. "It's a little early in the morning for you to be so . . . happy, Mike," said Wallis grumpily. "What's going on?"

"Bess says you and Louise come to dinner Sunday, okay, Hal?"

"Oh Jesus," groused Wallis, "what happened?"

"No, no, no," said Curtiz, who brushed past Wallis to grab the box of film cans out of the back seat. "Shooting go okay." Mike knew Wallis remained suspicious as he shut the car door and followed Curtiz toward the Administration Building. "Dailies look good, yes?" asked Mike.

"The dailies looked all right," said Wallis. "I have notes to go over with you." Always Wallis had notes. Mike could deliver the most beautiful, the most lyrical, the most incredible compositions, and still Wallis would have notes, which was okay with Mike because Wallis knew his business and could make good pictures great, and that was what Curtiz cared about, good pictures that became great.

They had reached the edge of the parking lot where the landscaping began when Wallis said, "Goddammit, Mike. Stop!"

Curtiz stopped. He turned to face his boss, his antagonist when a picture was in production. Mike looked all about; the nearest human was getting out of his car a hundred feet away, which meant this was as good a place as any to talk. "So, shooting go okay, Hal,"

Mike repeated, setting the box of film on the pavement, "only—"

"Only what?" demanded Wallis.

Curtiz inhaled deeply and let the breath out. "Only Ingrid not happy."

Wallis squinted at the director. "Ingrid is an actress making a good sum, an actress who hadn't worked in almost a year. Do I really care if she's happy or not?"

Mike thought about the question; it was a fair question. "You know me and actors," he said. "But Ingrid, she not happy because no Act 3. She shows how unhappy on set yesterday, and the camera see the confusion. Look at dailies from yesterday, and you see too. Christmas Baby need final Act 3 to make sense of character, or maybe I think we lose her."

"Whaddya mean, we lose her?" said Wallis. "What does that mean?"

Mike shrugged. "Don't know. She get sick. She make other actors unhappy. She walk off picture. Don't know, but bad for picture." Mike had been fearful that Wallis would lose his temper; but Hal was thinking and then nodding.

He leveled his gaze at Mike. "You know what?" he said. "You're right. We've got six or seven grand a week in these goddamn writers, and it's time they delivered. Enough of this bullshit. I want Act 3 done."

Curtiz had rarely heard such an outburst from Hal B. Wallis in all these years working together. Mike watched Hal bend down and pick up his film. When he had reached his full height again, his eyes shone like anthracite coal. Curtiz didn't know what to say, so he decided to just listen.

"Let's go see Renie and tell her this nonsense has to end," said Wallis. "And if she's not there, we'll wait in her office until she shows up. They're her goddamn writers, and that makes her responsible. As a matter of fact, Renie brought me this goddamn property and that makes her doubly responsible."

Curtiz held the door of the Writers Building open for Wallis and his film. Wallis was still grumbling: "They've had five months to give me a script—a complete script—and now I might lose my leading lady, and so they either finish the script or feel the wrath of the gods."

Curtiz felt himself gulp, and he followed Wallis along the hallway to Irene's office.

CHAPTER 48

Irene hadn't slept well, again. She knew her luck was running out and unless there was some miracle that resulted in a successful Act 3, Hal would come gunning for her sooner or later, and she wouldn't be able to charm her way out of it. But she didn't expect it to happen exactly seven minutes after forming the thought. Hal careened around the corner and into her office holding a box of film cans, and Curtiz followed immediately after.

"What's going on with Act 3?" Wallis demanded.

Seated at her desk, she froze. "I meet with the writers at ten," she said, looking up at him.

"To do what?"

"To go over the script. They try scenes, and we go over them and refine or throw them out and start over."

"Why is this taking so long? It never has before. Four writers and no finish."

"Hal, you're rewriting scenes every day and sending them to the boys, and they can't get their heads clear enough to find an ending."

"You know what I think?" he asked. "I think we're a laughing-stock for issuing an unfinished script to the talent. Telling them, 'Don't look at Act 3; it's not final.' And now Mike says Bergman is demanding the final act, and I don't blame her. Ingrid Bergman is not a difficult actress, but even she is questioning what's going on."

Irene fumbled for cigarettes; she couldn't find any. "It's going to happen, Hal. Just give them some more time. They're almost there."

"We are bleeding money on this cast as they sit around day after day, week after week. I finally got Warner to agree to give us time to get Act 3 in order, and your writers keep not doing it." He paused and continued to glare at her. "Maybe he's right. Maybe story editor is a man's job after all." And he stormed out, with Curtiz in tow.

There it was, the unkindest cut of all, from the man who always had her back. She sat stunned; mind a blank. The dark thoughts gathered; she had been wrong about this story; she was crazy to think she could ever be a producer; Mother was right all along. Get married, settle down, and forget this nonsense.

She reached for the phone and dialed the operator. "Can you please get me Brooklyn, New York? The number is West one, three seven one. Person to person from Miss Irene Lee for Mr. Aaron Diamond." Of course, he wouldn't be there, she thought as she waited. He'd be at a late lunch, or on a sales call, or—

"Is this *the* Miss Irene Lee," said a male voice, and the warm honey poured over her. She tried to match the tone, kiddingly, but nothing came to mind and no sounds escaped her throat. "Irene? Are you there?"

"I'm here," she managed. She swiveled her chair around to stare at the wall.

"Are you all right? What's happened?"

Why had she picked up the phone and called Aaron? She tried to reconstruct the thought process in her mind. Oh that's right, she was going to say yes to his proposal; that was it. She felt herself trapped inside a screenplay where she had been knocked unconscious and was coming to. She couldn't speak, but then, true to his nature, he waited, silently, patiently, while she wrestled Mother for her soul. *Just give up, be a wife, have children. That office is no place for a woman, and even the men who support you don't support you. A woman's place is in the home.*

She knew she had to say something. Then she heard her voice. "I just wanted to call and tell you . . ."

No. No, Mother, no. This job is my life. Whether it's here or some-where else, this is my life. Maybe that house on Hillsdale Avenue is your home and your life, but this office is mine. Go to hell, Mother.

"I just wanted to call and say hello, that's all."

"Well, hello!" he said pleasantly. "It's wonderful to hear your voice. Wonderful of you to think of me."

"What's new in the city?" she forced herself to ask to keep the conversation going.

"New in the city," he repeated. "Oh, there's a gas shortage. They doubled the value of the ration coupons, so each one is worth six gallons of gas instead of three. But nobody told the distributors, so all the gas got used up and now the whole state of New York is afoot."

God, that accent. Even now, with Wallis's knife sticking out of her back, she loved that accent.

She had fallen silent again.

"When are you coming home, Irene?" he asked.

"After production wraps. Not 'til then."

"How's it going, anyway?" he asked. "Your baby."

"Oh it's going, all right. It'll all be over in a couple of weeks. It's just been . . ." She groped for the words. "It's just tough going right now."

"I'm sorry to hear it," he said as if he meant the words. Why couldn't he be her boss, she mused. But then she would be leaning on a man when all she really had was herself. And she hadn't failed. Not yet, anyway.

"Listen, I've got to get going," said Irene. "I just wanted to say hi. So, hi, Aaron."

"Hi, Miss Lee. And thank you."

"Okay. Goodbye."

"Bye, Irene."

She held the phone by her ear long after the connection had been broken, thinking, just thinking. Sadness wasn't a feeling she tolerated in anyone, especially herself, but she felt it now, a deep, penetrating, soaking sadness. Slowly, she set the receiver in the cradle and swung her chair around to face the doorway.

And there stood both Epsteins. When her eyes met theirs, they became a new definition of awkward. "You didn't show up for our ten o'clock, so we came down," said Phil. "And your door was, you know, open."

"Yeah, I know, open," she sighed. She arose from her chair and smoothed her skirt. She realized she had set her cigarettes on the file cabinet behind her desk and took one out and lit it.

The boys had drifted inside her door and didn't seem to know what to do with themselves. They hadn't seen the script she found herself trapped within. So, the notorious wisecrackers of Warner Bros. waited.

"I told Hal to buy the play because I thought the story was too good to pass up," said Irene. "Burned-out American faces his past as the world erupts in war around him. And because I've got all these great writers, they'll turn it into a solid story for the screen. Great writers like the Epsteins who saved *Yankee Doodle Dandy* and made a thing of beauty out of *The Man Who Came to Dinner*. But now I've got to face the fact: maybe I was wrong all along. It can't be done—even you guys couldn't do it. Ilsa wouldn't get on the plane and leave Rick. It never made sense; it still doesn't. And in the end, Rick gives up. And that's no happy ending for Bogart." She sank into her chair again. "I miscalculated. Boy, did I ever."

Phil came over and rubbed her shoulder; she wouldn't have let Julie do that, but she knew what Phil meant by the gesture. "We're not giving up, boss. We'll figure it out. We want to make you proud."

She looked up at Phil, who had the gentlest brown eyes. "You were always my favorite," she told him.

"I know," Phil Epstein replied in satisfaction as his brother looked on.

CHAPTER 49

Julie was running, working up a sweat. He had never felt like he felt this moment, and he didn't like the feeling at all. The jobs had always just come, falling right into his lap. Up until this picture, this goddamn curse of a picture, everything had been fine. He knew the scripts they wrote were no different than the chum you threw overboard to attract fish. And the fish had been attracted, and the fish swam into theaters and ate the chum, and the Epsteins lived happily ever after.

Until now.

Julie cursed everything, especially their Epstein overconfidence that they could take this piece-of-shit play and turn it into something. They had begged Wallis to let them do it and now look. Hoisted on their own petard. Well, fuck poetic justice. Fuck Shakespeare.

Now Julie was running for his life, drenched in sweat and running. The morning was dense, warm, and humid, and the UCLA track deserted. He made ten laps without much effort because he had to think. The more he and Phil had tried to figure out the ending, the worse it got. Usually, a run like this would have made him feel like a million bucks. Today, no. Today he felt like crap because he was crap. They were crap. The Epsteins couldn't figure out how to end a picture! It was like they had been cursed. Renie and

Hal awaited their great idea that would save this picture and they had nothing. Koch even hand-held them to great insights, and Robinson had done more hand-holding, leading them through the dark, right up to the ending that nobody could figure out, not even Koch and Robinson.

He rushed home, showered, dressed, got in his car, and headed for Phil's house. On Holmby Avenue, Phil climbed in the car and by way of a hello said, "Let's go over it again."

"Let's not, and say we did," Julie replied.

Phil ignored him and said, "Rick hatches his plan in the café. He confesses to Louis that he's got the letters of transit, and here's the trap they'll set for Victor, right there in Rick's place. And Louis is in it for himself and sees recognition from the Nazis at capturing Laszlo."

"Of course," said Julie, hanging a quick right off Holmby Avenue and a quick left onto Beverly Glen. "That's the easy part," he snapped. "We got that far. Rick tricks Laszlo to come to the café. Then once Laszlo is there, Rick turns the tables and points his gun at Louis."

Julie did his best to remain calm. "Right."

"Ilsa's confused and she's already asked Rick to make the decisions," Phil went on, "so Rick says, 'Everything will be figured out at the airport,' and she goes along with him."

Julie gave a nod and kept driving.

"We've got to get the cast plausibly to the airport," said Phil. "Once at the airport, in the dark, Rick, Ilsa, and Victor are there, and they sort the mess out. The secret Rick's hiding is that he's going to make Ilsa live up to all she's told him about Victor and his greatness."

Julie drove up Beverly Glen through the green neighborhoods, blocks and blocks of beautiful houses and well-kept lawns. He decided to play along. "But we know that Louis has tipped off Strasser, who comes charging into the scene. There's a gun battle. Let's not quibble about how many times Rick shoots the Nazi, or whether he shoots him in the front or the back. The Nazi ends up dead on the ground."

Julie continued making his way up Beverly Glen and could see the intersection with Sunset Boulevard ahead. Yes, he could see it all. Strasser was shot dead at the airport and good riddance, and there ahead lay Sunset Boulevard, and Julie would turn right.

"We've finally gotten everybody to the airport and it all seems to hold together," said Phil. "Rick shoots Strasser dead, and seconds later the French police roll in and spill out of their cars. Louis, who Curtiz said and we all agreed was going to switch to the resistance side—"

"Yes, yes," snapped Julie as the light turned red at Beverly Glen and Sunset. "Louis is primed to change sides. So how do we show that, and how is it plausible for the audience?"

It was a long red light and they pondered it yet again, the million-dollar question: what would Louis Renault do or say to switch sides? And then it hit Julie. It hit him so hard he hit the horn with his elbow. Beside him, Phil grabbed his head as if the top might blow off.

"That's it!" said Phil.

Yes, thought Julie. And then he screamed aloud: "Yes!" The light turned green, and he eased his foot off the brake and onto the gas. "Yes!"

They both knew the line; they both now knew what Louis must say to take the heat off Rick. It was so obvious. It was hiding in plain sight all along. Louis must throw his own men off the trail of the obvious suspect standing before them, Rick Blaine, who held the smoking gun in his pocket. Rick was a hero for shooting the Nazi. Louis was a hero for protecting Rick. It was so beautiful, and so perfect, and how on earth did neither of them think of it until now?

"Oh my God," said Julie. "Oh my God. Wait 'til we tell Renie."

Irene was running later than she wanted to, but motivation was tough this morning. Not only didn't she have an ending for *Casablanca*, but she realized she was down to two pairs of stockings and now there was a shortage because of the war. What was a woman supposed to do with no stockings to wear? Go to work with bare legs? She wondered if there was a black market for stockings but figured if there wasn't, there soon would be. And then she thought the Wardrobe Department must have stockings she could pilfer, because certainly the actresses on-screen couldn't go around in bare legs. What good was it to be a female executive at Warner Bros. if you couldn't steal some stockings from Wardrobe?

As she ran around gathering her purse and cigarettes and script so she could head to work, the doorbell of the apartment rang. It was early for a messenger, but it must be a messenger. She careened to the door and pulled it open, and there was Aaron Diamond. Not only was it Aaron Diamond, it was Aaron Diamond dressed in a naval officer's uniform. For the second time in two days, she doubted her own sanity. Wasn't Aaron Diamond a civilian? Hadn't she just talked to Aaron Diamond, the civilian, in New York?

She reached out with her right index finger carefully and poked him in the chest, right above the tie clasp. Son of a gun, he seemed to be real.

"What . . ." she began, but in her dumbfounded surprise, *are you doing here* didn't follow.

He spread his arms wide like Jolson and said, "Coast to coast in seventeen hours! That's what TWA claims, and they were pretty close to right."

"And you're . . ." she began, pointing at his uniform, but as her dumbfounded surprise continued, deepened even, *in the Navy* didn't follow.

He looked down at himself and ran his hands over his jacket.

"Oh yeah, I'm sure I told you I'm in the Naval Reserve, and they've called me up. I'm on my way to the base in San Diego."

Without verbalizing an invitation, she stepped aside so he could enter. "I guess," she murmured, "I guess you told me."

"Well," he said as he turned inside the door, "surprise!"

Mixed in with the jumble of emotions of the moment, she knew she had to get to work. "Why are you here?" she asked. "How did you find me?"

He had removed his white hat and held it in his hands. "On the phone, you sounded very much like a girl—a woman—who needed a friend, but in the big moment, even though you had called me, you were too proud to ask for one. As for finding you, you're in the Los Angeles phone book." He gave a shrug that said, *And here we are.*

He glanced down at his wristwatch. "Listen, I know you're on your way to your job, so I'll give you my speech and then be on my way. I had seventeen hours to practice it, you know."

Oh my God, she thought as he was speaking, he's going to say that he's in love with me.

Aaron took a breath and began. "I know that first evening I made a big fat mistake and I promised I wouldn't do it again, but

I sort of feel I gave you the wrong impression of me, and I want to set the record straight."

"Okay," she managed.

"I like you. I like the way you think. I like all that energy. I like what you do for a living, and it doesn't take a genius to understand how proud you are of what you do. Whatever happens between us, I wouldn't change you for the world, because I think you're perfect. And that's why I said what I said that night. In my thirty-one years of life, you're the first and only perfect woman I've ever met, so I decided to say what came naturally." He looked up at the ceiling, and made a face, the face of one thinking, and said, "There, that's my speech in its entirety, I believe."

"I'm not perfect. Nobody's perfect," she managed. She felt especially imperfect this morning.

"Depends on your definition," he parried.

"And you came 3,000 miles to tell me?"

"Yes, ma'am. Well, that, and to report to San Diego."

She was all sorts of terrified, standing here alone with this man, because this couldn't be happening, and it was happening. A really great guy who probably wasn't Rasputin or a crazed killer thought she was perfect and had even pulled thoughts out of her head. He knew her well enough to promise that she wouldn't be sentenced to home life and children if they got married. How did he do that? He had sensed her distress on the phone and tracked her down all the way across the country and made a speech more beautiful than any she had ever read in a screenplay. And she simply could not let this man in. Into her apartment for a moment, yes. Into her heart for even a second, no.

With his speech concluded and work awaiting and the awkwardness piling up, she said, "Now what?"

"That's entirely up to you," he responded. "We're just a couple of little people, two tiny specks in this crazy world, and our problems don't amount to a hill of beans compared to what's going on. But I sure do like you and wish you the best. And wherever I go, you will go with me." He tapped his temple. "Up here."

She reached for her things and headed out the door, grateful at least that he had indeed not said he was in love with her. Well, he had used every other word in the English language that indicated he was, but not the big one. She reached back to make sure the door was locked, and they rode down in the elevator together. At the curb, his cab was idling. Behind it, a studio car awaited her.

He turned to face her and looked down from his great height. "Listen, I'd like to call you before I ship out, okay? I might do something crazy like ask how you feel about my speech, so maybe you could write your own speech."

This was all too strange, this moment so much like the one with Jack Janowitz in front of her other apartment 3,000 miles away. Back then she had joked and kissed him goodbye, and it occurred to her not to do either for fear of jinxing this one like she had jinxed that one.

"Yes, please call me," she heard herself say.

He nodded, and put out his hand for a handshake, just like on that first night. But as she clasped his hand, he seemed to change his mind and pulled her into an embrace and kissed her, just like he had kissed her the second night. In the five seconds the kiss went on, she determined the first one hadn't been a fluke. When he pulled away again, her head went for a little swim.

"Goodbye," said Aaron Diamond.

"Goodbye and good luck," said Irene, breathless. And he climbed in the back seat of the cab and off it went.

CHAPTER 50

Two hours later, after riding to the studio trying to make sense of what had just happened, Irene worked at her desk and did her best to force concentration on Robinson's latest notes and edits. God, the man was good. He had fine-tuned the scene where Ilsa is talking to Sam right after her arrival in Casablanca. Sam wheels up his piano, and instead of asking him to play "As Time Goes By" right off the bat, she starts out by pumping him for information about Rick. Where is he? When will he be back? When Sam says not tonight, she asks if he always leaves so early. Great character stuff for Ingrid to play to reveal she was once very much in love with Rick and might just still be in love with him. Casey's rewrite made her vulnerable, like a high school girl. And Casey had given more lines to Sam as he bobs and weaves, avoiding all the questions.

Irene realized that her writers had added such wonderful depth to the story and the setting and characters, some really beautiful stuff. And the dailies were looking wonderful as a result. But the lack of an ending tortured everybody, every minute of every day. A bad ending would kill them in reviews—reviews and word of mouth. The picture would tank and Warner would get rid of her. Hal's words cut into her each time they echoed: *Maybe story editor is a man's job after all.*

It was still quiet in the Writers Building before nine, so it seemed instantly odd when she heard the pounding of footsteps on the floor in the hallway. Then the boys hurried into her office and slammed the door behind them. She found this quite strange for a number of reasons, primarily, what in the world were they doing here on time? They were out of breath, their faces flushed, even the tops of their bald heads were flushed. They looked like a pair of peak-season tomatoes.

She stared up at Phil and Julie over her reading glasses. She didn't say anything; neither did they. Her stomach grew sour at the prospect that they had played another prank involving Colonel Warner, like the time they sent the new contract player a memo from Warner's desk saying he had decided to change the player's name to Irving Lowenstein and, "Come on up to my office so we can talk about it." Oh, the ruckus they caused when the rookie showed up in the chief's office and tried to convince him not to change his name to Irving Lowenstein.

Finally, when the Epsteins had begun to breathe more or less normally, and their faces had lost their fire-engine coloring, she took out a cigarette, lit it, and said in the form of a question, "Okayyyyy?"

"We've got it," said Julie, still a bit short of breath.

"We solved it," said Phil.

"Got what?" she asked, not daring to believe they had perhaps gotten it. The big it. The ending.

Julie said, "Remember how Hal said take everyone outside for the ending, and we moved it to the airport?"

"Yes, I've read it about forty times."

Julie went on, talking fast, like a character out of *Boy Meets Girl*. "Rick has a gun on Louis, and they watch Victor and Ilsa get on the plane. Strasser arrives on the scene and tries to stop the plane and Rick shoots him. Then the police come and Rick's obviously Strasser's killer."

"So now we need the big switcheroo where Louis changes sides, right?" said Phil.

"Right," said Irene, playing along and now very curious what they had up their sleeve.

Phil continued, "And so Renault announces the obvious: the German's been shot, and Louis looks dead at Rick, and you think he's going to say, 'Arrest Rick Blaine!' But he doesn't. Instead, he says . . ."

And in unison they told Irene what Louis must say.

Irene heard herself murmur, "Oh my God." It was such a perfect line and a perfect way out of the corner they had written themselves into that there must be something wrong with it. This line turned a key and unlocked a new possible ending. Rick didn't have to give up and go to a concentration camp. Rick could get away.

"We've alluded to it twice already through the course of the story," said Julie, "so that's already planted in the minds of the audience, but in a tense moment like this, they won't see it coming." He mimicked a right cross. "Pow!"

Irene felt a chill begin at the base of her back and spread through her arms and legs, serving as evidence she could trust the line the boys had given her. Then something strange happened that had never happened to Irene Lee before: tears welled up in her eyes and ran down her cheeks before she could even turn away. The boys saw it; the boys were eyewitnesses, and they stood there as awkwardly as Jewish guys could in any given moment.

"We . . ." stammered Phil, "we gotta go."

"Yeah, see ya, Renie," added Julie.

They struggled with the door as if they had never operated a knob before, and then they were gone.

She couldn't help but go on sobbing, she supposed from all these weeks and months of working and wondering and fretting and fixing in furious attempts to convert what she thought of as a lump of gold into fancy jewelry.

Or was she crying about Aaron?

She pulled a handkerchief out of the pocket of her jacket and wiped her face and blew her nose. Joan wouldn't cry at a moment like this; Greer wouldn't cry. It simply wouldn't do for anybody to see the only female executive at Warner Bros. in tears.

Her luck held; she pulled herself together without anyone any the wiser. But then she made the mistake of thinking about what the boys had left behind—the five most beautiful words she had ever heard: *Round up the usual suspects.*

And she started bawling all over again.

CHAPTER 51

Day by day, Phil and Julius worked at the remaining pieces of the unsolvable puzzle. Yes, Rick kills the Nazi, and Louis gets him out of a jam by telling his men to round up the usual suspects. But why does it make sense for Ilsa to leave with Victor? They tried every conceivable angle while also fielding Hal's rewrites, and the days passed, and then a week was gone, and another, and June became July.

Every day the shooting progressed. Paul Henreid joined the cast. Every principal was shooting now, and nobody knew the ending because an ending still didn't exist, even though pages and pages of script were written and performed and committed to film.

Phil had always relied on Julie when the chips were down; as the senior partner, Julie always had answers when they got in a jam writing a script. Julie always knew what to do. Now he didn't, but Phil could feel Julie's attempt at leadership, and for the first time in his life, it grated on his nerves. What felt worse, much worse, was meeting in their office in the Writers Building at night out of desperation because they were out of runway, and Wallis had called a meeting for eleven the next morning and expected the ending. So here they were, working into the night. The last night.

Alice sat at her desk, her arms crossed in front of her and her heavy-lidded eyes staring straight ahead.

Five minutes into their session, Julie said, "We've been through this every day for months. Why do you think it's going to be any different tonight?"

"Because we're out of time and we still haven't given them the final sequence," said Phil.

"They can't pin this on us. Koch hasn't done it. Casey struck out. Face it, we lost."

"No. If we can figure out the 'usual suspects' line, we can figure out the motivations for our triangle."

Julie covered his face with his hands in a dramatic gesture. "Give it up!" he pleaded. "So we get Klined. So what? So we go to Paramount or Universal. Who gives a shit?"

"I do!" shouted Phil, and the coiled-up springs inside him released. He shot out of his chair and loomed over his brother, who continued to sit slumped like a juvenile delinquent. "Renie's counting on us—you know that. I know that. We cannot let Renie down."

"She made a mistake," Julie yelled. "She's human—she makes mistakes! I refuse to go down for Renie's mistake!"

"We owe her."

"We owe her nothin'," said Julie. "She's as cold-blooded as everybody else in this town. And you're soft, Phil. Too soft."

Phil saw black. "You sonofabitch. Now it's soft to show some loyalty, some integrity? Those things don't apply anymore?"

"I'm a realist," screamed Julie, "which is a helluva lot better than some pansy who everybody walks all over." Julie jabbed a finger in his brother's chest, "At this point, it's every man for himself."

Phil swatted Julie's hand away. "Okay, fine," he shouted, "give up. If that's who you really are, who needs you?"

"Oh yeah, big shot?" said Julie. "Then how about this: figure it out any way you want. I'm going home." Julie rolled down his sleeves and buttoned the cuffs.

"Fine, you quitter," said Phil. "Leave me in peace and I'll figure something out, or I'll call Koch and work with him and figure it out. But we can't fail. She's counting on us." He took hold of Julie's wrist and added, "You know how important this story is. To everybody. To the world."

Julie wrenched his arm free. "Stop, your heart is bleeding all over my arm."

He grabbed his coat in a sudden move and headed for the door. "Good luck to both of you—you and your integrity." And off he went, the heels of his shoes echoing in the empty hallway. Then Phil and Alice heard him in the stairway and finally the outer fire door slammed, and they knew he was gone.

Phil felt spasms of physical pain in his gut. He could feel his heart pounding in a drumbeat that just about deafened him. He turned to Alice, who sat motionless, her face drained of color. Phil shrugged. Alice shrugged.

He drifted over to the window to catch sight of Julie's headlights as his car swung out of the lot and sliced into the night. He let himself drift to his left until the window frame was supporting him. He had his hands in pockets, and he tried to will his heart to ease up a little. When it didn't, he had an idea. He slid the curtain closed again and walked into Julie's office, where he found a new bottle of Glenlivet in the bottom left drawer of his brother's desk. He took it in hand and walked out to the common area where Alice continued to sit.

"I gave him this," said Phil. "Now I'm taking it back."

"Integrity in action," said Alice.

"You were an eyewitness," said Phil. "The bastard deserves it."

He broke the seal and unscrewed the lid, retrieved his coffee cup, and poured himself a healthy double shot that became a triple. He held the bottle in her direction, and she gave him a smile and little shake of the head that said, *Not in a million years.*

Down the hatch went the hot liquid in two swallows. About forty-five seconds and one giant shudder later, Phil felt the liquor hit his empty stomach with a cannonball splash. The healing began at once.

There was a knock on the door to their suite. Phil looked over and there stood Stephen Karnot, cigarette dangling from the corner of his mouth. He was a tall skinny guy with a full head of curly dark hair and a friendly face. Another wave of pleasure rolled over Phil courtesy of the Glenlivet. He said, "Hey, Karnot. How goes it with the proletariat?"

"It was fine until I heard all the shouting," he replied.

"You could hear it downstairs?"

"I imagine you could hear it in Barstow," said Karnot. "Do I get three guesses what it was about, and the first two don't count?"

Suddenly, Phil snapped his fingers, remembering. "Say, isn't this whole thing your fault? You're the one that found the play and convinced Wallis to buy it?"

"No," said Karnot. "Noooooo. Renie wanted me to write it up favorably for Wallis. Don't try to pin this on me, my friend. I argued with Renie up and down about all the problems. The police captain deflowering virgins. Sexual relations between unmarried people. Women trading sex for visas. And Rick—insufferable Rick and his self-pity. Bleh! It hasn't surprised me one bit to hear about all you writers trying and failing to make this stinker work. And now even you and your brother are at each other's throats." Karnot gave a faraway look. "I've already got it all thought out and scripted in my head: On my last day, I'm going to screw up my courage, march into her office, and say, 'Hey Renie, about that play you loved so much? I told you so.' And then I'm going to run like hell."

"What do you mean, on your last day?" said Phil.

"In two weeks, I'm off to Lockheed to make bombers," said Karnot happily. "They won't let me in the army because of, you know, my politics, but they'll give me the keys to a defense plant and let me make bombers. Whatever works for them works for me." He tiptoed over the threshold so he could tamp out his cigarette in the ashtray atop their low bookcase behind Alice's desk. "Don't let me keep you from your Academy Award, Phil," he cracked.

"Yeah, thanks," said Phil. He raised a clenched fist. "Long live the revolution." Karnot chuckled his way out the door and down the hall, free of the catastrophe.

Phil felt more deflated than ever. Julie was gone, and now the first eyewitness to the horrible traffic accident called *Casablanca* had confirmed that this had been a doomed operation all along. Phil thought about breaking down in tears, but Alice might find it unmanly. He breathed in, and out. In, and out. Then he turned to Alice and said, "Want to talk about the ending with me?"

She snickered. "You must be desperate." He didn't respond; he merely looked at her, letting the sadness come through.

"Oh, you poor boy," she said with a sigh. Then she mustered some insincere excitement. "Sure, let's talk about the ending! I already called home and told Mother to feed the cat and not wait up."

Phil found that adorable. Here Alice was, thirty-five years old—or was it thirty-six?—and still under the thumb of her mother. No, he told himself, focus. He said, "So, you know the *Casablanca* story, right?"

She smirked. "I've typed every page of every draft and every rewrite for four-and-a-half months. And I've read all the stuff Koch has added and Robinson's notes."

Phil felt his brain try to grab a time card and punch out, and he resisted the impulse. He kept looking at Alice; funny how neither Epstein stopped to appreciate what a gem Alice was. "I guess you do know the story," he said as he began to pace once more.

"Hal said, put the four of them—Rick, Ilsa, Victor, and Louis—at the airport for the climax and so there they are, and Ilsa says to Victor, 'I hate to tell you this, but I'm deserting you and staying here with Rick because I love Rick. I can't help myself.' And the schmuck Victor just stands there with his mouth open as he hears his wife say that she loves Rick in a way that's overpowering. In other words, Victor comes off as a cuckold, and the best we can do is to make Rick rationalize with Ilsa. He tells her she has to get on that plane because Rick is no longer the man she knew in Paris, that now he's a drunk who starts his day with booze at breakfast. To which Ilsa says, 'Fine, I'll start drinking at breakfast with you.' So now you've got one boozer creating another boozer."

He stopped pacing to try to focus on Alice.

"And after all that, she gets on the plane with Victor and flies off, and Strasser shows up and Rick fills him full of lead. Then Louis gets the heat off Rick by telling his men to round up the usual suspects. The end."

A silence ensued, into which Alice inserted, "Mr. Wallis is right. It does stink."

"After all these months with—" Phil counted them up in his head: Kline, MacKenzie, Koch, Robinson, and the two of them. "—six writers. All these months and six writers, and this is what we've got." He paced some more.

Alice stared at him for a moment and then gave a sigh. Not just an ordinary sigh, but a sigh worthy of Catherine the Great.

She said, "I have a question. Is this picture about three people and their heartaches, or is it about the world and the world's heartaches? Is it about sex? Or is it about ideals? Or, to use your word, integrity?"

Phil sensed she was saying something important, so he stopped and stared as she went on, "Because I'm hearing you describe a selfish man who's in love with a selfish woman, and meanwhile, this Victor is the one who really has something to offer the world, but all six of you are leaving him out of the equation. He sounds pretty damn attractive to me."

The fresh insight knocked Phil back on his heels. He sought the wall for support again. "You think Victor is attractive?"

"Oh yes!" said Alice. "All these new scenes you guys are giving him—he gets better and better!"

Phil considered another belt of Glenlivet but thought better of it to the extent he picked up the bottle and walked it back to Julie's desk. When he reentered the common area, Alice was removing her glasses. She dropped them on a stack of scripts and loose pages beside her big black Royal.

"Listen, I've typed every page of this mess, and so I know a thing or two about a thing or two. Victor is attractive as hell and he's not what you keep calling him, a cuckold, or a schmuck, or a weakling. I can take or leave Rick the way he's written, and Ilsa is torn between Rick and Victor for reasons I can't begin to understand because Rick really is a good-for-nothing drunk."

Phil resumed his pacing. "So?"

Alice didn't say anything; he gave her a glance and saw her rubbing the bridge of her nose with her thumb and fingertip. Then she said, "I saw a couple of pink pages—or were they blue pages? Somebody added a scene where Ilsa explains she left Rick in Paris because she learned Victor was alive and she had to go to him, right? It wasn't you guys because I didn't type it, but it was somebody."

"Right," said Phil.

"So, she already left Rick for Victor once. Rick was already second-best once because she knows in her heart she belongs with Victor." Alice leaned back and folded her arms and added, "And it just so happens that, oh by the way, Victor is the cat's meow."

Phil went back to pacing. "This is what you get with screenwriting by committee. Koch wrote that bit about Ilsa learning that Victor was alive—or was it Robinson? Hell, I can't keep anything straight anymore except to know it wasn't us." He stopped by the window and looked out into the night, thinking maybe he'd see Julie's car returning to the lot.

"I don't think so," said Alice, as if reading his mind. "I don't think he's coming back."

Phil skimmed over the entire incident in three seconds, culminating once again in the certainty that they must bail Renie out of this mess. He clamped down on his focus, despite the Glenlivet.

"Okay, so we've got Ilsa's POV of why she'd get on the plane. When it comes down to it, she can't leave Victor." Phil was at the window again, staring out at nighttime Burbank. "But what makes Rick send her away? If you go back to the play that started this mess, Rick is impossibly selfish and won't allow her to leave for any reason. He'll lie, cheat, steal, or kill to keep her with him."

Alice said, "Well, I remember when Mr. Koch added all that idealism to the earlier scenes. You know, all that backstory about Rick fighting fascists in Ethiopia and Spain?"

"Oh yeah, that's Koch all over," he said. "He'll beat you unconscious with politics and ideals."

To Phil, it seemed as if he were just meeting Alice for the first time. He said, "Where did all this insight come from?"

She rolled her bloodshot brown eyes. "Honey, I work at Warner Bros. and actually show up here at the office every day, so I see everything and hear everything that goes on, that's where."

Phil said distantly, thinking aloud, "So the ending is about sacrifice and not about murder and betrayal. Interesting."

Alice stood and stretched her back. "What's interesting is I make $1,700 a year, and you make that much in a week."

"At this moment, it doesn't seem very fair," Phil mused.

Alice said as she headed for the office door, "We're going to be here half the night, it looks like. I'd ask you to make us a pot of coffee, but you probably don't know how."

He called after her, "Ouch! That hurts, Alice!" But the truth was, he didn't.

CHAPTER 52

Dooley Wilson lay in his bed, awake in the night, as Estelle snored gently beside him. He found it the most reassuring sound in all the world. He grabbed the alarm clock beside his bed and tilted it toward a sliver of light beaming through the drapes: 4:50, meaning the alarm bell would ring in ten minutes. Damn—not enough time to go back to sleep but an eternity to lie awake. In the distance he could hear delivery trucks changing gears on Beverly Boulevard and roaring by on Temple. This morning he thought: six weeks on this picture at $350 a week. That's . . . why, that's $2,100! It's enough for a down payment on the house Estelle always wanted.

He thought about the Martin Beck Theater and Little Joe Jackson. He thought about Ethel Waters, Rex Ingram, and Katherine Dunham. About the footlights on Broadway and the steady work. And he thought, *You know what? Hollywood ain't so bad.* He felt a smile emerge on his face as the alarm sounded at five o'clock.

He pushed the button on the alarm as Estelle shuffled into the bathroom to brush her teeth then moved on to the kitchen.

"You have another full week, Dooley?" she asked forty minutes later after he had bathed, shaved, and dressed. She made flapjacks today in the old skillet and sliced him fancy bread while sausages sizzled. She was so happy lately—she had vaulted out of bed!

"Sure looks like another full week," he answered. "They keep adding scenes, reshooting scenes, and working on the last act, and so we keep sittin' around." He thought back to the previous week on Stage 8A. "Nice folks there. Nicest folks you could imagine."

"They must be," she said as she finished preparing his plate. After she had set it before him, a stack of flapjacks, fancy toast, and sausages, she said, "Close your eyes, sugar!" And he did. She said, "Ta-da!" and when he opened his eyes, there sat by his plate a glass jar with golden contents.

"What in hell?" he murmured.

"It's real maple syrup! From Vermont!" she enthused. "They had it at the farmer's market! Nothin' is too good for my man, my movie star!"

It didn't matter that within five minutes his knife, fork, fingers, and the cuffs of his shirt were sticky. He ate the flapjacks, the toast, and the sausage in quick bites and after a cleanup at the sink, he slipped on his jacket, kissed Estelle goodbye, and gave her ass a good long squeeze.

"Thank you, baby," he said as he kissed her a second time, a long, wet one.

He stepped out into the humid summer morning feeling the love of a good woman. His good woman. The studio car awaited, the driver dressed as always in a dark uniform with a black cap. Under the cap, his hair was gray and his expression blank.

"How's it going, Denny?" asked Dooley as he slid into the back seat.

"Can't complain, Dooley," said the driver as he eased the door closed behind Dooley. It hadn't been until about the third week that the driver with the gray hair had adjusted to driving a Negro to the studio every day.

The turning point seemed to be the day Dennis was especially quiet, and Dooley could feel his sadness. Dooley had dared to ask about it and found out that Dennis's daughter had taken some narcotics at a party with an actor in the hills and ended up in the hospital. Dooley expressed the shock and concern that any man would, and after that day they had discovered something to talk about: Virginia and her recovery. Lately she had been doing so well that Denny and Dooley had moved on to other topics, like Denny's days as a bit player in Westerns at Columbia and Dooley's run on Broadway. And, of course, they had the war in common, and Denny recited the latest about the war as if it were box scores from the ball game.

This morning, Dooley learned that the Germans had bombed Allied bases in Ireland, and that the mighty Nazi offensive on the Eastern Front was ready to crush the Reds. It all sounded mighty grim—so grim that Denny changed the subject. They were on Cahuenga when Denny said, "So Dooley, tell me about this picture you're making. I've never driven a featured player to the studio for seven straight weeks. Are you redoing *Gone With the Wind*?"

Dooley laughed, his stomach full of flapjacks, maple syrup, and love. "No, sir. It's a picture with Mr. Bogart and Miss Bergman about doings in Casablanca. Lots of fine actors and a wonderful script, except for the fact there's no ending. That seems to be bothering some of the folks quite a lot."

Denny was glancing at his passenger in the rearview mirror with genuine interest. "And you have a big part in this picture?"

"I wish I could describe it to you, Denny," said Dooley. "It's the kind of part I didn't know a colored man could get. I play Mr. Bogart's best friend. I sort of take care of him through the picture. It's . . ." He struggled for words. "It's the best time I've ever had."

They had just rolled through the studio gate when Denny said, "That makes me happy, Dooley. I can't think of anyone who deserves it more." They pulled up at Wardrobe and Dennis jumped out to open the door for his VIP. "Break a leg, my friend."

"Thank you, Denny. See you at 6:30."

Thirty minutes later, Dooley was in wardrobe but not in makeup; he would be called for makeup if any of his scenes were to be reshot today. And one never knew when the director would order a scene to be reshot, so sitting around was sort of like playing Russian roulette. He strolled down to Stage 8A in the glare of morning sunlight and adjusted to the sudden lack of brightness inside the soundstage door. Past a maze of plywood walls dressed as Moroccan stucco and the army of busy technicians, he found a row of chairs that hosted Dooley's rogues' gallery of new friends.

Sydney Greenstreet sprawled in one of the camp chairs and next to him, leaning forward in a now-familiar SS uniform, sat Connie Veidt. "Ah, Dooley, just in time," growled Greenstreet.

Dooley sat down and whispered, "In time for what, sir?"

The SS man confided in a clipped accent, "Sydney said that he has a surprise for us."

Greenstreet put a finger to his lips and glanced about. "A surprise for us, gentlemen. Just for us. And perhaps for Mr. Rains, if we choose. If we put it to a vote." He motioned for the other two to lean forward. "I have brought a pie."

He revealed the news with utter delight, as if he had unsealed a tomb of the pharaohs to discover immense wealth. Dooley couldn't decide if the actors were playing a trick on him.

"I have baked this pie myself," said Greenstreet with pride. He leaned forward still further. "It's a cherry pie. Because, as you must know, the Bing cherries are in season." He glanced both ways to assure privacy. "Plus, this cherry pie has a secret ingredient I discovered myself." He leaned so far forward he almost fell over. "I added cherry schnapps."

Dooley was certain now: this man wasn't joking. This man was serious. Sydney hadn't really stopped talking about food for at least four weeks. He told stories of buying food, cooking food, serving food, and consuming food.

Veidt leaned back in his chair, crossed his legs, and held an elegant finger in the air. Everything Mr. Veidt did was beautiful. "You know, I have had cherry schnapps," he said with gravity, "and yet, I am quite certain, I have never tasted a cherry pie." He thought some more as Greenstreet glared at him. "Yes, yes, I am certain of it."

"Egad, Connie!" said Greenstreet. "Do they have no Bing cherries in Germany?"

"Yes, they do," Connie considered, "but the best explanation I can give you is that they do not seem to concoct the cherries into a pie." He said this with great thought, great deliberation.

Greenstreet gave the German a solemn, jowly look, and suddenly guffawed so loudly that some of the crew stopped and stared.

"Quiet please! Quiet please!" Lee Katz shouted from deep in the soundstage. "We are shooting Scene 250!"

Veidt pulled out the script sitting beside him on the chair and thumbed through the pages. "Ah, Rick and Ilsa in the club."

Dooley thought what a strange world he had found himself in, drawing a salary for sitting with these gentlemen day after day. He had heard that Mr. Greenstreet was earning $3,750 per week for the role of Ferrari, and Mr. Veidt an unbelievable $5,000 for Strasser. Meanwhile, Dooley made just $350 and was happy as a clam to get it.

Off a ways, deep on the soundstage, Bogart and Bergman rehearsed a scene. Dooley could hear her say, "Richard, Victor thinks I'm leaving with him. Haven't you told him?"

And then Bogart said, "No, not yet."

"But it's all right, isn't it?" she said with distress. "You were able to arrange everything?"

Bogart said, "Everything is quite all right."

"Oh, Rick!" she said pleadingly.

Bogart said, "We'll tell him at the airport. The less time to think, the easier for all of us. Please trust me."

Rehearsal ended with a great flurry of talking and rushing about among the crew. But none of this concerned Dooley, or Connie, or Sydney. They sat there relaxing at—Dooley glanced at his wristwatch—9:30 in the morning. He felt almost guilty to receive money for nothing but sitting around.

Connie Veidt slouched in his chair, his long, thin legs jutting out like a praying mantis. He was looking at the great heights of the ceiling and said, "Sydney, when may we enjoy this pie of yours?" The fellow was so refined, his voice like a little song.

"Not until lunch, man!" Greenstreet growled. "It's in the icebox in my dressing room!"

It was now that Dooley happened to notice a fellow forty feet or so down the soundstage, standing by the sound-baffled wall in what seemed to be great tension. He was bald, and wore a scowl, and leaned by the wall with sleeves rolled up and his arms folded tightly at his chest. Then another man walked up to the bald man, a very tall fellow holding a pipe and wearing a matching, glum expression. They conferred, and Dooley felt bad for these men because, far from lounging about as Dooley and his companions were forced to do, these two seemed ready to fly into a rage or burst into tears. Then Dooley remembered, oh, this was one of those twins who wrote the screenplay. He had met them in the commissary many weeks back. The bald fellow took notice of Dooley watching them and said something to the tall man, and then the pair approached.

The bald man said to the three actors, "Did they, uh, did they tell you what you'd be shooting today, by any chance?"

Sydney shrugged. "The call sheet listed me, so I reported."

Attention fell to Dooley, who said, "Me, too. I was on the call sheet."

"No one has spoken to me this morning," said Veidt. "All I know is that now they are shooting Scene 250. We heard them."

Dooley thought that these men had the look of the condemned about them. They were pale, unshaven, and disheveled, almost as if they had slept in their clothes. Greenstreet said with a sweet smile, "These are the writers."

"Some of the writers," said the tall man. "Two of the writers."

"And you're here to learn what they plan to shoot because they need your ending," Sydney added with a dash of cruelty. Dooley thought it marvelous the way this man spoke, and how he could put two and two together.

"I can only imagine," continued Sydney, "that you are, as they say, at the end of the plank. But I must tell you, this has been a most delightful way to spend the summer, awaiting your Act 3 and getting paid to do it."

"My wife certainly thanks you," Dooley piped up, to which Veidt chuckled softly.

"Tell your wife I said, 'You're welcome,'" said the bald man.

Connie stood to his great height, every inch the soldier, and arched his back, letting out a groan. He looked into the face of the tall writer, matching him inch for inch. "The SS wishes to know the plan. You see, my studio has inquired about my availability for another picture."

The bald man interjected, "The plan is we meet with Wallis at eleven this morning and hash out the ending once and for all, or everybody's fired."

"Excellent," said Veidt with a cold smile. "I will inform Metro of my pending availability."

Greenstreet gave another chuckle, as if the lives of the disheveled weren't really at risk. And yet Dooley couldn't help but feel bad for both, the way they looked, the sorrow and frustration visible in their worn faces. Such a strange thing—their misfortune had made Estelle Wilson the happiest woman in Hollywood.

CHAPTER 53

Pulling into the Warner lot, Irene knew that today was judgment day and that the meeting Hal had called for eleven o'clock would settle Act 3 of *Casablanca* and, likely, determine what would happen August 1. Hal's patience had been exhausted by all of it—writers who hadn't gotten the job done, actors who whined and complained, and Irene herself for insisting he buy this property. Warner had said this was a man's job, then Wallis had agreed. Had she failed because she was a woman?

As she parked her car and walked to the Writers Building, she formulated plans for what she would say to her parents about the job change. She could never tell them that Jack Warner had shown her the door; the tale she told back home would depend on where she could find a safe landing spot at another studio or perhaps with a book publisher in New York. Yes, she thought, that was the course to take, permanent relocation to New York. And in the next instant, she scolded herself for the very thought.

At twenty past ten, Phil appeared at her office door looking like he hadn't slept. He clearly hadn't shaved. He confided he hadn't been home at all since the previous morning, and a late-night creative session with Julie had ended in disaster. Phil was paler than death and dazed and needed a friend more than a boss or colleague. She encouraged him to run down to the commissary for a late breakfast or early lunch, but Phil said no. He had realized some things and wanted to air his thoughts while he was still clear-headed enough to get them out.

He sat in the chair by her desk, leaning forward, hands clenched together, as if about to be sick. She lit a Chesterfield and waited. After a while, Phil said, "You know Alice, right?"

She nodded. "Your secretary."

"Yes. Alice Danziger. After Julie and I argued, he stormed out, and then Alice and I had a talk. She's read everything up to this minute, every draft of the script and all the rewrites, and I'm going to confess a lot of what I'm about to tell you came from Alice."

Irene wasn't surprised. The conversations she had had with Alice, most of them in the ladies lounge, had revealed Alice to be one sharp cookie. "I'm listening," said Irene. She knew to be careful of Phil at this moment. She liked and respected Phil. Of course, she loved them both, but Phil didn't have Julie's edge, which could disrupt conversations and screenplays alike.

Phil detailed what the brothers had argued about, and at that point, Irene asked him to pause so she could walk to the coffee table and pour Phil a cup from the pot that the script readers had gotten started.

The coffee seemed to revive Phil a little, and he told Irene what Alice thought of Rick and Ilsa, that Alice didn't care for either character in the screenplay, but she loved Victor's character and was offended by any talk that Victor was a lesser player in the drama. He was, in fact, the one who saw a bigger picture than the two weak souls—the married woman and the hard drinker who fancied themselves in love.

"Alice mentioned the new scene from Koch, or was it Robinson, where Ilsa told Rick she hadn't shown up at the Paris train station because she learned that Victor wasn't dead. She went to Victor in Paris out of a sense of duty and perhaps of love." Phil looked at Irene and added, his voice hoarse, "The biggest thing was, Alice said that the blue pages made it clear Ilsa had already left Rick behind for Victor once—why shouldn't she do it again?"

Irene weighed the statement. "So that's what gets Ilsa on the plane."

Phil nodded wearily. He said, "Maybe Koch or Robinson already understood this motivation, but Julie and I didn't. It solves a third of the problem of who stays, and who goes, and why." He pulled a folded piece of paper out of his pants pocket. "After Alice said that, she and I talked some more, and I jotted down a few ideas, you know, to fine-tune what we've got. Smooth out the rough spots." He stared at the paper.

Irene smiled at the thought of Alice Danziger bringing clarity when all the writers could feel was pressure. Imagine what Hal would say at the idea of a million dollars in talent and production unstuck by a secretary.

"I'm not thinking very clearly," said Phil, "but it seems to me the key thing now is what Rick says to Victor and what Victor says back to Rick that will square it for each other and the audience. That's what I tried to do—give them those lines that clarify why Rick stays and why Victor wants Ilsa with him as they walk to the plane." He rubbed a meaty hand over his face and his eyes.

She looked at her watch. "I'd love to see what you've got, but we're meeting with Hal in ten minutes."

"Shit!" said Phil, instantly revived. He shot to his feet and added, "I've got to go brush my teeth and get washed up. I don't want the guys to see me like this."

She looked up at him, feeling exultant for reasons she couldn't begin to pinpoint. "You know what you look like? You look like somebody who gives a damn, and that will mean a lot to Hal."

Phil rubbed his unshaven cheek. "Maybe that's my problem—I give too much of a damn." Phil rushed out toward the stairway to the second floor while Irene contemplated the meeting to come. Hal would not be dragged down by these mere mortals, these writers. The writers might fail him today, but Irene knew damn well that Wallis himself would not fail. Wallis the high lord of council would write the key pages himself if that's what it took, and she would stay there beside him, at his right hand, come what may and no matter that he had delivered unkind cuts.

Julius had spent the night sleepless after thundering home in record time and collapsing on the couch so as not to awaken Frances or the kids, Jimmy and Lizzie, and perhaps trigger another argument when things had been relatively quiet since the reconciliation. He then lay there replaying in his head the argument with Phil. He didn't really mean it about throwing in the towel; it occurred to him that he had left because he couldn't face failure in himself. He and Phil were the best, but maybe even the best couldn't fix every single concept that somebody dragged in the door. Maybe this stage play was too broken for anyone to spin into gold, even the Epsteins and Koch and Robinson.

But then, as the clock hit four in the morning, Julie came to accept that maybe the code to making this story work could be broken, but he and Phil hadn't managed it yet. Maybe the mighty Wallis was right to throw thunderbolts at their feet.

An hour later, at five, with the first rays of the sun, Julie changed into shorts and a T-shirt and went for a run on the UCLA track, a long, exhausting run in the oppressive July heat, even now at dawn.

He wanted to wear himself out of every ounce of frustration, punish himself, and cleanse the poison he felt within that had made him turn on his own brother, his other half.

An hour and seven miles later he dragged himself across the threshold of his home and showered and dressed for the morning. There would be no thought of avoiding the studio today, not after the blowup with Phil that had resulted in no plan for what to do next. Frances was up and puttering around the kitchen, and the kids were up. Sleepy, but up.

Frances informed Julie that the studio had called: writers meeting at eleven o'clock. She poured him coffee without another word, and he ate a bowl of oatmeal, kissed the kids goodbye, and headed out toward his fate. Should he stop for Phil per usual? No, Phil would have gotten the call for the meeting, and he wouldn't wait for Julie. Phil would just make a beeline for the studio because of how much was at stake.

Julie pulled open the door to the Writers Building at 10:52, in time to see Phil hurrying from Renie's office into the stairway heading upstairs. Julie felt an ache at the glimpse of his brother, then cursed his own weakness at feeling it. He walked to the door of Renie's office to assess the situation. She was gathering a big, tangled mess of scripts and loose pages, a yellow legal pad, and pens and pencils. She looked up at him.

"Well, well, well," said Renie, "look what the cat dragged in." Her tone revealed she knew pretty much everything.

"So, my fink of a brother spilled the beans," said Julie.

"Whatever you do," said Renie, "don't use that line in a script." She assessed him head to toe. "Go get your stuff. I'll see you in the boardroom." As he turned, she added, "And Julie? Today of all days, don't make trouble." A wisecrack tried to coalesce in his mind. But then he judged the look in her brown eyes and the wise-crack evaporated. He nodded silently, bounded up the stairs, and charged into their suite.

He expected to find Phil there but saw only Alice, who forced a smile. "Good morning, boss," she said with a disingenuous flair.

"Where is he?" asked Julie.

She nodded toward the men's room across the hall. "He grabbed his shaving kit."

"Jesus, you mean he stayed here all night?"

"He did indeed," said Alice. "I left at about 1:30, but he decided to stay and keep working."

Guilt crushed Julie like the sixteen-ton weight in a cartoon. He said nothing further but gathered his versions of script and notes and pages in various colors and headed down the hall to the boardroom.

It was stuffy in there already, despite small, oscillating fans that worked in each corner. Hal sat rigidly at the head of the table, his fingers entwined on the tabletop. Renie was settling in at her usual spot. Curtiz spun a pencil on the polished table surface as Koch sat lighting his pipe. Then Robinson appeared and filled the doorway; in another reality he might have made a crackerjack defensive lineman.

At eleven sharp Phil rushed in, clean-shaven and smelling of Old Spice, but with a bleeding gouge on his neck. The brothers said nothing in acknowledgment of each other, at least nothing the others could intercept, but Julie could feel no hostility from Phil and that was just Phil for you. Stick to the task at hand and don't hold grudges.

Wallis began, "There are 6,000 Paris Jews counting on me." He looked about him. "In my mind, this picture is dedicated to those people. They're dead or in concentration camps, and in *Casablanca* they're represented by the old man and his wife trying to learn English by telling time. And the Amsterdam banker. And the woman selling her jewelry, and the Norwegian willing to die for Victor Laszlo." He shrugged. "That's the stakes. If we find an ending, the picture will triumph and the Paris Jews will have a voice. If we don't, it bombs. We fail.

"So, we need to wrap up Act 3 today. We're going to sit here until we hash it out, and what we produce is going to be final. What we produce today is going to be shot starting tomorrow, and it had better be good." He unfolded his fingers and said, pounding the tabletop with his index finger, "No, it had better be perfect."

Julie watched the others stealing glances, and what came to mind was all those times Charlie Chan would announce to the assembled cast, "The killer is in this very room."

"Well, I've got a date," said Robinson, "so let's make this fast." It was a funny line that only Koch laughed at this morning. But Julie had to hand it to Robinson for trying to ease the tension everyone felt.

Before Wallis could play high school principal, Irene said, "Actually, Phil and I were talking, and he's got some ideas how we might be able to work some of these things out."

Julie felt his face flush and knew at once everyone could see it. Renie looked him in the eyes and flashed her sweetest smile, which only served to deepen Julie's shame.

Phil pulled out a folded piece of yellow legal paper and flattened it out atop the three-inch-thick stack of *Casablanca* ephemera in front of him. Then he opened his script and flipped through the pages. "Let's start with Scene 232, blue pages," said Phil. "Rick and Ilsa in his rooms at the club. She tells him she can't fight it anymore and she left him once and can't do it again. She wants Rick to do the thinking for both of them." He turned some pages. "Now referencing Scene 250, blue pages. Ilsa in alarm says to Rick that Victor thinks she's leaving with him, and Rick says he hasn't said anything to Victor yet but assures her 'everything is quite all right' and 'we'll tell him at the airport.'"

"Correct, we're shooting that today," said Curtiz.

Phil kept flipping pages. "We'll skip all the back and forth during the crosses and double-crosses with Louis and Laszlo and focus on the four principals after they arrive at the airport."

"Right," said Wallis, following along in his script. "Casey and I figured out that Victor has to be involved at the airport for any of this to have a chance of working. He's got to be an active participant."

"Agreed," said Phil. "But, as Howard postulated, we need Victor to be out of the way so Rick and Ilsa can say what they need to say to sort out who's flying off and who's staying, and why. So Victor will have to go put their luggage on the plane—it's not the best reason to lure him off, but for lack of anything better, then okay." Phil paused a moment, deep in thought. "I'm going to give full credit here to our secretary, Alice—"

"Alice Danziger," Renie interjected.

Phil nodded. "—for the realization that Ilsa already left Rick behind for Victor once, back in Paris, so why shouldn't she do it again?"

Robinson said, "Because Ilsa has already stated to Rick that she can't possibly leave him again."

Julie had been waiting for a chance to jump in on Phil's behalf and said to Robinson, "But we read your notes to Hal. You said Rick realized there were bigger forces at work here. We can play that card now. Rick can say it to Ilsa at the airport. And how can she argue?"

Renie piped up and said, as if reciting a poem, "We're just a couple of little people, two tiny specks in this crazy world, and our problems don't amount to a hill of beans compared to what's going on."

Julie looked at her and said, "Wow, that's good! Where's it from?"

"I just heard it recently," she said in a strange little voice, not at all like Renie's.

Hal was writing it down. "Let's work with that."

"Right," said Phil. "So the lines we gave to Rick about how he's a saloon keeper who starts drinking at breakfast—those things he says to get Ilsa to leave—forget all that. It's bullshit. Irrelevant. Now we're talking about higher stakes: the world in flames." Phil motioned to Hal, "It's 6,000 Jews in Paris, or a million in Warsaw, for that matter."

"Exactly," said Koch. "Rick has to confront her. He has to ask, how can you even think of leaving Victor when he may be the one who saves the world?"

Julie added with a nod toward Renie, ". . . since the problems of two little people . . ." He paused. ". . . three little people don't amount to a hill of beans in a world in flames." Julie jotted the line on his notepad.

Renie said, "How about, 'don't amount to a hill of beans in this crazy world'?" Julie kept writing and acknowledged the refinement with a nod.

"Okay, let's think this through," said Wallis, referring to his script with the current pink and blue pages inserted. "Rick's got a gun on Louis and tells him to put the names of Mr. and Mrs.

Victor Laszlo on the letters of transit. Ilsa hears this and panics—she thinks she's staying with Rick. Rick tells her she's getting on that plane and he's staying behind with the gun on Louis until the plane is away. She protests, but he reminds her that he was supposed to do the thinking for both of them, and it all added up to the fact that she belongs with Victor."

Wallis looked at the script and said, "I love these lines, where Rick tells her she's part of Victor's work and she's what keeps him going. If she were to send Victor off alone, she'd regret it. But they'll always have Paris. They'll have the memories."

Koch had been following along and said, "Then Rick tells her he's got a job to do because he's decided to take up the cause and fight the Nazis, and she can't be any part of that. He says he's not trying to be noble—"

Julie added, reading his notes, "—but she has to understand that the problems of three little people don't amount to a hill of beans in this crazy world."

"Wow!" Renie exclaimed.

Julie said, "At which point Laszlo comes back, after Rick has made his point and Ilsa has given in to it."

In the pause that followed, Phil said, "Now we're into the hardest part. How does Rick square it with Victor and allow him the dignity he deserves? And it was Alice who was singing the praises of Victor, who she thinks has really become a strong character after we've added to Henreid's part."

Wallis said, "Remind me again why I should be paying you two Epsteins when I could just be paying your secretary?"

Phil said, "Alice made me see that I had been looking at Victor all wrong. He's not a weak character—how could he be? She reminded me that he's really fucking Charles de Gaulle. He's a strong character and he needs to match Rick move for move at this moment by the plane." Phil referred to the script again. "Scene 262, Rick admits to Victor that Ilsa had come to see him the previous night for the letters of transit."

"Yes," said Wallis, following along. This had been one puzzle of the script nobody could solve, the touchy relationship between Rick and Victor. "Does Rick respect Victor? How do we show it?"

Phil referred to his notes. "I have Rick saying something to Victor such as, 'She did her best to convince me she was still in love with me so I would give her the letters. I knew it was a lie and she was doing it for your sake, but her heart was in the right place, so I told her she could have the letters.'" Phil looked up from his notes. "So, in effect, Rick is conceding that Victor is the better man, the winner. But we, the audience, know the real story is different."

Silence fell over the room. "Holy shit!" said Robinson.

"Holy shit," Julie heard himself echo.

"Victor keeps his wife and his dignity," said Wallis as he leaned back in a mixture of astonishment and relief.

Julie said, "So then, Rick hands the letters of transit to Victor, man to man."

Koch said, "And we can give Victor a socko line, something like, 'Welcome back to the fight. I know we're going to win.' Something to get the people up out of their seats."

"Oh my God," Renie murmured. "Oh my good God!"

"Fantastic," exclaimed Curtiz. "This I can shoot. This is worthy of the people in Paris." And he lifted himself from his chair and exited the room to return to the set.

Wallis vaulted up and caught the door before Curtiz could close it. Hal hollered down the hall, "Sally! Get a stenographer in here, PDQ!" He reentered the room, closed the door again, and said, "Okay, now we're going to go through everything at the airport one more time and nail down each line. I'll have Sally order us some lunch because we're not leaving this room until we've got it all and the rhythm is right and it's typed up and we do a reading. It's all got to be perfect."

Wallis and Renie lit cigarettes. Howard relit his pipe.

Phil pushed his chair back and arose. He staggered to the window and opened it a foot, and Julie could feel that the outside temperature far exceeded the inside temperature. Julie stood and walked over to his brother. He put a hand on Phil's back and felt the dampness there. They looked at one another. Julie gave a little shrug; Phil gave a little nod. Apology offered and accepted. Julie thought to himself, *Boy, am I proud of my brother.*

CHAPTER 54

At 8:40 at night, as Bogart ran lines with Sluggy and the dog watching, an unexpected knock at the door gave all of them a start. A studio messenger stood on the other side and, when the door opened, handed Bogart an envelope and hurried off, presumably to make other deliveries. Bogie opened the envelope to find a thick set of pages on green paper with a new final sequence.

"What is it?" asked Sluggy.

"Looks like a new ending!" he raged. "What color is this? Green? Green! They're down to green paper!" He counted the pages and then glanced at the clock. "It's almost nine and here's an eleven-page rewrite, and we're supposed to shoot it in the morning!"

"They can't do that," said Sluggy with the outrage of a supportive wife—God bless her, she had laid off the sauce long enough to help him prepare the old ending, before this new ending.

"Oh, can't they?" said Bogart. He felt himself slipping into a panic. "How can this thing be any good if they're rewriting up to the last minute? I'm screwed. My first big picture and I'm screwed."

He wanted to drink; he wanted to get bombed, but instead he learned the new lines as best he could and then went to bed like a good soldier and got up like one. Mary drove him to the studio in silence except for the radio, which reported big Nazi gains in Russia at the Don River and talk of Nazi plans to seize the Suez

Canal. Bogart's gloom deepened as he went for wardrobe and makeup and then paced around Stage 1. It was 8:30 in the morning, and the temperature already neared eighty degrees. Not a dry eighty but a humid, miserable eighty. Every day this month had sweltered, and the thermometer had topped 100 a couple of times. By now he was accustomed to Stage 8A, the Rick's set, but for the finale they would use Stage 1, which had been set up as the Casablanca airport at night—more proof that this picture was doomed, shooting an entire airport sequence inside on a soundstage!

Against one wall was forty feet of airplane hangar, roof and all, with the tail section of half a plane visible in the back, and a telephone stand set up near the open front. Claude Rains walked in, then Connie Veidt, and Curtiz was there—preoccupied, but there—conferring with Edeson about the camera angle near the telephone stand. In the air hung fog courtesy of smudge pots of glycerin, which gave off an odor that Bogie knew all too well. He had never liked it. Effective, yes, pleasant, no.

Sixty or so feet past the front of the hangar sat the all-important plane that would carry Victor and Ilsa out of Casablanca, a dummy contraption built smaller than full size by the Prop Department since Stage 1, as big as it was, wasn't big enough to hold a full-size, twin-engine plane of the type required. As Bogart assessed that plane over yonder, it disappeared as the special effects guys and camera assistant ran another fog test. A couple of fellows were wetting down the concrete floor of the soundstage from here to the plane with a fire hose as Bogart paced.

Henreid and Bergman walked up, keeping their distance from the spray of the fire hose. Henreid was dressed in a white suit with a white fedora and Bergman in a tan suit and a tan hat with a wide black band on it—she had been wearing that outfit for the past two days. Victor's usual facial scar had been applied by the Makeup Department. Henreid, a surly fellow who rarely smiled, surveyed Bogart, Rains, and Veidt and said in his usual deadpan, "Who died?"

"What time did your scripts arrive last night?" Bogie asked Henreid and Bergman.

"Nine-thirty or so?" said Ingrid.

"Oh at ten, perhaps?" said Henreid.

In his however many years at Warner Bros., Bogart had never seen anything close to such chaos as this. He had been on much more lavish productions, like the pictures with Cagney, and he had always received a finished script before shooting began. Always. But on *Casablanca*, the lines kept changing as the paper went from white to blue to pink. Then changes of changes of changes were a weird color they called salmon. And now changes of changes of changes of changes were the green he had received last night.

At this uncomfortable moment, with the principals standing about, Irene Lee, the boss of the writers, drifted into view with the dialogue director, Hugh McMullen.

Bogart looked down at the pages in his hand. The idea of the camera rolling and the star delivering the wrong lines filled him with dread. He took a step toward the story editor. "How can you give us new stuff twelve hours before we're supposed to shoot?"

"Did you ever read Homer?" asked Irene Lee. She was an annoying little woman who had no business on the set, as far as Bogart was concerned.

"Homer?" he replied. "What the hell are you talking about? Homer?"

"I'll lend you my copy of *The Iliad*," said Lee. "Life among the gods on Mount Olympos was never boring. Kinda like the way it is around here." Bogart couldn't think of anything to say to that, and then she added, "I promise you: we got the lines right, which is all you need to worry about."

"It's not just the lines," he shot back. "It's the interpretation of the lines. We've got to have time to internalize the material."

Bergman was off several paces and said, "He's right. The camera sees everything, and it will see our confusion when we're not clear about our motivations."

Henreid said, "This would never happen on the stage. You rehearse, you rehearse some more. You work it out with your fellow performers. This . . ." He waved the green script pages. "This script-by-committee business—it's ridiculous."

Bogart said to Henreid and Bergman, "She says they got the lines right, but I don't even know what that means." His voice rose. "So they got the lines right. What does that mean?"

Curtiz had stopped fiddling with the camera setup, attracted not so much by what was being said, Bogie thought, but by the tone of the words. "What's the problem?" he asked in typical Iron Mike fashion, less a question and more a demand for information. Bogie never liked to go toe-to-toe with Curtiz because no one could predict what the Hungarian would say or do. He could lose that temper in a fraction of a second and scream at anyone who bucked him head-on, and Bogart hated to be embarrassed in front of the company. But somehow, he forgot all that at this critical moment and got close enough to the director to feel inferior to his height.

"The problem is," said Bogart, speaking slowly for emphasis, "we just got all these new pages late last night and you're going to want to shoot any minute and we don't know the lines. This is the key moment in your picture, and I know you, Mike. You're going to stick that camera right up my nose, and the world's gonna see I don't understand these lines."

"We need time," said Henreid. "We have the lines; now you've got to give us some time with this script and with each other."

Bogart knew from the pages he'd already studied that Henreid had little to say in this climactic sequence here on Stage 1, so it was likely he was just helping Bogart out and that was good; Bogie had rarely felt comradeship with Henreid or with Bergman. Feeling it now would help.

Ingrid moved closer to the fray. "Yes, Michael," she said with more edge to her voice than Bogart was used to hearing, "it's important we have some time to go over these pages."

"They're green pages," said Bogart, drawing out the word green with the best sneer he could muster as he looked over at Irene. "I don't think I've ever seen green pages in my life!"

Curtiz said, "No, no, Bogie, lines very good. Lines perfect. Story works. Paris Jews."

Bogart wondered if Mike had lost his mind, which he summed up as, "What the fuck?"

Hugh McMullen, who Bogart hadn't minded on the production, cut in with, "It's really very good material."

Rains and Veidt were off a ways by the opening to the hangar, just watching. So it was pretty much everyone who was anyone, standing around hearing the discussion. Bogart forced himself to remain silent and glared at Curtiz, waiting for what the director would do next. But with the burden now squarely on him, Mike did something Bogart had never seen him do, not on this picture or any of the ones preceding it. Iron Mike took a step back. A silent step. A small step. But it was a step back, and he wasn't exploding or saying anything at all for many seconds.

"Art and I work on car shot, complicated shot," said Curtiz after that long pause. "You work on lines." He reached out his hand in the direction of Irene. "Script pages?" he said. Another demand. She handed over her set of green pages. He glanced at the page on top. "Scene 259. We start there, in car. Car pull up, four leads get out. Rick and Renault go back and forth a little, up to Ilsa first line. We shoot that, then take lunch break, okay?"

Irene said, "So, three lines for Bogie and two for Claude this morning?"

"Sure, easy, even for lunch bums," said Curtiz. Bogie looked about him at the others; nobody moved. "Go," said Curtiz quietly, flapping his hands at them as if shooing away pigeons. "Learn five lines."

He walked off and Bogart remained rooted to the spot, unnerved that they would indeed be shooting new material this morning.

Irene said to the actors, "I know this is important. I know it's not ideal. I know you're not happy. Can we please run through the final-final and talk about it a little bit?"

The annoying little woman turned and looked about the hangar set with its open ceiling and trusses. Behind a prop telephone stand sat a long table under an industrial pendant lamp, over near where Rains stood with Veidt. Lee walked that way with McMullen following dutifully. Henreid drifted over toward the table, and then Bergman. Bogart trailed them all.

Irene Lee looked up at Veidt and purred, "Good morning, Connie."

"Good morning, dear Irene," he purred back. Rains gave a little laugh.

Irene stood at the head of the table and said, "I'm not going to kid you. This was the toughest problem I faced since Intro to Physics at Carnegie Tech, trying to get Ilsa and Victor on that damn plane while Rick stays behind." Bogie looked at the other three principals; everyone's attention was full on the woman that Hal and the writers called Renie. She proceeded to walk them through the new pages and Bogart just kept silent. Silent and fuming.

After Lee had talked a while, the dialogue director chimed in, saying, "This is wonderful stuff to play. Rick is noble at the hardest moment of his life. Ilsa's in turmoil but resigned. Victor displays dignity as he stands toe-to-toe with his romantic rival."

Lee said to Henreid, "And then you get the key line in the whole picture. After Rick gives you the letters of transit, you welcome him back to the fight. And the line that should raise the roof is, 'This time, I know our side will win.' It's the line of the picture—you give the free world hope with your delivery of that line." She paused. "Did you hear the news this morning? We don't know what's going to happen. It doesn't look good, and we can only hope."

Bogart blanched at the idea of Henreid getting the best line in Bogie's picture. McMullen seemed to understand and flipped through the pages to find a key line and said, "Then there's this awkward little moment, Scene 264, after it's been sorted out who's going and who's staying, Rick uses his last ounce of emotional strength to say to Ilsa, 'You better hurry, or you'll miss that plane.'" He looked at Bogart. "That is a hero."

The little Irene shook her head and then shrugged her shoulders as she said, "It all works. It's hard to remember how exactly we got here, but we're here and it works."

Bogart couldn't decide how much of this made sense and how much was a con job. "Does Hal think it works?" he asked Lee.

"Oh he does indeed. We went through every line, over and over." She scanned all the faces about her and said, as if she were six feet tall instead of five, "And now, with the ending final, we can shoot a number of set-up scenes from earlier in the story in the next week or so." The actors watched her. "Any questions?" asked Lee. Nobody said anything and she added, "Okay then, I'll leave you to it. Break a leg." And she strode on her tiny legs toward the camp chairs set up by the wall of the soundstage.

"Can we talk, Hugh?" Ingrid asked of McMullen, and they drifted off. The conclave of actors broke up and Bogart felt a little foolish for raising such a stink because it sounded like Lee and the writers had finally worked through their issues.

He lit a cigarette and studied this morning's lines. One, after exiting the car: "Louis, have your man go with Mr. Laszlo and take care of his luggage." Two, while handing the letters to Louis: "If you don't mind, Louis, you fill in the names. That will make it even more official." And three, as Louis begins to write: "And the names are—Mr. and Mrs. Victor Laszlo." No big deal. But in the back of his mind, he had already begun to dread the afternoon, when the lines would be long and the pressure would be brutal.

Within an hour, with the annoying little story editor still sitting there watching, the four principals climbed in the big Buick to begin the final sequence. Rains drove with Bogart next to him, and Henreid and Bergman in the back seat. The scene began with the car pulling up at the hangar as a French police orderly spoke a weather report into the telephone. The four got out and Edeson dollied in. Henreid walked off-camera to attend to the luggage. Cut. The second setup was Bogart and Bergman as he handed over the letters to Louis and announced he should write in the Laszlos' names.

They broke for lunch and at one o'clock resumed work, and by then Bogart felt panic welling up within him as Curtiz described the next setup. Mike wanted a dolly-in as Ilsa says, "Why my name, Richard?" And he tells her, "Because you're getting on that plane!" Then she had a line and he had one, then he had a speech and another speech and Mike wanted to roll through all of it in one chunk. The lines were similar to the previous script, but different enough to trip Bogart up.

Bogie tried to focus on all the lines. He took out a cigarette and struggled to light it, his hands shaking. God, he needed a drink. *Last night we said a great many things. You said I was to do the thinking for both of us . . .*

He looked up and there, twenty feet away, stood Bergman with the dialogue man, going over the lines. She had, what, three sentences? He had two speeches! He could feel despair descending over him. He hated everybody. He hated that little woman for delivering eleven pages at the last minute. Wallis for allowing it to happen. And Mike for pushing, pushing, pushing. He glared at Curtiz and Edeson as they marked off the beginning and end of the dolly move. It would all be shot in one take that ended in a close-up of Bogart—Mike had said so. One fucking take, two script pages, and a close-up.

Bergman walked up to Bogart and then studied the script some more. A fresh bank of glycerin fog rolled in as she looked up at Bogie and said softly, "All right, Rick, convince me that I must leave with Victor." She said it with a smile and she meant to be collegial, but the smile lit a fuse.

His nerves buckled. He turned away from Ingrid and hissed at Curtiz and Edeson, "This isn't right! We can't shoot this thing now. We all need time to prepare. I've got two speeches here in close-up and I don't know the goddamn lines!" He didn't care he was bucking Iron Mike or that the very proper Ingrid stood just past his shoulder.

Curtiz said, "No! Stick to schedule! We take our time, get this done, stay on schedule!"

"Bullshit!" screamed Bogart. "I want twenty-four hours, do you hear me? It's got to be written in my contract somewhere, twenty-four hours to learn new material! This is nuts. Just, nuts!"

Bogart turned around and Bergman had vanished. He spotted her fleetingly through the fog, way back by the scale-model airplane.

Curtiz stormed up. "Must shoot now," he barked, motioning at the camera and dolly. "Not too many lines! Schedule."

"To hell with the schedule, Mike. Just to hell with it!" Bogart snapped. "I'll be in my dressing room, trying to learn all the . . . not-too-many lines."

He headed for the edge of the set, then the soundstage door. Irene Lee stood nearby. As he glared at her, he stripped off his trench coat and hat and threw them toward her. He punched through the door into high sun in the blazing July heatwave. The pavement broiled; he could see heat rising on the street between looming soundstages. In all these years, playing gangsters and hillbillies and Mexican bandits and even a vampire, he had never snapped. Just say the lines, he would tell himself, and take the paycheck. But as he pounded up the street toward the sanctuary of the star bungalows, he knew there was no turning back.

CHAPTER 55

Wallis was on the phone with Wald when Renie appeared at his door. "Hal, we've got a problem," she panted. He wasn't used to seeing her disheveled, or perspiring, or breathless.

"I'll call you back," he said to Wald and hung up.

"Bogart just walked off the set," said Renie. "Too many new lines."

"Shit," said Hal. He shot to his feet and headed toward the door. "I'll kill that son of a bitch," he hissed.

She stood in the doorway and stretched her arms across it, clutching the frame on either side. "No, you don't."

"Get out of my way, Renie!" He intended to steam past her, but no part of his brain could accept violence against Irene. When he saw she wasn't about to move and he couldn't bluff his way past, he screeched to a stop. "Move."

"Nope. He's got a point."

"Don't push me. I'm telling you. You have no idea what thin ice you're on."

"The hell I don't," she shot back. As her eyes bore into his, he could see she was near tears. "This was a man's job all along."

He wanted those words to hurt when he had said them; now he was sorry they had found their mark. He glanced down at his watch; 1:30 on a perfectly good afternoon and he knew nothing was being shot on the *Casablanca* set, and the magic was there for the taking. Those people in Paris could have a voice, if only.

She continued to block the door, and he took a breath. "Okay, say your piece, then move."

"Bogie has got to sell us on everything—the way we sat here yesterday and worked it out, it's all about his performance. The other two are reacting to him, and he's feeling the pressure. I didn't realize all this until I saw his face this morning."

"What were you doing on the set this morning?" said Wallis.

"Doing every goddamn thing I can think of to see that this picture works out, that's what," she hissed. "I'm not associate producer and never will be, except, hello, I already am."

"They would never accept that title in a woman," said Wallis. "It's tilting at windmills and I didn't have time to waste trying. I still don't. It's nothing personal. It's business."

She no longer blocked the door. She had dropped her arms. "I figured that out. I get it," she said. "Doesn't make it easier, but I get it."

His practical mind had taken over again, and he could imagine all those actors sitting around, those very expensive actors. And there would be the chief reviewing the numbers and pouncing. Irene nodded to the right, toward the wall. "Is Emerson up there just for show?"

Hal didn't respond. He knew a point was coming; he braced for it.

"Do not be too timid and squeamish about your actions," she recited. "To me, the thing to do is go see Bogart, and tell him you understand. Tell him about Paris. I think he wants a fight, but don't give it to him. Make him be a big boy. He's a pro, and I bet he'll come through if you remind him of it."

Wallis felt his entire body capitulate. He sensed she was right as soon as the words met his ears. He also knew that none of the men working in the building would have had the guts to do what she just did. He paused another moment to gather himself.

"Okay, let's go," he told her. She smiled a big, glorious Renie smile, the kind he hadn't seen in weeks, and they walked out of the building together, side by side. Damn, it was hot. Midday-Los-Angeles-in-summer hot. These days, the internal struggle was do I get there as fast as possible to get out of the heat? Or do I move slowly to save some strength?

They reached the door to Bogart's dressing room by the tennis court. Wallis had decided along the way that they should go in together—it was his way of acknowledging her value. He would never tell her that, but he could show her.

As he was about to knock, Renie said, "You go on in. He hates me; I can tell."

Wallis nodded and rapped on the door with his knuckles.

"Yeah?" Wallis heard Bogart call.

Hal pushed open the door, stepped inside, and closed it as Renie walked away. His eyes adjusted from the brilliant sunshine left behind, and the air conditioning washed over him. Hal took a moment to assess the situation. Bogart sat on his sofa to the right of the door, green pages resting in his lap. His shoes were off and he propped his feet on the low coffee table, which also held his chess board with a game in progress, half a bottle of bourbon, and an empty glass.

Bogart noticed Wallis noticing the liquor. "Help yourself," said Bogie.

Hal shook his head no, shoved his hands in his pockets at the implication of the bourbon, and drifted deeper into the room before turning to face the star. "I heard there was some commotion on Stage 1," he began.

"That's one way to put it."

"And you don't like the ending."

Bogart dragged the last bit of life out of his cigarette until the glowing paper burned his fingers, prompting him to tamp it out in the ashtray. He exhaled a long line of smoke. "I don't know whether I like the ending or not. You see, we've only just met."

Wallis measured his words before he said them. "That wasn't some whim, that set of pages you're holding," he began. "That was my story editor, my director, and four of my finest writers sitting in a room with me working out a perfect ending."

Bogart shot Wallis a surprised look. "Perfect ending," he grumbled. "Blue pages, pink pages, orange pages, green pages. You know what all that adds up to? Crap. Bad reviews."

Hal kept Renie's guidance front and center. "Maybe," he said, "but I don't think so. I've been watching the dailies for going on two months, and this is a very good picture. It's the picture you always wanted."

"*Falcon* was the picture I always wanted," Bogart shot back.

"Nope," said Wallis. "When you signed your new contract, you told me you wanted a starring role that wasn't a George Raft hand-me-down. You said you wanted an A picture with your name above the title. You wanted to be in the company of Davis and Flynn. And here you are."

"Do you make them do what you want me to do?" he asked, waving the green pages.

"Sometimes. It comes with the territory." Wallis awaited a Bogart riposte and was surprised when he didn't receive one. "You're every bit as good an actor as either one of them. Better maybe."

As cynical, as grouchy, as depressed as Bogart could be, Wallis knew the acknowledgment had hit home. "Look at you," he pressed on. "You didn't drive off the lot. You stayed here and studied your lines. I think I rest my case."

Wallis drifted over to the other end of the sofa and sat down. He thought of Renie again. "I've never seen anything like this story, Bogie. It came in right after Pearl Harbor. It touched Miss Lee first, and then it got ahold of me. And then Mike. You see all those beautiful people out there that he hired. They all had to get the hell out of Europe or die, and now they're playing themselves on-screen. Themselves! Can you imagine? They've all lost parents or brothers or sisters or children. And by being in this picture, they show the world who the Nazis are exterminating."

Hal pulled out his handkerchief and wiped his eyes and nose. "And yesterday," he went on, "we figured out the ending. And it works. It works." He let out a deep sigh and looked into Bogart's surprised brown eyes. "The world needs this picture."

Bogart was many seconds behind the speech, absorbing it. Then he shook his head, and it was clear the anger had left him. "Okay, okay," he said, "give me thirty minutes alone with my new friend here and I'll come back ready to shoot. Thirty full minutes with nobody rousting me."

Hal studied Bogart, then studied the bottle on the table. "What about your other friend?"

"I won't touch it—take it with you if you want." Hal stared at the bottle, considering, but knew it wasn't an issue and headed for the door. Outside, he leaned against the closed door and wiped his eyes again.

Back on First Street, he found Renie sitting in the shade on the bench they sometimes shared. She was smoking nervously.

"Well?" she asked, her face tense.

Hal nodded. He didn't say anymore. He didn't need to. Renie's face settled into a smile, and she chuckled to herself.

Wallis said, "I'm going to the set. Bogie said he'll be there in half an hour—I'll tell them." He hesitated. "You coming?"

"I'll be along," said Renie. As he started to walk away toward the entrance to the stage, she said, "Hal?" He turned. "Thank you," she said. She smiled, and then he did. They probably wouldn't ever have sex, he thought to himself, but they had this, and this was pretty good.

Inside Stage 1, Ingrid felt that, after all these weeks, she finally knew Ilsa's mind and how to play Ilsa, who owed too much to Victor to leave him. Wallis had told her the censors would never let Ilsa stay with Rick, so she knew intellectually how the story must end. Now she knew emotionally that Rick would give her a shove toward her duty. Victor loved her so much that he couldn't go on to save the world without Ilsa at his side, and that fact rejuvenated her. Ingrid now saw Ilsa as the emotional compass of the picture, and she couldn't wait to play her scenes, even though the end of the picture neared and after that, another abyss.

With Bogart gone a long time, Ingrid asked for the nearest telephone, because she had felt an impulse to call David Selznick. "Ingrid, my darling! I know you are shooting or I would have called you! The jungle drums are pounding all the way from the Sierra Nevadas, my darling. It's like a Tarzan picture, the way the drums are pounding."

The stage began to spin around her. "I don't know what that means, David," she said. She found Americanisms exhausting. But his tone—his tone sounded so promising.

She heard Selznick laugh on the other end of the line. "Did you know," he said slowly, "that the mountains terrify poor Vera Zorina? She fears something might happen to those gorgeous legs of hers."

Ingrid's mind flashed through the facts. *For Whom the Bell Tolls* was shooting this moment in Nevada with Gary Cooper and Vera the dancer, George Balanchine's wife.

"Balanchine is having a fit every time his wife walks on uneven ground," sang Selznick. "It's glorious, Ingrid! Zorina can't think about acting because she's worried she will break a leg!"

Ingrid began to laugh, a grateful, delicious laugh at the irony of it. She had lost the part of Maria, the part she had wanted more than anything in her career, to a delicate German ballerina, and now that poor girl was foundering in the mountains. "How can we help her, David?" Ingrid asked. "The poor girl. She must be careful of those beautiful legs."

"My thought exactly, Ingrid!" said David. "My thought exactly. I'm going to give Adolph Zukor a call over at Paramount to see if it's possible we can help Vera out of all that danger."

"They tell me I will be working here another week or ten days," she whispered. "They're going to want some other new scenes because they've figured out the ending. Do you think it's possible that I can start another picture at once? This picture? The picture of my dreams?"

"Sit tight, finish your job, and we'll see," said Selznick. A commotion distracted her—ripples of commentary from the crew that Hal Wallis was on the set. She hung up in a hurry and rushed back from the phone at the far end of the soundstage onto the airport set. She found Paul Henreid leaning forward in his camp chair, playing with his fedora. Claude Rains sat in his chair inside the hangar, and he was reading a magazine. Hal Wallis, the boss of bosses, stood between them, with Connie Veidt standing beside him to lend menace.

"So, how are we doing?" asked Wallis, whose eye now caught on Ingrid as she ran to her chair beside Henreid.

"Oh fine," purred Claude Rains as he studied photos in the magazine on his lap.

"Ask Mr. Bogie how we are doing," said Henreid with undisguised displeasure.

Bergman settled in her chair, careful not to expend an ounce of energy or make any sudden move that would require an adjustment to wardrobe or makeup. All she could think about was Maria—that part in *For Whom the Bell Tolls*—and precious Vera and her legs. Ingrid felt herself ready to burst, but wrenched focus back to the here and now. She owed Wallis and this band of actors her allegiance.

"I just spoke with Mr. Bogart," said Wallis. "He'll be along shortly. He said to give him thirty minutes."

Rains stood and said, "Good, there's time for a little walk." Ingrid watched him saunter off. She couldn't imagine why he would care to venture outside in the broiling heat of afternoon. With all the willpower she could muster, Ingrid worked on her lines on the green pages. But every so often, a scene played out before her eyes. It was a ballerina in a tutu falling from the rugged cliffs of Nevada.

CHAPTER 56

From her spot in the shade of the bench, Irene could see the heat rising in waves from the pavement of First Street and the avenues branching off toward the soundstages. She sat considering the problems that had oppressed her a day earlier. Thanks to a great many people, especially unsung hero Alice Danziger, the script had been conquered. Her fractured relationship with Wallis had been healed. Only the fates could know if Jack Warner would hold to his threat and remove her from the lot. One issue remained now, the big lug of a Navy man who had showed up at her door the previous morning and made the most beautiful speech she had ever heard. What to do about Aaron Diamond?

"Well, hello there," called a silken voice. "I wondered where you had gotten off to." She looked to her left and there stood Captain Renault in the next spot of shade over, about fifteen feet away. He looked quite handsome in his uniform and cap as he smoked a cigarette.

She motioned to him and patted the bench beside her.

He walked through the heat and said as he sat, "How kind of you." She didn't really know Claude Rains; what to say next eluded her. She needn't have worried.

"The last time we spoke," he said, "I had just started the picture, and you gave me some coaching on how to treat the good captain. How are you feeling now? Has it worked out for you?"

"The rushes are wonderful," she replied. "You are everything I imagined that Captain Renault could be."

He smiled a warm Rains kind of smile and said, "I suppose that's because I am Renault—your writers captured me pretty well, right down to the lechery."

Irene laughed. "That's my boys. They told me they were writing it just for you, and they did."

"Your boys?" he asked.

"Phil and Julie Epstein."

"Ah," he said. "And you don't mind the lechery in his character?"

"My God no," she said without thinking. "I love it!"

Rains dropped his cigarette butt on the pavement and stepped on it. "You know," he said quietly and paused before continuing, "my dressing room is just around the corner. Maybe we should go in there and cool off for a little while in the conditioned air."

She realized her error. He was such a charming and magnetic man, and she had been living with him for eight long months. Or, she corrected, living with this character all these months. It was so beautifully perfect, the invitation. She felt as if he had snuck in and replaced the blood flowing through her veins with champagne. "Will it get me my letter of transit?" she asked, not caring if it seemed like flirtation.

"It will get you anything you like," he answered. He reached out and took her hand, and she not only allowed it, she caressed his fingers with her thumb. She liked Claude; a little interlude sounded like fun. Maybe it was exactly what she needed to celebrate the conquering of the script. If only life were that simple.

"I truly hate to say this for a number of reasons," said Irene, "but I think I'm spoken for."

"You think?" said Rains. "Well, come with me before you're certain." He arose and tried to assist Irene to her feet. She hesitated and then stood.

"I've been trying to deny it for a while now, but I can't," said Irene. Rains looked at her with curiosity, and then with admiring resignation. He gave a little chuckle.

"Whoever he is, please tell him I'm jealous," said Rains. It was a dreamlike moment, Irene with Captain Renault.

They still held hands, and she shook her head clear and pulled him toward Stage 1. "Come on, Captain, let's get you back to the set. And you had better know your lines."

As they walked inside the door of Stage 1, Irene heard the assistant director call, "All right, everybody, let's get ready to roll!" and the place came to life as if a switch had been thrown. Rains let go of her hand and walked off. Lighting men attended their grip stands; Art Edeson, the DP, appeared with his camera assistant and dolly operator. The hair and makeup people hovered, and a man from Wardrobe held Bogie's trench coat, newly pressed, and his fedora, awaiting the star's arrival. Deep into the set, Wallis stood, hands in pockets, examining the prop plane.

Stand-ins for Bogart and Bergman were being assessed by the camera people, and the lighting was adjusted. Curtiz was working on dolly moves—wheeling the camera up to the stand-ins who stood looking at each other. They did it once. They did it again. Camera technicians marked the distance from the lens to the stand-in's faces with a tape measure. They checked the key light; they checked all the other lights, waving hands to see where each light shone, and adjusted flags and white cards and reflectors until the pair was lit perfectly.

The stage door opened and heels clicked across the concrete floor. Irene turned, and here came Bogart, stone-faced. The Wardrobe man held out Bogart's trench coat and he slipped it on. "Thanks, Leon," said Bogart as he was handed his fedora. The star walked to the spot held by his identically dressed lookalike. "Thanks, Russ," said Bogie to his stand-in. Then he said, louder, "Sorry, everybody."

Rains picked up his chair to move it out of the way. As he did, he said, "Sorry? I found myself a tractor. It's a Fordson and a beauty. I'm going to order it at the next break." He stopped in his tracks, looked over at the star, and said with a subdued smile, "Thank you, Bogie."

The lighting and camera guys double-checked all the measurements and lighting characteristics of Humphrey Bogart. They adjusted the reflectors and a bounce card to send light into Bogie's face on close-up.

Rains took his place for the scene at the standing desk fifteen feet from the marks of Rick and Ilsa. Bergman's stand-in stepped off the mark on the floor and Ingrid stepped on. Just to check the sight lines, Bogart turned to Rains and said, "Isn't that right, Louis?"

Rains shot back, "I'm afraid Major Strasser would insist."

Connie Veidt's ears perked up and he called, "Major Strasser always insists," and Bogart and Rains laughed, along with some of the crew.

As Irene watched, the camera crew fine-tuned their two-shot of Bogart and Bergman at position one, then again after the dolly rolled to a stop to shoot past Ingrid's shoulder onto Bogart's face. The cameraman said to Bogart, "Adjust your hat up a half inch higher on your forehead."

Bogart made the adjustment. "Better?"

"Yeah," said the cameraman, "thanks." Two dolly operators moved the camera back to position one. "Ready, Mike."

Wallis was looking at his stars on their marks. Ingrid stood close to Bogie. Irene heard Bogart say to Bergman, "Are you ready to be convinced?"

Ingrid laughed and replied, "Yes, convince me."

Curtiz gently instructed Ingrid on her two positions—position one as Rick announces the names that go on the letters of transit, and position two as she rushes up to him in a panic. He asked if she understood. She did. "Camera rehearsal!" called Curtiz.

Wallis walked up to Irene and led her farther into the shadows. She knew Hal didn't want to risk interfering with the energy of the director or performers. Everything mattered now. How would Bogart do? Would the new ending hold? Did Bergman have the answers she needed? How would the prima donna Henreid behave? Since the writers meeting had broken up at 6:30 yesterday, Irene felt this would be a home run if only the people on this stage could execute the plan.

It was all up to Mike now, Mike and his players. She watched Curtiz study his script and check with Continuity to make sure everything taken before lunch would match what they were about to commit to film now.

All was in readiness. The boom mic hovered into place over the heads of the players. Irene could feel her heart pounding in her chest. She loved this life—loved it so much. "Rehearsal with camera," Mike reminded. Then, "Action one."

"And the names are Mr. and Mrs. Victor Laszlo," said Bogart in a pickup.

"Action two."

Ingrid stepped into her mark next to Bogie, who had his hand in his coat pocket with the intention being he had a pistol in there to keep Louis in line. "But why my name, Richard?"

"Because you're getting on that plane!"

"But I . . . I don't understand. What about you?"

Bogart's stare held on Rains. "I'm staying here with him until the plane gets safely away."

Ingrid said with dazzling intensity, "No, Richard, no! What's happened to you? Last night we said—"

The camera had settled beside Ingrid and looked into Bogie's face, and Irene held her breath to see if Bogart had really learned the lines.

"Last night we said a good many things. You said I was to do the thinking for both of us. Well, I've done a lot of it since then, and it all adds up to one thing: you're getting on that plane with Victor where you belong."

"But Richard, no, I . . . I . . ."

Irene wondered where Bergman had found this new reservoir of feeling.

"Now you've got to listen to me," said Rick to Ilsa. "Do you have any idea what you'd have to look forward to if you stay here? Nine chances out of ten we'd both land in a concentration camp." Bogart was on, and intense, and he turned to Rains. "Isn't that right, Louis?"

"I'm afraid Major Strasser would insist," said Rains with be-musement. Irene felt a surge of love for this man who had helped her sort out life in a five-minute conversation.

"Cut rehearsal," said Curtiz.

"Maybe getting laid mellowed Mike," said Wallis.

"Mike got laid?" whispered Irene.

Wallis nodded. "One of his quickies, while Bogart was away."

Curtiz was pacing, looking at the script, maybe replaying what he had just witnessed in his mind. "Camera not on you, Ingrid, so more force! Must convey desperation. 'But why *my* name, Richard?' *My* name. Get it?"

"But why *my* name, Richard?" she repeated with greater urgency.

"Yes!" said Curtiz. "Up!" He said to Edeson, "We shoot Renault lines as inserts." Curtiz fell silent and paced some more. Then he turned to Bogart.

Irene noticed Hal's intensity as he studied Bogart's every move.

Curtiz said, "Bogie? Your line, 'You've got to listen to me.' *Got.* Punch word even more! Otherwise perfect," said the director. Bogart smiled the faintest possible Bogart smile and nodded almost imperceptibly. Curtiz turned to his people. "We shoot."

"Rolling camera!" shouted Katz. The dolly moved back to position one, and makeup was freshened on the stars.

"Turn the air off, please!" said Al Alleborn. The hum of the air conditioning ceased, and the space fell remarkably silent.

Just as Curtiz pointed a finger and prepared to call action, a voice called, "Hold it!"

Wallis strained to see. It was Fran Scheid, who said, "Airplane!" Seconds later, all could hear the engines of a plane droning overhead. It happened a lot, airplanes busting good takes, but Fran had caught it in time.

In twenty-five seconds Scheid gave the all-clear, and Curtiz rolled on a take. Bogart nailed his speeches and Bergman delivered her lines intensely. Curtiz ordered that take to be printed and shot another, also perfect. Then Curtiz directed isolation shots of Rains saying his two lines.

"He's cutting in the camera again," murmured Wallis.

Irene felt herself floating in a dream. She thought back to every twist and turn since that afternoon with Jack Janowitz, then the evening she had first held the play in her hands and read it, and experienced that sensation of importance. And then flash cut to this moment.

Mike moved on to the next page of script, the two stars on their same marks. Irene kept watching from the shadows. The stars rehearsed in position, scripts in hand.

Forty feet away, Bergman was looking at her script as she said, "You're saying this only to make me go!"

"I'm saying it because it's true," said Bogart. "Inside of us we both know you belong with Victor. You're part of his work. The thing that keeps him going. If that plane leaves the ground and you're not with him, you'll regret it."

"No!" said Bergman urgently.

"Maybe not today, maybe not tomorrow, but soon, and for the rest of your life."

"Oh my God, they're good," Irene whispered.

Twenty minutes later Curtiz had ordered the camera rolling, exposing film, no scripts in hand this time.

"But what about us?" said Bergman, the camera over Bogart's shoulder to shoot Ingrid's close-ups.

"We'll always have Paris. We didn't have it—we'd lost it—until you came to Casablanca. We got it back last night."

"And I said that I would never leave you," she said in little more than a whisper. The writers intended this to be a desperate declaration, but Ingrid had interpreted it her own way.

Bogart took her by the shoulders. "And you never will. But I've got a job to do too. Where I'm going you can't follow. What I've got to do, you can't be any part of."

Nothing more came out of Bogart. He kept holding her by the shoulders and said, finally, "Line?"

"I'm not good at being noble," said the girl monitoring the script.

Bogie rolled right into it without hesitation, "I'm not good at being noble, Ilsa, but it doesn't take much to see that the problems of three little people don't amount to a hill of beans in this crazy world. Someday, you'll understand that."

Bergman slumped slightly before him. He smiled wistfully. "Now, now. Here's looking at you, kid."

Irene felt herself sway as if she might faint. She grabbed Hal's arm and leaned into him.

"Cut!" called Curtiz.

"We did it, Hal," she whispered. "We did it."

EPILOGUE

Alice Danziger worked at Warner Bros. another twenty-five years before retiring in 1967.

Joy Page failed to use her career as a means of escape. Instead, at age twenty she married actor Bill Orr in 1945—Orr would oversee the Warner Bros. television empire of the 1950s and '60s, until Jack fired him in 1965. Joy divorced Orr in 1970 and died in 2008 at the age of eighty-three.

Dooley Wilson would continue his career in film, on the stage, and finally in television and die on May 30, 1953, at age sixty-seven after buying a home for Estelle, who followed him in death in 1971.

Conrad Veidt would live less than eight months after completing his work in *Casablanca*. He died of a massive heart attack while playing golf at the Riviera Country Club on April 3, 1943.

Sydney Greenstreet remained a darling of Warner Bros. through many more films in the 1940s and retired in 1949. He died in 1954 at age seventy-three.

Claude Rains remained busy as a leading man and then character actor for another twenty-five years until his death from cirrhosis of the liver in 1967.

After *Casablanca*, Paul Henreid enjoyed a long career as an actor and director of motion pictures and television into the 1970s. He died in 1992 at age eighty-four.

Ingrid Bergman would go on to make *For Whom the Bell Tolls* after *Casablanca* and earn an Academy Award nomination as Best Actress in the role of Maria. She would win a Best Actress Oscar for her role in *Gaslight* in 1945 and another for *Anastasia* in 1957. She died in 1982 at the age of sixty-seven.

Humphrey Bogart went on to make twenty-eight more pictures, earning an Oscar for Best Actor in *The African Queen*. He died in 1957 at the age of fifty-seven.

In recognition of their success with *Casablanca*, Philip and Julius Epstein were promoted to producers at Warner Bros. and translated their script for *Mr. Skeffington* to the screen in 1944 with Bette Davis and Claude Rains. The picture returned a strong profit, but the experience of cajoling a performance out of Davis soured them on the producer role. Phil and Julie remained a successful writing team until Phil's sudden death from cancer at age forty-two. Julie continued to write screenplays alone, his last the sleeper hit *Reuben, Reuben*, released in 1983. He died in 2000 at ninety-one.

Jack Warner got revenge on Hal Wallis at the 1944 Academy Award ceremony. When *Casablanca* was announced as the winner for Best Picture, Warner beat Wallis to the stage and accepted both the Oscar statuette and the glory of the win. Warner survived changes in Hollywood to become the last of the studio moguls. He remained married to wife Ann until his death in 1978.

Hal Wallis never forgave Warner for the Academy Award incident. He moved to Paramount Pictures in 1944 and continued his unparalleled success as an independent producer. He earned another fortune as producer of many of Elvis Presley's hit pictures and scored a late-career triumph with *True Grit* in 1969. Wallis died in 1986 at the age of eighty-seven.

Irene Lee's sixth sense regarding North Africa paid off at the beginning of November 1942, when a U.S. task force zeroed in on Casablanca, French Morocco, to establish a foothold in northwest Africa. With post-production of the film complete and the premier scheduled for early 1943, *Casablanca* was rushed into a splashy November premiere in New York City that was sponsored by the Fighting French Relief Committee and France Forever. *The Hollywood Reporter* stated that the "lucky break" of events in North Africa would result in a "surefire box-office smash."

Irene remained at Warner Bros. She asked Hal if she deserved a bonus for nurturing *Casablanca* through the production process. He responded, "That's what you're paid for." She continued to work for Wallis at Paramount and is credited for giving career breaks to Burt Lancaster and Robert Redford, among others. She married Aaron Diamond on August 27, 1942, six weeks after *Casablanca* wrapped; their daughter was born in 1944. Aaron would become a real estate mogul in New York City until his sudden death in 1984. At that point, Irene began a second career as philanthropist, overseeing the disbursement of their $100 million fortune to medical research—including AIDS research—and the arts. Irene died in 2003 at the age of ninety-two, having fulfilled her mission to give away all their money and secure in the knowledge that without her, there would have been no wartime screen masterpiece.

Casablanca earned Academy Award nominations for the music of Max Steiner, the editing of Owen Marks, the cinematography of Arthur Edeson, the supporting actor performance of Claude Rains, and the lead actor performance of Humphrey Bogart. The Epsteins won Academy Awards for their screenplay and Michael Curtiz won for his direction. And *Casablanca* was recognized as the Best Picture of 1943 and, indeed, as one of the most magical of all time.

QUESTIONS FOR DISCUSSION

1. What did you find surprising about Irene Lee's position at Warner Bros.? In what ways was she a "second-class citizen," even though she was a studio executive?

2. Irene's goal was to become a producer at the studio. How successful was she in this quest? In what ways did she buck the system and provide creative input beyond the scope of her job?

3. What challenges did Dooley Wilson face in Hollywood? How were African Americans portrayed on the screen at this time? What was your reaction to these attitudes? In what ways did Hal Wallis and the writers confront the racism of the time in crafting the character of Sam?

4. How would the casting of Hazel Scott as Sam have changed the dynamics of *Casablanca*'s storyline?

5. What were some of the ways the war touched the home front and the everyday lives of U.S. citizens?

6. Name some of the actors who fled Europe because of the rise of Nazism. What did you find surprising about their stories?

What was your reaction to the number of exiled Europeans who appeared in *Casablanca*?

7. In what ways did Frank Capra's confrontation with the Epsteins reflect the dichotomy of the United States and Soviet Union as allies?

8. Irene read of 8,200 Serbs exterminated by the Nazis, and Wallis reacted to 6,000 Parisian Jews forced from their homes and sent to camps. How and why did news of these atrocities, both of which were reported in the United States in 1941, surprise you?

9. Which contributors do you see as being key to the creative development of *Casablanca*, and why?

10. What surprised you about the way motion pictures were written and filmed in 1942?